Getting Witchy With It Anthology

Book 5.6.7

Copyright

Table of Contents

GETTING WITCHY WITH IT

SALEM 2023

WILLIAM SCHLICHTER   JEANEVA CHRISTIE   MAGAIDH DUNBROCH   ANDI LAWRENCOVNA   R.N.A

MICHAELA CANE

ANYTIME AUTHOR PROMOTIONS

ONE

Getting Witchy With It

WILLIAM SCHLICHTER

One

"Get your ass back to base—right now!"

Warrant Officer Stryker covers the speaker on the cell phone, not that it keeps most of his commanding officer's beratement from spilling forth. "Yes, sir. I'll tell the reporter from the KFVS 14 News we're needed back at base while they search for this missing child." He must hold the phone away to prevent the further barrage of curses from damaging his ear drums.

Stryker gives the reporter a nod before directing his statement at the black man built like a linebacker standing next to him. "Gunny, give me a couple of men to stay with the convoy, and have the rest work in with the searchers where needed."

The reporter signals the woman holding the camera emblazoned with a fourteen on its side. Throat clear, the reporter gives the "we're rolling" sign. "I am sure the Copeland family appreciates any aid in locating their missing daughter. The Army doesn't normally assist in missing person searches."

Stryker will never be selected as a PR representative, but he knows he can fake it long enough to ensure this news broadcast keeps him from a court-martial. He first must correct her before he answers the implied question. "Ma'am, we're not the Army, we're a Marine detachment escorting a convoy to Fort Leonard Wood. In this instance, we are proud to have been given an opportunity to help the local community. It's what we do."

A cohort of off camera voices give a coordinated Marine *Hoorah!*

Once filming concludes, the Gunnery Sergeant joins Stryker. "You going to catch hell for this, Sir?"

Stryker must glance up to meet Gunny's gaze. "Not if she shares my remarks on TV. The media loves to play up the evils of the American military. I made the Marines look good. Way better than we would appear parked on this two-lane blacktop doing nothing, while half a town searches for a missing child. I'll take the reprimand."

"You said this was a shortcut."

Stryker uses the truck door as a shield while he pulls the slide on his M&P. The brass shell winks at him. He secures the weapon in a hidden holster at the small of his back and covers it with his coat. "I grew up in the next town over. This route would have cut an hour off our trip through southeast Missouri as long as Grandpa wasn't out on his tractor using the road to get to the next field. I couldn't have known there'd be a missing child, or that the county sheriff closed the road during the search."

The Gunny pats his right hip. His muscles keep the fabric tight and with no excess to hide his own KA-BAR. "Fifteen tan military trucks hauling more military equipment on their beds will make a hell of an opening shot on the news. Most people don't know what we use this equipment for, but it sure gives the appearance like we're prepping for combat. That drone the reporter uses must be the station's new toy. The family seems happy for the help, even if the local sheriff's face doesn't look thrilled to see someone of my obvious background in his jurisdiction."

Stryker closes the truck door. "Most of the people who live here are decent, but there are those who have never left the county."

"You can keep the cousin-marrying kind around here. They tend not to appreciate my complexion."

"Yeah, when your uncle's also your father, you shouldn't take issue about someone being born with a permanent tan."

The Gunny snorts. "I'll have to remember to lay off the bass in my voice."

Stryker allows a chuckle. Most people won't understand the brotherhood soldiers who share a foxhole have with each other and for that he won't apologize. When the enemy opens fire at you, skin color and a whole lot of other social conventions lose all meaning. It's the heart of the man that matters. "One of the main reasons I had to escape this area—too much ignorance."

"You had to escape rusty pickups and moonshine-drinking bigots. I grew up in gun-free Chicago where they shoot you for your shoes."

"We don't need to one-up who grew up the worst. You'll always win."

Stryker studies the field of unmown grass where over a hundred and fifty people keep a slow pace an arm's length apart. Some poke walking sticks into the waving fronds before them. He's no doubt all of them fear overlooking a clue that will lead to locating the missing child, and yet none of them want to be the one to discover the body. They all pray she's still alive.

Hope is a cruel mistress.

Gunny remains at parade rest. "I know they need to find this kid, but I sure don't want to find her out here."

"Better she got lost out here and faced exposure, than being found in some creep's basement." Stryker heads toward the sheriff running the show. He offers his hand to shake.

The man gives a "crushing fingers" grip as he gives three strong pumps. "I'm sure this will cause you some issues with your commanding officer, but we're glad for the assistance, uh…" he fumbles for a moment, not sure of Stryker's rank.

"I'm a warrant officer, Sheriff Burke." Stryker doesn't need to read the golden name plate on the officer's chest. As a teen he had had a run in with Burke and is shocked the sheriff doesn't seem to remember. "Stryker is fine."

Burke has gotten no less imposing since Stryker left his hometown for the military and, even with his combat training, he's not sure he can take this mountain. He won't bet on his Gunnery Sergeant to beat the sheriff in a fair fight either. "Where can we be of the most use?"

Burke surveys the scene before him like a king inspecting his holdings. "Most of the men and women in the field are not experts in search and recovery. It's why we put them there. I'm using the FMO, Find the Missing Organization volunteers in the wooded area where I've greater concerns a clue can't be missed. They're highly experienced in search and recovery."

Stryker bets Burke hates that part of the FMO uses biker volunteers. The man is likely still a bit old school when it comes to people who ride hogs. The subtext of the sheriff's remark isn't made about the bikers. It's clear he believes the child is in the wooded area, but he can't ignore the field. "Gunnery Sergeant Goodman here has *military* search and rescue training."

The sheriff never makes eye contact with the black man as he speaks. "Useful. You find anything, you call for my men." Burke's issues his next command as if speaking to a field hand. "Now, don't you touch nothing. I don't want you contaminating any evidence. I want to get whoever took this little girl."

If this situation doesn't need their focus on the missing child, Stryker is more than willing to move out of the way for Gunnery Sergeant Goodman to pummel Burke. The man has been sheriff too long and needs someone to knock him down a few notches. Inform him how his old school treatment of people doesn't fly anymore. "What's her name?"

Burke chews as if he has bile in his mouth. "Sloane. She's a Copeland."

Stryker wonders if she's related to the Copelands he went to high school with. "We'll do all we can to find her, Sheriff."

Goodman waits until he and Stryker are out of earshot. "I don't think the sheriff likes me much. Kind of reminds me of Buford T. Justice if he were a bodybuilder."

"Man's a mountain, and the rumor when I attended high school was he ran the town his way including who got elected to town council. A lot of people owe him, and he kept Springwells clean of major crimes."

Stryker and Goodman join the crowd being directed by a woman who likely needs heels to reach five feet. Pinned to her jacket are dozens of buttons, each with a face. Most are women and young girls with a few little boys sprinkled in. From the hairstyles, some of them have been missing since the 1980s. Stryker wonders which button contains the image of the woman's child. He has no doubt a woman with her disposition finds other missing people because she couldn't locate her own lost child.

She speaks with a loud and experienced voice, "You will never know how much all of you here today will mean to this family. I know many of you have never done this before—that's why the FMO members are all in these blue shirts." She tugs at her own shirt. "Follow their lead. Thank you for all you're doing. I need my B team to stay. The rest of you please be careful."

More than half the crowd breaks away to search. The woman now addresses those who remain in the blue FMO shirts. "Unfortunately, all of you have done this before. This wooded area is dense. It will be more difficult to search than most of you have experienced, but we need to try and stay an arm's length apart. They'll be bringing in a couple of human remains dogs tomorrow, but the Sheriff wants us to search before the family sees them."

Human remains dogs signal an end to all hope the little girl will be found alive or maybe found at all. Stryker has no children, but in combat when a Marine doesn't return, and they can't go after him, it's not knowing that pains the most. It must be horrid when it's a child. He has brought home every fellow Marine lost during combat. Stryker hopes he can do the same for Sloane.

"It's a steep gully in there and after a good rain it floods. I think it will be best if we work down from this high end to the area that connects with the creek. Those of you with waders, we want you to head back upstream in the water. Use your probing poles. It's shallow, but there are spots that drop off, and Missouri is the cave state. As with yesterday, if anyone spots anything suspicious, call for the deputies. We don't have any leads on whether anyone may have taken Sloane, and we want to preserve all evidence in case someone is located."

Goodman waits until the crowd breaks and moves into the trees. "They seem focused more on evidence over locating the little girl."

Stryker hates when evidence is more important than a life. "You've been on these search teams before? Don't you think the authorities know the girl is dead and they want to nail whoever has hurt her?"

"Your sheriff bothers me. I can see why my family never came for a visit."

Stryker pokes his staff into some leaves. It's one of those freak life occurrences. Being halfway around the world and discovering there's a connection to the stranger next to you. Goodman's uncle lives in Stryker's hometown. "I haven't been back since high school graduation."

The Gunnery Sergeant must hunch down and dip under branches as he moves deeper into the trees. "My uncle never let me visit him there. After meeting the sheriff, I understand why. He's the type to arrest a man for driving while black. Next time, no more shortcuts."

Stryker swore he'd never return to Springwells. His curiosity of how much his hometown changed got the better of him. "No argument there. Let's find this little girl."

With the density of the trees, the searchers become more spread out. Stryker forces himself to keep a slower pace. They aren't on a ten-mile run before breakfast. It takes time to probe the accumulated stacks of leaves and dead brush, so no clue is missed. "If she was dragged in between all these trees, it was by a smaller person."

Gunny lifts a branch, so he doesn't have to crouch to duck under it. "You tend to forget, Sir, we are some huge dudes."

"At least we're well equipped to handle a Momo if we run into one in here."

Gunny gives a crooked grin. "Let's not joke about bigfoot-esque monsters in the woods."

"Gunnery Sergeant Goodman, I never thought you'd ever be rattled. You charged those three men who emptied their full magazines at you and never blinked."

"Those towelheads didn't know how to aim. And I saw the Fouke Monster. After that my mother moved me to inner-city Chicago. I ran into the worst monsters there. Dogs and cats. Dogs and cats." Goodman sinks the end of the hiking pole not into earth but through an object under the forgotten autumn leaves. His stomach bubbles as the sound's not quite unknown. At least not in his memory. He hates the stereotype, but he does love chicken. His mother would get a whole bird and crack the bones. Whatever the tip of the pole hit sounded like cracking bone.

Stryker halts his probing. "Find something?"

Goodman tugs his work gloves from his belt. He stares down at the undergrowth. "Not sure." He slips on the right glove and kneels. "I don't want to contaminate evidence, nor call the deputies needlessly." Gunny pushes away from the leaves, careful not to move the pole. It's covered in wet earth, not mud, but more as if the dirt protecting the object. Even through the brown smears, it's clear he smashed through the yellowed cranium of a human skull.

Stryker's glad his own height allows him to peer over the Gunnery Sergeant's shoulder. He blurts out as if relieved. "That skull's too large to belong to a child."

"I was thinking the same."

Stryker adds, "Closer to Springwells they found bodies belonging to those who died on the Trail of Tears when expanding the highway. And we used to find arrowheads along the creeks. This might be one of those lost souls. I know they sure sparked a lot of ghost stories."

Gunny breathes not realizing he's been holding his breath. "Better I not move until the experts come collect the evidence. In this dense tree growth, we could lose the skull."

Stryker straightens up, glancing around for any of the blue shirts. Somehow, they're alone in the woods. "I'll have to go back to the edge of the tree line to call the deputies. I don't want to sound cold, finding this person might bring closure to another family, but it will put a crimp in the search for Sloane."

"Do I leave this pole stuck in the skull?"

Stryker ducks under a tree branch attempting to retrace his exact steps. "You're the search and rescue expert."

"I think it's been here a long time." Goodman brushes away some leaves again to be able to examine the skull better visually. "Lifting the pole straight up should prevent any further damage. Trying to hold the pole in place might upset any forensic evidence."

"Do what will prevent the most upset to the skull."

Goodman bites his bottom lip and lifts the probing pole slow to reduce further destruction. The moment the pole tip clears the skull—

Stryker mashes his eyes shut. It helps with the ringing in his ears but not with the pain inflicted from the half dozen branches he smashes through on his way to the ground. By the grace of a holy being or blind dumbass luck, he was in another Hummer when an IED took out part of his squad. He'll never forget what was left of that Private. Or the feeling of the percussion the blast caused. The moment the pole tip cleared the skull, an invisible force flings Stryker through the tree branches with the force of an IED. Part of his brain says no way it's an IED. Not in the backwoods of Missouri. The other part must locate his Sergeant. If someone rigged that skull to blow, he's right in the path of the blast.

Stryker's body refuses to get up. His mind debates who would bother to leave a skull in the middle of the woods–where no one goes–rigged to detonate. There are more caves in the state than any other and many are unknown and unexplored making them the optimal location to dispose of a victim.

It pains him and he hopes it is not in his head, but Stryker calls out, "Gunny!"

Seconds. Minutes. He hopes not hours have passed before he gets his arms to push his body up. A concussion will put me on the bench for a few weeks. "Gunny!"

Blurry lines remain in his vision, but Stryker can't wait for his body to correct itself. They may not be in a firefight, but someone attacks them. In combat, movement is life. "Gunny!"

No answer.

Stryker will settle for even a moan of pain. Any sign his Gunnery Sergeant—his friend—still breathes.

He detects the slight slope in the ground, which he had noticed near the edge of the creek bank. That tumble down might hinder him. He blinks rapidly, clearing some of the blurry lines.

His vision clears, revealing some mystical fairy tale setting with a woman in a royal velvet cloak in the middle of the forest. Even with the cloak's hem floating in the water, Stryker notes she's barefoot. If she had an apple, or if there were seven extremely short miners next to her, it couldn't be more of a fantasy. Even under heavy enemy fire sometimes his mind wanders. Stryker can't help but notice how plain her face is. Maybe he expected a woman appearing in the woods to have the most repugnant of features—

warts and all like a witch or be so beautiful would be impossible to believe she's real. She might be from a time when respectable women didn't paint their faces. He shakes off the wool gathering to focus on the woman's actions.

She unclasps the cloak. It flutters from her shoulders, revealing her naked form.

Stryker doesn't understand all her mumblings. He expects it to be Latin but it's not. He makes out part of what she says about renouncing the Christian faith and then she promises to be faithful to the Devil—body and soul.

With that declaration, her body spasms and contorts almost as if she is having a seizure. She drops to all fours still convulsing, then defined muscles consume her. As she becomes the figure of an Olympian bodybuilder, each muscle swells, gaining mass. Her body explodes in size to that of a bear along with growing dark shaggy hair.

Stryker swears she transforms into a black panther, but he knows no such feline exists. He reaches behind him, locking his hand firm around the handle of his M&P. Now's a good time for Gunny to wake up.

The full conversion takes mere seconds, ending with her growing horns. The feline-creature raises up on thick stocky legs, glaring flame red eyes down at Stryker.

Some primitive part of his brain should be soiling his underwear but the part that has faced combat keeps cool and draws the M&P ready to fire at the monster's center mass. In the same moment, the creature leaps and unleashes a scream to bring death. Stryker fires. Part of him hopes the thunder-crack of expending the round will draw the deputies. He's prepared for the impact of the monster but not for a side tackle. It catches him off guard and as he and the Gunnery Sergeant tumble out of the path of the horned feline, the M&P skips across the ground and plops into the creek.

The horned feline stomps past them, turning more like a bull than a surefooted cat.

Gunny recovers from the dive and springs to his feet, K-bar in hand. "Get up, Sir."

Stryker struggles to breathe but follows his Sergeant's suggestion. He half stumbles toward the creek. Mythical or not, it will take more than one bullet to bring down a beast of that size.

The Gunny slides his right foot back and side steps the creature as it charges past. His knife tastes blood but doesn't reach any vital organs.

The monster rears up on her hind legs to be taller than the Marines. Stryker must abandon his search for the M&P to avoid the beast's attack. He joins Goodman as if they are two linemen prepared to halt the offensive charge. The two Marines make eye contact.

Gunny orders, "Singapore."

Then they both focus on the feline creature. They brace for the attack. As they take the brunt, they each move under the opposite arms, locking in a shoulder hold that allows the pair to flip the beast on her back. She snarls, snapping her jaw, flails her forearms and kicks with the back without being able to unpin herself from the combined strength of the two Marines on each side of her. Their practiced move saves them from being mauled, but neither can release the monster to do her any damage without facing fatal injuries from her front paws.

Stryker struggles to keep the beast trapped. "What now, Gunny?"

"You're the commanding officer, Sir."

In other words, it's his shit-show now. Stryker can't hold on forever. Even with his constant physical training, the struggle wears at his muscles and Gunny must be in a similar state. The explosion should have brought the deputies by now. "Go for my weapon."

Without warning, both Marines break their hold and race for the creek. It takes the feline creature a few seconds to realize she's no longer being held down. She overturns, landing on all four paws ready to pounce.

Stryker reaches the water first. Goodman spins around KA-BAR in hand to cover the Warrant Officer. No reason both of them should get in each other's way fumbling for the M&P.

Stryker laces his fingers around the gun's handle. His next move seems almost in slow motion against the charge of the demon-snarl of the feline creature. Stryker spins around, water spilling off the weapon. He takes aim and squeezes the trigger. Twelve *booms* deafen the gully. Twelve Teflon coated copper rounds puncture the creature.

It skitters to a halt and collapses.

"Think they'll let me mount the head in the barracks the way you rednecks display your deer heads?"

Stryker keeps the M&P aimed at the creature's center mass. "She's not dead yet, Gunny. Taking her head might not be a bad idea."

"Monsters like this never die."

Stryker approaches slow, giving the creature a wide berth. "Got to finish them with a head shot."

The feline creature's breath quickens almost as if she's hyperventilating.

Gunny swings around the monster opposite Stryker. "What is it?"

Stryker shakes his head. "Bullets brought it down. That's all I know."

"Just because it bleeds doesn't make it easy to kill."

With each quick but labored breath, the beast diminishes in size until reaching the form of the human woman.

Crimson holes spilling little blood decorate her stomach and shoulders.

Gunny halts not wanting to get to close to her. "What did you hit her with?" Then he scrunches his face. "Where did the woman come from?"

Stryker keeps out of her reach. "Box said zombie killers. Claims to open up and explode inside a target. They cost about two dollars a bullet."

"I know my next investment."

"As for the woman I think the skull is hers." Stryker aims at her forehead. "What are you?"

She spits her words along with flakes of blood. Most of what she says sounds like some ancient language. The tone delineates cursing. "I have been living on these lands for a hundred years."

Stryker doesn't ask a question. "And kidnapping children."

"They are pure, untainted by the darkness. The darkness that surrounds you. What did you do to earn such a black mark?"

Stryker fires. The bullet splatters her eye and explodes out the side of her face, trailing bone, blood and brains behind it.

Her skin grays and flakes away like ash. Her underlying muscle tissue darkens and falls off her carcass like well cooked meat until her bones crumble into dust, leaving only the skull.

"No one's ever going to believe this, Sir."

Stryker lowers the M&P to his side removing his finger from the trigger, executing the discipline that prevents an accidental firing. "I don't believe it myself, Gunny. I don't know what we stepped in, but we aren't going to easily wash this off."

"What about the little girl?"

"When this creature appeared, she was near that overhang by the creek."

Gunny slips a flashlight from his BDUs and marches through the water. He shines the light into the back of a cave. "There are some clothes in here. They can't belong to an adult."

"Find one of those blue shirts. Let's find peace for Sloane." Stryker drives the heel of his boot into the remains of the skull, shattering it.

"Feel better?"

"No." Stryker kneels. "I'm sure not going to let these pieces be held by Burke." He gathers the smashed fragments into a handkerchief.

"Who we going to report this to, Sir?"

Stryker shakes his head. "I don't know. Someone who won't put us in a padded room and give us a medical discharge."

The Marines don't speak until they reach the edge of the tree line where they are greeted by the Sheriff and an armed contingent of deputies.

Burke is the only one without his sidearm drawn, but his hand rests on the gun as if he's Wyatt Earp. "You better have a grand explanation for discharging a weapon during an active search for a missing child, soldier."

Stryker won't take the bait and he hopes Gunny knows not to say anything either. This is not the time to correct the man they aren't soldiers, but Marines. He didn't think of how all his expended rounds might scare the civilians. "We found Sloane."

"And killed the man who took her." Burke doesn't ask a question. He's the type to approve the execution of child molesters.

"I fired on," Stryker breathes, "*At* some animal. Felt too large to be a dog but too small to be a bear. Maybe a mountain cat of sorts. We fell into the ravine trying to scare it away before we knew Sloane was gone."

Burke removes his hand from his pistol and waves for his deputies to lower their weapons. "American's finest at their best. At least you found the child."

Skyler hates these little interrogation rooms and who doesn't know now that a group of people watch from behind the mirrored wall. Probably enjoying popcorn at his debriefing.

The door opens. Stryker's only thought, send in the clowns.

The white shirt and black suit is indicative of Hoover's FBI, however, the man fails at giving off the Men in Black vibe without the Ray Bans, and he doesn't have the indignation of a CIA agent. However, he's got shadow government written all over him. "Warrant Officer Stryker."

"And you are?"

"Don't worry about that." He places a small metal case on the table. He flashes the shattered bits of skull before snapping shut the lid.

Stryker pats the table in a mild drumbeat. "Bet you can't tell me what that creature was either?"

"We aren't sure. Might have been an Ozark Howler."

Stryker has heard a few tails of the overgrown wildcat.

The agent continues. "There are some who consider it a Dark Dog of Death found in British legends, but likely she's a witch of sorts. They tend to enjoy feasting on young children. Many of these supernatural creatures don't leave behind corpses for examination."

"You looking to ship me to some forgotten Arctic base?"

"No. In fact, after this incident we would like you and Gunnery Sergeant Goodman to consider transferring to a special unit of which I have oversight." He places a file folder on the table. "I'll give you some time to think about it. If you decide to go back to being a regular Marine, then sign this non-disclosure agreement and the official story will be that missing girl was killed by a bobcat."

Stryker makes no movement toward the folder. "And if I decide a transfer is in order."

"The official story remains, but you can stop monsters before they murder anymore little girls."

Stryker glances at the metal case and then at the folder. "I won't chase monsters without my Gunnery Sergeant."

The government official gives Stryker a nod. "Your Gunnery Sergeant attacked an Ozark Howler with nothing but a knife. If you didn't want him on your team, I was going to request he be transferred to my security detail."

END

The Hollow

MAGAIDH DUNBROCH

Edited by Hana Blue C. Charshade Press charshadepress@gmail.com

Prologue

The Hollow. It was a dank, watery prison of endless pain and suffering, and the dead kept it. Their broken voices choked the air. Their pain-drenched wails stretched endlessly in the wind, reminding her she wasn't one of them; but she wasn't *not* one of them. The frigid night should have chilled her, yet the enchanting ivory evening dress she wore felt too warm. She trudged through the endless knee-high waters that made up this place. The beautiful glittering pearl gown staining the water behind her like a ghostly procession.

Stopping at a tree whose gnarled trunk ascended from the black water, stretching endlessly into the black sky. Carnelian light spilled from a hollow in the trunk, staining the surrounding water below it.

The molten center illuminated her pallid face as she immersed her torso below the water, sitting on bent knees reverently before it. The wound seeped a dark liquid, which she covered two fingers in, swiping it over her forehead. She traced an upturned crescent moon and dagger on her skin. The image wept from the liquid ichor. She sniffed, barely able to smell the putrid blood that was the tree's offering. A gentle smile graced her lips as she washed her fingers in the oppressive water, bringing them up clean to pray to her goddess. The backs of her thumbs touched nail to nail below her elongated index fingers; the sign of the Goddess.

She prayed silently, staring into the fiery pit of the tree, hoping against hope that today would be the day she could step through the gash into the Underworld. As she prayed, her whole body vibrated with energy. She envisioned herself stepping through the carnelian light, being called to the Eternal River, to the Elysian Fields, which she had been promised once upon a spell. She grew weary of this eternal night. Tired of walking on legs that were constantly wet. Legs below the surface, scratched the ground with skeletal toes. A tight breath escaped over her tongue, a tear slid down her cold cheek.

She stood, hearing the plopping of a soul trudging through the water. The plopping and splashing of the forced footsteps alerted her to its presence and brought her to her feet. Kissing her thumbs, she thanked the Goddess for her prayers. As a bloated and bleeding hand grasped her shoulder, she allowed it to turn her, and didn't flinch. Nor did she cry out in fear as she stared into the rotting, slimy face of the corpse who had been called to oblivion instead of her.

This one, an Anubi, the long snout of its jackal face was missing. Its long teeth bared in a grisly smile forevermore. It looked down at her with dead milky eyes. Its chest still rose and fell, like its body needed air, just a reflex from reanimation. Muscle memory of its life before death.

She took great care to remove its hand from her person and reached back into the tree, bringing forth a wickedly curved blade and handing it to the Anubi, who stood above her. It growled, echoing its unease through the watery glade. She smiled gently and stepped aside so that the tree's embers illuminated it.

"You had better find heart for where you're going. Anything less than viciousness will not be tolerated." She snapped, taking another step back as the tree's gap widened and flared.

Flames writhed, pulling at the Anubi against its will and singeing the wet flesh as it tried to escape. She snarled at the beast. *This was a gift it clearly wasn't ready for.* The Anubi looked at her with pleading eyes before she let loose a bolt of blue ice, knocking it back into the tree. The frostbit skin of her arm didn't hurt as she inspected it, already knitting itself swiftly back together.

The tree quieted. Only one was permitted to leave tonight, even if its suffering hadn't hardened it at all. The Goddess needed fodder, after all.

One

She had never grown accustomed to the sound of her toes clicking on the stone floors. The water always hid that telltale feature from her. If she had anything to say about it, she would never step foot in the castle. In the night, she could imagine herself being whole. Here, though, it was one reminder after another that she was not whole, in appearance or mind. She slunk around corners, the light from the torches never casting a shadow from her body, not even the pieces that were still intact. Not even the captivating dress that caressed her once sensual curves; its magnificence, falling like a waterfall behind her, was never graced with a shadow. *Shadows were for the living.*

Had she a beating heart it would have constricted painfully realizing it wasn't a dress, but a nightgown made by her treacherous lover. A gown that had stolen everything from her. *Sure, he said she would gain so much more by accepting the spelled gown, but he had not given her all the information.* A chuckle brought her out of her pondering. She never had recollections except in the castle. Another form of torment he subjected her to. She turned to see a figure sitting at the table, his dark boots propped up on the deeply carved top, looking very much like the pampered king he believed himself to be.

"I heard you coming." His deep satin voice filled her with a dangerous nostalgia. A nostalgia that was equal parts revulsion and desire. Just like it had for so many nights previously.

"I haven't yet," she replied snarkily, crossing her arms in front of her, hoping the barb would hit him in his manhood. His visage burned into her memory now. She didn't need to look at him to know that a smile crossed his alluring dark lips. Her eyes remained focused on a pillar away from him. The wooden leg screeched along the stone floor as he pushed from the table and padded heavily toward her, consuming her vision. *Thank the Goddess she couldn't smell him. It might undo her resolve.* She couldn't remember his scent, only how it had made her feel. Her stomach turned, remembering the lightning that coursed through her, how her stomach tightened in anticipation, and how her skin craved him. It all quickly faded as she fingered a pearl bead, remembering the memories of the gown. He angled his head down at her, flicking a hand through her body and chuckling.

She bristled at his rudeness. *He did that every night, seemingly just to put her in her place.* She turned from him.

"The Anubi has left, the scythe given to it, though I think its torments have left it weak and far softer than the Goddess would appreciate. Losing your touch?" She sneered. Her head whipped roughly around as he pulled her arm, spinning her into him. He glared at her with his beautiful cognac eyes, rimmed with full dark lashes and perfectly strong features. He whispered into her ear.

"It's funny that you bring her up like you're privy to her needs, yet it is she who keeps you here, Velaryon."

The sound of her name on his tongue kindled the memory that once set fire to her stomach. Valaryon remembered her features while alive. Her white hip length hair, icy sapphire eyes and full breasts were the envy of every female. She had been a true beauty. He smirked as she tried to pull away, the pain of the past welling up. Every Time she saw his mauve skin, muscles fit to bursting with wavy maroon hair it sent her over the edge. His sharp, angled jaw and intense calculating eyes drew her in. His hands found every tender spot she craved them to touch. She loved and hated this game. She knew he loved using his magick over her like this.

Her stomach tightened, her skin crawled as she tried to rebel against his charms. Something inside her mind told her that fighting was the only way to break free, and then it would scream 'go to him.' She stood on the precipice of drowning each night to distance herself from him. Something he allowed her to do, to torment herself. Then one crick of his finger and she would crave him. She hated herself for allowing it as he sidled up against her back, his evident desire pulsing against her bottom. One moment she was corporeal, the next a wraith. She should be thankful for times like these, the times that allowed her to become whole again thanks to his magick. The times that he freed her from her prison and she could again feel what it was to be alive, or something close to alive. *Even if he was the reason she wasn't.*

His hands deftly unbuttoned the dainty buttons that lined her long back. He slipped her hip length, snow white hair to the side before the gown slid like water from her body. She felt his fingertips tapping along her shoulders, over her collarbones and down to cup her breasts. Her skin prickled at his touch. *It was always the same, always the same sensation as his magick turned her to flesh and blood.* Blood that now made her mound of venus ache. She had said so many times she wouldn't let him do this again, that she was stronger than her lust, but tonight proved her wrong again.

Every time he licked or kissed her neck, traced her nipples with a claw, it drove her wild. Wild with a desire that burned through her. It was one of the few things that she could remember of her former self. Passion that flooded her being, and the feel of his cock inside of her. Something that not even this pale existence could scour from her memories. She turned toward him, allowing him to scoop her up, his hands cupping her bottom and spreading her legs wide as he pushed her against the heavy table. He took one hand from her bottom to free his cock and sheathed himself inside her.

Velaryon moaned loudly and called his name as he buried himself in her, deep enough to grind on the delicate nerve cluster that sent lightning wracking through her core. She reached up, grabbing his curved, onyx horns, pulling his head down to bite her nipples as he continued to fuck her. He carefully transitioned to the ground so that she could ride his massive frame. Her hips bucked and rocked back and forth as she ground herself against him, seeking a pleasure only she could entice. Her core heated as she chased her passion with reckless abandon. No matter how many times he searched for that nerve cluster, he never found it. She had tried so many times to picture someone, anyone else, beneath her.

The way his body and cock moved inside of her, for her pleasure, almost seemed like they were created specifically for one another. She could feel herself clenching as she rubbed herself against him, the pressure and heat in her core building, driving her wild. Her breath grew ragged as she neared release, and she finally looked at him. He bit his lip. Gavril rocked his hips beneath hers perfectly. Reaching up, he grabbed her throat, applying enough pressure to make her breath shallow, enhancing her experience as he held her to him as she came. Velaryon's body tightened around his cock as her release swept over her. The building fire extinguished too soon for her liking.

He didn't waste a minute before he rolled on top of her, his hand still constricting her throat, though not from malice. The other he placed on her bouncing breast, pinching her nipple harder with every pound of his cock. Her passion rose again, quickly. He fucked her hard. She couldn't help but gasp in ecstasy as he pulled her closer to him, burying himself fully in her. His cock hit just right and sent an explosion. through her. He knew when she came, she could tell because he fucked her harder, to the point she feared she would go insane or be torn apart.

Velaryon enjoyed his breath on her in the moment. The sweat their bodies produced as they undulated against one another. Every time she raked him with her nails, he smiled and groaned, changing the pace of his stroke. She relished the power she had over him. Maybe that's why she continued in this disgrace. It was the only power she had left. Her body seized as she felt total release and peace every time his cock gave her that ultimate gift. Likewise, she always knew when he was close. He kissed her, and his strokes became long as he pulled her into him. Her hips hurt, splayed wide for that long as he finally succumbed to his pleasure, and brought her to hers.

For a time, it was as if they were normal lovers, laying together in a sweaty embrace. When the passion wore off, without a word, she felt herself drift back into the lonely sense of drowning and regret that held her captive. She stood, disgusted with herself for once again abandoning all resolve for a few brief minutes of bliss. The gown glittered around her at his whim, encasing her sweat drenched body once again in her white chains. He sat arrogantly now on the corner of the table, eating an eple. Attraction filled her senses again, remembering how instantly she had fallen for him.

He was the forbidden fruit, and with her first taste of him, she had lost everything. *That was his game, though, allowing random memories to seize her while she was in the castle. Memories that would affect how she interacted with him, that would keep her from realizing her power and being able to break free.*

"Why do you insist I come here every night?" She wrapped her arms around her as she whispered, not really to him. The memories of who she was were fading from her thoughts, thanks to his magickal control. She was scared. Scared of the Incubus that sat before her. His glistening mauve skin, the rippling sexy muscles, cognac eyes and onyx horns intrigued her, though she didn't know why. He didn't even look like a textbook Incubus. He laughed heartily.

"You sent the Anubi on his way this evening?"

Nodding, she looked behind her into the darkness, hearing the whispers of her glade call to her. He looked questioningly at her.

"Tomorrow you will have two visitors. You shall send two to the Underworld."

Velaryon nodded absently, staring into the darkness. She jumped as she felt his hand on her cheek, his thumb caressing her lips and chin, angling her attention from the dark. He chuckled as she pulled away and tried to bite him. The darkness had whispered who she was, enough that it had sparked a memory, and she stepped away from him, toward the black, glaring at him. He smiled devilishly.

"I can't wait to see you tomorrow. Let's hope that your shadows do not interrupt us again. For your sake." He picked up an eple and crushed it in his giant fist. She ran down the dark halls, diving into the water that would lead her back to her watery prison and away from him.

*****

She sat on a moss-covered boulder, her white garment splayed about the dark waters delicately. Her snowy hair reflected in the ripples, clashing with the grey, scaly mess that her once milky smooth skin had become. *Another torment he let her have, the memory of her delicate beauty. How mortals had craved her features and complexion. It was nothing more than an inconvenience now.* Why, night after eternal night, did she look through the ripples at herself? It never brought her anything but grief. She tried to drown out the splashing and choking sounds of the glade and those tormented there. Honestly, she should take comfort in the fact she would never become a slimy, bloated corpse like them, but she couldn't.

This was a part of the nine hells. A watery grave of torment and terror. She was their keeper, their taskmaster. The overseer for the traps and torments that Lord and Lady Death surmised for the unworthy that ended up here. It was she that doled them out. Velaryon wasn't sure how she had ended up here, in such a prestigious position as most would consider it. She wasn't sure who she had prayed to alive, but now, in her death, she prayed to Andraste; the Goddess of death and reanimation. *Who else could have allowed her to transition into this, whatever she was?* It was to Andraste she prayed to, asking for her beloved Goddess to end her suffering and usher her through the world tree to her eternal rest.

It isn't an eternal rest, Velaryon.

"I know it's not for them, but for me it would be."

When their torments here are finished, just like in the other eight hells, they are called to the Underworld as part of the horde. They do not transition to peace. There is no peace for the damned.

She knew the words to be true. Still, she fought against them. "The Goddess will hear my prayers when it is right for them to be answered." Velaryon whispered vehemently, with unyielding devotion. She molded her fingers into Andraste's symbol and ignored the incorporeal whispers. The shadows and shrieks were all she had. Apart from their company, and the tiny bits of news they brought her, she was alone. The rest of the bodies here weren't much fun to talk to. Murders and rapists, thieves and liars. Lecherous fools and lesser beings she refused to entertain for the sake of her sanity.

Not that it mattered. Gavril would give her different memories or no memories, depending on his mood. At times, her former self battered and bludgeoned at the walls of her mind, trying to break free of the cage that imprisoned her. Only to have another, stronger one placed upon her. The walls close in every time; the terror filled drowning experience washed over her, stealing her breath and making her skin crawl. She wanted to claw at her body, to climb free of the dead smothering skin and be reborn into the cold light of daybreak where her lungs could gasp clean air unburdened. Velaryon supposed that was why she allowed Gavril to control her so. He was a slight breath of fresh air, the last sweet breath before she drowned each day. Then she remembered that last sweet breath she had been craving was instead the boot that kicked it from her body— the reason for her endless torment and anxiety.

She slapped the water, hearing the shadows skitter and chitter their amusement at her suffering. She couldn't hide it. Anxiety and fears reverberated and intensified in this place. Another torment that Lord and Lady Death had so graciously bestowed on the hollow, her watery glade. *Hopefully not realizing that its caretaker would also be affected.*

They don't care about you. You are here for a reason. Caretaker you might be, but you earned your place in this shit hole Velaryon.

Velaryon shook her head as she waded through the water, refusing to listen to the disembodied whispers.

"I did not. Andraste would not leave me here after granting me reanimation. It is a gift from her to her followers, a second chance." She breathed heavily, trying to outrun their cutting words.

It's your prison. You can believe whatever you like. You don't know your own mind, but we do. We REMEMBER the truth.

Velaryon ripped at her hair, frantic. A corpse burst free of the water, gulping and sputtering, begging for help. She couldn't let it escape its punishment. The shadows kept berating her into insanity. She rushed the corpse, slamming her fist into its tainted mouth, releasing a burst of ice down its gullet in her anger. It screamed briefly before sinking back into the water. She peered in after it, watching it reanimate and start the torment of its drowning once more. It might have broken free that time had she not lost herself. She screamed as she was ripped through the water back to the world tree.

She cursed silently. *It had been only a few minutes since last night. How could it be night again so quickly?* She sat in front of the tree, staring at the carnelian embers she so desperately wanted to walk through. She prayed to Andraste to save her, to call her home to the Underworld so that she may swim the Eternal River and finally ascend. A tear slid down her cheek as she heard a pair of mismatched splashes behind her.

She stood slowly, allowing the tree's light to engulf them. She watched them with dead eyes as she reached mechanically into the tree twice, bringing forth short swords for the rotting mortals. One had been massive. He leered down at her, unafraid. His companion showed more care, tapping him and shaking his head. The dumb one shrugged his shoulders.

"She be the Winter Witch dummy."

Two

I believe it's long enough, don't you?" Gavril's satin voice rang out as he nipped at her ear. He sauntered past her. She ogled him as his muscles flexed, his hair swayed and hungrily drank in how his wet cock looked as he put his midnight trousers back on.

"It's always *long* concerning you," she quipped, crossing her arms over her naked breasts. *He never let her keep the garment off this long. It was only off while they were fucking. Once he had his pleasure, he forced her back into it.* Her heart beat wildly as he drew near. His mauve skin looked so smooth and perfect wet. She instantly hoped for round two as he kissed her neck. She groped him through his trousers. *Even not aroused, he was a delight to play with.* He pushed his hips into her.

"Oh, I meant your memories. It's been long enough since you've had them. Don't you think so?" She pushed him away, instantly on guard. He smiled at her as he raked a hand through his shoulder length black hair, picking out a stray strand like he had said nothing alarming.

"Why, why now?" she stuttered. Her mind couldn't fathom his reasoning. It wasn't hard, since her mind wasn't what it used to be. He reached out and ran a hand down her neck, over her collarbones, gently cupping her breast. Her core ignited again, prickling her skin and her nipples. He pushed her back onto the tabletop, splaying her legs as he pulled up a chair and sat. Velaryon arched her back as he feasted on her. He paid special attention to the delicate nerve cluster between her thighs, licking and sucking. Heat overtook her, as she writhed into his face. He reached up, caressing her nipple, flicking and pinching it as the other hand's fingers slid into her. She moaned, feeling like she was going to explode, the pressure steadily growing inside of her.

His hot breath and wet tongue on her cunt were her favorite game. Gavril would bring her to within an inch of release, only to pull away and pound her with his fingers. He rose from the chair and leaned over her delicate body, sucking on her tender nipple. His fingers pulsing in and out of her, using his thumb to rub her cluster; faster and faster. His lips drew the air from her lungs as he kissed her;continued his game, allowing her this time to come on his hand. The demon that kept her captive bent and kissed her tender flesh, tasting her, then pulled her from the table. With a firm hand on her shoulder, he pushed her to her knees.

Still trembling from her climax, she pulled free his hardened cock and pressed the tip against her lips, flicking her tongue out and teasing the tip. Gavril breathed heavily. Grasped the back of her head, entwining his fingers in her hair, pulling her head into a cadence with her mouth open, swallowing him. Velaryon's tongue traced his swollen cock inside her mouth as her throat expanded for him. Her hands felt his hardened quads, tracing lazy circles on his inner thighs and massaging his manhood. She loved hearing the frenzied breath leaving him as he moaned for her, her name. The power over him she had in that position.

He pulled free from her mouth and tossed her to the floor away from him, reaching down and pulling her ass toward him. Gavril didn't wait for her to get comfortable on the stone floor before sinking his stiff cock inside her. She craved the way he fucked her, how he wrapped himself around her, reaching over her shoulders to caress a breast while the other hand massaged her mound and pressed her tighter against him. She reveled, feeling her wetness on him as he fucked her within an inch of her life. How he held her as they came together and even more when the embrace ended and she could be free of him.

"I don't see what that has to do with my memories, or lack thereof, Gavril." Velaryon turned on him, no longer under his spell. He snorted and kissed her cheek.

"Someone," he paused briefly, "has requested you. Someone who would be very upset to learn that your mind is not as it once was. That you were free of the memories that still haunt them. Consumed and destroyed."

This piqued her interest. *Had the Goddess Andraste finally come for her?* She smiled shyly, carefully turning away from Gavril. Lightning wracked her body as she felt his hand upon either side of her head. The searing magick rebuilding the ruined paths he had damaged so long ago. Then he let go, just as she thought the pain would finally overtake her and save her from her torment. She stood rigidly, fearful if she moved, she would fall apart. Her head swam and sickness overcame her. She wretched on the floor, then felt better. She turned to see Gavril smirking at her as she touched her body.

Her fingers stilled as she felt the gown. She pulled it up, revealing her bone legs, and raged at him.

"Another trick? Why get my hopes up, Gavril? What is the point of this torture?"

He laughed at her.

"I said your memories would come back. I did not say I would release your curse."

She thought about that for a moment. Actually thought, clear and concise. Not the jumbled mess of incoherent nonsense that had plagued her for so long. Her hand erupted in ice. It did not burn her or singe the dead flesh as it had last night. Had he meant to give her magick? The innate ability to control her winter magick and protect herself was intact. Everything that Gavril had taken away from her, he had given back. She threw out her frozen hand at him, directing the shards of ice to encircle and consume him. Her ice winked out as Gavril stepped through them. He had sent her back to her own plane. Here, the shadows warred and whispered against her.

"I think you should be more grateful, Velaryon, that I was gracious enough to give you back something that means so much to you, for him."

Coldness overtook her. Had she not been so stunned, she would have relished the feeling. Her breath became ragged and her memories flooded her, allowing her to become excited once again. She looked around, unable to contain her elation, pushing past the strangle hold that Gavril had placed on her. For the first time, fresh air was at hand. She touched her face, raking the scales and pallid skin from her cheek. Dank blood oozed and Gavril laughed wickedly.

"No amount of self care will change your appearance, Velaryon. Isn't that what they say about *true* love? It matters not what one looks like, only what's in one's heart. But then again," he cackled louder, "you don't have that either."

She tried to ignore those painful words, to push down the ache that threatened to tear her chest apart. The stabbing, stifling pull of despair that he had created with not only his words but his presence. That she had done to herself so long ago because of him. She glared as Gavril walked to the table and sat down regally before the food she could not smell or taste, and snapped his clawed fingers.

Velaryon felt him before she saw him. Smelled his tobacco musk that she had loved about him. It had been so long since she had laid eyes on him, fear radiated from her. Her mind shrank back in on itself as her memories took hold of her consciousness, playing back the memories of her fall into darkness and arrogance that she should have never nurtured. Her third eye wrested control of her vision as he approached, and she let it.

*****

Velaryon sat inside a stone chamber, emerald plants growing all around, and delicate citrine light fluttering through the windows of the keep. She marveled at the precise circles and shapes that she had painted on the smooth surface of the floor. Painstakingly, she had replicated the ancient and long dead text perfectly, mixing her blood with the painted pigments of a filled soul gem and faery wing. The crimson casting circle illuminated as she spoke.

Gnirb htrof eht nomed Gavril fo yromem, tel mih eb tneivresbus ot em.

Morf ym doolb eh lliw esir, rewop ni eht sih sdrow tonnac yned.

She felt the pull of power tear through her veins. It drank from her mana stores as the scribed words glowed brilliantly. She stumbled, not expecting the spell to consume so much of her energy. Velaryon cried out, falling to the floor as the spell severed. Through a glowing slit between dimensions stepped the most beautifully horned demon she had ever seen. Their eyes met. She felt a tug from somewhere deep inside her. He inhaled sharply and smiled at her. Something she was not expecting. The stories of demons instilled terror and fear in mortals, but they had always drawn her to them, and now she had one of her own to control.

She stood ogling his impressively muscular, naked form. His eyes bore into hers and she blushed. Her excitement grew, realizing she had just become one of the most powerful females in all of the Faedoroth; knowing she would rival the Gods with her newly summoned power. Velaryon raked her eyes over him, suddenly unabashed, her core heating.

"Are you ready to do my bidding, slave?" Her voice filled with haughty huskiness. She shuddered as he licked his lips. Enough, she shouldn't be so girlish, she was the Winter Witch. Only one man should have the power to have sway over her. Her beloved, he taught her everything she knew. Her heart skipped as her memories of him faded.

"I, Gavril, am at your disposal, my queen, but first you must set me free from my prison." The demon motioned toward the faintly glowing circle that was his cage and she nodded absently. Something in the back of her mind told her not to, screamed for help. The dark recesses of her mind called out for her love. Her mind grew hazy. He would set things right. The demon stroked his cock lightly, causing her to blush again. "The words, your highness, sweep them away and I will sweep all your worries away." Velaryon nodded. She should have taken more care, but he was so polite and handsome. It was cruel to keep such an intelligent being caged.

He nodded as she swiped her foot over the bloody paint, smearing the words. The demon rushed her, enveloping her in a kiss, and all she knew was Gavril. She heard her love shouting and tried to pull away, but the demon held onto her, kissing her. It felt right, she melted against him. His footsteps were close. The heavy oaken door shattered and blew into the room, drawing her attention. Gavril looked lazily around her at the disruption. She turned and smiled as her love rushed in shouting.

"Send him back, Velaryon. Do not fall for his false charms!"

Her shoulders rose in a halfhearted shrug as she started mouthing a spell. Her love faded from sight, his emerald despair filled eyes the last thing she saw.

Heavy footsteps thundered behind her. Only today there was no door to break between them. He stopped a hair's breadth away from her, so close she could feel his hot breath and remembered how she had loved him. She had wanted her memories for so long. Just to see him again. Velaryon turned and stuttered. He was more handsome than she had remembered. His hair had become salt and pepper, and the beard he once wore was gone; revealing a strong jaw. Even while frowning, he turned her stomach to butterflies. She worked up her courage. He glared over her at Gavril and growled. She jumped and finally shyly whispered.

"Hello, Kharon. It's good to see you."

To Be Continued in 2024

Visions

JEANEVA CHRISTIE

<u>One</u>

The sound of scraped hull sounded through the control deck. Ella knew there wasn't much that could be done about the damage that was about to happen. She'd seen it years ago in a vision, a vision that would lead to a new life, a new people separate from their origins. She had done her best to hand pick those she thought best suited to what was to come. Some there were no choices with, they were an inescapable part of the visions.

"Is it time?" came her symbiont, Gree's whisper in her mind.

"Yes." Ella thought back as she hit the abandon ship alarm. Granted no one had read the system's readings yet and it might be considered presumptuous of her, but Ella already knew what was coming.

"Then we will hope for the best." Gree was staunch in her reply.

The sound of running feet could be heard coming from the Captain's quarters. She wasn't exactly looking forward to the confrontation with her mate, Jovander.

He rounded the corner in a disheveled state. His hair was actually standing on end and it was apparent his uniform had been donned in haste. He was still sealing the front as he barged onto the bridge.

"What the hell? What happened?" He yelled as he headed for the Captain's seat where he could monitor the ship's systems.

Ella glanced away. She knew shit was about to hit the fan.

"A vision?" He screeched when he looked up and discovered her looking away. He'd come to hate her visions and the way they often dictated their lives over the years.

As she turned to face him, she lifted her chin and looked him squarely in the eyes. "Yes." Was all she said.

"How long?" He asked.

She had to wonder if he meant until something catastrophic happened or how long had she known. The latter would only lead to an argument, another in a lifetime of arguments. When he repeated himself, she decided to ignore the second possibility and answer the first.

"Any moment. I wanted to give the crew as much time as possible to reach the life pods."

"Well at least there is that." He said in exasperation.

"You better get strapped in and help me deal with what is coming then." He said as he continued to study his screens. "I'm seeing some damage but nothing bad yet."

"I'm not sure what the damage will be, but I know that it will force us down on the nearest planet, Mepuvir. It's believed to be uninhabited by sentient life forms."

"Believed?" Obviously he'd caught that distinction in her remark.

"Yes. There is a life form that we will encounter. They will be integral to our survival on the planet."

"Alright, good then. At least there is a chance."

As Greella sat at her console she was thankful he hadn't said anything more. It wasn't always easy to live with the foreknowledge she had. She brought up the readings for the planet below. She had already programmed the landing spots for the pods and knew exactly where the ship would need to land. The pods were going to be spread out in a jungle and needed to forge their way to various rendezvous before meeting up at the ship's landing area.

Each pod was equipped for the survival of its assigned crew of six except the medical pods. They were all specially equipped for the sciences and life support needed to colonize and survive. The med pods each had a med bay hence their five passenger crews.

She was just relaxing into her seat when the whole ship jolted and more alarms started blaring.

<u>Two</u>

D*amn her and her secrecy.*

Jovander did care for his mate. After a few centuries with a woman you did tend to develop feelings even if they weren't exactly the all consuming romantic kind of love. Greella was the woman he had spent a lifetime with and she had borne his children, of whom he was very proud. But still there were things about Ella herself that he had never come to terms with, namely her visions.

"Did you know about this?" He asked his symbiont, Jov.

"You know that Gree tells me most things. But we agreed years ago that it was best that the sharing go no further than us." Jov answered.

"And you wonder why I have such a problem with that. My own damned symbiont is keeping secrets from me."

"Yes and you know why. All the two of you did was argue. It wasn't good for the children let alone the two of you." He could hear the exacerbation in Jov's mental voice.

"Yeah well the children haven't been children in decades." Ander snorted as his fingers flew over the keys of his console. He looked up to see Ella at her console working as well. He looked back just as the ship rocked. His console lit up with alarms and a cacophony of sound blasted his ears.

"Ah, Fuck!" He'd never felt the need to use the ancient term before, but if there ever was a time it was now.

"Well that pretty much sums things up," came Ella's reply.

"Were you able to program the landing zones?" He asked.

"Yes. They are all set and I have our course programmed as well."

"Did they all make it onto the pods?"

"All of the crew made it to pods but not in the configuration they were supposed to. One of the engineering pods is light, one crew member and med pod one is heavy, an engineer. I'm pretty sure it's all how things were meant to be," she said.

"Right, just as things were meant to be." He bit out.

He watched as the many warning lights went out on his console and the blaring alarms silenced. He couldn't keep the ship flying, but they had managed to stabilize it at least temporarily. They should be able to land. If they were really lucky they would be able to use it for their survival.

"Have you gotten off an SOS?" he asked.

"I've sent out the SOS and messages to Doar. I'm not sure we'll get an answer, though. There aren't enough comm satellites between here and there. I think we'll be here for the long haul." She looked up at him as she said the last.

"The long haul? What about the children?" The thought of never seeing his children again had his heart seizing in his chest as if the spike of adrenaline weren't enough.

"I know." She said as tears filled her eyes.

"Are you sure, there was nothing that could have been done?" He searched her face as he asked, but he knew the answer even as he asked. Slowly she shook her head from side to side as the tears tracked down her cheeks.

"Nothing." She sobbed.

Sighing he bowed his head. Deep down he knew it wasn't her fault. He knew she would never do anything to jeopardize their relationship with their children. This was hurting her as much as it was him.

"I know, babe. Chin up. We need to strap in and stay alert. We'll be hitting the atmosphere in a few moments."

Three

"B*uck up. You knew this was coming,*" said Gree.

"*Doesn't help with the emotions any,*" sobbed Ella.

"*You don't have the luxury of feeling those emotions right now. We have a ship to land. Or have you forgotten?*"

"*Right! Like I could forget. I've lived with this vision on repeat for over twenty damned years.*" Ella hiccuped as she wiped at her eyes.

Most visions were fleeting. They came and they went, happening in close order. There were some, though, that came over and over again and took years in the making. They were the most vivid and often the most traumatic. She had known for years before her first pregnancies that they wouldn't last. The first years of their mating were filled with miscarriages. Each one had been a heartache she thought would never end.

When Ander found out that she had known, he became so angry with her. He refused her bed for years. Not that she had felt it as a great loss. Don't get her wrong, though. Ella liked sex just fine and Ander was an exceptional lover. He just wasn't the man she fell in love with all those years ago. But matings on Doar were dictated by their symbionts and the elders. Everything was decided well before they were even born.

All in all, things could have been worse. After all, she did care about Ander and she knew he cared about her as well. Eventually, she had known it was time to try for children. It had taken a bit of convincing and manipulation, but she'd finally gotten Ander back in their mating bed. They'd had two children in close succession. Their son, Carator was already well on his way as an ambassador's apprentice. Their daughter, Syranna was a captain in her own right, although she flew a much smaller trading vessel between the planets of their star system.

If her visions hadn't already shown her their reunion she would be completely devastated. Even so those visions were fleeting and there was no telling how many years in the future they were.

Ella had just managed to get strapped in at Jovander's urging when the ship started to shake further as they broke through the atmosphere.

"We're coming down way too fast, Ander."

"Yes I know. Get ready for me to hit the brakes," came his cryptic reply.

Just as they broke from the upper atmosphere the ship jerked and slowed marginally as the brakes engaged. Ella could feel her cheeks stretch tightly across her facial bones as her stomach almost hit her throat in reaction. The view outside the ship's view screen was blurred at the speed they were descending.

"Come on baby. Slow down, dammit." Ander whispered to the ship. As if the ship would hear his coaxing and obey. He'd always held some intimacy with his ships. A woman could become downright jealous of the way he talked to his ship, but she knew she had nothing to be jealous of. He filled her bed each night, even if it were only to sleep.

The ship started to shake even harder as it finally started to slow. Ella kept a close eye on her console to make sure they were coming down in the right area. If things went well they would be landing at the southern end of the continent close to a beach where there was plenty of room for a ship of this size.

"Do you have the landing gear ready to engage?" She knew he had his hands full keeping the ship on course, but readying the landing gear was critical.

"In five, four, three, two, one…" he said as she felt the stabilizers lower and the mechanical air brakes engage.

Ella grabbed at the arms of her chair in anticipation of their landing. There was no telling just how rough it might be.

When the ship finally hit the sandy beach, she watched their view screen as their vision was obstructed by flying sand. They bounced several times and she could hear the metallic screech as one of the stabilizers was damaged. Suddenly they were careening at a tilt across the sand and they could see the ocean coming closer and closer.

"Please tell me that a water grave is not part of the vision?" Ander asked.

"Oh hell no, I hope not," wincing, she stared in horror out front of the ship. Then suddenly and inexplicably their progress slowed and they came to a rest some distance from where the waves crashed onto the shore.

"Damn, that was close. I hope to hell that it's high tide now or we may still need to be concerned."

Four

The ship had come to a stop about a hundred feet from the shore. No telling if that would be sufficient spacing for high tide on this planet. Ander was grateful that the ship had stopped so abruptly. He could only assume they had come up against something that had stopped their forward motion.

"Well that was damned fortuitous." He said.

"Yes. Not sure what stopped us, but I'm so relieved we aren't resting at the bottom of the ocean," replied Ella.

"Let's do everything we can to analyze the ship's status, then I think we need to talk." He huffed.

Sighing Greella replied, "Right. I'll start on hull breeches and damages."

"Then I'll start on ship-wide systems before we review the engineering, medical, botanical and other individual systems." Ander said as he started running scans.

After a solemn sharing of the damages to the ship, Ander scrutinized Ella. Did she look guilty? How long had she known? Clearing his throat he decided to get some answers.

"How long?" he asked.

She squirmed and looked away as she replied, "Years."

"How many years?" he persisted.

"Many years."

"Ella!"

"Decades, alright? I've been getting visions for decades!"

Sighing, Ander shook his head. Decades and she hadn't said a word.

"Go easy on her. You know these visions can play havoc with her emotions," said Jov.

"Yes, well they aren't exactly easy on mine either," he replied. *"What about our children?"*

Actually that was a good question to be asking. "What about Carator and Syranna? Will we see them again?"

"I've had visions of them in the future, albeit long into the future," she sobbed out.

"Do you know how long?" he asked as he got up to go to her.

"Centuries at least," she got out between hiccups and sobs.

"That long?" he stumbled as he took in her reply. Reaching her he pulled her up from her seat and into his arms.

"Yes," she wailed as her head came to rest on his shoulder. Ella's body shuddered in inconsolable weeping.

Ander was angry and devastated at the news, but ultimately he knew she was in no better condition. Picking her up he carried her towards their cabin. She needed rest before they discussed this any further. Besides he could always get some of his answers from Jov.

Laying her on the bed he climbed in behind her.

"How fucked are we?" he asked Jov.

"You know how these visions go. Sometimes she gets a complete vision and they happen soon after. The more catastrophic happen in bits and pieces over a long time. The bits and pieces are scrambled and it takes a long time to piece them together and know what is coming," Jov answered.

"Okay, I get that. But how long has she been preparing for this?" he asked.

"The better part of the last decade," Jov said.

"What? How?" Ander was surprised by the reply.

"A ship had to be designed that would give the crew as much chance at survival as possible. All of the life sciences that might be needed. Research capabilities. The best equipment and labs. We had to make sure that the database of information was as complete as possible." Jov said.

"We?" Ander asked.

"Yes, we. Gree, Ella and I have worked on this for years."

"But how?" he asked in surprise.

"While Ella did all the physical stuff and advocacy to make sure an adequate ship was developed, Gree and I communicated with the other symbionts to influence their hosts. Of course we also ran scenarios between us to make sure we were as prepared as possible." Jov's reply was matter of fact and concise.

Ander had known that Gree and Jov often kept Ella's visions to themselves, but this was different than anything he'd known about.

"What about the crew? Do any of them know?" he asked.

"None of the hosts know. We may have had some influence with the symbionts to insure that some of the hosts joined the crew." Jov answered.

"She even picked the crew specifically?" he asked.

"Well, yes of course. We had to make sure that we had the best for survival. Also, some of them appeared in her visions," Jov said.

"This is a lot to take in." Ander mused.

"Get some rest while you can. There is much more to know and do." Jov answered before Ander felt himself drifting off to sleep.

Damned symbiont, was his last thought.

<u>Five</u>

lla woke up snuggled against Ander. Peering over her shoulder she saw that he was sleeping soundly before she lifted his arm and scooted to the side of the bed. A trip to the bathroom was a must. Besides a need to relieve herself, she felt like her eyes were puffy and her face was dry and coated in a layer of the salty remnants of her tears.

"Feeling better?" asked Gree.

"As much as can be expected," she replied.

"Yes, well it's time to put that aside and get to work," said Gree.

"Has Jov indicated just how angry he is?" she asked.

"He isn't exactly a happy camper, but he's coming around." Gree offered.

"At least there's that." Ella sighed as she washed her face.

"You need to get on the comms and see if you can reach any of the pods." Gree said.

"Yes and we'll need to check the vicinity with external scans before we venture out." She agreed.

"Best get to it then,"

"Yes, mother," Ella replied.

"I am not your mother," Gree huffed.

"Well then don't act like it," Ella huffed back while making her way back to the bridge.

Gree spent the better part of an hour trying to reach the life pods with no success. Between the distance, terrain and damages to the ship any factor could be the culprit. Eventually, the pods would make their way closer and they would be able to communicate.

In the meantime she and Ander would have to do what repairs they could manage on their own. There wasn't really anything that could be done about the outer hull. They would need Beryl for that. As a metallurgist he'd be able to locate metal on the planet sufficient to make the repairs.

That didn't mean they'd be getting off the planet though. The hull breach had caused damages to the drives that wouldn't be fixable for the foreseeable future. They really needed all the crew for a full assessment.

She was just starting a scan of the vicinity when Jovander joined her on the bridge.

"Feeling better?" he asked.

"As much as can be expected," she replied.

"Good. Anything to report?" he asked as he took his seat in the captain's chair.

"Communications are down. I'm not sure of the cause, but I can't raise any of the pods," she said.

"Okay. Any speculations?" he asked.

"We haven't checked the exterior of the ship to see if it might be an issue with comms relays. It could also be a matter of distance and terrain. Perhaps something in the planet itself is causing the issue," she sighed. "I'm just not sure, yet."

"Right. Have we scanned the vicinity yet?" he asked.

"I'm doing that now, We're on the southern tip of the continent. The pods were all programmed to land in clearings I located in the jungle north of us. It will take them weeks to arrive at our location. They're going to have to clear a path to get here," Ella replied.

Ella was staring at her screen when she felt Ander lean over her chair back.

"What are these?" he asked, indicating the moving dots on the screen.

"Lifeforms," she said.

"Any details on them," he asked.

"I'm waiting for the scans to complete before I bring up the stats." Ella continued to broaden the scope of the scan. The number of lifeforms weren't really that many close to their location but the further north they scanned the greater number of lifeforms they saw.

"Think any of them are sentient?" Ander asked.

"Yes, actually," Ella said.

"Statistical answer or do you know from your visions?" he asked.

"Both actually. A planet this size typically has at least one sentient lifeform. My visions actually indicated that there may be more than one. I'm not positive, however, because I never saw myself speaking with them verbally." Ella said.

"How do you know they're sentient then?" he asked.

"It's more a feeling and the actions I saw," she replied distractedly.

"Ella, let the scans run. I think it's time you told me about your visions." Ander said as he spun her chair around to face him.

Taking a deep breath she looked up at him. She was actually surprised when he didn't appear angry. "What do you want to know first?"

"You said you've known for decades? What did you know first?" he asked as he searched her face.

Ella closed her eyes as she thought back to her first visions. "The first visions were short. I'd see and hear the blaring alarms and the two of us sitting on a bridge." She took a shuddering breath. "I could feel my future emotions of fear and loss."

"So all you knew was something catastrophic was going to happen?" he asked.

"Yes."

"You didn't know when?" he asked.

"No. There was no point of reference to when," she said. "As the years went by, I would get bits and pieces and I wasn't sure if they were related or not, until about a decade ago. Then the bits and pieces started to coalesce. It became apparent that we would be on an exploratory vessel. I knew we would be forced down on an unknown planet. That's when I started planning. With Gree and Jov's help I was able to advocate for better life sciences on our ships. I started looking for the crew that would be needed." Ella said.

"Wait. You started looking for the crew a decade ago? But that makes no sense. They were still children," he exclaimed.

"Not exactly, children. They were in their final years of general education. I needed to make sure they were steered towards the education and careers we needed," she said.

"Did you know who, already?"

"Some I've known would be involved for decades before they were even born. Others were more a choice down the road as they proved their aptitude and education. It was still a guessing game until a few years before we left. Then visions of the crew coalesced as well. I knew who we needed and I did whatever it took to make sure they were chosen."

"Damn, Ella. You handpicked a crew to crash land on this planet? What about their futures? What about their families?" Anders' voice rose as each question spilled from him.

"Ander, you know I have no control over the visions. All I could do was make sure we were all as prepared as possible," she looked away. "I wouldn't wish harm on any of the crew. Nor would I wish for the heartache of leaving behind family."

"What about their mates? We're the only mated couple on this voyage." He rasped.

"I know. But the visions…" she trailed off.

"The visions? What about the visions?" he asked.

"Have you looked at gender ratios for the crew, Ander?" she asked.

"No. Not really. Gender doesn't have anything to do with how well a person can do their job," he replied.

"Right. Well there is about a 1:5 ratio of women to men on the crew," she said.

"Alright. And?" he asked.

"And we will be here for centuries at least. Eventually, we will need to start populating the planet," she said as she studied her hands.

"Wait." Ander shuffled as he thought about that. "But you don't have a 1:1 ratio."

"No we don't. And a 1:1 ratio with this size of crew wouldn't work." Ella said.

"What do you mean?" he said as he grabbed the seat next to her and plopped down.

"Each of the females will have to have children by multiple men in order to ensure enough diversity for the following generations," she stated.

Ander's head hit his knees as he took in the information. It took a few minutes before he rose up and stared at her. "You're going to mate with other men?"

Ella looked at Ander in surprise. He looked totally devastated.

"Ella? Are you replacing me?" he asked.

"No! Gods, no!" she replied. "How could you think such a thing?"

Shaking his head he stared at her. "You just said the women would have to mate with multiple men."

"Oh Gods, Ander. Them, not me," she stammered. "We're already mated! They aren't. They are young and they can adapt better."

"What about the diversity and numbers?" he asked.

"Yes, well… You know how difficult pregnancies are for me. I'm not sure I could be much help when it comes to populating this planet."

"But perhaps in time, we can try again?" he asked with a hopeful look.

"Yes, Ander. We'll try again," she replied with a smile.

Six

"Are you seeing this?" Ander asked.

"Yes, I assure you I can see as well as you can." Ella replied.

"But… those are dragons," he replied.

"Yes. I'm quite aware of that," she replied with a smile.

Ander was so excited at their discovery. They had exited the ship and explored around for the better part of the day. It was early evening when he heard roaring in the distance. When he looked he'd discovered distant specs high in the sky. At first he'd thought maybe he was seeing another ship. But then the creature had flown closer and he'd been shocked by what he saw. An honest to Gods dragon flew above.

"You knew?" he asked.

"Of course. They are one of the sentient lifeforms on the planet."

"Are they dangerous?" he asked while watching the dragon. Soon it was joined by a second dragon.

"Well I suppose any lifeform can be dangerous, including us." Ella said as she shaded her eyes with a hand. "But we need them."

"We need them?" he turned to look at Ella with a brow raised.

"Yeah. We need some of their DNA to survive on this planet," she replied.

"Their DNA? Are you fucking kidding me? How the hell do you propose we do that?" he asked.

"Carefully and very diplomatically," she said.

Find out more about Jovander and Greella's descendants in Scents and Sensibility, Book One of The Mepuvirean Prophecy.

Find out more about the crew in the upcoming series Origins of Mepuvir.

To find out more connect with Jeaneva and join her newsletter at https://jeanevachristie.com/link-in

The Witch Next Door

ANDI LAWRENCOVNA WRITING AS FAITH ALEXANDER

<u>One</u>

Carey knelt in the dirt along the side of his house and stared at the dead and dying flower beds he couldn't seem to keep alive no matter how hard he tried. Black weeds ran rampant in the soil. The dark roots curled around the green sprouts and damned if it didn't just add to the house's air of "witchery."

There.

He'd said it. *Thought it…*

He'd admitted it for all the stupid fools who claimed the same as they walked by at night.

His house looked like it belonged to a Goddess-damned-witch and his presence wasn't helping matters. In terms of aesthetic, the dark grey painted siding and black tiled roof weren't helping his "I'm not a witch" avowals either. That most people said they saw floating orbs in the windows at night or ghosting around the perimeter… well…

Was it his fault that his pipes were old and there were tiny holes in some of them that let out steam? Or that the wiring had needed to be updated for nearly a century and sometimes bulbs just happened to flicker when no one was around?

*Nooooo…*but people still came to gawk like they thought it was ghosts!

And Carey liked his anonymity. He liked flying under the radar, going unnoticed, being left alone.

Being known as the Witch Next Door was NOT helping his peace of mind!

People actively seemed to hunt him out BECAUSE of the house's reputation. And then when those same people, tourists and townsfolk both, saw him…well…

Between his dark hair, darker eyes, and too pale complexion, he'd been called a vampire and the emo-goth-wannabe most of his life. Everyone always laughed, wanting to know if the high neck shirts and the black button downs hid all his tattoos beneath the cloth…

He just burned really easily!

…and it wasn't because he was a vampire!

"Witch" was technically a new one, but he wasn't sure he liked it.

Didn't "not" like it…

It just felt…sacrilegious? Insensitive? Titled as a "witch" in Salem where the name had a history that needed to be remembered and honored for the tragedy it entailed not as some new-agey-moniker that didn't really seem to harken back to the trauma of the past…?

Maybe it was just him.

Especially since most of the town folk made some sort of claim to the original witches who were murdered here, and he had none.

"Then why are you here?" was the first thing most people asked him.

So he might have a "slight" connection to the past, but that was mainly on his step-father's-uncle's-sister's side.

Yeah, he knew how that one sounded too.

Aunt Mary had kept in touch even after his parents split and he moved out of state with his mom. Carey'd always liked the old woman because she was kind and caring and never seemed to care about what anyone said about her, and he always wished he didn't care as much.

The house had been her sole possession, and she'd left it to him.

No idea why.

Seriously, not a clue.

He was living across the country in Nebraska when this lawyer showed up at his door and handed him the deed.

"Let me know if you wanna sell!"

Apparently, there was a market for haunted houses…especially in Salem.

But Mary'd willed it to him, and he didn't want to dishonor her by giving the gift back, or at least not trying it out for a while.

But the damn weeds were going to be the death of him.

"Vinegar, salt, and Dawn dish soap."

He jumped at the deep, accented voice that came from over his shoulder.

Carey jumped so badly, that he fell back into the grass on his black jeans and ended up scrambling away like he was being chased by Brad Newgate in junior high intent on "seeing if the vampire could swim"…in the nearest toilet…

Well, the little shit can certainly run!

Carey managed to get his breathing under control…because at no time had Brad ever had a British accent nor lived in Massachusetts. And last Carey knew, Brad was in a penal institution in South Dakota for, well, it didn't matter except that he was not getting out in a long, long time.

Apparently, this new stranger though…

"Brad Newgate."

His eyes opened wide in disbelief—

"Just kidding. I couldn't resist. It's actually worse than that." The man held out a hand and Carey stared at it like an idiot. "Ichabod Proust. My mum was a huge Washington Irving fan. It's quite embarrassing really having to introduce myself these days. I'm you're new neighbor. Thought I should introduce myself since you were outside."

Carey knew his mouth had dropped open in shock. Had…had *he* read his mind? That wasn't like…possible…right?

The man's smile grew wider, his hand still extended like he could do the same all day.

"Pardon?" Oh Goddess, now *he* sounded like a Brit…only not…which just made him a fool and he was incredibly flustered by everything.

His eyes cast around surreptitiously for a place to go hide and die.

The expression on the man's face never changed. "Ichabod Proust," there was a little shake to the man's hand now to draw Carey's attention back to it. "The Witch," the stranger tipped his head to the house beside Carey's, "next door."

Carey couldn't help but follow that unspoken directive.

They shared a side yard between them. The same yard that Carey had been muttering and swearing at since early that morning.

Ichabod's house was the opposite in entirety to Carey's. White siding with a slate roof, it had a front porch that had rocking chairs and a small table on it, inviting guests up for a quick spot of tea before they saw the sign that read "The Witch is Out" on the door.

Wait…so…*he* really *was* a witch?

The man laughed out loud. If it wasn't for the complete absurdity of it all, Carey would have said that the clouds seemed to agree with the merriment, flying out of sight so as not to obscure the sunshine illuminating the warm smile on Ichabod's face.

Brilliant, Carey snarked in his own head.

"That's the spirit!"

The innocuous hand, long-fingered and beautiful with its single ring and swirling black stone, decided not to wait any longer and made the descent towards Carey's answering fingers.

When he'd decided to raise them, he didn't know, but there it was, that moment when they'd touch, and it felt like something—

"Magical."

—was about to happen.

He pulled away before it could. With clumsy movements, Carey forced himself to his feet and turned aside, wiping at the smudges of dirt and grass he was certain covered him from his fall into the same, using the moment to catch his breath, figure out what the hell was wrong with him, and why the man—

Wait. "Witch?"

Ichabod laughed. "First, call me Proust. No one calls me Ichabod, not even my mother who named me. And the only ones who call me Witch," the man waggled his eyebrows, honest-to-Goddess, "are the ones who I make magic with."

It was clear what he meant by the turn of phrase.

Carey knew the moment he flushed hot from the man's words.

Because Carey was embarrassed for the man…not because that brilliant smile made his heart beat faster or…he swallowed against the lump in his throat, hands moving to clasp in front of him in a completely natural sort of way. His face got warmer with the lie.

Ichabo…Proust…Witch.

"Wait!"

Witches were women…right?

The madman laughed, but Carey caught the slightest of flinches that crossed the man's too-high cheeks. "It's a long story, with a torrid history, but sex doesn't really matter for the name. It's more an attitude thing."

Carey had no idea what that meant.

Proust waved the words away with a flippant twist of his fingers. "Professionally speaking, Mr. Goode, yes, I'm a witch. Séances. Love potions. Scrying. I do it all. Gems and omens and ruins and candles. You know…witchy things." The man's gaze turned intense when they caught Carey's again, the pulse that had tried to calm speeding to new life at his neighbor's stare, "But my lovers call me witch because I'm magic in bed, and," he shrugged, a reprieve to the tension filling the empty space between them, "who am I to argue with the truth?"

A chill tracked down Carey's spine that had nothing to do with fear and everything to do with lus…

He shook his head, hands rising to press against his eyes, blocking the sight of the man in front of him.

Firstly, no one was supposed to be that open.

And, two…also…whatever, Brits weren't supposed to be that open!

No offense to all those lovely British people that Carey didn't know but had always wanted to meet weren't supposed to be that open and here was a truly gorgeous specimen standing in front of him making lewd, suggestive comments and Carey didn't understand what was going on or how to respond or even anything at all because it was a jumble in his head and WITCH!

"Breathe, mate. Just breathe. It's all right, I promise. I'm not going to hex you or anything, I swear."

When had Proust stepped closer? Why were his hands so soft against Carey's cheeks? Was that spark he felt growing in his stomach indigestion or—

– *Magic* –

Deep blue eyes stared into his and Carey couldn't pull his gaze away. The witch drew in a deep breath. Carey followed suit. Honeysuckle and jasmine and a hint of something earthier filled his lungs. He breathed deep of the man's scent, let his eyes drift shut while being held in Proust's arms.

Warm lips brushed against his in a not-quite-kiss. "Breathe."

The word zinged through him like he'd been electrocuted, except the feeling felt far, far too goo—

He pushed away, saved from falling back to the ground by his tormentor's hands somehow catching Carey before he toppled.

Proust let him go without hesitation when Carey pulled back.

He still couldn't seem to catch his breath. "You enjoy making people uncomfortable." It came out more as a question than the statement Carey had intended.

"I enjoy pushing boundaries, fair enough, but not making people uncomfortable. Getting them past their discomfort; making them look at the reason behind it, yes, I do quite enjoy making people do that, but not to be cruel."

For all Carey might wish it was that way, he couldn't argue that his neighbor's tone and deeds didn't seem to be intentionally cruel. Not that he was going to pretend he believed the other man's good intentions, if those intentions could even be considered good.

Witches weren't good, after all.

"Oh, I'm a very, *very* naughty witch," Proust's teeth snapped at Carey and an image formed in his head of being eaten by the far too attractive man.

Proust reached for Carey again, and for a moment, Carey considered allowing himself to be taken.

He stepped back into his flower bed, boots sinking into the muddy loam he'd been weeding.

"Shit!"

The word slipped past his lips with a growl. His pant leg caught in a thorn bush and as he tried to pull free, his fingers caught on the sharp prickles which drew red furrows down his skin.

Proust drew in a clipped breath.

Carey'd forgotten the man was there as he battled his Aunt's flowers.

His head snapped up when the witch grabbed Carey's hand in his own and pulled him bodily from the bush. Those blue eyes seemed darker now, midnight rather than bright summer sky as they stared into his own.

"You should be more careful, Carey."

Transfixed.

He stood transfixed by his neighbor as Proust raised the hand he'd captured to pale lips and pressed a kiss that tingled through Carey's skin to those small abrasions from the thorns. That tingling touch slid over Carey's fingers and up his arm, sank to settle deep in his gut where the butterflies churned around that spark like moths to an open flame.

Funny, but he'd never wanted to be burned so badly before.

"A pleasure meeting you, Mr. Goode. And please, come to my door anytime. My magic's always open to you." Proust offered a final, parting, grin, and released Carey.

He turned and walked away, and Carey watched the man go.

There were movies in which the heroine stood gape-mouthed at the hero as he walked by. In that moment, the audience always knew that those were the two that fate had meant to put together in their story.

That didn't happen in real life.

It wasn't supposed to happen in real life.

Carey raised a hand to his cheek, feeling the heat of his blush against his skin. He looked down at his other hand, so recently kissed by thorn and lips, except the scratches were gone, almost like he'd just imagined them.

"And Carey," he looked up at the witch who stood on his porch, one hand on the knob waiting to push the door open. "Sorry in advance."

Carey frowned. "Sorry for what?"

Proust's smile grew wider, and something in Carey's gut twisted, not in discomfort, but in anticipation of what was to come. "You'll see."

Without waiting for a response, Proust opened his door and disappeared into the house next door.

In the front window, the signed flipped over:

The Witch is In

Two

"Well, that was unexpected."

He spoke to the emptiness of the house, unable to keep the thought to himself.

The man he'd went to meet next door was still staring awkwardly at Proust's front door right where he'd left Carey.

For a mugg—

"Fiddlesticks."

He fought the curse back.

Proust had grown up with magical stories in the media, devouring tales of boys with scars who fought villainous warlocks to save the world...

So most of his terminology came by way of Rowling.

Which probably was most definitely not accurate.

He'd studied magic for years and KNEW that ninety-nine percent of what was in those books wasn't accurate, but still, the names lingered. When you grew up in a world that believed in witches and wizards because of the words of a writer, it was hard to get away from the terms that decorated those pages or filled the ears from movie screens.

So, when Proust looked at Carey, there really was only one thing to call the beautiful man...

Which, for copywriting purposes Proust steadfastly refused to think in his head.

But Carey was absent any spark of magical aura to his being. It was clear as daylight, written on the man's fair skin. He was horribly, terribly, miserably mundane in a completely exceptional way. He had no magical talent or aptitude at all.

What he did have though, that ran deeper than a spark, was a Well.

Proust knew that made no sense.

How could someone not have a spark but still be a well? Spark implied combustion. The ability to make magic...ping! If Carey were to utter an enchantment, pick up a tarot card, throw down the runes...nothing, absolutely nothing would happen.

But from the moment Proust had walked up the street a week ago, he'd felt the man drawing from him. It was addicting, the feeling, the relief that came from having the excess energy Proust produced drawn off and redirected so he wasn't on constant overload like most practitioners of his level.

Surprisingly, being drained of his energy was an incredibly relaxing prospect.

…Erotic…

Shut it! Proust paused in his staring, turning his awareness inwards towards that voice in his head, speaking out of turn, answering the same.

It was a dangerous game, engaging with that *otherness*. Acknowledging it. Answering it.

Agreeing…

Laughter filled his head and he leveled a hard stare at his reflection in the window, refusing to look left at the other image filling the glass before him.

No, much better to focus back on his little Well kneeling back in his flower beds, trying to make roses grow with will alone.

Maybe a little bottle of fertilizer. A trinkle of magic splashed in to keep the beetles away from the man's plants.

As a thank you…for drawing off Proust's excess energy…draining away the strain, as it were.

A few things Proust could help *drain* from the other man in return, if the Well would just give him a chance.

That bright flush to the boy's cheeks. Delicious.

Yes…

No! He grit his teeth against the laughter filling his head, forcing himself to turn away and stop looking at the Well next door.

In truth, it was safer to give the Well a wide berth.

He was here to watch the man, protect him, keep him safe…even from himself.

Proust shook his head.

Carey was…that place were excess magical energy could pool before being drawn forth to be used by another practitioner.

Wells were extraordinarily rare.

And extraordinarily dangerous.

Not because of what they were, but because of who could use them…

Which was anyone.

Anyone could use a Well. Anything with any magical talent. A witch. A warlock. The ghost of a witch or warlock. Surprisingly, priests were also actually incredibly adept at using wells for themselves, but that was usually for making "miracles" happen or convincing a congregation that someone or other be "healed" – a feat that only lasted a few moments when the sick walked away from the well of the priest's benediction.

But Proust was definitely not a priest.

And he had no intention of draining his Well dry…

He paused mid-step as he stood in the front room of his shop.

I mean...

He could envision a certain situation which involved draining the very handsome, completely unaware of his own appeal, innocently alluring magical *Well* dry…but that sort of thing was not exactly the type of magic that Proust was worried about exposing the man to.

Convincing Carey to try it…that was another matter entirely.

But, again, not what Proust was worried about.

The excess magical energy Proust shed as easily as sweat seemed to gravitate to the other man and fill Carey up. Again, not in a bad way. It made Carey, well, it made Carey like that silly battery-bunny! The one that kept going on and on. Without proper care or surveillance, someone would come along and steal Carey from the world with careless inattention, or, worse, malicious intent.

And Proust was damn sure not going to let that happen. Especially now that he'd met the man.

Wells were supposed to be a sacred mecca for witches to commune with.

To be protected and cared for because of their rarity in a mundane world that magic could barely touch.

'Course, there were always a few who just wanted to take and take without care.

Who thought it was their right, no matter the cost.

Proust forced his fingers to unclench at his sides.

The spirits in his house rose up at his anger, at his fear.

Mary Goode had spent a lifetime protecting the Well she'd claimed as her own a long time ago. She'd made sure that the ghosts that haunted Salem, the witches of years past, the ones forced savagely from the world in sparks of fire and the ones that came after to repair the horrors committed here, knew that her nephew was to be protected.

Those same ghosts would fight like hell to keep Carey safe, and they'd fight with Proust so long as he intended the same.

Glass chinked against glass behind his back.

He refused to turn his head and look back at the window he'd just vacated.

How many had come to this town over the years to try and coral the magic and power steeped into the earth for their own purposes? How many more would come when word of the Well reached them?

You could create an empire with a man like Carey beneath you.

But there was only one reason Proust wanted the little Well beneath him, and it wasn't to suck the magic from the boy's veins…

Not *that* magic at least.

Damn…that wasn't even the other voice in his head, that was Proust's alone.

He looked at the sigil carved into the frame above the door.

Mary's sigil for safety and protection. It was imbued with her love, and her conviction. Her gift to whoever claimed the house when she was gone.

Both houses, really.

One for the Witch. And one for the Well.

She hadn't told him what he was getting himself into when she wrote Proust to come to town. When Mary had written him asking for him to cast an enchantment to protect her boy, he'd thought it an odd, simple task, allowing himself to think that the old woman made the request because she was slowing down in her years, and Proust was still searching for his peak. He hadn't expected her *boy* to be not a boy at all. And he hadn't expected Carey to be all that he was either.

Proust had owed Mary.

As much as he hated it, the woman had saved him when no one else would risk it.

She had a habit of finding lost souls to save, even ones as broken and betrayed as Proust. She'd helped him make something of his life; *more*, he thought, than either of them had ever thought was possible, because of the Goode Witch.

He'd be damned if he repaid that unconditional kindness with disregard.

If looking out for her *nephew* was the cost, it was a debt he was happy to pay.

Especially since it wasn't much of a hardship at all.

He wanted to protect the Well with the sweet face and far away eyes. There was something to the way the man had knelt there like he was hiding in his own front yard that Proust wanted to tear away and show to the world. He wanted to help relax those tense shoulders and watch the man come apart beneath him, give in to pleasure which didn't seem like something the young Mr. Goode was used to enjoying.

Poor sod.

61

Or was that *Lucky Proust*, since he was the one who would reap the benefit of breaking the man out of his shell?

Glass rubbed against glass in an ear-piercing screech.

Proust flinched, lewd thoughts spiraling down deep.

Now was not the time for them. He had an appointment coming in an hour or so. Even witches of his caliber needed to prepare.

And if those preparations included a brief double-bubble-cauldron-crockpot concoction to ward off weeds…well, it was all just part of the job.

Fingers trailed across the back of his neck and he couldn't suppress the chill that came with them.

Maybe something with a bit of protection too, since that *was* why he was here.

<u>Three</u>

Carey couldn't help looking over his shoulder every now and then to see if his neighbor was spying on him. He had the feeling of eyes on his shoulders, staring out at him from what had always been an empty house to his knowledge.

Actually, it was a house he barley remembered at all.

Despite spending summers with Aunt Mary, he couldn't recall ever actually seeing the bright cheery residence next door, let alone meeting anyone who lived in it.

Which made no sense…

Because it wasn't like houses sprung up in the middle of the night…

Unless you were a witch?

And *the witch is* in…

Don't be a dolt, Care. Witches aren't real.

There was a beat of silence where even his brain held its breath, waiting on a response that wasn't coming.

His brain held its breath…*get a grip, man!*

Ichabod Proust was not a real witch. He wasn't psychic. He wasn't magical. He just was…

Handsome. Breathtakingly attractive. Comfortable in his own brand of uniqueness. Highly intuitive.

But not a mind-reader.

…

See! Nothing.

Carey told himself to stop living in a make-believe world of witches and wizards.

He was far too old to believe in that sort of thing.

Besides, Carey didn't need anyone in his life, especially not some fanciful British man pretending to be a sorcerer.

Carey was not the sort of person who enjoyed or needed the attention of others. He did his damnedest to never need anyone.

Everyone around him was always so…greedy.

He couldn't explain it. But it just felt like the people he got close to always wanted more from him than he was willing to give.

Ichabod would be just like everyone else, wanting to torment the "goth" kid, or sleep with a "vampire," or hang around for a while until Carey invested himself in the relationship and was left reeling when it ended.

His shoulders slumped forward as he reached for another weed.

It wouldn't normally be a problem, but the man was…attractive. Like…unfortunately hot.

With the accent, and the crisp linen shirt and the tall frame hidden behind the posh clothes Carey desperately wanted to see beneath…

He was NOT a sexual person. The one experience he'd had with Bryan Fuller in college had been a disaster. They'd dated for a month, and it had been a month of pestering from the other man to do more than Carey felt entirely comfortable doing. So he'd finally given in if just to shut Bryan up, and he'd spent the next month trying to pull himself out of a depression he didn't understand. Days of feeling weary to the very depths of his soul, of eating food that had no flavor and listening to music that had no soul. He lost thirty pounds in less time than it took to…do…something…very quickly.

Carey groaned at the memory.

Aunt Mary was the one who finally noticed and slapped some sense into him. Literally. She slapped him and it was like she cracked the cold shell that surrounded him.

She didn't ask what had happened.

He didn't tell.

But she said if he was going to go about giving pieces of himself away, he should be smarter about it and protect his heart first.

He still didn't know precisely what that meant. Hadn't been tempted into a relationship since then regardless.

She'd probably murder him if she found out he was tempted by Mr. Proust.

But she wasn't here to protect him, or rescue him, or talk to him anymore. All that was left was her house, and Carey had to admit that her home did bring him peace, and that he was grateful for the comfort it offered.

It had only been a few weeks, but he'd never felt as content, as *full*, as he did while in the space.

Having someplace to call home, to work from, was wonderful.

He'd put his *sun allergy* to good use in school and gotten a degree in programming. Such good use, that he had firms all over the place wanting to work with him, and willing to let him work from anywhere if he just said yes. And he got to choose his own schedule most days, which was another blessing too.

While Carey might not like being around others, he did crave the contact. He recognized from enough sessions with therapists over the years that his anxiety about social situations came from past experiences and how he expected others to react to him, not reality, and that he was an extrovert who had learned to be afraid of that part of himself a very long time ago.

Bartending on the side was a nice, safe way to fulfill his need to be around people, without being expected to engage beyond a drink order with them.

Mild-mannered geek by day! Mild mannered alcohol-enabler by night…

A real-life superhero!

He snorted into his weeds.

Made sense though that he and his superpowers would end up living next to a witch…

Carey shook his head. *What even was a witch?* And who went around *saying* they were a witch to people?

It *would* be cool to meet a witch though.

He'd lived most of his life being nicknamed after a supernatural creature. Meeting one in real life seemed…he didn't know.

But he wasn't opposed.

With another sigh, which he was doing far too many of this day, he gave up on his weeding and retreated inside his house.

Next door, an elderly man was walking up the steps towards the sign hanging there.

Carey refused to think about what it would be like to make his own appointment with the magician.

Four

Proust managed not to shout at the old man standing before him disparaging his hard work and giving him the haranguing of a lifetime.

It wasn't Proust's fault that the wife the man had come looking for had moved on.

No medium or witch or whatever could connect with a soul that had crossed over.

Maybe a reaper. A reaper might be able to. But READ THE SIGN ON THE DOOR!

He. Was. A. WITCH!

Gramps was lucky Proust gave the man a refund when he realized he couldn't make a connection.

Goddess, but what a *wanker*.

He was referring to them both with the thought. Himself for time spent being nice. The codger for being a ruddy codger!

The bottles and jars on the windowsills began to shake with Proust's ire.

Beneath his feet, the floorboards squeaked in offering to swallow the offender whole.

It was one of the few nice things about owning a haunted house, and being able to commune with the spirits within it. The ghosties had a tendency to like their chill uninterrupted, and took unkindly to being disturbed. It's why witches were so welcome in the area. Who wouldn't want to communicate with another, even if you were dead?

But when he got agitated, the spirits got agitated, and currently, he was fuming.

A knock sounded at the door.

The old man shut his trap instantly, looking from Proust to the entrance, no doubt wondering if this was some spectral ploy to silence him or if the patron was real.

Truthfully, Proust was wondering the same. He wasn't expecting another visitor today. His calendar was relatively free as he was only just starting his practice here in Salem.

A wave of his hand opened the door. The little show of magic was the sort of thing most people passed off as a parlor trick. Proust rarely argued semantics with them.

Standing right there, outlined by the sun behind him, dark clothes making him a pseudo-spectre in the doorway, was his neighbor, hand upraised, ready to knock again.

Saved by the Well.

Proust couldn't help his smile at the man's timing. "My," he turned his wrist over to look at his watch, "4:27 is here, Mr. Garney. Please excuse me."

It was clear on the old man's face that he wanted to continue his argument. The codger wanted to tell the man at the door that Proust was a charlatan and to get out while he could. Proust wasn't sure how many more ways one person could call another a liar, but he knew that denying Garney the chance would likely make the man apoplectic.

He knew better than to tempt Karma, but he just couldn't help himself.

With a rather valiant show of self-restraint, the bloke shoved past Carey in the doorway and stomped down the stairs, red faced and ham-fisted. Muttering disparagements as he went, but he did go.

Proust tipped his head to the side and grinned after the grandfather. "Another satisfied customer."

Carey managed a sheepish laugh in response to Proust's words.

In the silence that followed, Proust raised his eyebrows, arms rising to cross over his chest, fully aware of the way the shirt hugged his shoulders and upper body, the button down deliberately fit to show him off best to another's eye.

With a grimace, Carey stepped through the door.

There was a silent sigh that echoed through the house when the man's feet settled inside the threshold.

Proust released the breath he'd not realized he was holding.

A faint look of confusion crossed Carey's face at the not-sound, but it passed quickly. "You...you really tell people you're a witch?" His chin nodded towards the door he'd entered through and the sign hanging upon it.

"Worse than tell, I'm afraid. I come from a long line of distinguished practitioners. Whole family's magic." That those same men were also assholes...well, Carey didn't need to know about that.

"Really?"

Proust shrugged. "Why not?"

Lines formed on Carey's forehead. He looked from Proust to the room, at the jars and candles, incense and cards, shelves and shelves of books, and finally towards the table at the center of the space with the Tarot atop it.

Proust watched the man swallow, wondering what question Carey would ask next now that he was asking.

"I thought boys were supposed to be wizards and women witches?"

Ahh yes, one of the usuals he had to field.

"Men," if Proust emphasized the word, who would say, "can be either, though there's a rather nasty connotation about wizards and especially warlocks. Witches are much more common these days, so witch I am. Though I suppose wizard would play as well."

A faint blush crossed over his neighbor's pale skin at Proust's response.

He was doing his level best not to read too far into Carey's thoughts, but the male was damn tempting. Out in the garden, Proust hadn't been able to resist. He was lucky that in the house, there were other things that required his attention, and so he kept better hold of his thoughts and where he let them wander indoors.

"So, what? You have a wand somewhere where you cast spells to make your morning coffee?"

"That's what coffee machines are for, I'm afraid. Or Starbucks. I am partial to a morning macchiato. Mostly people come to me to try and connect with the recently deceased, make a spell to help with catching someone's eye or keep someone interested in the bedroom."

The poor man's eyes got wide as saucers. "Spells for the bedroom? I don't—"

Keep torturing the lad, the voice purred, enjoying Carey's bright blush and sharp breathing.

Proust looked over Carey's shoulder to the glass orb hanging in the window.

It wasn't so much a frown that crossed his face as something more, something darker and dangerous.

Of course, as dangerous as Proust could be if he wanted, what was held in that sphere was more so.

Witch balls usually were.

They held the spirits of evil sorcerers, so the legends said. Most true witch balls were well hidden, buried beneath running water, cast in concrete at the bottom of the deepest pit. Risking whatever was inside them getting out...

Not good.

When he'd left England, *Goddess*, a lifetime ago now, he'd taken the orb with him. He'd had to. The damn thing rather clung to him, in a magical sense, probably because he'd been the one to create it in the first place. His witch ball, pieced together from sea glass Proust had claimed from every place he'd visited, wasn't smoothly round or filled with a branching tree to trick a sorcerer within.

No, the orb tinkling against Proust's window was jagged and flawed and cracked where his magic had melted all the pieces of glass into one being. It was the truest witch's ball he'd ever seen, holding all the malevolence of his magic within its pieces, that part of himself he didn't trust, that could tear the world apart if he let it.

That whispered: *claim the Well. Make him ours. Use him.*

Like the old man, Proust curled his fingers into fists at his side. Acknowledging what was within that glass only gave it power, and Proust knew better than to offer it his attention.

Never!

He couldn't help his violent response to the jail's demands.

The orb did its version of a roar, swinging on its thin cord and tapping against the glass of the window.

Carey turned to look at it for a moment but gave it no more notice than that.

The lack of attention rather pissed the ball off more, which made Proust rather proud of the ignorant little mortal ignoring all the magic contained in that mundane hung of melted sand.

He offered a silent sneer at the glass, more mental rebuke than physical, and forcibly turned his gaze back to his guest.

Snubbing the orb better revenge than anything else Proust could have thought of.

With an exaggerated wave of his arms, perhaps a teensy bit of wind-whispering, Proust bowed forward, setting the chimes around the room chinking, his guest's dark auburn hair to blowing in the breeze, witch ball forgotten, words and whispers and questions ignored.

He rose with that same flourish fingers spread wide to calm the currents fluttering the pages of the open books around him.

"Welcome to my world, Mr. Goode. What can the spirits aid you in today?"

A simple enchantment. Ritualistic words.

Carey stared at him, mouth open, pulse speeding at the big vein in his throat. "Uhm," the Well laughed nervously, but it was tinged with something that hinted almost at wonder.

It took most people more than a little wind magic to make them believers.

Hand raised in the air, Proust rolled his fingers like he was running a coin over his knuckles. He knew the deck of Tarot cards on the table even better than the back of his hand. With each twitching spasm of his digits, the cards unwound themselves from their deck, beginning to dance in the air, shuffling to the desires that only they were privy too, that Proust would read when he sat down at the table.

Carey's mouth gaped wide at the display.

Oh yes, wonder and hope, a dark little thread of cynicism dancing in the deepest shadows of the man's gaze.

Everyone wanted to believe in magic.

Everyone who wasn't was just a little bit the cynic too.

The deck settled into place on the velvet tablecloth, a faint tremor to the cards that he doubted Carey would recognize, only a highly skilled practitioner able to sense the need to move imbued in the inanimate objects.

Proust turned and pulled out one of the chairs, looking over his shoulder for his newest client – *lover* – to take a seat. "What will your fortune hold, Mr. Goode?"

An Elemental Like Me

R.N.A

One

"There you are. I've been looking for you, Little Witch."

Chills crawled down my spine, as my nerves reawakened. I felt him stalk toward me until his breath tickled my ear.

"For a hundred years I have waited, searched because you left me behind. Now, here you are."

He was right, *I did.* I refused to be a possession to *anyone.* Whether I loved and cared about him was beside the point. We were too powerful, too destructive together. Our magic created chaos.

So, I ran away.

"Here I am," I tried to steel my shaky words, trembling even still.

"I didn't answer your summon immediately, because you hurt me greatly. You've torn a hole into my soul and shredded it. However, despite what you think, I am not you. I will not abandon you."

I sighed, feeling his body against mine, memories swirling of our passion so long ago.

"I only summoned you, because I needed your help."

I turned around trying to put some distance between us, but I saw the hurt lacing his eyes on his handsome face. A face I had dreamt of for far too long.

It wasn't that I *didn't* love him. I just…*needed* to find my own way without the chaos. Without feeling like I was a possession, not an equal.

"You know the price for my help, Little Witch. *Your body is the token I require."* His dark eyes flashed as he straightened, holding his head high and confident. The familiar warlock I knew him to be.

"Whatever, fine," I told him as I began gathering the candles I had laid out, grounding myself back into the earth before exiting the circle I created in the clearing. The night was brisk as I vanquished every candle.

Before I had decided to summon him from the realm I had left behind, I *knew* he would be angry, but I was desperate. A new evil was lurking and terrorizing the town and people I cared about for the past five years.

I also knew that our combined magic would stop it. Begging was not something I ever did unless it was sexual. Sex with him was amazing, so I didn't mind the price. *Hell, I craved him just as much.*

"Do you want me to tell you why I need your help, or do you want payment first?" I asked, the night settling around us, making his features loom.

He conjured fire in his hand, appearing in front of me.

"No apologies, Miri, really? You left the realm to come to *this* planet, and you don't have anything else to say to me? Did I truly mean nothing to you?"

I could see and feel the heat of his torment.

He was an Elemental like me, and we were some of the best there were in our home realm.

"I'm not ready for that conversation, I need to think more first…"

"You always did love to torture me." He extinguished his flame.

I held out both hands to prove a point as fire burned around my palms.

"As if you didn't return the same torture! You know we created chaotic magic together, and you were consumed with it. I refused to feel trapped. I needed to pave my path without you. You would've never let me leave willingly Samson!"

He stepped closer. "Of course not! Is this really what you thought of me all this time? *I loved you.* You didn't want to do the mate-binding ritual. *I chose you.* The only prisoner that I owned was this," he was on me at once, cupping my center over the long thin dress I wore.

A startled groan escaped my lips. "I *never* wanted to own you, Miri, and I'm hurt you think so ill of me. Makes me question if you truly loved me at all to paint me so horrendously. Our chaos was always fitting, don't you think?"

He exhaled slowly as I bit my lip to suppress the moan.

My body always did like to betray me.

"You're an asshole, Sam."

"Takes one to know one, Little Witch." He removed his hand, and I sighed, my heart racing at finally having its other half near me again.

We had a lot to work on.

"Come, follow me, and I'll explain the situation. My cottage is a couple of miles from here. We'll figure out the rest together." I turned away from his penetrating stare as I felt my magic electrifying through my blood, aching to tangle with his again.

I put the candles and supplies from the second summoning away in my bag, putting my thick coat back on, along with my shoes.

"I will listen, but I'm not promising anything. I wouldn't want you to think I was your *captor,*" he muttered bitterly, and I huffed a breath.

I had much to apologize for, and I needed to admit how much of a coward I was. We were young and reckless, and I got scared when he mentioned the ritual. *I wasn't ready.*

Instead of communicating, I had it in my head that he would never understand and wouldn't let me leave. So, I fled and started a new life in a new world. I thought the heartache would go away with time as my soul battled with my impulsive decision. *It never did leave though.*

The heartache only became easier when I found distractions and friends to care about. The past five years have been troublesome, but it didn't compare to the hole in my heart from leaving him behind. I didn't deserve his forgiveness, and I was clueless about how to even begin to tread down that road.

The first step was the summoning and hoping he answered. When he didn't, I tried again on the next full moon. I was surprised when he appeared, finding it risky to be in the circle too, but I needed him to trust me again. *Or try to, anyway.*

As we walked those miles, I could feel his brooding from beside me as if it were its own magic. I wanted to form the words, *I'm sorry, Sam,* but they didn't come. Letting him cool down was probably best, not talking until we reached my cozy cottage.

The cottage was draped in greenery with plants and vines all over the outside. A large herb garden decorated the backyard, the low fence was wood and crooked from the years, and the front yard held colorful flowers. There was a lake nearby and all the quiet I could ever hope for. The only company I had were the forest animals and my black cat, *Salem.*

I came across her when she was a kitten ten years ago, and she has never left my side since. Not that I minded, she was a great companion and seemed to understand me when I muttered to myself day and night or planting and growing, plus spell work.

"The place suits you," Sam mentioned quietly once we stepped onto the threshold.

"Thank you, it's homegrown," I smirked; his eyes lit up once I snapped my fingers and the candles were lit all around the stone cottage.

My favorite part of being a witch, the convenience.

"It's peaceful and quiet… I see the charm," he said as he looked around.

The inside was as green as the outside. Vines and plants hung everywhere and various shelves full of jars of ingredients, *no toads or eyeballs.* There was a set of stairs in the far corner that led to my bedroom which was open and could be seen from the bottom floor.

I kept important books and spells upstairs next to my bed in another corner by my dresser.

"Where is your bathroom?" He looked at me finally.

"It's out there," I pointed to the window at the back corner of the house. There was a huge clawfoot porcelain tub, big enough for multiple people.

"Why on earth are you living like old times? There's electricity and water—"

"*I know. I have* running water, but as an Elemental, do I really need to? This lifestyle is simple, and I grow all these amazing plants. What, do you live in a mansion?" I raised my eyebrow, and he shrugged, looking away from me.

"Something like that. Why not live comfortably?"

I scoffed. "*This* is comfortable, Sam… Do you want some tea?"

I placed my cauldron tea kettle on the stove and used my fire to light it after filling it with water from the sink.

"Have a seat, my home is your home while you are here," I gestured to the forest green couch in the middle of the room with two matching chairs and a table between.

"Is it?" He questioned, and I could hear his bitterness.

Geez, someone is butthurt.

I ignored him while mixing different herbs in the tea that would hopefully calm him down more.

The water boiled for five minutes; once done, I poured the hot tea into two green teacups, brought them over to the table, and placed them onto the matching saucers.

His brown eyes watched me, and I got a good look at him finally. *He looks the same.* His hair was still brown, freshly groomed, no five o'clock shadow, and he smelled like a thunderstorm.

My favorite scent after all these years. Any time it stormed, I was always reminded of him, and I would sit outside wishing I made other life decisions.

Sam looked as if he still held his great shape underneath the dark layers of clothing he wore. My mind wandered, wondering if he still tasted as I remembered, but I stopped myself. *It wasn't the time to ponder the what-ifs.*

"Are you hungry?" I asked, distracting myself from gazing at him all night while walking back into the kitchen.

"No."

My heart skipped a beat as I yelped when a chirp from the open window startled me.

It was only Salem. I was wondering where she had gone off to. I didn't want her at the summoning ritual, so she scattered off.

"Hey girl," I scratched behind her ear, and she meowed quietly as if returning the greeting, "we have a visitor tonight."

She hopped onto the counter after licking my palm.

"Glad to know you don't live alone," I heard him say as I cut a few pieces of bread and buttered them, "is there…a man in your life?"

Answering immediately to shut that conversation down, "No. Just me and Salem."

I felt the tension leave the room as I walked back over with the small plate.

To my surprise, she was rubbing against him as he scratched behind her ear.

Me too, Salem. Warm his heart for me since I ruined him.

"She likes you," I said sitting in the chair across from him.

"At least someone in this house does," he murmured while looking at me and picking up his cup.

I behaved and kept my comments to myself, blowing on the steam before sipping the hot tea. My shoulders relaxed immediately.

"So, tell me what the problems are before you run me out again. Will it be another hundred years this time? *Forever?*" He looked hurt as he said it, sipping his tea.

Salem jumped up and lay next to him, and my heart warmed. *Looks like she's telling me something.*

"Samson, for what it's worth, I *am* sorry. For leaving without a word and for assuming the worst of you. It wasn't fair to you."

I held his gaze. Part of me dreamed of the day I'd see him again if only it were under better circumstances.

"I'll consider your apology… Why didn't you ever come back *at any point?*"

I held the cup in my lap, looking down with shame. "I'm a coward. Do not think I didn't feel guilty every day for the past century… I couldn't face you or my pride. I knew I fucked up, and that I hurt you badly."

"Tell me the truth. Why did you leave?"

Slowly moving my eyes from the cup to him, my eyes misted. "I wasn't ready for the mating ritual. The commitment… I couldn't do it at the time. Fear, I guess. Being tied down or stuck. I made the impulsive decision to open a portal and leave our realm to come to this one."

76

His nostrils flared as he fought within himself. Complicated emotions and thoughts were dancing in those brown eyes that reminded me of mountains and the dirt I grew plants with. He was earth, and I was a disappointment. My woes were earned and deserved for hurting him.

"I will not ask for forgiveness; I know I do not deserve it. I don't deserve your help either, but *this* isn't about me. Some innocents will be hurt, and dare I say it, *friends,* if we don't stop the dark magic from spreading."

His expression cleared, changing into mere concern. Sam leaned forward, placing his teacup back on the saucer.

"Why in the *fuck* is there dark magic here?"

I sighed deeply, finishing my tea and placing it back down. "I'm not the only witch here. I've been trying to keep it from spreading to other parts of the land; so far it has held for the past five years until it didn't."

"What. Happened." His eyes flashed.

"I think there are multiple forces involved... I can't do it on my own anymore. I know you and I can take them on together. We were always stronger together than apart. I was too blind and selfish to see."

"You were... I will help you. Tomorrow we will set out, and you'll show me around your world. Then, we'll plan from there. I need to assess and see how dire it is."

I nodded, reaching for his hand with tears in my eyes. "Thank you... Do you want it to be on the bed or couch?"

He pulled his hand away as if I shocked him. "I'm not asking for that right now. *I will call upon it later at a time of my choosing.* I'll take the couch; go to bed."

He went about taking off his long coat, and I stood up. "Okay... Goodnight then."

Salem scattered off as I climbed the stairs. Halfway up, I turned to look at him.

"I'm glad you are here, Sam. There are more blankets and pillows on the corner shelf there," I pointed to the nearest corner of the room opposite where I stood on the steps.

"Goodnight, Miri."

I sighed and continued my way up. He settled in on the couch, taking his boots off and closing his eyes.

Since there was no privacy, I undressed, feeling his eyes on my naked body. Part of me hoped he'd be less angry eventually.

After I put on a white slip, I crawled under the covers as Salem hopped in next to me, curling up at my side.

I heard a finger snap, and all the candles were extinguished. It wasn't long before I fell into a dreamless sleep, hoping for better outcomes.

***

Over the following few weeks, I showed Sam around the forest I protected and the town nearby. *How the energy fell immediately once we were in town.*

"The land here is tainted. But by whom?" I remembered him saying as we walked through town.

I introduced him to the friends I had. One was a local bartender, another in law enforcement, a local gardener, and the bookshop keeper. All of us had gone out one night, and I introduced them to Sam. I told them he was there to help. They gave me a look, knowing otherwise. *To which I ignored,* but they liked him, nonetheless.

After that fun outing, he told me he liked my friends and didn't blame me for wanting to keep them safe.

The hostility and hurt eased between us and it soon felt amicable. *Him, more so than me.* I began to sit next to him at dinner and tried to give him privacy when he bathed outdoors.

I couldn't help but watch him in wonder, remembering our years together so long ago. I began to question if I ever truly stopped loving him. Our weeks together since I summoned him had proved that *yes, I still did.*

Aside from my foolishness, I realized I craved that mating ritual the more I was around him. After I apologized multiple times for the past, we stopped talking about it. The present and future were the only concerns, the rest would come together somehow— *whatever that would consist of.* As long as my friends were safe, along with the town and the forest I cared about, then I'd consider it a success.

A couple of months passed.

Sam came outside while I bathed one morning in the overcast weather.

I didn't cover myself as he stood feet away, letting his eyes rove over the rose bath I was submerged in.

"Do you regret not doing the ritual?" He asked so quietly I wondered if I imagined it.

"I do," I murmured as he looked off into the distance.

"Could you ever love me again?"

What's with all these questions all of a sudden?

"Who said I ever stopped?"

He turned and made his way closer, kneeling beside the tub.

By the Gods, he's handsome. It stole my breath away as he lightly ran his fingers across my collarbone.

I felt the familiar connection of us spark under his touch, emanating from my bloodstream.

"I have a proposition for you. I figured out how to defeat this dark magic. It would be eradicated permanently. I will leave the door open if you want to go back to our home realm or stay here. Visiting is also optional after we finish what we need to. I don't ever want you to feel trapped. You are thriving here, and I will not be the one to break your heart and take your peace away."

My eyes misted as I gazed wistfully at him. With my heart torn open, I basked in his light touch.

"I appreciate that… What do you have in mind?" My spirit knew the answer, but I needed to hear him say it. *If this was his way of forgiveness.*

He moved his fingers up my neck before cupping my face, rubbing his thumb on my cheek.

"As hurt as I was, I understand your reasons for leaving. I only wish you had told me a century ago... I would've given you the space you needed if you were uncertain."

I leaned into his touch, closed my eyes, and placed my hand on his.

"I never stopped loving you, not even for a moment. The craving of your body, the yearning… I had hoped I'd see you again someday. The century without you was lonely, and I don't ever want to feel that again. *I forgive you for all of it.* I will only ask this once as I haven't changed my mind in a century…"

I opened my eyes as tears filled them; he leaned closer.

"Will you complete the mating ritual, binding yourself with me forever? I only want to spend the rest of my life with you, magic, body, and spirit. Whether you stay or go, my place has always been with you. I will give you a couple of days to think it over. If the answer is still no, then I will leave if you request it once we're done. *No sexual payment is needed. Unless you wanted to give me a parting gift before I'm sent away."*

His lips were soft when they met mine, and my blood heated in response. *I haven't felt those lips in a century, and I nearly cried over it. I needed him more than words could ever describe.*

When he pulled away, I opened my mouth to speak, but he put a finger there. "Say nothing, just think it over. I'll see you this evening. I'm going into town to strategize. Relax and enjoy your bath."

He dipped his hand in the water, heating it back up for me. I found the gesture touching as he stood up with one last longing glance before walking away. Watching him and feeling speechless, he disappeared beyond the trees.

I already knew my answer the minute he asked. There was a shame that still bothered me. I should never have left him a century ago, and I had ample time to make up for it. I needed the ritual as much as he did.

So, after my bath, I prepared. I made the oil, and the ingredients for the feast afterward, cleaning up the place. After watering the plants, the storm clouds rolled in as intended.

Back in our home realm, if a witch or warlock were an Elemental and found themselves amidst a soul mate, a ritual could be done. It involved blood and a storm. The combining of magic during sex was the ultimate bond and functioned as a marriage too.

A circle was to be drawn up with soul-binding runes and symbols. Certain candles were lit, but for Elementals, we had to light them ourselves. The key was for us to use our magic and share blood during a great storm. Fire, water, current, air, spirit, blood, and earth. Sex occurred once everything was chanted and going. The storm had to be in full swing.

So, I waited.

I stood in the pouring rain I conjured with my hair down and wild while wearing a thin black robe.

He sauntered over from the trees at last. Soaked like I was, he made his way toward me. It was nighttime, but I could see him as if it were still twilight because of the storm I had brewing in the distance.

"I've missed how your rain felt, my love," he said so heartbreakingly that I pulled him into my arms, merging my lips with his.

I tasted his heartbreak, the longing for me, but most of all, I tasted his everlasting love. So unconditional that he deserved so much better. *Yet, he still chose me.*

When he slipped his tongue inside to play with mine, his hands gripped my hips before one of them went to my nape. I was helpless against him, pure passion pushed me further.

Once we pulled away, both of us were panting. His gorgeous brown eyes remained locked on me.

"Gods, you are sexy," he breathed out, leaning his forehead against mine and cupping my cheek.

"I don't need time, Sam. I've prepared it already, now it's up to you to help me complete it. The lake is nearby with painted runes and needed materials ashore. *Create the circle. I am yours forever."*

The rain poured then, and I knew it was *his rain.*

I cried tears of joy, missing how magical we truly were together in our chaos. *Yet so complete.*

"Lead the way."

I grabbed his hand with a pure smile, one he mirrored. It seemed as if he were crying too, but it was hard to tell with the pouring rain.

Disappearing and reappearing at the lake, I snapped my fingers. Flames erupted on half of the circle, plus the candles. He finished lighting the rest.

The wind picked up as I released his hand. There was a goblet and the dagger I'd stolen that he intended to use for the ritual a century ago.

"So, that's where the dagger went," he said, following me.

I disrobed and watched him create the circle around me. The water splashed from the lake behind us, then lightning came. Thunder sounded as he paused and stripped naked before completing the circle.

My nerves were on fire as I felt our magic already beginning to wreak havoc. The circle was safe with us in it.

Sam kneeled in front of me, grabbing the dagger as I mimicked him. We slit our palms wide open, letting our blood drip into the goblet at the same time.

Our storm was raging all around us. Fire, water, current, air, spirit, blood, and earth.

We repeated the following chant:

"Through time and space, life and death, we will never be parted again. Let love guide us into the future, and may our magic prove fruitful as it continues its universal way from atom to atom. My blood to yours. Our spirits entwined forever. Let my love guide you. My magic is yours. All of me belongs rightfully to you. And so it is and will always be."

Once the goblet was mostly full, we each drank half until it was finished. The dagger disappeared, along with the goblet, as if the universe gave her blessing.

I kissed him ruthlessly. A powerful kiss that erupted in flames circling us. Ignoring the muddy earth beneath, I pushed him down and straddled him, running my hands up his slick chest.

"Here is the oil," I told him as I reached for it and poured half into my hand before pouring the rest into his.

Smearing it all over his body, I lightly touched his face before rubbing some on his hard cock.

He groaned, gripping my hips as he sat up to smear it on me.

"You are perfect chaos, Miri. I love you. After a century too long, let me fuck you as you deserve."

"I love you, Samson. *Please do but allow me to finish by riding you.*"

His lips found mine as I moved off him and grounded myself on all fours, digging into the mud.

"Let me have just a taste," he spoke into the wind that picked up.

As he licked my pussy, I cried out. Just when I was edging closer into orgasmic oblivion, he stopped and kissed my ass cheek.

"Together, Miri."

"Together," I repeat, moaning as he entered me finally, gripping my hips.

Increasing his pace, a fire twister swarmed around the circle, cutting us off from the world.

Slamming ruthlessly, I tilted my head back, a sign that I wanted him to pull my hair as he fucked me hard.

With a fast smack to my ass, *he did.*

"Fuck, you are as perfect as always. I missed that tight pussy of yours. *That's the only part of you I own forever. She's my prisoner.*"

I cried out, feeling my inner walls swell. *It's been so long; I feel untethered and wild. Like our Elemental magic. Electricity brimmed my veins.*

"Yes, that's it. Let go, my love, I will join you in forever."

His hand held the front of my throat as he whispered, *"I love you,"* in my ear.

Despite the roaring wind and loud cries from me, I heard him. When I finally sought oblivion, I spasmed as I screamed, my hand cupping his head behind me.

He roared as he spilled into me, his thunder, my rain. *Our wind.* Our blood and fire. *Water and earth. Our love is forever forged.* Completed at last.

Our spirits were merged.

My pussy answered his roar as she clamped down, tightening around his girth.

"By the Gods, Miri, *my Little Witch. My equal.*"

He eased his grip, our Elemental magic in full swing.

I wasn't done yet.

Grabbing his arm, I pulled him around before pushing him into the mud.

His laughter echoed. "There she is. Come claim what's yours once more."

I climbed him, sinking onto where he was still thick and hard.

He played with my breasts as I rode him, nipping and curling his tongue while teasing my nipples.

"You are perfect too, the reason for *my chaos,*" I told him before he looked up at me.

Then, he licked up to my neck, sitting up fully. Wrapping our arms around each other, his lips molded to mine.

When we came together again, both of us roared into the wind. Fire and electricity transformed our blood as we ignited, unharmed by our magic.

As we caught our breath, the fire tornado disappeared, but the rain still poured.

"I love you," was all we said until we stood ready to face whatever came ahead.

We burned our clothes and cleared the runes as intended. The circle and oil disappeared.

The way back was insightful as he carried me.

"It's like I can feel myself, but I can feel you too. It's so strange."

His smile was breathtaking. "We really are *one. My Gods, what a fucking fantastic feeling.*"

I giggled, kissing his cheek.

"I hope you're ready for what's ahead," I told him as we reached the cottage.

"Anywhere you are, is where I want to be. *Always,*" he told me while letting me down.

I leaned into him, feeling the truth in his words.

Our storm died down, but our inner heat didn't as we made love all through the night. There was more peace than I could ever dream of.

So, when the time came for us to eradicate the dark magic plaguing the world—it was a battle of storms. Dark magic and Elemental magic. Our storm overpowered theirs due to the mating ritual, and I loved Sam for his proposal.

We stood in the streets after the defeat, staring at the destruction heaved upon the town.

Once we finished cleaning up the town, I looked at Sam and asked, "Now that our purposes are served. Are you in a hurry to go to our home realm, or will you stay here with me for a while? Let our love enjoy the peace for a while without distractions…"

He pulled me closer, placing a soft, gentle kiss on my cheek.

"Through time and space, Little Witch."

We shared an equal grin as the sun parted through the clouds, showing the dark storm was over.

I had my mate, and we had infinite time to figure out the rest of our story.

The end.

Leverage, Locked

MICHAELA L. CANE

<u>One</u>

Denae played the ribbons through her hands, still leaving the corset settled on the bed beside her. On the black comforter, the red satin shone bright and dangerous, with the long ribbons promising all sorts of possibilities. She tucked one hand into the edge of the corset again, noting again how rough the inside was.

"Ray, can you come here?"

He muttered something she couldn't reply from the bathroom, and so she stood up and went over to watch him shave. "That thing...you really want me to wear that tonight? To a Halloween party? Fuck, my brother David'll be there!"

"It's Halloween!" He swiped shaving cream from his face with a towel and turned back to her. Bare-chested as he was, with that giant pentagram hanging from his neck like it always did, he looked more the devil than he would once he put on his costume.

She reached up and twitched a few fingers through the beard that he'd shaven to a point, and then up along the thinly shaped sides. "You do look like a devil today."

His hands wrapped around her waist, pulling her in. "And you'll be my devilette."

She wanted to protest that he wasn't making sense, but his lips cut her off. He tasted like that cinnamon gum he loved, the taste so sharp that it nearly burned her lips. When he pulled away, his hands tightened on her waist and he bent his lips to her neck, sucking.

Wetness pooled at her center, and she squirmed. "You want me all hot and bothered."

He huffed a laugh against her neck, sending a shiver down her spine. "Please."

This was such a bad idea. The possibility of wearing such a skimpy costume, and to a public party where her friends and her brother and his friends would all be there to see her...

"We'll just stay a while." He nuzzled her neck, his tongue darting out. "And then we'll come home, and I'll take it off you."

She swallowed down desire, picturing that. Having him peel the corset off of her...maybe even tying her wrists with those ribbons before he fucked her silly...all that and pleasing him would be worth the cost of a little bit of embarrassment, surely? And what was Halloween for, if not playing the tramp?

Her eyes went back to the corset spread across the bed, and the flouncy black skirt still sitting in its box by the nightstand. "Okay, babe, but you're gonna have to help me."

Ray sucked the skin of her neck in, pulling a whimper from her throat, and then pushed her gently out of the bathroom before turning back to the mirror to finish his shave. "Gimme one minute to finish this and put on my shirt, and you couldn't stop me."

Denae stared at him for a moment more, the words were so dark, but then she turned back to the bedroom to face her costume.

I can do this. Lots of girls do.

In a quick second, she'd stripped down to her lacy red underwear, bought just to go with the corset. Later on, she'd want Ray to appreciate it, but right now, she just wanted to get this over with.

She'd already loosened the ribbons, but now she picked the corset up, lowered it toward the ground, and stepped into it. Then she tugged it upward, past her hips abdomen until she was pulling it up over her breasts. It was a tight fit, even with the ribbons loosened, but she got it over her nipples.

The material was rough on the inside, more like untreated leather than silk, and itched at her skin as if she were laying flat on sand. Thinking twice about her decision, she went to either push it down or turn to look in the mirror—she wasn't sure which even as she tightened her grip on the hem above her breasts—but then Ray was behind her.

She felt him gripping the ribbons, and gasped as he tugged so hard that she fell forward, hands coming away from the corset top and landing on his bed.

"That's it, baby. Stay there."

She wanted to protest, but the corset was tightening on her, wrapping to her body like a second skin, rough and heavy. Her breaths felt stuck in her lungs, a lump of frightened air in her throat.

"Ray, I don't think—"

"Shh." He tugged again, and she felt the material tightening on her ribs, pulling against her sides. Why was she staying bent over? Why hadn't she pushed him back? "Just like that."

The tugging stopped, finally, and she felt his hands moving at her back, tying the ribbons. When he pulled her upright by her shoulders and whirled her to face him, she felt her cheeks reddening, and still couldn't find words. His eyes all but glowed with desire, his mouth parted, and he ducked down to suck her lips between his own, sucking in the little bit of breath she'd had to spare.

When he stepped back and sideways, she was left staring at herself in the mirror. Her breasts were pushed up and rounded by the material, her waist looking impossibly small. Her brown hair had been teased and curled earlier to perfection earlier, and hung down to her collar bone as if the ends rested on her breasts, highlighting them.

Before she could find words, to tell him how uncomfortable and scratchy the material was, how it made her itch and want to hide beneath the comforter until she looked more like herself, he'd grabbed the black skirt out of the box. To her surprise, it was one wide, flouncy line of fabric. He wrapped it around her waist so it hung low on her hips below where the corset released her hips in something of an hourglass. He buttoned the one large button there to secure it, tucked the ribbons into the back of it, and grinned.

"Denae, you're a vision. Let's go before we're late, yeah?"

Staring at herself in the mirror, Denae could barely breathe. She couldn't go out like this.

But she also couldn't find the words to protest.

As if he knew she'd been enthralled by the costume, Ray pulled the red stilettos she'd bought for the night out and knelt in front of her. He lifted her right foot and slid it into the uncomfortable shoe, so that she teetered above him, and then did the same with her left. When he stood straight, he eyed her like a designer.

"You look different." Her whisper hung in the air, and he acted as if he didn't hear her.

He twisted a curl behind her ear. "A little more makeup, babe, yeah?"

She looked in the mirror again. Her breasts rose and fell with the shallow breaths the corset forced from her, and Ray stepped behind her and all but pushed her forward toward the dresser and her makeup. But instead of pulling her makeup bag closer, he plucked something from his top drawer and handed it to her.

Mascara. She *never* wore mascara.

But, obediently, she plumped her eyelashes with the stuff. And when he handed her a dark, smoky eye shadow that she never would have chosen, followed by a bright red lipstick, she used those too.

Her throat dried, looking at herself. "I...Ray...I think I'm too exposed in this." She brought up a hand to tug at the upper edge of the corset, hoping to pull it tighter, and he grabbed her wrist before she could.

Then standing behind her, he leaned down to peer over her shoulder, grinning. "Don't fidget, babe. You look gorgeous."

She shook her head. This was maybe, possibly, pin-up gorgeous. Play bunny gorgeous. But it was *not* her.

And, worse, the rough innards of the corset felt more abrasive than ever.

"It's not comfortable. The inside of this thing—"

"Shh." He nipped at her neck, hard, and she let out a gasp that hurt her ribs. "Keep protesting, and I might have tie up your hands with that extra ribbon so you don't ruin the effect. You wouldn't want that, would you?"

Denae saw her own eyes go wide within their smoke.

Her boyfriend didn't sound at all as if he were joking.

***

Denae wouldn't have thought she could be more uncomfortable—not with only Ray present, anyway—but the car took things to a whole new level.

Ray's Camaro never left her feeling relaxed, the way it offered up every bump in the road like a miniature carnival ride, but tonight it seemed like Ray went out of his way to hit potholes, take turns too fast, and generally offer up the roughest ride possible.

And, though she knew it should have been the opposite, the corset seemed to tighten on her. She squirmed within it, trying to get comfortable in the bucket seats, but her breaths were hard and shallow. Her breasts looked like round, white balls offered up by the torturous thing, and she was amazed each time she glanced down and didn't see a rash spreading upward from the line of fabric, the way it constricted her.

At a stoplight, Ray reached sideways and reached up beneath her skirt, toying with her red lace undies. She slapped at his hand half-heartedly, too focused on the feel of the corset to really reprimand him, but he responded by tugging the fabric up so that it felt more like a thong than it should have, and in the worst way possible.

He caught her hand before she could reach down and adjust it, and she stared sideways at him. "Don't adjust it," he whispered, squeezing her wrist, "because I've got you right where I want you."

Denae blinked. His eyes looked darker. His jawline harder. And his hands were so tight on her wrist...

She glanced down, almost expecting to see a bruise forming, but the skin was unmarred.

You're imagining things. Your fault for letting him talk you into this ridiculous get-up.

And besides, she told herself, they'd see her brother at the party. Earlier, that had seemed like a horrifying embarrassment.

Now? Well, now...she felt a little bit comforted by the fact that her cop brother would be around if she needed him.

She took a deep breath, staring forward through the windshield, and tried to ignore how her underwear was biting into her now, and how the corset's inner lining seemed to be abrading her with each breath.

Maybe she'd just get there and ask her brother to take her home.

David was nothing if not protective when it came to the women in the Fredricks family. He'd not think twice about deserting a party in order to take care of his little sister.

At the next light, Denae forced herself to relax back into the seat, and she was so focused on what she'd say to her brother that she barely reacted when Ray reached across her to unlatch the glovebox.

His hand came out with a leather pouch, but she barely had time to recognize that the fabric of it seemed to match the lining of the corset before he'd opened it up and dumped a silver locket into his hand. He held it up for her, as if he meant to hypnotize her with it.

The necklace was pretty. A short silver chain, with an oddly shaped pendant. "Put it on, love?" he asked, and she opened her palm to receive it without thinking.

It was heavier than it looked, but fit perfectly. The chain was just loose enough to feel comfortable around her throat, the odd, diamond-encrusted pendant hanging above her breasts as if pointing to them.

Anything to keep him happy till we get to the party. Then, I'll find David and be out of there. I don't even know if I want to see Ray again after this.

The thought was so sudden, it shocked her. They'd been dating for five months. There'd never been a hiccup till tonight. Maybe he was a little forceful, but she liked that.

Or, she had, until tonight.

She fingered the pendant, and looked to him to say thank you....

And couldn't.

Her chest tightened, a flutter of panic speeding her heart rate. She tried to open her mouth again, to say something, but her lips remained shut, as if glued tight by the crimson lipstick that matched her corset.

Ray glanced sideways to her, grinning, and then twitched aside the collar of his shirt, undoing the top button and turning so that she could see a gleam of silver at his neck, as well.

"You've got the lock, Denae, and I've got the key. Ray's got your tongue, dear."

Denae's hands shot to the back of her neck, to where she'd just fastened the necklace clasp, but she found only unbroken chain.

This is impossible. This is fucking impossible.

"Making fun of my magic. Silly girl." Ray reached sideways and patted her knee, then gripping it through the skirt. "No more talking for you for now, okay? Let's see how you do without that argumentative tongue of yours."

Swallowing, Denae kept searching her hands along the chain, but found nothing. When that impossibility seemed true, she wrapped her hands around two bits of the chain, and yanked with all her heart.

But instead of breaking in her grip, the chain sent a hot zing of electricity circling her neck and into her hands, and she heard a pained squeak come from her mouth.

All she could do without opening her lips.

David was right. Ray's really a fucking witch who does fucking magic.

Still driving, Ray reached up and took the arm closest to him, and laid it in her lap. She let him, doing what she could to simply control her breathing.

The corset seemed tighter and rougher around her body now—thicker, too—and she wondered what he'd done to it.

When he pulled into the tavern parking lot, he unbuckled his seatbelt and then leaned sideways to whisper into her ear. "Don't bother trying to cry. I won't let you do that, either. So, be a good date, won't you? I have some things to talk about with your brother."

<u>2</u>

Ray was right about the fact that she'd blend in.

Despite her discomfort, the pain of the strange corset and the silencing of her voice, Denae found that her appearance was the least of her worries. Everywhere she looked in the tavern, women pranced around in clothing that just barely shied away from being obscene, showing as much leg and breast and midriff as the men's eyes could take in. Among them, Ray looked debonaire—the tall, dark-haired devil with a gleam in his eye, a pitchfork in his hand, a pentagram visible around his neck like some demented Olympic medal...and her on his arm—and Denae blended in perfectly.

At the bar, he bent to whisper to hear. "Smile."

And she did, her lips lifting despite the fact that she'd have preferred screaming or crying.

"You can open your lips enough to drink. No talking. A mixed drink, I think?"

Denae couldn't answer, which Ray clearly knew. He ordered a porter for himself, and a purple-colored cocktail for her.

Obediently, and with a smile, she took it from the bartender whose eyes had been hovering on her exposed breasts as he'd poured her boyfriend's beer. When she sipped it, she wanted to gag on the strength of it, but Ray's voice in her ear ordered her to enjoy it...

And then she found that she did.

Her heart nearly stopped, realizing that she wasn't just silenced when he told her, and smiling when he told her, but enjoying what he told her to enjoy. And still, tears wouldn't come.

Ray tucked her hand around his bicep and pulled her toward a lounge area in back of the bar. Men smoked cigars with women sitting nearly in their laps, but in a small favor, Ray simply pulled her down to sit beside him on a leather couch. Her thigh flush against his, she could feel the energy of his touch when he ran his hand down her arm, and then along the line of her breast.

The rough fabric of the corset seemed to tighten against her whenever she thought to move away from him, constrictive and rough on her skin, and so she leaned into him with a smile, and enjoyed her drink. When the waiter came around, Ray ordered another round for the both of them, and she had no way to argue, or even to frown.

At her neck, the lock seemed to pulse when she touched the chain, and so she stopped doing that, too, even before Ray could remind her not to fidget.

When her brother appeared, dressed in overalls and cowboy boots and a button-up Henley to pretend he was a farmer rather than a cop, Denae was three drinks in, drowning in unshed tears and liquor. One of her legs was crossed over the other, toward Ray, the stiletto dangling loose from her toes.

David froze upon seeing her, but Ray only grinned and waved him over. Then, he leaned in to whisper in her ear. "You can speak what I want you to speak. Be friendly. The loving girlfriend. Or don't. If you never want to speak to your brother again, that's fine by me."

The corset seemed to vibrate on her, rough and tight, and her heart shivered. Ray's grip was loose around her, his arm relaxed, but his hold might as well have been a pinch collar on her windpipe.

David sat down across from them, eyes pointedly on hers and then on Ray. "Good to see you two." His eyes came back to hers, sitting on her gaze suspiciously.

Ray chuckled. "Not going to hug your sister?"

David's cheeks went red, his lips tight.

Denae found that she was allowed to force a laugh. "He's never seen me dressed like this." She swallowed, heady with the sound of her own voice. She could talk again. "Never will again, either."

David blinked at her. Took a sip of his beer. "Sis."

The word all but throttled her heart, and the necklace pulsed against her throat. She thought to say "Bro", which would have been completely out of character and perhaps told him something more, but the jewelry didn't allow it. Instead, she smiled, knowing it looked more genuine than it should.

Ray hummed beneath his breath. "I hear you're doing well at the academy."

"I am." David's eyes lingered on Denae's for another moment, but then he met Ray's gaze. "I hear you've been cornered for a special assignment too."

Eyes narrowing, David glanced sideways to Denae. "Where'd you hear—"

"The walls talk." Ray shrugged, grinning. "But considering your new line of...interests? We thought we should tell you that Denae's converted to my lifestyle. We're going to elope."

Oh god oh god oh god.

Denae tried to jerk her head sideways, to stare at him, but the motion was muted. She found herself all but lifted by the heavy leather of the corset, giving Ray a long, loving-looking kiss on his cheek. Her lips lingered, her heart gagging on the emotion in the kiss, and she heard David cough pointedly.

For another second, she still couldn't pull back. She felt her breasts being pushed higher by the tightening corset, showing way too much skin, and then Ray chuckled and hugged her sideways as if he were the one who was embarrassed. "Denae, you're embarrassing your little brother."

Tears built behind Denae's eyes, her throat choking on air without showing it, but her lips smiled.

She looked back to David, who'd gone white as a sheet. "Denae, you can't be serious—"

"It's okay, David." The lock at Denae's throat pulsed, though she doubted David saw any sign of the hidden magic there. "I know what you said. What you warned me about."

Ray's hand snaked sideways and took hers, and she wasn't able to either release or squeeze it so tight as to offer up a signal, let alone a cry for help.

David's face went flat—emotionless in a way she'd never have thought possible—and he settled the beer on his knee. Somehow, in overalls and a farmer's get-up, he looked every bit the cop she'd seen just a few weeks before when he'd stopped by their parents' house for a family dinner.

Their mom's birthday had been a good one. Ray hadn't been able to come, and neither had David's girlfriend. It had just been the four of them for her birthday, like old times. Dad had given their mom a painted portrait of her prize-winning Saint Bernard, Lucky, and she'd nearly fainted for happiness. David had given her a gift certificate to her favorite spa and an I.O.U. for a mother-son lunch-and-movie date. Denae had given her a stack of new thrillers that she felt sure she'd love, and a scarf she'd seen her fawning over but which was too expensive for her to be willing to splurge on for herself.

They'd had a good night. And then, as she and David had been leaving the house, he'd pulled her aside before she could jump into her car.

"Can we talk? Now?"

She'd laughed at him, being so serious. "Yeah? What about?"

"Ray's practicing witchcraft."

She'd choked on a laugh, unable to decide whether to punch him or turn around and drive off. "Are you drunk? Or do you just want me to date one of your friends instead."

He'd pulled her further from their parents' front door, muttering under his breath. "I'm signed on to a new unit. I can't tell you the details, but trust me, I know. When I saw the two of you the other night, I did some digging on him and—"

She'd hit him, then, hard in the shoulder. "You're doing background checks on my boyfriends?!?"

"No!" He'd grimaced, shoving his hands in his pocket like he'd done all the time as a teenager. "But you need to break up with him. For your safety, Denae, and the position I'm gonna be in..."

"Excuse me?" She'd been laughing before, but that humor was long gone. "This is about you?"

"I'm gonna be *hunting* witches, Denae! You understand that? And I'm not the only one. You'll be in danger." David had stepped back, sighing. "You probably already are. I don't know if I can protect you if his name comes up."

Denae had cocked her head, staring and waiting for the punchline. "Is he cheating on me? Is that it?"

She'd never considered that, but compared to what David was telling her...

"That's probably what I should have said." David had frowned. "Would you believe me and break up with him if I told you that?"

"Jesus, David, seriously?" She'd rolled her eyes. "Not now."

David had kept going after that. Telling her all sorts of things about witches, about the unit he'd be entering, and about signs that Ray had cast spells in order to get to where he was a financial advisor to a major company. He'd made her laugh with all the stories, and gotten angry when she had taken him less and less seriously.

And then, in what now felt to be the worst mistake of her life, she'd gone home and called Ray, and invited him over, and told him all of that, and they'd had a great big laugh over how her little brother was making up crazy stories because he didn't like his sister's boyfriend.

The tavern's music had gotten louder since they'd come in, and the DJ producing it gave a shrill, unintelligible announcement that somehow translated to 'Last Call' through the microphone's distortion.

David was sitting back in his chair, frozen and staring into his drink. Ray patted her arm and picked up their empty glasses. "I think I'm going to get another round. David?"

Her brother stared at him, and then drained the last few sips of his beer and nodded. "Yeah, thanks. That's the least you could do after stealing my sister, huh?"

Ray laughed. Denae felt a smile on her lips.

She'd thought his absence might allow her to speak. To at least frown, but she'd been wrong.

The necklace went hotter around her throat as Ray walked away, the corset going so tight that she felt her breaths becoming more shallow even as the smile on her lips grew. David looked over her shoulder.

"Are you happy, Denae? Because if you go off with him...it's not gonna be safe for us to be...family. I'll disconnect, it's fine. I've been thinking about it. Mom and Dad would die without you. But me...they already know my career's gonna take me out of state."

Denae's heart twitched, and her throat burned just like the tears she couldn't shed. "That's good of you," she said. "Ray's good to me. You could...do something else."

David's gaze shot back to hers, burning into her. He leaned forward, glaring. "Now who's putting themselves above the family?"

The question stabbed at her. She'd accused him of making their parents worry with his career choice. Been mad at him when he'd told her she should study something other than advertising so that she could follow in the family's legacy of 'doing good'. Theirs was a family of teachers and lawyers and cops and firemen. Not advertising gurus and marketers.

For her to tell him to quit being a cop, so that she could date a witch...her gut bottomed out with the awareness of what she'd just suggested. The selfishness of it.

"We're eloping. I'm happy." She smiled, knowing the expression looked real, and the necklace pulsed.

"It's gonna kill Mom if she loses you. So, don't let him take you away from her, alright? You can't." David pursed his lips, staring at her. She knew he was right. "What are you not telling me?"

Liquor burned in her throat, threatening to come up, but she knew the spells wouldn't allow it. The corset would tighten into her chest and hold the vomit in before it came to that.

"Nothing, David. Nothing. You just...have to leave us be, okay? I'm with Ray now. I love him."

David leaned forward, hands clasped. "And he loves you? He treats you good?"

Denae forced herself to nod. The roughness of the corset constricted around her ribs, burning at her skin as it abraded her and she attempted a deeper breath. And then Ray was headed back to them from across the room, drinks in hand, and she waved to him.

3

In the car, Ray left her trembling in the passenger seat, burning with pain. And, patiently, he explained to her that he'd already hired a moving company to clean out her apartment. He'd transferred to a job in a city three hours south, and they'd be moving in a few days. The resignation letter she'd need to send to her boss was in his email, and he'd give it to her that night, and she'd have no need of doing anything but telling her parents the great news. He'd already called them, too, and arranged for them to come over for dinner the next night.

She was his leverage, he needed her to understand. Leverage against her brother and those like him, who'd hunt witches down and kill them. With her being a witch, or at least attached to one, David would protect them. No matter the cost to his own career and sanity.

"But that's not to say I don't love you, Denae. You're great in the sack, and gorgeous to boot. Just look at you now. I think we'll leave that corset on for a few days and let you really get used to it. Along with the locket." Ray laughed. "What a uniform, huh?"

Denae shrank into herself, barely hearing him. The locket pulsed, hot against her skin, and the leather on the inside of the corset ate into her, hard and abrasive and tight.

Ray began talking about removing the skirt and her panties, and she pressed her legs together, but he reached sideways and pulled them apart with barely the press of a finger. She couldn't resist, and her lips were so tightly held together that the whimper he brought up barely escaped her throat.

Laughing, Ray ran his hand up her thigh, touched her core, and she was wet for him. Because of him.

Foot to the gas, he sped up, talking about what he'd do when he got her home, and how the resignation letter could wait for the morning. They'd had such a great night out together, after all. Such a hallmark of a night.

Denae swallowed, but another knot came to her throat. Her fingers twitched up to the necklace, aching to try again to tear it away, but Ray laughed as a jolt of electricity sent her hand flying back to her lap, red with the quick burn he'd offered her in reprimand.

She closed her eyes, wanting to see anything but Ray and the inside of his car, but flinched back from David's gaze staring back at her. Accusing, and lost. Hurt like she'd never seen him.

She'd lost her brother that night, in choosing Ray over him. She'd seen it.

And tomorrow she'd lose her parents, and David would hate her for it.

Words and tears burned at her, but wouldn't come.

She crossed her arms over her ribs, feeling the heavy corset beneath her grip, and gagged on the smile Ray forced to her lips.

GETTING WITCHY WITH IT

SALEM 2023

ANYTIME AUTHOR PROMOTIONS

JAY LEIGH BROWN   ELLE BEAUMONT   MIRANDA SHANKLIN   RACHEL RAWLINGS   LORI DIANNI
SEDONA ASHE   J. TRUESDELL   A.M. MAHLER   ARTEMIS CROW   CREA REITAN   BRANDY SLAVEN

Hexy Beast

JAY LEIGH BROWN

Chapter One

"Steiner Jones can go fuck himself," I fume to Hex. "He thinks he's so hot, so perfect, so...so...unattainable! His mother probably told him he slid out gift-wrapped. UGH. The only thing he's God's gift to is narcissist statistics. I don't know why I ever lusted that asshat." Tugging on the sleeves of my sweatshirt, I fold them over each other one more time to make sure they stay knotted around my waist. I reach up and scoop up my hair into a messy ball and quickly slide an elastic around the ball of hair. A twinge of guilt terrorizes my insides as I consider how selfish it is of me to waste a full-moon solstice on casting a date, but I have two huge life events coming up.

Hex meows in agreement, strolling languorously along my workbench. His shoulders roll as he slinks and prowls, carefully weaving his sleek black body around the scattered mess of ingredient-stuffed glass jars. I step around the giant cast iron cauldron and lean against the counter, bending down so Hex can rub his cheeks across mine. The diesel engine rumble of his purr vibrates through my face, down the flushed column of my neck, and straight into my heart, soothing my doubts. "Am I being selfish? It's not like the world will end if I don't have a date for these things." He springs off the thick wooden counter and leaps to my shoulders, curling himself around my back. His purring is interrupted when he nips my ear and then licks his rough tongue over the bite. I reach up and scratch his ears while he butts his head into my hand.

"I'll give him a week. And I'll make the rest of the week about him, I swear!" I mutter, pulling my old Smashing Pumpkins T-shirt away from my sticky skin. The cauldron is at a rolling boil, the fire beneath crackling. The steam is making the environment of the small, but not smothered, cabin humid. The cauldron hangs from the cross beams over a recessed fire pit in the workroom on the eastern side. The walls are bathed in green and purple light. Not because I'm burning spelled candles, or the lights mean anything regarding my magic, I just love the ambiance green and purple create. LEDs can cast one hell of a mood-stoking glow.

Hex leaps off, his paws barely touching the counter before hitting the floor. One more jump, and he's circling the old, white oak book stand holding my great-great-grandmother's thick grimoire. He carefully steps over the ancient pages, each paw landing on the wood, dragging his tail down the sides until it hooks in and flips a section of pages over. "Hex! Bad ki—" his head whips around, his chrysochlorous eyes narrowed. "Panther. Bad, bad panther," I amend, biting my lip and squeezing my hands together in front of me. If I whip them out in a plea to Hex not to damage the grimoire my mother doesn't know I have, he'll piss all over the precious book of spells just to make a point.

He sits back and licks a paw, his eyes following me as I inch over, unable to tamp my curiosity at what spell might be on the page. Càit a Bheil thu a'Dol is scrawled in slanting script across the top of the page. Botanical illustrations edge the flowing spell.

Hex yowls plaintively, then reaches up and bats my face. "Dick move, Hex! A familiar should know that the minimum

requirement to perform another's spell is being able to read it." I glare at the enormous feline, who now sits grooming himself like he's the King of the Craft. I straighten and brush a stray curl off my face. "I swear if you get a single hair in the crack of those pages, I'll shave you barer than a baby's ass," He sniffs, launching himself back to the counter that runs along the entire wallbehind the cauldron.

I watch him saunter the length of the thick wood, mesmerized by his swaying hips and twitching tail, my eyes drooping under the weight of my guilt and the sauna-level heat I need to cast. By the time I realize what his intentions are, it's too late. I'll never be powerful enough to stop time. My body starts, my knees bending, my toes digging into the dirt floor. My left elbow bends, cranking back as my muscles bunch and catapult my body forward. My right hand reaches, fingers spread as wide as my eyes, to accommodate the sheer desperation of my quest. But Hex has already reached the folded, wrinkled pieces of paper on which I've painstakingly crafted my spell. He sits back on his haunches, his head rotating in slow motion, his eyes locked on mine as his paw reaches out and calmly swats the bundle of paper off the counter. My voice fills the cabin, reaching my ears long after it tore out of my throat like the last sheet of my spell from my notebook. My disbelief warps in the steam, becoming distorted as it bounces around the periphery, avoiding the trajectory of my carefully curated list. A fingernail bends and breaks as my digits close around the edge of the countertop, halting my forward progression. All my research and hard work, all the sleep-deprived hours I spent outside of studying and working, sail through the steam like Ra atop his chariot, flipping stem over stern until landing neatly in the fire.

I'm not stupid nor talented at healing enough to attempt retrieval. My heart cracks, denial echoing in my ears, as I tear my gaze from the fire. Hex isn't the least bit repentant, staring haughtily down his nose as he grooms his ears. I push off from the counter and walk across the space, sliding down when my back hits the opposite wall. This is the spot, right here. This is the bit of packed earth that will absorb my body as it rots. Because I'm done. I'm never getting up. I'm going to sit here until there is not a molecule of oxygen left in the room, and then I will gracefully retire from this life. The whole production has been a shitshow on my end anyways.

I bend my legs, drawing them up and tucking my nose in the space between. My patellas punish me, mocking my dry orbs by grinding them into their sockets. No wonder Steiner found me unattractive. My knees are knobbier than Seabiscuit's. That was why I added a pinch of cardamom. The chai tea mainstay was a twofer, promoting both lust and sweetness. A kind man wouldn't care about my bony knees. He'd be making intense eye contact with me when he wrapped his callused hands around them and spread them apart. Hell, a little courtesy might be all it takes for them to fall open.

None of that matters now. Dusk has retired. A crushed velvet night sky rests over a brilliant moon, so pregnant with light I can visualize the surface. The time to mix and cast has arrived,

and here I sit, spell-less and defeated. Now is my opportunity to create, to build the perfect partner for Drexa's wedding and Litha.

102

Hex yowls.

I close my eyes and let my shoulders sag. The cabin is quiet. So quiet I can hear the soft thump of Hex's feet landing in the dirt, right after a bit of sap explodes under the cauldron. The thread of magic between us reels shorter as he approaches me. I lift my heavy head before he stops. "I have never, never been so angry at you. I want you to leave Hex. Get out of my sight. What you did...," I trail off, trying to find words big enough to contain the ocean of betrayal between us. He meows, sitting up on his hind legs. One paw reaches out, displacing the molecules of oxygen and nitrogen, reaching for me. His cry is plaintive, urgent almost, imploring me to look at him. "Don't touch me," I hiss. For the first time since we chose each other, the thought of touching Hex makes me sick to my stomach. That revulsion is followed by a wave of grief so intense it sucks the air from my lungs. Finally, the tears come.

My shoulders shake as dual streams of grief soak into my pantlegs. I bite my lip, forcing my heaving breaths, razor-sharp with pain, to cut through my swollen pharynx. Hex has never done something like this. We spent two days glaring at each other and not talking once. I locked him in my room by accident, and he shit on my Lumineers T-shirt on purpose. Two days later, he insisted we take a wrong turn. I found my new favorite thrift shop and three vintage '80s hair band T's. That afternoon was magic. He found me a portal to a happy place. Hex and I ironed out our differences, and I got to check three bands off my ultimate collection list.

Plunk. The sound of something heavy enough to sink snaps my head up. I survey the room. Everything appears to be in place. Except Hex. He's laid out at the end of the countertop, stretched, spine arched as if the morning sun were heating him back to peak pliability. My eyes narrow. Hex is judiciously ignoring me.

The logical part of my brain is telling me that noise sounded like something falling into water. But how? Hex wouldn't dare fuck with my cauldron. I push up from the wall with a groan and wander over to the grimoire. I hadn't planned on doing anything with the book other than manifesting some of the powerful vibes surrounding the text. And I'm not even in the same stratosphere as my great-great-grandmother. Her power was legendary. Mine is laughable. She changed the world. I change my underwear. We aren't in the same league. It won't hurt me to attempt the words. They should be harmless over a cauldron of boiled water. I hadn't added the base.

"Ophioglossum lusitanicum" Hesitantly, I sound out one of the ingredients. My index finger hovers over the page, wanting to run down the thick, hand-pressed page, but I don't want to spread any harmful oils that could decrease the longevity of the precious book. Hex yowls encouragingly.

"What has gotten into you?" I huff, whipping around and shaking my head, my eyes widening entreatingly. My palms are wide open, ready to receive and answer on behalf of the rest of me.

"You are acting so...so weird. What is going on Hex?" Hex isn't just my best friend. A familiar is more than a partner. We're an extension of each other. We overlap. We share energy, emotions, goals. Our connection is so much more than empathetic. We're like a living representation of a Venn diagram. Spiritually and emotionally conjoined at the heart. So, I don't understand why he's suddenly acting irrationally. I close my eyes and breathe, reaching for the connection between us.

I breathe. Inhaling and exhaling until I push my own stress and worries aside enough to sink into the part of me that is Hex. What I find bowls me over. I stumble back from the grimoire as the room tilts. Pressing my back against the wall, I lay my hands flat next to my thighs, letting my tears flow freely as I hang my head in shame.

"Hex, I'm sorry. I'm so sorry," I mumble, hiccupping. My poor panther. He's so frustrated. He longs for...something, so much that it pounds through his heart and mind at an exponentially increasing frequency. I am the worst witch ever to walk the face of our Mother. Desperation to make things right with him, I force my eyelids to crack open. "Whatever it is that you long for, I'll help you get it. That's what I'll cook tonight. A spell for you. Can you show me what you need? I promise I'll do everything in my measly power for you. I'm a dick witch for not Seeing this." Corbeau fur lifts over his left eye as the right side flattens. He turns his head and stares at the grimoire.

Oh. Duh. "You've tacked all of the signs onto a stick and clubbed me with it and I still didn't figure it out," I murmur, staring at the grimoire with trepidation. I step towards it, gripping the edges of the podium to maintain my balance. The heat and my doubts are leaving me dizzy. "I'm going to think out loud for a minute," I whisper. "Bear with me." Inhale. Exhale. I close my eyes, sending a promise to make time for self-reflection with a quick prayer to the gods to take my shame away. I have no room for it if I'm going to help Hex. All thoughts of creating something for myself have flown the coop. I deserve all the she-can't-get-a-man looks and patronizing comments headed my way in the near future. It isn't like I haven't suffered through them for years already. Being a good witch for Hex is far more crucial to my well-being than buffering the judgment of a bunch of uppity bitches, excuse me, I mean witches, I don't give a rat's ass about. They don't mean shit in the grand scheme of my life.

Hex means everything. He leaps up, carefully landing each paw outside of the leather edges. He drags me out of my tumbling thoughts with a softly sputtering meow, his tail lashing gently against my cheek. "I hear you. I'm willing to try the spell. I'd try any spell for you. But I can't read it. Even if I have all the ingredients, I...I don't know if I have the otherworldly oomph for this." His tail slides down my cheek one more time, curling around my chin to pull my face to his. My breathing slows as I sink into depths of smaragdine and gold. He tilts his head, then leans forward, oh so slowly, and nips my cheek before rubbing his over the sting.

A nervous titter bubbles out of my throat as I try to cover the sharp inhale his bite elicits. I reach up and stroke his thick, gleaming, atrous fur. How many times have I longed to be enough

to spell Hex into a shifter? How many times have I tamped down forbidden desire, watching his muscle bunch under rippling fur? How many sighs have been uttered helplessly, their weakness no match for my secret dream of turning his airy cat laugh into a low, masculine chuckle. The kind that curls over the delicate shell of my ear as his stubble grazes my cheek.

Oh my God. Oh. My. God. Blinking, I step back, drawing away from Hex. I imagine a brick wall being put around my heart and my mind, each brick being laid at superhuman speed. Hex has fallen in love. That's what this is. The truth smacks me in the face like a block of fired clay. I feel the universal veracity of this fact in my bones. My jaw shakes as I suck in a bit of my cheek and bite. I'm such a weakling I can't even bite down hard enough to draw blood. The bitter copper I taste on my tongue is metaphorical.

This is Karma, laughing and frolicking, as she brings all my ineptitude and insecurity home. She's like the shittiest delivery guy ever, kicking my box of vibrators up the walk until they've spilled all over my porch for the neighbor's viewing pleasure.

Go ahead and dance honey. I'm already well aware. For once in your cosmic existence, you're going to be wrong. I'm coming through for Hex. And then we're going to sit back and clink sweating glasses of sweet, sweet victory while you reevaluate your entire schtick.

I step back up to the podium. Hex is always there for me. It's time to stuff my childish fantasies away and be the witch he deserves. "I can only promise my best. I swear Hex, if this is something you need...I'm here. If you think you can guide me through this, I'm listening. I'll do everything for you, including believing in myself." He grins.

Licking one of his sharp incisors, he lifts a paw and taps the incantation at the bottom, meowing firmly. "You want me to practice the incantation? Who's going to cook?"

Hex leaps to the counter. He's so light on his feet there isn't a wobble from the stand. He saunters down the countertop, weaving through my mess without touching a single jar while looking back and smirking at me, lifting the end of the thin scar that slices vertically over his right eye and down his cheekbone. "You? You're going to mix?" He stops and glares, affronted. "Gimme a break Hex. Of course, I think you're capable. But you're also a cat. Isn't it more your style to let me and my primitive opposable thumbs do the dirty work of measuring?"

He rolls his eyes and points to the grimoire. Right. I scan the ornate, slanted script on the bottom half of the second page. I roll the sounds around in my mouth, exaggerating the shapes of my mouth like a toddler as I emphasize different syllables and work the word like a toddler just learning to speak. Occasionally Hex meows, letting me know I've nailed it.

Beads of effort roll down my neck, turning the groove of my spine into a runnel of perspiration. My cheeks are flushed. Wisps of breakage curl into spirals contracting like my vocal cords as I throw myself into learning the spell my familiar wants me to cast.

Casting isn't just about measuring and mixing and reciting. Otherwise, the spawn of my kind would be potentially wreaking havoc on the world each time they got out a plastic pail and mixed up a dirt salad. The materials we use aren't concrete. They have multiple properties.

Plants are grown in different soils and under unique circumstances. And don't get me started on Animalia. That's a whole new can of...um...worms. A witch can, and should, fastidiously cultivate her ingredients, her tools, her amplifiers and dampeners, and the environment in which she casts, but none of that means jack squat if she doesn't have magic. If she doesn't cultivate and commune, if she doesn't nurture the source of her thaumaturgy, she will lose it. This is why I'm the source of such ridicule. Born of an incredibly powerful wizard and renowned witch, the world had expectations for me before I drew my first breath. I love my parents. I really do. But they're no different than the rest of my community.

I spent every day of my childhood and teens wishing I had been born without magic. I prayed fervently to any god who would listen to make me someone else. Someone who only made sustenance when they cooked. Someone who went to public school and had friends without agendas. An average person who had a sliver of freedom to discover the kind of person they wanted to become. My saving grace was Hex. He *chose* me. He tapped into my piddling connection to magic and loved me anyway.

I will do this for Hex. I will connect to my magic and grovel and plead for Hex. I will burn every drop I'm allotted in a blaze of selflessness if that is what this spell requires. I've never been comfortable with the intention aspect of magic, but I find myself burning with it as I practice the invocation.

My focus is so intense I don't notice what he's throwing into the pot. Notes of sweet cherry leave a tart aftertaste before blending with vanilla and tobacco. Middle notes of bergamot and cardamom rest upon a bed of conditioned leather and simmering spice lift, curling out of my cauldron. The scent fills my lungs and clings to my skin, caressing me. I'm so hyper-focused on producing a clean, crisp chant and putting all my love for Hex into my words that nothing is getting through.

Until I notice the rhythmic shifting of my legs. My knees are rolled in, my thighs clenching and releasing hard. My nipples are throbbing. My voice has changed. My tone is lower, practically sultry, my cadence slowing. I stop chanting, pressing my hand to my chest, only to realize it's heaving. My core is dripping, and it isn't with sweat. I lean on the podium, grasping the thick wood hard so my fingers don't slip. I lean over the grimoire, rolling my head on my neck, obsessed with the way the wet cotton of my T-shirt is pulling against the tight skin over my shoulder blades. It feels so good, pulling and pressing against my skin that my mouth falls open and I squinch my eyes shut.

At least Hex is too busy tossing crap into his potion to notice I'm about to cum all over the cabin. I purse my lips and pant through the rising tide inside of me. Electricity zaps across my breasts, arcing into a puddle between them. Heavy sparks slide down over my soft, rounded belly, under the waistband of my cotton sweats, and skitter across my pubis.

No! No, no, no, no. Please Karma, I'm sorry, I take it back, please; please don't let me do something so incredibly selfish like give in to the biggest orgasm I've ever felt brew! I spread my

legs, widening my stance, and stand straight up, tugging my shirt away from my skin. I lock my knees, praying they don't wobble. Steam swirls, heavy with the delicious, masculine aroma of sex in a cauldron.

I've never had an orgasm I haven't given myself. I've dated scads of Chads, but I've never gotten past third base. My vagina is drier than a desert by the end of the evening. Eventually I gave up. I'd rather spend my evenings studying or working or curled up in a mass of texturally pleasing blankets with Hex. There is no modesty revolving around nudity amongst witches. It's not a matter of shyness or embarrassment. I just haven't found the guy that turns me into a water witch.

My thoughts fragment as I gather my reserves and restart the chant. I must do this for Hex. I reach deep and pull out all the stops. I thrust my insecurities aside and dip my hands into my well of my magic. For Hex I'll ram my arm into that dark, dank pit and break every bone all the way up the socket when I hit the shallow bottom. The assault between my legs meets the challenge. The energy coalescing between my legs solidifies, sliding between my dripping labia like a thick finger. It strokes and circles around my swollen clitoris. I throw my head back and grit my teeth, doing my best to spit out the words of the enchantment between my teeth. I back up, leaning against the wall, no longer needing the grimoire.

One would think this amount of output from the cauldron would wash out the lights. The purple deepens to an oily black. Soft fur slides across my most tender skin. The inside of my wrist, the arch of my foot, my belly. The echo of Hex's bite resurfaces on my cheek, and the three thin scars where once he protracted his claws and swiped them across my left buttcheek sting like hot honey.

My chant dies. My occipital bone grinds into the wall as the energy between my legs spreads my opening and enters me. Rough and thick, I feel the magic bend like knuckles and begin to stroke the patch of magic inside my cunt. They scissor and spread and undulate as the legerdemain rubbing and circling my clit starts to vibrate. My shoulders slide down and brace against the wall as my pelvis bucks, riding the sexual sorcery between my thighs. Guttural moans replace the mystical poetry I should be crooning over my cauldron. "Hex...I can't...make it...stop...I..."

My body explodes like a supernova, every nerve ending in my body frying, burning to ash, and reforming over and over and over again. Waves of purple and black and emerald flow through me. The last thing I see is verdant green, flecked with halcyonic diamonds, closing around the darkness until only a slit of onyx is left.

***

"It's time to wake up, baby girl."

"Mm hmm," I hum, lifting my hands over my head and arching my back. My toes flex and my butt clenches as my hip grinds into the soft dirt I'm lying in. *No wonder cats stretch like this so much; it feels fucking fantastic.* I yawn and take the proffered hand, pulling against it to swing my upper body into a sitting position. A glass of water is thrust into my face. "Thanks," I mutter,

tipping it back and draining it in a few gulps. I swipe the back of my hand across my mouth in a half-hearted attempt to wipe off the streams of water that escaped both my mouth and the glass. "Wow, my mouth was dry. That was the best water ever." My head loll to the side and I take a not-so-delicate sniff. *Thank the gods.* I'm surprised I don't smell like a dead yak from all the sticky sweat I can feel still clinging to my skin.

Something isn't right, but I can't bring myself to care. My body is loose and languid, after that feline stretch, and I feel blissfully content to just reside here on the dirt floor of my cabin. Hell, there are probably lots of things I should be doing right now, but wasting this mystically majestic state I'm currently riding would be a grave sin. I giggle.

"Baby, let me help you off the floor."

I lower my voice and repeat. "Baby, lemme help you off the floor." A fit of hysterical giggling erupts. I draw up a knee so I have something to fall forward on. "Ow," I giggle as my head droops, and I smack my eye on my knee. My next breath fills me with the heady, tasty scent of my own sex. My kitty feels nice. "Rawr," I tell her, crinkling my fingers into claws and taking an appreciative, if slightly wild, swipe at my lucky lady bits.

That reminds me of Hex. Some of my high fades. "Hex!" I call. "Have you seen my cat?" I ask the stranger sitting in front of me. "He's black. Very shiny. Pointed ears. Big, beautiful, bangin' green eyes." I lift my paw and eyeball the distance from my wavering hand to the floor. "I'd say 'bout yay tall. He's a big guy. Fucking magnificent really. Have ya seen him?"

The man chuckles. His laugh is rich and deep. It's hearty, like a good stew, and smokey, like whiskey that's too expensive to drink. I lift my bobbling head and squint at the stranger crouched in front of me. He's squatting, his elbows resting on thick thighs. He's got black sweatpants on, but his feet are bare. His hands are loosely clasped in front of him, leaving me a clear shot of his ripped abdomen and ridged pectorals. Shaggy black hair brushes his shoulders. He's got a firm chin, a lovely square jaw, and a dusting of dark stubble that deserves a jacket slung over the shoulder and an expensive watch upon his wrist. His nose is long and straight, not too narrow or turned up. But his eyes...his eyes are brilliant. And his pupils... My face screws up in confusion. I press my hands into the dirt and sit up straighter. "Where did you say you came from? How did you get in here?"

"You let me in. I came here with you."

I reach out, my arm finding my target with no sway. My high is evaporating quickly. The steam from the spell Hex and I were doing is gone, but that intoxicating scent lingers everywhere. I brush a lock of iridescent hair from his right eye and gasp when I see the scar running across his eye. "No. No. Hex, that spell was for you!" I draw my arm back and cover my face with my hands. It isn't enough to hide my sob of shame. "I fucked it up for you, didn't I?" I ask, choking on the words.

He swings over and sits beside me, pulling me onto his lap. I snuggle in, sighing when he lays his chin on my head and wraps his arms around me. "You're right; the spell was for me." His voice

rumbles through me, calming and soothing, affecting me the same way his purr does when he's in cat form.

"But I thought—"

"We aren't thinking anything. Hush, let me speak. For once. I don't want any miscommunication between us." I shut up. He's human now. He deserves to talk. I can't be mad he hushed me. I would have said the same thing. He runs his fingers up my arm, then across my cheek, tucking a lock of hair behind my ear. "I know exactly what you were thinking when we started the spell." "We didn't start the spell!" I protest. "We were just practicing. And then, as usual, I fucked it up," I complain bitterly.

"You didn't fuck it up. We completed it. Beautifully. Do you have any clue how much magic you tapped? I'm so proud of you baby. You did it. We did it." I freeze as he drops a kiss on my head. He laughs. He nuzzles my head to the side and rests his lips against my cheek. "You were right," he whispers. "I didn't need to change to find love; I needed to find a way to return it. We belong together. You must have known I'd never let another come anywhere near your...cauldron." He quirks an eyebrow and grins before carefully removing me from his lap. In the blink of an eye, he's feline.

He meows plaintively, wanting something from me. Was that it? Was that all the time we got? My high is completely gone. My heart feels like it's going to wither, bereft after being impossibly full. He holds a paw up, halting my tears. Slowly he shakes his head and starts backing away from me.

"No, Hex, wait, don't run off!" He turns and bounds away, leaping up on a side table, pushing open a window, and disappearing outside.

By the time I hit the window, I'm running on four paws.

Moon Witch Rising

ELLE BEAUMONT

<u>One</u>

The scent of rosemary invaded River's senses, calming her otherwise frazzled nerves. Harvest Moon: Crystals and Herbs, the Forrie family shop, *always* soothed her, maybe because she'd grown up on the floor, playing with gemstones long before she knew what their properties meant.

But in this moment, the overpowering fragrance of the herb did nothing the quell her mounting anxiety. The sigils her mother and brother had set in place were lighting up like Christmas bulbs.

"Shit, shit," River muttered, backing up as she stared at the front door. All around it, the sigils blinked. Of course, something would go awry the first time they left her in charge of the shop.

At twenty, River always griped about her distinct lack of magical abilities. *You're a changeling, clearly.* She could hear her twin brother, Oliver, snickering. He had nothing to worry about; he'd inherited both lines of magic through their parents. They were all witches, except for River, of course. She was a mundie but had the ability to See the Others through their glamours. Like she'd been caressed by the power, but not imbued with it.

While she couldn't perform a simple spell, River *could* whip up a mean meatloaf, and that, in and of itself, was magic.

But hurling the bacon-wrapped loaf wouldn't save River, not now.

River bolted for the checkout counter and snatched her cell phone. Her hands shook as she scrolled through her contacts and tapped *Hot Will*. It rang for what seemed like eons, then went to voicemail.

"Come on, William," she huffed.

Jars shook on the wooden shelves, bouncing so violently they tumbled over the edge, shattering as they hit the floor.

"Shit." She tried calling William again—voicemail. River refused to call Oliver or her mother. She needed to prove she could handle herself, but dammit. If the shaking didn't cease, they would not have any product left to return to.

And then it stopped. The remaining jars no longer danced precariously close to the edge of the shelf, and the glowing, angry sigils faded until River no longer saw them.

She sidestepped the mess toward the shop's door and pushed it open. Wellesley Center appeared as it always did. Cars parallel parked against the curb, the oak trees whispering to one another as their reddish-brown leaves danced in the soft breeze.

Golden light poured from the other shops, splashing onto the sidewalks. All of it appeared normal, except for the giant clock looming above her. The hour and minute hand spun backward, and the gold accenting the black and green seemed to shimmer.

111

"What is going on?" River whispered, spinning on her heel as she looked around for whoever was pulling these magical strings. If River thought she would find a villain around the corner, twisting their proverbial mustache, she was gravely mistaken.

She stepped closer to Harvest Moon's door, and as her hand fell onto the handle, a body collided into her.

"Excuse me!" River stumbled back then steadied herself, readying to round on the rude moron. "Watch where you're f—William?" She squinted at him as he bent over, sucking in precious breath.

Normally, Will's wavy chestnut hair was gelled back, but fresh out of the gym, it curled and licked at his sweaty forehead. The idea of him being drenched in his body fluids should have disgusted her, but it gave him a primal look. Especially as the beads ran down the tip of his upturned nose.

He narrowed his dark brown eyes. "Saw you . . . called," Will gasped, his hands firmly planted on his knees as he dragged in another lungful of air.

River looked off to the side, then back at him. "So, you ran the entire freaking way?"

"No." He stood, flashing a toothy grin that made her stomach flutter. "I ran from the gym to here," he said with a shrug. "It's been a day. You called when I got out and I dropped my phone—into the damn storm drain. And the Bentley's battery is dead, so I couldn't drive here. I didn't want to chance something being wrong so . . . I ran."

She blinked, letting it all sink in. "You left Baby B behind?" Will cherished his car. If it came down to saving either Oliver or Baby B in a fire, River was certain he'd choose his car.

Will turned his attention to the door of the shop, lifted a brow, and not-so-discreetly sniffed the air. "Was someone here?"

River's brows knit together as she watched him. *What is he doing?* She glanced around, sniffing to see if she could smell anything.

"No. At least no one that I saw." Although someone had to be around to set off the sigils. Rather than stand like a fool on the sidewalk, she motioned for him to follow her inside. When they crossed the threshold, she stepped aside then shut the door and locked it behind Will.

He knew, of course, that the Forrie family was full of witches, except for *her*. River suspected Oliver had set him to the task of protector while they were out of town because he was never this ready to run to her aid. Ever.

Not that she didn't want him to be.

Spirits. Sometimes she lulled herself to sleep with fantasies of Will with his arms around her, and his cupid's bow lips pressed to hers . . .

Will sniffed the air again and glanced around. "Are you sure no one was here?" His low, gravelly voice broke through her thoughts. The muscles in his jaw twitched in annoyance—tension?

"Yes, I'm sure."

He walked over to one of the shelves, half its bottles lining the floor in shards. Will's face was so damn serious as he stared at the floor, she thought he was going to bore a hole into it.

"Someone *was* here, River." Will squatted, his nostrils flaring as he took in a deep breath. "Yesterday, maybe."

"I wasn't here. I was cat-sitting." She wasn't sure why adding her whereabouts felt necessary, but at the declaration, he only arched a brow.

She realized, belatedly, Will was saying someone *had* been here, not that they *were* here. That somehow he knew?

"I'll help you clean up, but then you need to come to my place." He picked up the large pieces of glass and brought them to the trash bin by the register. "If you need anything, we can grab it before we head out."

River chewed on her bottom lip. "But your car is . . ." And she'd be alone, with Will, in his apartment. Her heart tripped a few beats, and she tried her best to keep from smirking. This wasn't anything more than her brother's friend helping her out, and yet River's cheeks still burned from the possibilities.

"I know. I just need to call roadside assistance." Will grabbed the broom and dustpan next to her and started cleaning up.

"Let me do that and you can call whoever you need to." She crossed the room and grabbed the handle, but Will didn't relinquish his grip, only glancing down at her. Tension flickered to life on his face, just for a moment, and River nearly missed it.

She swallowed and jerked the broom out of his grasp, breaking the spell. *Whatever that was.*

The shop wouldn't clean itself, and River had no desire to explain the leftover mess to her mother when she returned.

Two

Will's apartment complex was twenty minutes from the shop, in the heart of Newton at The Ravens. From the outside, the building was crisp, clean even, with its hard edges and modern gray and black tones. Nothing about it screamed *home* to River.

She followed him to the front door, and he swiped his card. The entire thing felt as impersonal as a hotel. River winced as she filed in behind him and shifted her bag on her shoulder.

"It's so quiet," she whispered. "It also smells like a furniture store."

Will shot her a look and cocked his head to the side. His jaw muscles no longer leaped, but his shoulders hadn't eased from his ears since he'd run into her. "Quiet is good."

"No. It's lifeless and boring. Where is the personality—the community?"

He scoffed at her and headed toward the elevator, the matte black doors contrasting with the white walls. "Not everything needs to be colorful, Rainbow Brite." Will's eyes flicked to her hair, which was currently violet.

While she enjoyed her brightly colored wardrobe, River had opted for a teal cable-knit sweater and dark-wash jeans.

Even that seemed like a world of color compared to the complex.

The ride upstairs was quiet, but River couldn't help but notice how the air thickened when the elevator stopped. She'd never been inside Will's personal space, and yes, he'd been Oliver's friend since she could remember . . . but he always seemed so untouchable. So beyond her reach.

So much better than her.

Intelligent, worthy of being on the cover of *GQ*, loyal, but so damn serious! And he was on the verge of taking his bar exams—a freaking lawyer. She supposed no one could be absolutely perfect all the time.

Will opened his door and motioned for her to follow.

River had conjured an image in her head on the way over of what his apartment would look like, and it was nothing like this. She thought there would be an art piece or two hanging on the wall, perhaps even a sophisticated mood light. But there was none of that.

Gray walls, white cabinets, silver light fixtures. It was all washed out.

"Home sweet home." Will placed his keys in a bowl next to the door and shot her a look over his shoulder.

"Is it?" River's voice squeaked out. "Where is home?"

He chuckled and shook his head. "*Things* don't make a place home."

"Maybe not, but sentimental belongings do." She let it go at that, but Will was staring down at his phone, texting whoever was on the other end rapidly.

His entire living space was larger than her family's home.

River placed her bag down and crossed the floor to the massive window that overlooked the city. Spirits! She didn't realize how tall the complex building was. She sucked in a breath and glanced down, her stomach fluttering.

The view was breathtaking from above. The clouds darkened and the lights below gave off a golden glow. From here, the hustle and bustle were almost peaceful looking. She wished she could push all the buildings off to the side so she could see the full moon in all its glory. Even from where she stood, she could see the orange-tinged orb.

Will touched her shoulder, and she stumbled back into his firm body. "Sorry, it felt like I was falling." She spun around on her heel, and he was much too close to her.

He offered a crooked smile. "Yeah, you get used to it." Will cleared his throat and took a step back. "Listen, River . . . there is something I have to tell you." His brown eyes flicked away from her, and she touched his forearm.

They had never shared a heart-to-heart before, but they knew one another enough to *trust* each other. "Hey. You can tell me anything."

His phone rang, and he pulled away. "Oliver. What is it?"

River's shoulders sagged. She didn't want him telling her brother how incapable she was, but she supposed they needed to know . . .

"Oliver? Can you hear me? What book—hello?" Will pulled the phone away from his ear and glared down at the screen. "Something's going on. Do you know about a book in the store?"

She swallowed and pressed her fingers to her temple. A book? The only one she knew about was in a safe at the back of the store. It had simple spells in it, ones used to enchant herbs to make them more potent or bring out a crystal's property all the more.

"Y-yeah." Her brows furrowed as Will moved toward the window and glanced upward. "What is it?" River's heart thrummed wildly in her throat.

"You need to head back to the store and grab the book." A pained expression formed on his face as he turned to look at her. "I can't go with you."

"What? No. You have to. Something or someone has already attacked Harvest Moon." She gawked at him as if he'd sprouted another head. "I'm not going back alone!"

"Listen, River!" Will growled, but it didn't sound human. It was low and she could feel it in her belly. "I can't leave my apartment until tomorrow, and you can't put off securing the spell book. If I could go with you, I would in a heartbeat." There was a raw edge to his voice that tugged at River's heart, but as she psyched herself up to go alone, Will brushed his knuckles down her jawline.

She inhaled sharply and leaned into his warm touch. How many times had she wanted a moment like this? But as she glanced up at him through her lashes, she saw his eyes flicker between a brilliant hue of gold and their usual dark brown.

"William?" she whispered, backing away. "What's wrong?" Had someone put a hex on his apartment? *But who, River, who? Who knows that I'm by myself with Will as backup?*

He swallowed roughly and balled his hands into fists. "I can't let you go alone," he grunted and turned away. "We need to hurry because I don't have a lot of time."

The fact he wasn't answering only sped up her heart. "What are you talking about? Not a lot of time until what?"

"Until the moon takes over."

<u>Three</u>

*S*hut *the front door.*

Will was a werewolf? Of course River knew they were around, but Will—she'd known him since elementary school!

River snapped her mouth shut and rubbed her eyes. "Excuse me? I'm just learning this now?"

Will stormed up to her and she danced around him, shaking her head. "Come on, River. We don't have a lot of time left. Once the moon rises above the city, that's it."

Wolves didn't maintain their *human* senses. They lost them to the beast within and the feral creatures often terrorized local forests. She'd heard a local pack often camped out in the Needham Town Forest, letting their instincts take over, all the while hiding from society.

But Will—William Robert Wallace was a werewolf!

She rooted herself in place, crossing her arms. "I'm serious, William."

"And so am I." He narrowed his eyes at her. "If I have to carry you to your Jeep, I will."

Somehow, instead of inspiring fear, the idea elicited the delicious image of her being draped over his shoulder, and perhaps a loud smack to her backside—*focus, River.*

Will stepped forward, his muscles visibly tensing as he readied to grab her.

"Okay!" she blurted and walked toward the door. "But what am I supposed to do if you . . . you know, wolf out on the way?"

"I'll do my best to hold back, but if I do . . . don't come near me. Let me run away."

That didn't sound like a terrible idea. A massive wolf running through the streets of Wellesley, letting everyone see the oversized beast snarl and howl. However, if it came down to him pinning his furious eyes on her or running down the road, she'd choose setting him loose any day.

River bit her bottom lip and knew that she'd regret this, but there was little choice. "Fine, let's go."

***

Twenty minutes seemed like an eternity in the car with a sweating Will seated beside her. He clutched his side, grunted, and occasionally swore under his breath. She couldn't imagine what it felt like fighting herself, struggling with control like that.

When she pulled up to the curb in front of the shop, she took a moment to survey the area. All the shops were closed for the evening, their lights dimmed.

River slid out of her Jeep and turned to glance at Will, who was quickly making his way around the bright purple vehicle. His face was strained, eyes tight with what she hoped wasn't pain.

She hesitated in front of the door. There was the nagging feeling that something was inside, waiting for her. But Will was with her, and knowing he was Other comforted her a little more. He wasn't defenseless.

River opened the door, forcing herself to walk across the hardwood and toward the back room. Small wet footprints wound their way from the entrance to the desk in the far corner. A small, black safe perched on it. That's where the book was, but footprints . . .

"Shit!" Will blurted from out front.

A small creature leaped out at her, baring razor-sharp teeth and claws. Gossamer wings flapped so quickly that River could scarcely see them move at all.

She yelped, swatting at the pixie. It was no bigger than a crow, but its clawed hands scraped at her face, stinging.

Will barged in a moment later, snatching the pixie out of the air. Fury blazed in his eyes, changing them to deep gold again. He squeezed the creature until it wailed in anger and pain. "Why do you want the book?"

"*She* wants it back. It belongs to her," the pixie spat in a bird-song voice.

"Who is *she*?" River prompted, finding the nerve to move closer to inspect the teal-limbed being. They had a narrow face, amethyst eyes, and short white hair. They wore a simple pair of breeches and a laced-up tunic.

"Queen Mab," the pixie said through a vicious smile, showing off their needle-like teeth.

Will snarled and tightened his grip on them. "Grab the book, now, River."

River rushed forward, shakily entering the code to the safe. When it popped open, she scooped the book out. The old brown leather was cracked, but the gold lettering remained intact and almost possessed a holographic quality. *Magic*, she supposed.

"Wait up front," Will instructed in a tone so low, it sent shivers down her spine.

She held the book against her chest and darted from the room. He was going to kill that pixie, wasn't he? She shook her head, swallowing the bile that threatened to expel itself.

Spirits forgive her.

A high-pitched scream filled the shop and River gasped, dropping to her knees as she clasped her hands over her ears. Then, as quickly as it came on, it ended.

"William?" River blinked and her ears popped from the shriek. She turned on her heel to face the back of the store and Will emerged from the hall, his eyes glowing and his body hunched, like he was readying to pounce. "Are you okay?"

"I'm fine." He drew closer, and in the dim light of the shop, he looked *primal*.

River's pulse leaped but Will moved closer until his chest was brushing the book. "Are you sure?" her voice escaped her in a husky tone. Despite the fear racing through her, there was an aura surrounding Will that lured her in, and she wanted to taste his lips.

His eyes flashed between their natural state and the golden hue, almost hypnotizing her. "River, I've wanted to kiss you for years now. If you don't want me to . . ." Will dipped his head down and captured her lips between his. He smelled of his cedarwood cologne and something distinctly musky. His fingers slid up her neck, into her hair, securing her in place.

Spirits! Her fantasies had nothing on this moment, and as his body pressed firmly into hers, River wanted more. But as much as she wanted to wrap her arms around his neck, she didn't want to relinquish her hold on the book. Not yet.

Will grunted and picked her up, her legs wrapping around his waist. He plopped her onto the register table, now at eye level with her.

River chanced placing the book down beside her and when she did, Will pressed his lips against hers, coaxing her mouth open with his tongue. His hands pulled her closer to him until the seam of her jeans pressed into her just right.

She moaned into his mouth as he shifted against her. Through the haze of her arousal, River remembered the moon . . . Will was running on borrowed time. They both were.

"William," she murmured against his lips as she pulled away. "The moon." She closed her eyes, tilting her head back as his lips traversed her cheek then down to the spot between her neck and shoulder.

One moment he was kissing her, and the next pain blossomed so brilliantly that she gasped and shoved him away. Blood trickled down his chin, but his teeth—no, fangs—gleamed in the light.

"Run," Will growled, then grinned as he dropped to his knees. Bones cracked as he shifted, and human limbs elongated until they were a wolf's, covered in fur as dark as midnight. He was beautiful, but he was not *Will*.

And he'd bitten her.

River choked on a scream. She snatched the book and bolted from the table, but it didn't matter how fast she was, he was faster and larger. He was going to devour her!

Will leaped forward and she dove under him. He crashed into the register table, stunning himself. Turning around, he licked his muzzle and readied to leap at her again.

As adrenaline coursed through her, River's head started to spin. Was it the bite taking effect? Her vision darkened around the edges, and she stared at the beast hurtling her way.

He was ready for her to dart beneath him this time. With her free hand, she grabbed the broom and smacked him hard enough that the handle snapped in half. The wolf only shook his head and growled at her.

If he wanted to eat her, he'd have done so by now. He was playing with his meal first . . .

The notion sickened her.

"William!" River screamed, then weightlessness washed over her, and the last thing she saw was the floor rising to meet her.

Four

An intense wave of heat stirred River from her slumber. She groaned. Every muscle felt as though she'd run the Boston Marathon. She tried to push the stifling blankets off her, only for her hand to brush bare skin.

Skin.

The pixie, the book . . . *Will.* She squeezed her eyes shut, then dared to glance down at her chest. His dark hair filled her vision, and his soft snoring roused her all the more.

River glanced around them, realizing she was back in the office. Maybe after he shifted back, Will had carried her in . . .

She brought her hand up to rub at her face. This was a mess. The whole thing was a horrible, bloody mess.

The clock on the wall said it was eight, which meant she had two hours to open the store. Yet, all she could think about was if she had shifted last night, too. With the full moon and a fresh bite, it was perfect for a newly infected wolf to turn.

River whimpered.

Will jolted into an upright position and scanned the room, and River didn't waste any time rolling away. She almost wished she hadn't, because he was entirely naked. Every contour, every muscle, every blessed piece of him was on display.

"River, are you—" He sniffed the air, and she had to wonder if he could sense the change in her. He'd know, wouldn't he?

"Did I . . . am I . . . ?" She placed her hands on her head as panic rose within her. "Did I fucking shift too, William?"

His eyes flicked to her shoulder, and he paled considerably. "River, I'm . . ." The apology never left his mouth. Will stood and approached, but didn't touch her, only sniffed the air. "But you didn't." His brows furrowed, and he cocked his head. "You're . . . not infected." He drew in another lung full of air. "Different, but . . . not a wolf."

The notion was almost as impossible as keeping her eyes up and not on his pecs. She'd wanted him before, but there was a new hunger—*need* really—that desired to be sated.

"Different, how?"

"I can't explain it," he said, searching her eyes. "Not you entirely."

Wonderful.

River raised her hands and lightly pushed on his shoulders. "We can figure it out later, but for now, you need clothes. Oliver keeps a spare set in here." She turned away from him and walked toward a wooden shelf. On it was a pile of neatly folded clothes. She might have been more than freaked out about the situation, but Will was still naked and standing six feet away from her.

His long toned legs led to six feet and two inches of glorious muscle.

She blinked. *Focus!*

River crossed the room and handed him the clothes, but her attention was drawn to the floor, where she'd dropped or maybe placed the book. She scooped it up and stared down at it.

Through a hazy memory, she recalled what the pixie had said. "Queen Mab wants the book back . . ." River turned to face Will just as he was pulling the T-shirt down. She swallowed roughly and wiggled the book in her hand.

"I don't know. We'll have to talk to your mother about it. Oliver knows nothing. He would've mentioned it to me."

River sucked in a breath, nodding. "Listen, about last night—"

"We don't have to talk about it," he rushed out. "I wasn't in my right mind. We can pretend it never happened."

Those words, though simple, devastated her. Outside of the bite, their kiss had been a moment she'd longed for. She was confused, hurt, and amped up over the stupid book, let alone the mess with Will.

Instead of laying into him about the ordeal, knowing it would only hurt one of them, she schooled her features and popped her lips together. "Pretend what didn't happen?" She forced the words out in a cheerful tone. "Anyway, we have the book, we defeated the lone pixie, and tomorrow Mum and Oliver return. We survived day one."

Will's lips turned up in a crooked grin.

One day left.

A lifetime of trying to forget last night ever happened.

About the Author

Elle Beaumont is a writer who loves creating vivid fantasy and science fiction worlds in the young adult genre as well as new adult. She lives in southeastern Massachusetts with her husband and two children. When not writing or chasing around her children, she can be seen crocheting, candle-making and taking care of her animals. More than once she has proclaimed that coffee is life blood and it is how she refrains from becoming a zombie.

Discover more on www.ellebeaumontbooks.com or sign up for her newsletter to keep up to date on the latest and greatest! www.ellebeaumontbooks.com/newsletter

Find Elle on her social media at @ellebeaumontbooks on Facebook and Instagram

Duplicity

MIRANDA SHANKLIN

This is dedicated to all of those who are still lost and wandering, trying to figure out who they really are.

<u>One</u>

When she lost her job, she took it as a sign. She has been working in that field for twenty years and became burnt out years ago. She's become cynical and regards everyone with suspicion. That's what happens when you work in the legal field, on either side. You're always finding creative ways to cover or explain what your client did or gloss over it completely.

She has always had trouble with her hands. They always hurt, and it's getting harder to hold onto objects. She drops almost everything she picks up. After three surgeries, her typing speed isn't what it used to be.

She has always taken what life handed her and has done the best she could with it. She had never intended on raising twins on her own, but she's proud of them and what they've accomplished. If they would only listen to her on one more subject, but they both shut her down.

She had exposed them to many different religions during their youth. It's important to her for them to find their own paths. She would rather take them with her on her path, but that isn't for her to decide, and she has known that since the doctor handed them to her, and she looked into those tiny faces.

Those tiny faces have grown into adults now. However, they still live with her. She doesn't mind; she actually likes that they both still live here.

She walks in the house from the shop she opened and listens to their argument from the doorway from the kitchen to the dining room. She came in too late to find out what they're arguing about but almost laughs at her son's argument.

Amorphous puffs out his chest proudly and arrogantly talks down his nose at his sister. "I am the man, the only man, which means the man of the house. I was born first, so that makes me the oldest. I am the one who gets to make these decisions."

Her daughter Amora doesn't even try to subdue her laughter. She laughs in his face. "Where the hell did you come up with all that?"

His arrogance slipping, he shifts his weight. He hadn't expected her to outright laugh at him. He straightens his spine. "I have my ways."

Astral hates it when they fight, especially when one is wrong and digs their heels in. She chuckles under her breath as she responds to her son.

"Am, you are not Mr. Know-It-All. Your grandfather owns the house, and we rent it from him, so he is therefore the actual 'man of the house,' and you two were born by c-section. They pulled you both out at the exact same time. You were the same weight and length, and even had the same amount of hair. You two have been equal since before the day you were born."

Amorphous deflates at his mother's words. He mumbles, "I hate being the only man in the house. They always gang up against me," as he slouches his shoulders and drags his heels on his way to his room.

Astral calls down the hall after him. "Am, honey, that's not what I meant. You know I don't take sides. I was trying to make sure you had all the information. I don't even know what the argument is about."

Astral sighs as she stares down the hall her son had walked down. Her daughter starts to talk, and she snaps her head up to look her in the eye, her anger barely contained.

"I don't want to hear it. Until you are both here to tell me what's going on, I'm not listening to any of it. You've gotten good at manipulating a situation to make yourself look good and everyone around you bad. You seem to forget I can see through your bullshit."

Am quietly closes his door after listening to his mother's scolding of his sister. It makes him feel better when he's reminded his mom doesn't buy into her act. She had already given him a ridiculous name, the least she could do is help him out every once in a while.

Before Astral can make it to Am's room, he comes out, pushing past her. "I'll be back later."

She doesn't respond, and he doesn't wait for her to. He glares at his sister as he passes her on his way out the door.

Astral wishes she could figure out what's going on with him. That's the first step in bringing her twins back into harmony. They may not want to recognize the importance of that, but she does, and she'll keep working and try to fix this. If only they aren't so stubborn.

Amora stands in the same place Astral had left her. The difference is now, she has her arms crossed over her chest, her hip cocked out, a red face, pinched lips, and her eyes are barely a slit.

Astral notices the anger in her daughter but has no intention of dealing with it. As she walks past Amora, she chuckles. "You look like your grandmother when you do that."

Amora's eyes open wide, and her mouth drops open as her arms fall to her side in shock. She isn't sure what just happened. She's really close with her mother, and this is the first time her mom doesn't let her explain or listen to her.

Am gets to his girlfriend's apartment and as soon as she looks at him, she steps out of the doorway to let him in. As she closes the door, she takes a deep breath, preparing herself for the onslaught of emotions that's about to hit her like a truck.

She starts to turn and before she knows what's happening, she's against the door while Am kisses her, and his hands are everywhere at once. It takes all of her willpower to put her palms on his shoulders and push him back.

They stare into each other's eyes for a moment. Both have swollen lips, red faces, and are breathing heavily. When she pushes, Am only pulls the top half of his body away from her so she can still feel him up against her, making it harder not to give in. As an empath, its difficult to separate her feelings from those around her. This is one of those situations where it's important that she concentrate and make sure she reacts based on her feelings and not his.

When Am realizes she won't answer his unspoken question, he knows he'll have to make the next move. "Bree, I need you. I love you. Please."

She knows he won't take this well, but it's how she feels she needs to respond. "I love you too, Am. You don't need me. You want me so you can forget about what's going on at home. I don't want to be your distraction." She untangles herself from him and walks away.

Am leans against the door for a couple of minutes with his head drops, taking deep breaths to get his body under control again. His pants are still a little uncomfortable when he follows her into the apartment.

Bree sits in her oversized chair with a blanket over her lap and a book in her lap. She isn't sure if he'll come in or leave, but it'll be completely up to him. She looks up from her book when he enters the room. However, when all he does is walk in, flop on the couch, and sit there pouting, she returns to her book. They've been together for three years, he should know by now that pouting won't work.

Am sits on the couch, slumped, watching Bree. It gives him a chance to study her. She thinks he uses childish antics to get what he wants, so she ignores them. He actually uses them to study and gather information about the people around him. She does the same thing with body language. She just doesn't realize it.

Bree blows out a frustrated breath, puts a bookmark in her book, and glares at Am. "You really want to do this now? After, I'm assuming, another fight with your sister?"

Am laughs. "Well, I think it's safe to say you aren't talking about sex. That tone I'd be afraid you would cut my dick off."

Bree raises her brow at him. "Really?"

Am rolls his eyes, sits up on the couch, leans forward, putting his elbows on his knees, and gives Bree the most intense look she has ever seen. "Bree, I can gauge your mood, general health status, general mental status, and whether you either like or want to talk to the person you're talking to by your body language and social cues. However, as far as I know, there isn't a person on this earth who can read your mind to know what you're thinking. So, when you ask if I really want to do this, you're going to have to be a little more specific because you spent the last half hour ignoring my existence."

Bree hadn't expected this. She has never seen this side of her boyfriend. She's thrown off her game with his words. She doesn't want him to know this, so she continues, "I didn't tell you what you feel. I told you the emotions you're broadcasting. I'm an empath, as you know whether you want to believe or talk about it, so I have no control over whether I feel your emotions when you're sending them out that strongly."

He scoffs. "It has nothing to do with empath or emotions. It's all about body language. You're as bad as my mom, always trying to tell me I'm a witch, and I need to embrace my heritage."

Fire flares up in Bree's eyes. As a full witch, she believes wholeheartedly he needs to accept his gifts, but it's not her place to tell him that. He's walking on thin ice.

She responds in a deceptively calm, quiet tone. "I've never, not once, told you that you need to embrace your heritage, accept your gifts, or anything along those lines. I asked why you haven't, and you explained, and that was the end of the conversation. Don't you dare blame me if you feel bad about not doing something that has nothing to do with me."

He narrows his eyes, and his body stiffens at her words. He can't believe the audacity she has. "Really? So, the altar over there, and the rituals you do, while I'm here, the spellcasting, all of that isn't you trying to tell me to just accept it and move on?"

Bree's eyes pop open so wide, Am hopes they don't pop out of her head. "Wow. Egotistical much? Not everything I do is about you. In fact, most of what I do has nothing to do with you. I do my rituals and spell work because I'm a witch, which doesn't have anything to do with you."

Am deflates. "So, you're like my family. You don't think or care about me. It's all about you."

Bree looks up at the ceiling. "Goddess, help me. Am, you realize it doesn't have to be one way or the other, right? There's a happy medium here. Would I like you to accept your gifts? Yes. Am I going to pressure you into it, or even ask you to? No. That's a very personal decision that only you can make. I'm not going to love you any less or any more, whichever decision you ultimately make."

He paces. "I wish it were a personal decision; it would make things so much easier. That's what my sister and I have been fighting about. Until we either accept or officially deny our, what did you call them, our 'gifts,' we're both connected to them. We both have to accept or deny them. I want to at least look into it, and she wants nothing to do with it. Whatever is done, we both have to do the same thing."

Bree opens her mouth to respond, but Am stops her, raising his palm out and shaking his head. "Nobody is allowed to help. We have to come to our own decision on this. I only told you so you would understand what I'm dealing with."

She nods and smiles a mischievous grin as she lifts the blanket in her lap, showing Am she has no clothing on from the waist down. He's at her chair in one step and has her on the couch in another. She has his pants undone before she lands on the couch. She may not be able to help him with his decision, but she can help him to know he isn't alone, and he's loved.

<u>Two</u>

Amora watches her mother and brother both walk away from her, again. This is what always happens. Am tries to bully her into doing what he wants, their mom walks in, they stop talking because they know she isn't allowed to help, then she's alone again. She's always alone.

She has no idea what Am is thinking. He wants to turn her into a complete cliché. The loner girl, there's something different about her. We think she's a witch or something. Yeah, let's add that to the pile of other things that are already being said about her. Of course, Am is in his own little bubble and doesn't even know what they're saying about her.

The universe gives her someone who's her complete equal and supposed to be by her side for her entire life, and he abandons her. Now he wants to make her life more difficult.

Then to make it worse, her mom doesn't help. She tries to keep her witchy stuff subtle, or where we either can't see it, or when we aren't home, so she doesn't influence our choice. However, she makes comments like 'my daughter who wants to ignore the gifts she was given' or 'my daughter who wants to deny a piece of herself.'

Am has his girlfriend he runs to; Amora is left on her own. As if she knew, Amora's best friend who moved away last year video calls. Amora smiles as she answers and walks toward her room so she can talk to her friend privately.

Kristin's smiling face and bubbly personality have Amora lighting up in no time. They catch up since their last call a couple of days ago.

Kristin's smile fades. "What is it? I can see it in your eyes. What's going on?"

Amora chuckles as she lets out the breath she had been holding. "Kris, I don't think I can tell you. Nobody is allowed to help me with this one. This is something that Am and I are supposed to decide on together, but we're on opposite sides."

Kristin rolls her eyes. "Mor, you and Am are always going to be on opposite sides. I can't believe nobody has figured it out yet. You were born at exactly the same time, were the exact same weight and length, one boy, one girl. You are the Yin and Yang, Sun and Moon, or however you want to look at it. He has always had his happy little bubble, and you've always felt out of place. You two are always going to be the exact opposite of each other."

Amora is lost in thought for a few minutes. Sputtering out words occasionally, such as one with black hair, the other blonde; one fair skinned, the other olive.

Kristin waits for her to work through all of it in her head. When Amora looks back at her screen, she has narrowed eyes, and her nose is scrunched up in anger.

"You knew. That means you're involved in all this and never told me. You let me think I was alone in this, and then you left."

Kristin's eyes popped open as wide as they would go, and she held her hands up in surrender. "Whoa, whoa, whoa. I had no control over any of that. And I never let you feel alone. Just like tonight, when I feel you're feeling alone, I make sure you know I'm here for you. As far as the moving, it was the last thing I wanted to do. Some thought with how close we are that I would unintentionally influence your decision. After you and Am make your decision, I can come back. I'm just pissed they didn't make Bree move. I mean Bree and Am are a lot closer than you and me; they're in a relationship."

Amora holds her hand up to make Kristin stop talking. "Kris, I know it's unusual for you to know this much information, and I don't know any of it, but you're doing a huge info dump on me here. Let me catch up. Did you just say that Bree, my brother's girlfriend, is a witch just like you?"

Kristin smiles with a sneaky grin. "Because she has been open with him about it from the beginning, she got to stay. So, since they made me move away, and you're so close to having to make your decision, I figure it won't hurt to tell you. Now, I still can't help you with your choice, but I'm a great sounding board. I can listen while you talk through whatever you need to talk through; just don't ask my opinion or what I think because I can't answer those questions."

Amora snaps her head around to look at her friend's image on the screen. "Wait, with the way you're talking, it sounds like I've been surrounded by witches my whole life. How do I not know that? How could I have not noticed anything?"

Kristin giggles. "It took a lot of work. Everyone let out a sigh of relief when it came time for you two to decide. Then you would find out about all the witches, so they don't have to be so super vigilant when there was a chance you might stumble on them."

Amora furrows her brow, thinking hard about something. "Hey Kris, how are Am and I supposed to make this decision when we're always going to be on opposite sides?"

Kristin lets out a long breath. She knew a question like this was coming. "Oh honey, I have no idea. It's an impossible situation. I think you two need to sit down and actually talk, instead of arguing. You're both always trying to make the other one hear you. Maybe sit down and agree to listen to each other, then come to an agreement you can both live with."

Still halfway lost in thought, Amora responds, "Yeah, that sounds like our only option. I'll talk to you later, Kris."

Amora disconnects the call without waiting for Kristin to say anything else and sits on her bed. Kristin has given her so much information that it takes a while for some of it to process. She lives in a witch community and has never known.

<u>Three</u>

When Am gets home, he sees Amora's light still on. He takes a deep breath and sticks his head in her room. He finds her sitting on the edge of her bed, staring at the floor. As soon as he starts talking, her head snaps up, and her full attention is on him.

"Hey, Sis. I hate when we fight like that. I'm sorry I was such a dick. We need to find a way to work this out, though."

She nods, clears her throat, and gestures for him to come in. He sits on the vanity chair facing her.

He can see it when she comes to a decision by her face going from that of a lost child to one of a determined adult. He waits to see if this is good or bad.

Amora looks her brother in the eye and speaks in a calm, confident voice. "First, we both need to agree to listen to each other. We're really bad at that. We try to talk over each other and interject our own opinions. For this to work, we have to actually listen to what the other is saying and then respond to it."

Am lets out the breath he has been holding. "I agree. I think that's the only way we're going to come to a decision."

Amora relaxes. "Oh, good. I was afraid you would dig your heels in. Anyway, Kristin called me tonight and opened my eyes to a lot of things I hadn't seen before. I don't know how much of this you already know, but I'm going to tell you to make sure we have the same information."

Am furrows his brow in confusion but gestures for Amora to continue. Amora tells him everything Kristin had told her. By the time she's done, Am is pacing.

He stops and looks at his twin. "It all makes sense now. All the bits and pieces we've picked up over the years; when you put them in there, everything comes together."

Amora nods. "Yep, that's the line of thinking I was on. Keep going."

When he gets to the point that had Amora staring at her floor, his face drops. His eyes snap up to hers. "No."

The moment that both of the twins understand what their decision means, Astral, Bree, and Kristin all feel it. There's a shift waiting to happen. All three women race for Amora's room.

Astral is across the hall, so she gets there first. Nobody is allowed to help, especially now that they know what their decision means. Astral sees the aura around the doorknob and knows if she touches it, she won't get into that room. She'll most likely be thrown away from it.

Bree doesn't bother with knocking. She flings the front door open and almost has her hand on the knob before Astral can grab her arm and stop her.

Bree speaks in a tone that says she's barely hanging on. "Astral, I know the rules, and I will gladly pay any penalty, but I'm going in that room. As their mother, I can't believe you aren't already in there."

Astral lets out a laugh that sounds half crazy. "I don't give a fuck about who's allowed to help or not. I wouldn't stand out here in the fucking hallway if it wasn't for that." She points to the doorknob and the aura around it.

She rips her hand from Astral's grasp. "Is that…?"

She continues her angry pacing. "Yep, an aura placed by the Norns. Nobody is getting past that."

Kristin had entered silently. "I can but not while it's blue. Blue is they know but don't fully understand. After they fully understand, I can get through. It will be orange."

Astral and Bree stare at her with raised brows, laying the question out there without saying it.

Kristin sighs. "I am a Norn in training. Not that I was given a choice. Amora is my charge to protect, but she became a friend. That's why they removed me. I'm sorry but when I enter, I can't take either of you with me. If you try to enter, you won't like the results."

Astral throws her arms in the air and lets them flop back down. "Of course not. It's only my children."

Kristin snaps her head around with narrowed, glowing eyes, her hair flowing as if a breeze were flowing through the hallway. "Astral, do you know who your children are? They're the Yin and the Yang, the Sun and the Moon, the Light and the Dark. They're the balance of the universe. This is the single-most important decision of their lives as it involves the entire universe. So, back off and let me do my job."

Bree interrupts, "Astral, don't you dare move. Kristin, it's orange. Please go help them."

Astral falls to the floor as her muscles no longer hold her up. "What have I done?" She watches the door as all the comments she has made to her daughter, and all the times she pushed her son, replay in her mind.

Bree sits in front of Astral and takes her hands. "Astral, I need you to understand something. You didn't see it because you didn't want to. It wasn't made obvious to you because it would have influenced the way you treated them. Only they can make the decision. You were chosen because you can handle this."

Astral's eyes snap from the door to Bree. "Of course, I can handle it. That's not what I'm worried about. I don't care what their decision means magically, I could have done so much more to make their childhood more enjoyable for them before they got here."

Bree gave her a small smile. "Which is why you didn't know. They needed the childhood they had. You were a terrific mother to them. I couldn't be more in love with your son."

Astral grabs Bree and hugs her tight, holding onto her in the hope her son would feel it.

******

Kristin enters the room to find the twins facing each other. She takes a deep breath and approaches them.

Without looking away from her brother, Amora talks to her. Kristin notices silent tears streaming down her face.

"Kristin, you don't want to be in here right now. I'm sure you know if Am and I accept our gifts, then he becomes the light, and I become the darkness. If we don't, the world falls into chaos because there will be no balance."

"Yeah, I know all about it. I'm in training to be a Norn, like my mother before me. I'm here to help you with whatever decision you make. Are you sharing everything with each other?"

Am responds this time. "Yeah, almost done. Can you tell Bree I love her?"

"If your decision leads to that needing to be done for you, yes."

Amora turns to Kristin, who doesn't react to the skin on her face that's moving like she has tiny snakes under her skin, or the dead look in her eyes.

Amora is clearly trying to intimidate her. "Now would be a really good time to go."

Kristin ignores her and looks at Am. He is the one who has silent tears streaming down his face now as he sees what has become of his sister. He's also glowing with a white aura. They can't stay in the same room much longer. They need to be far away from each other.

Kristin points at the door, and it flies open, causing Bree and Astral to jump to their feet. Bree stands there, taking in the scene expressionless. Astral is crying as she looks at her children. Bree came prepared; Astral did not.

Kristin sighs again. "Bree, I need you to get Am and Astral far away from here. I have Amora."

Bree nods, drags Astral behind her, and just before she reaches Am, everyone focuses on Amora.

"Mommy? Please help me. What's happening to me?" Amora sounds like a scared child.

Astral breaks free from Bree's grip and runs to her daughter and wraps herself around her in a hug, holding her precious little girl tight to her chest. Over Astral's shoulder, everyone else in the room can see Amora's evil smile before they both disappear.

Kristin yells into the air. "Damnit, Amora!"

They hear an echo of fading evil laughter.

Kristin looks over to Bree and Am. "The goal was to get you two far away from each other, and that was accomplished. So, I guess you get to stay here. Bree, keep him safe."

Bree nods and turns to Am. "Come on, Baby. Let's get your things; you're moving in with me at my apartment."

About the Author

Miranda Shanklin lives in Central Illinois with her husband, two children, and the family security system, a hundred-pound lab named Fido. Paralegal by day, mom/wife by night, she writes during those rare but precious moments of downtime. An avid reader her entire life, Miranda's dream was to someday become an author. That dream was realized in 2015 when her handsome and intelligent husband said three beautiful words: go for it.

Hexed In the City

RACHEL RAWLINGS

<u>One</u>

A witch, a wand maker, and a warlock walk into a bar—not together or entirely in that order. It sounded like the beginning of a bad joke but it was the beginning of a bad night, one I hoped to turn around before things got too far out of hand.

Easier said than done.

Jacob Orly - the wand maker - sat at the end of the bar with slicked back silver hair and a lightweight beige jacket zipped up to the collar of his button-up dress shirt, ordering another round as if he didn't have a care in the world.

Of course, his carefree attitude changed the second he saw me walk in. The moment I entered his peripheral he hopped off his stool and took off for the rear exit, running out on his tab and the warrant for his arrest.

To the untrained eye, Orly seemed like any other unassuming tourist visiting a historic mill town. Short stature and wiry frame—I guessed his weight to be somewhere in the neighborhood of my own hundred and twenty-five pounds. His bland appearance made him seem less threatening.

But Jacob Orly was a dangerous man who pedaled power out of the trunk of his car, selling wands to any average Joe on the black magic market, heavy emphasis on the *average*.

Trading magical wares to ordinary people was something the Arcane Magical Authority took seriously, putting Jacob Orly near the top of the most wanted list.

A tip came in just as my shift ended. I'd been tracking the wand maker for weeks. Hecate herself couldn't stop me from following up on the lead. *Maybe Hecate should try a little harder next time.*

I should have followed protocol. I could have turned it over to the practitioner on duty.

Shoulda, coulda, woulda.

I sloshed through oil-slicked puddles, hop-scotched my way over bottles and cans littering the street from overflowing dumpsters, and skirted around a herd of alley cats feasting on scraps that had been tossed out from the noodle shop adjacent to the bar. Orly darted left around a corner and almost gave me the slip.

Almost.

If I'd learned anything in my short time with the AMA, it was that cardio was one of the most important skills an agent could have. It was also a skill I had yet to master. I relied on stealth, stalking my prey like a lion on the Serengeti until I was ready to pounce.

I cut left around the corner in the same direction as my suspect. I was closing in and gaining ground until I got hit with the magical equivalent of a baseball bat to the solar plexus.

Another important lesson I'd yet to learn - never chase down a lead alone.

With less than five years under my belt, I was a rookie by most agent's standards and subject to constant ribbing by my peers. As the daughter of two prominent magical officials, I was considered a rising star by my supervisors - which led to more ridicule and an overactive desire to prove myself on my merit rather than my last name.

So far, I'd say I was doing a bang-up job. My parents and the department disagreed.

Case in point, I let my suspect get the jump on me. The magical blast knocked the air from my lungs and my head into a dumpster. *At least Orly's products work.* Confirmation the wands packed a real punch upped the charges against him.

"I love watching you work." A familiar pair of black biker boots that used to share a closet with my Doc Martens stepped into view just as my suspect slipped out of my line of sight.

"Yeah? I thought so. I mean, it was obvious. What with the way you bailed on me and our relationship - all telltale signs of how much you love me and my work."

I tried not to think about the ingredients of the dumpster stew that soaked into my jeans - or Griffin's whiskey-colored eyes that held the same subtle burn as the aged alcohol - and peeled off the greasy burger wrapper that clung to my elbow.

My ex hadn't said anything about *loving me* per se but I knew what he meant. With Griffin Wildes, you had to read between the lines.

A skill I'd perfected throughout our relationship.

After a year and a half, it became exhausting and a large part of the reason why our relationship had deteriorated to the point of him skipping out on the rent and transferring to a different precinct.

"I called in the tip, Morgan." That was as close to an apology from Griffin as I was likely to get. He held out a hand and offered to help me up.

I grabbed hold of the upper right corner of the dumpster instead and hoisted myself up off the filthy cement. After I picked a piece of what I hoped was gum from my raven waist length hair, I resumed the chase.

With a glance over my shoulder, I offered as much gratitude as I could muster. "Are you coming or what?"

The invitation to tag along must have meant more to Griffin than I realized because he smiled in response. But not just any smile--*the smile.*

It was different from the deviant curve of his lips and devil may care attitude that drew me to him the night we first met. No, this one was private, reserved for me, and far more dangerous.

The smile that settled onto his lips held the power to melt the block of ice that had encased my heart since the day he walked out on me—and the other parts of me that I had locked away.

Parts that yearned for one more touch, one more kiss.

For the love of the Goddess, Morgan, gird your loins and get your shit together. You cannot screw this up.

Orly got the jump on me again, dodged down another alley, and then out of sight.

I was sensing a pattern. One that would land me behind a desk pushing paper and processing other detectives reports or worse, put an end to my career at the AMA. I needed to bring Orly in and put an end to his black-market business for good.

With one last trick up my sleeve, I removed the amulet hanging from my neck, pricked the tip of my right index finger, and rubbed a small drop of blood across the face of the crystal to invoke the charm.

"Tracking spell?" Griffin asked, reaching for the magical GPS disguised as an antique family heirloom.

"I thought you wanted to help." Old wounds and my temper got the better of me and I smacked his hand away from the amulet with more force than the gesture warranted. "You know better than to get your fingerprints on it. You'll scramble the signal."

"I'm sorry," Griffin uttered the two words in the English language - or any language, for that matter - that I never expected to come out of his mouth.

Two words I waited months to hear and were powerful enough to knock my world off its axis. It was a shame he hadn't said the words when they would have meant something.

"Wow. I've been waiting a long time to for you to say that. I wasn't sure I'm sorry was actually in your vocabulary."

We're not doing this. We are not doing this. Focus, Morgan. Focus. Easier said than done with my ex hanging around.

The tracking charm warmed in my hand and began to glow, bringing my attention back to what mattered: serving the warrant and making the arrest. The light shifted from a soft amber to bright orange as it zeroed in on a location.

"He's not moving. It looks like he's hiding in the theater down on Main Street." I started down the alley, heading back toward the main drag when Griffin grabbed my arm and pulled me back.

"Hang on a second." His grip loosened and his hand slid down my forearm until his fingers intertwined with mine.

Nope. Absolutely not. We have been down this road and know exactly where it leads. Heartbreak. Do not be lured in by eyes the color of storm clouds, a strong jaw, and chiseled abs.

"I'm supposed to be working. You're supposed to be helping." Every warning bell and whistle went off in my head and I tried to shake my hand free of his.

"Just listen to me. Please." Griffin pleaded, but he released me. "I screwed up, okay? Is that what you want to hear? There is *so much pressure*, so many expectations dating a Byrnes, but I shouldn't have listened to your father when he told me I wasn't good enough for you."

The desperation in his voice was the straw that broke the broom. Ten months of bottled-up anger, heartache, and suspicion that my family had played a major role in our breakup burst free.

"Oh my, Goddess. Now, Griffin? You want to do this now?" I pushed against his chest, forcing him to step back and put a little distance between us. "It took the better part of a year for you to offer an apology. Your timing sucks. As usual."

"Yeah? Well, I waited a long time for the right time to talk to you, Morgan." Griffin raked his hands through his chestnut hair, gripping the roots for a moment before his fingers combed through the ends. "Trust me, it doesn't exist."

"I find it hard to believe that you couldn't have found one opportunity that wasn't in a disgusting alley *and* in the middle of a run?"

A year ago, I would have swooned over his apology, fallen into his arms and turned my back on the pain he caused the morning I came home from a double shift to an empty apartment.

But too many moons had passed for that.

"Why couldn't you just send flowers or a card like a regular guy?" I tapped the crystal, willing it to send me a ping with Orly's location and a reason to walk away from Griffin that didn't give the impression I was still hung up on him.

"Because I'm not a regular guy and you are not a flowers kind of girl."

As much as it pained me to admit it, Griffin wasn't wrong.

The most powerful warlock born outside of the old bloodlines, nothing about Griffin - from his well-defined abs to his tousled brown hair and five o'clock shadow or his ability to wield magic - was regular.

And I had never been big on cut flowers. They wilted and withered--nothing says *I love you* like a vase of long-stemmed decomposition.

"That may be the first time you didn't argue with me." The corner of Griffin's mouth turned up in a lopsided grin.

"Well, statistically speaking, you were bound to be right at least once." I pinched the bridge of my nose and dipped my head to hide the blush I felt on my cheeks when memories of our arguments and subsequent make-up sessions stoked old flames, warming me from the inside out.

Or maybe that was just the tracker charm pulsing in my hand.

"Statistically speaking." Griffin's laughter rumbled up like a slow rolling summer storm. There was a spark of confidence in his amber eyes as if he knew he was winning me over one smile at a time.

Like Hecate, he is.

I shook my head with the hope of clearing away my distraction, but all six feet, seven inches of it was still standing there in the alley with me, towering over my five-foot frame.

The amulet pulsed and scorched my palm. Where my good senses failed me, the charm's increasing temperature set me back on track.

It was a damned good thing, too. If I stood there staring at Griffin's irritatingly handsome face any longer, I ran the risk of losing my perp—and my heart.

Two

"Orly's still in the old theater. Let's go before he moves and the tracker wears off." If I lost the wand maker, my badge would be the next thing to disappear. "I'll take point."

With Griffin watching our backs, I led us out of the alley and out onto the sidewalk lined with old buildings that had been patch worked into a popular shopping district. My calves and lungs burned as we double-timed it up the street to the intersection of Columbia and Main.

"I need to add more cardio into my exercise routine." I pressed my hand between my ribs and my hip to ease the stitch in my side from huffing it up the hill.

"What exercise routine? Wait, don't tell me, the one you're starting on Monday." Griffin teased while scoping out the theater. He jabbed me with his elbow and pointed toward the second story. "The top windows are still boarded up. That leaves the front and rear doors. We'll flush him out."

Thank the Goddess magic had its limitations. No flying - hovering is about the best we can manage - and no teleporting. Witches and Warlocks could bend reality but our feet were still firmly planted in it. If Orly wanted out of that theater, he would have to do it the old-fashioned way.

"Piece of cake." I tucked my chin against my chest, closed my eyes, and sent up a little prayer to the Goddess for luck.

Thanks to Griffin's delay in the alley, Orly seemed to be under the impression that he gave us the slip.

The wand maker strolled out through the front doors of the dilapidated theater like he owned the place. He even stopped to check his reflection in the glass door, brushing away the dust and cobwebs he collected in his hair while breaking into the old playhouse.

With a wall of granite rock behind us and the buildings butted up tight together like row homes, there was nowhere to hide, and we didn't exactly blend in. Orly would have spotted us the moment he turned around.

"You had to say it out loud." Griffin groaned, echoing my thoughts. "You jinxed us."

"*I jinxed us*? *I* almost had him." I pointed my index finger at myself before turning it toward him. "You're the one who decided to waste time with a heart-to-heart back behind the bar."

"It wasn't a waste of time." The hard set of Griffin's jaw and clipped tone of his voice left no room for counterarguments. "At least, not for me."

With one hand gripping my waist and the other my shoulder, he spun me around, backing me up until my spine pressed against the lamp post. He leaned in, molding our bodies together and his lips against mine.

The kiss held everything good about what we were and the potential for what we could have been. But it wasn't the unbridled desire that liquefied my lace panties. No, our relationship never lacked passion. There were always fireworks whenever Griffin and I were together.

In and out of the bedroom.

This kiss was different from the first and last time his mouth claimed mine. It was the slight tremble in his hands before he gripped me tighter. The millisecond of hesitation before he deepened the kiss. The way he savored it like a starving man would a morsel of bread.

Griffin needed me.

Not my name and what that could get him or the dowry dangled like a carrot on a stick by my medieval father to entice the right warlock. Me. Just me.

Griffin melted the last of the ice encasing my heart and that scared the ever-loving hell out of me.

"You've got one shot, Morgan. Make it count." Griffin provided the perfect cover - eager lovers who'd stopped for a kiss on their way to something more.

I hoped Orly was convinced because Griffin's performance certainly worked on me.

Damn. The kiss had been a cover.

His words in the alleyway replayed in my mind. He apologized for the way things ended but he never asked me to take him back. *Double damn.*

The guise violated my rule about public displays of affection but his plan worked. As much as it pained me, I had to give credit where credit was do. Griffin was quick on his feet and I was glad to have him as a partner when I ran the streets.

In the sheets? That remained to be seen. But I didn't have time to overanalyze past, present, or future relationships.

That's what I paid my tarot card reader for.

My target headed west on Main toward an old residential area with half a dozen abandoned properties and three routes of escape.

Orly never looked in our direction, ignoring what appeared to be a happy couple making out across the street. He flipped up the collar of his light jacket and pulled it snug against the back of his neck. I doubted the thin cotton provided much protection from the damp, cold air that had settled in between the rock walls surrounding the old mill town at night.

Cold never bothered me while I was on the hunt. Adrenaline kept my blood pumping and my body temperature up. Coincidentally, close proximity to Griffin caused a similar effect.

The wand maker reached the corner and stepped off the curb into the crosswalk without heeding to traffic or the flashing signs. *When you're already wanted for illegal magic, what's one more charge for jaywalking?*

The window of opportunity Griffin provided with his kiss was closing fast. I needed to make the most of it.

"He didn't even look both ways before crossing the street." I pulled the standard issue stun Umarex Brodax air pistol from my holster, peered over Griffin's shoulder and lined up the shot.

Unlike its traditional counterpart's steel BB ammunition, the Authority's version of the pistol had been modified to fire .177 caliber stunner charms.

I fired two shots. The wand maker ducked down an alley and slipped out of sight before the first charm left the barrel.

"What in the name of Hecate?" I holstered my weapon and pulled the tracking charm from my pocket.

It went cold.

Orly made us when he came out of the theater and we hadn't realized it. He was better than I gave him credit for. It wasn't often I underestimated my opponent but it only had to happen once for the perp to go free.

"He fell off your radar?" Griffin took the charm from me, turning it over in his hand. "I didn't think that was possible."

"Neither did the Authority." I plucked the useless stone out of his palm and shoved it in my coat pocket just as Orly popped out of another alleyway and back into existence two blocks away. "Over there. Come on."

If Orly had perfected a spell that disabled a tracking charm, the Arcane Magical Authority was in serious trouble. With a single enchantment, Jacob Orly rocketed himself from the bottom of the top ten to number one on the AMA's most wanted list.

And I planned on knocking his ass off the roster entirely.

We chased after the wand maker but for each block we gained, we lost two. It looked like at least one of Orly's incantations worked correctly.

"Thousands of spells to choose from and he picks *festina lente*?" I asked between deep breaths. The harder we ran, the less ground we covered.

"Can you blame him? He's wanted by the Authority." Griffin breezed past me, arms and legs pumping with the technique of a seasoned track and field athlete.

"And this is why I could never be a criminal. I hate running." My lungs burned and leg muscles cramped. My body was at its limit. I was out of breath, out of steam, and struggling to catch up. "People do this for fun?"

"For the orgasm-like endorphin high." Griffin chided, throwing down a gauntlet he knew would rekindle my competitive streak. "Come on, Byrnes, pick up the pace, or I'll bust him for you."

"Like Hecate." Muscles I hadn't used or even known were involved in running ached but I pushed harder and matched Griffin's stride. "And for the record, there are ways to have an orgasm that don't involve running a marathon."

"*Orgasm-like* and I never said it was *my* preferred method. Just that I've heard people say that's why they run." Griffin looked straight ahead but I could see the corner of his mouth tip up from his smile. "Personally, I'm not trying to run a race. I like to take my time, a slow and steady pace."

"I know all about your methods and techniques." I teased, sounding breathy and hoarse and for all the wrong reasons. "I've experienced all your best moves firsthand, remember?"

"Every glorious detail." Griffin chuckled but his laughter had the bitter edge of regret. "It doesn't have to be something we talk about in past tense, Morgan. *We* don't have to be past tense."

Memories of late nights and later mornings spent tangled up with Griffin left me scorched, inside and out. At least running down a perp had one positive. It provided an excellent scapegoat for my flushed cheeks and elevated heart rate and body temperature. Griffin shoved me off the sidewalk and into the street right before we came under fire.

Orly had more than one trick up his sleeve. Knockback spells.

A blast of energy that had been intended for me smacked Griffin in the chest. He flew backward, hitting the sidewalk hard enough that he bounced. His head took the brunt of the impact when he connected with the sidewalk the second time.

"Griffin." I forgot about Orly and making the collar, changed course, and rushed over to his side.

Losing the wand maker meant I would get probation instead of the promotion I'd hoped for but I couldn't leave Griffin injured and alone. Not after he saved my ass and not after the Goddess gave him the sight to see his wrongs and the wisdom to ask forgiveness.

He laid motionless on the sidewalk, limbs limp at his side, and he didn't appear to be breathing.

"Griffin, don't you dare leave me again. Not like this." I dropped to my knees beside him and yanked the leather corded necklace from around my neck.

The small vial that dangled from the cording was standard issue and contained a concentrated health potion. When given the right dose, the potion could mend broken bones, heal superficial wounds, and stop internal bleeding, saving an agent's life

But if administered incorrectly, an Airmid brew could be lethal.

Blood pooled in a grim halo around his head. Fingers pressed against the soft hollow on the side of his neck by his windpipe, I checked for a pulse. It was thready, but there. His chest rose and fell on a short, shallow breath.

I removed the dropper cap from the small bottle, gagging when the potion's pungent odor wafted up to my nose. After prying open Griffin's mouth, I emptied the pipette onto his tongue.

Seconds ticked by and nothing happened.

The potion should have started working as soon as the brown, syrupy liquid coated his taste buds. Panic gripped my heart like a vice when it didn't. *What if I have a bad batch?* There wasn't time to weigh the risks of side effects which ranged from loss of taste to seizures or cardiac arrest.

I was losing him. Again.

So, I made a hip-fire decision and gave him a second dose.

Three

Still, nothing happened. I straddled his waist and slid my hands under his shirt. Twelve months had passed since the last time I touched Griffin intimately, but I knew every inch of his skin. Every scar, every birthmark. Muscle memory drove my hands over the hard planes of his muscular body.

Fingers splayed over the expanse of his bare chest, I opened my third eye, tapped into the ley line running beneath the old mill town, and invoked a Salutaris spell.

Confervo, emaculo, percuro.

I used my body as a conduit for the earth magic, pulling it straight from the line and funneling it into Griffin while repeating the spell two more times.

His body thrummed with the magic that coursed through his veins in search of injuries to be healed. I focused the energy from the ley line and the spell on the most significant one--the trauma to his head. Griffin's eyes fluttered opened. His pupils were dilated and his pulse elevated, but we'd worry about that later.

Griffin was alive and that was all that mattered.

"What, no mouth-to-mouth?" He rolled to his side, groaning behind gritted teeth, and inched his way up to a sitting position. "Holy Hecate, I feel like I've been electrocuted and my mouth tastes like I gargled with dumpster water."

"I don't want to know how you know what that taste like." I resealed the useless vial, tucked it back in my pocket, and made a mental note to visit the Authority's herbalist to swap it out for a new potion.

"Back when we first started dating, the case with the goblin." He touched the back of his head, eyes widening when his fingers came away covered in tacky blood.

He'd been healed from the inside out, but the physical evidence of his injuries remained.

"I remember, but you didn't say anything about a dumpster." I got to my feet, offering Griffin a hand when he tried to do the same on his own. "I kissed you when you came home. Gross."

There was no point in asking if he brushed his teeth or gargled before he kissed me that night. I already knew the answer.

"Thanks for saving my ass." Griffin laced his fingers through mine and squeezed my hand.

"You saved mine first." I slipped free of his grip and jabbed my finger into his chest, the reality of what could have happened rocking me to my core. "You didn't even know what spell he fired."

"You're supposed to go easy on me." Griffin rubbed his palm against the spot where I poked him. "I'm still recovering."

"You almost died from a knockback. What if it I couldn't heal you?" I blinked back tears and wrapped my arms around my midsection, hugging myself tight and closing myself off from him.

The sudden crash after the adrenaline rush wore off left me jittery and raw. Griffin's near-death experience had me in my feelings—feelings I thought I had long since gotten over.

But there was no getting over a warlock like Griffin Wildes.

"I made the mistake of living without you once, Morgan. There was no way in hell I was doing that again." He pried my arms from around my middle, draping them around his hips, and pulled me into a hug. He tucked my head under his chin and breathed me in, the way he used to when we spent our days off spooning in bed. "I miss the way you smell, like honeysuckle and summer storms."

"Griffin, I don't know if I can—."

"Don't, please don't say it." His pressed his lips against my forehead in the barest of kisses. "Hear me out first."

"It's just, this is all...." I buried my face in his chest to avoid meeting his gaze. It was all too much, too fast, and it terrified me how much I still wanted and loved him.

"Your dad was in my ear the entire time we were together, whispering about how I wasn't good enough for his daughter, for the Byrnes family. Like I was just after the money and prestige." He sighed and I felt the weight of his next words in that one breath. "The thing is, he was right. He rushed to rephrase part of his statement when I went rigid in his arms. "Not about the money and prestige. At least, not in the way he meant it. I didn't want you because of your name or your money. That never mattered to me. And yet, at the same time, it mattered. It mattered a hell of a lot because what did I have to offer? Nothing."

"I only ever wanted you, Griffin." I tilted my head back until our gazes locked. The pain in his eyes almost took my breath away. "I loved our apartment, our life together. I loved you. That was enough for me. When you left the way you did, without telling me any of this, it broke me, Griffin."

"I know, Morgan, and I will spend every day of my life making it up to you, if you'll let me. I don't blame you if you won't but I need you to understand that I needed to make something of myself first. I needed to have something to give you."

"I understand that but what I don't understand is the way you did it, Griffin." I shook off the memory of walking into our apartment, empty of every last shred of evidence that he'd been a part of my life.

"I was weak. I wouldn't have been able to walk away from you or the Authority if you were there." Griffin cinched his arms tighter around me, as if he were afraid that I would pull away.

"You left the Authority?" I didn't keep tabs on him when he left and assumed he transferred to another region.

"I started a freelance agency." Griffin unwrapped one arm from around my waist and pulled his wallet from his back pocket, flashing me an independent agent badge. "I give the orders, which is easy since I only have one employee at the moment, but I take the cases I want, when I want."

His brows pinched together, and a frown settled onto his face when he remembered that I'd been working a case and the perp had gotten away.

"I'm sorry you lost the wand maker."

"It's mostly not your fault. Besides, I could use a vacation anyway." I would have preferred a *paid* vacation but when life gives you lemons - buy vodka.

"I don't suppose you'd want to finish this conversation over a drink at the Emporium?" Griffin winced, as if the question pained him and he regretted asking.

"It's going to cost you more than drinks, Griffin Wilde." I informed him, as we stepped off the curb and crossed the street, heading for the bar at the bottom of the hill. "I'm talking appetizers, entree and dessert."

"Is that—."

"Orly," I answered before Griffin could finish the question. *The Goddess works in mysterious ways.*

The scraggly wand maker's horrible sense of direction and unreliable magic led him right back to us.

Orly stood in the middle of the street slewing curses that would make a bridge troll blush. He tried to blast us with another spell, but the wand misfired. Orly snapped the bum wand in half and tossed the pieces on the ground. He pulled a replacement from the inside pocket of his trench coat, extended his arm shoulder high, and took the shot.

So did I.

I unholstered and fired my modified Umarex Brodax faster than a gunslinger in a high noon quick draw. Orly went down from an immobility charm with the first shot.

The wand maker refused to give in but the more he struggled, the tighter the spell wrapped around him. He lost his balance and hit the sidewalk, unable to move his limbs.

It was a shame his mouth still had full range of motion.

Orly shouted a colorful variety of hexes and curses, my personal favorite being perpetually lukewarm coffee. My cup would never be hot and never be iced.

The man was loud enough to wake the dead. Dogs and cats from the apartments above the stores took position at their windows and erupted into an unholy chorus, alerting the locals to our presence. Light flicked on in the third story of the building across the street.

"I need to call this in before some townie stumbles on to us." I reached into my coat pocket for my cell and walked over to Orly as I dialed the number for the Arcane Magical Authority.

Dispatch picked up after the first ring. "AMA. What's your emergency?"

"This is Byrnes. I need a ride."

"And how many people are in your party?" The Authority's operators were trained to keep the calls short and sweet. No idle chitchat.

"Just one. Jacob Orly."

"We have your location, Agent Byrnes. A car is in route." Dispatch ended the call. Back up was on the way.

"Your new friends will be here to pick you in a couple of minutes. If you play nice with them, they'll play nice with you." I bent down to check the magical netting, slipped the Brodax out of its holster and removed a charm from the chamber.

Orly muttered one last curse in my ear.

"Well, that was naughty, Jacob. What did I just say?" I squeezed the BB hard enough to pop the plastic shell and let the charmed liquid inside drip out onto Orly's chest.

Agents were immune to the spell, a safeguard in the event we were overpowered and lost our weapon. We were immune to hexes, too. Something I took pleasure in explaining to Jacob Orly.

"You can't hex your way out of this, wand maker." I pulled back my onyx locks, revealing a protective ward tattooed behind my ear. "Good thing too, because that coffee one.... That was straight up diabolical."

Griffin waited by the streetlight, staying out of the way until the other officers arrived and stuffed Orly into the backseat. When the taillights blinked out of sight, he made his way up the cobbled brick sidewalk, falling in step beside me.

One down, one to go.

I yanked another black magic dealer off the streets and closed another case but my night was far from over. I still had unfinished business with the warlock who crashed my collar.

"You know, I happen to be in the market for a partner." Griffin draped his arm over my shoulder and tucked me against his side.

The double entendre wasn't lost on me.

"What, and leave all this behind?" I made a sweeping gesture with my arm, motioning to the magical hot spot historic town I had been assigned.

"Morgan, I—."

I turned to face him, fisted my hands in his shirt, and stood on tiptoe to close the few inches between us, and rendered him speechless with a kiss. His arms enveloped me, pulling me tight when I deepened the kiss, hinting at possibilities to come.

Possibilities I wouldn't have thought I would be open to when I started my shift hours earlier.

"I know, Griffin. How about you start by buying me that drink?"

Griffin walked back into my life the same way he walked out--without warning. He had a habit of blindsiding me and this was no exception.

But Griffin wasn't the same warlock I fell in love with twelve months ago.

He was better. Every step of his journey led him back to me. I envisioned this moment a million times and it always ended the same. With me turning Griffin away.

His fate was in my hands, our fate was in my hands, and realizing I didn't want to throw it away surprised me. He'd asked for a second chance and I wanted to give it to him. It wasn't going to be easy. We had challenges, both old and new, ahead of us, but we would face them together.

A witch and a warlock walked into a bar...

The End

If you love stories filled magic and mayhem, be sure to check out my other Paranormal Romance and Urban Fantasy Romance books.

www.rachelrawlings.com

Newsletter

https://view.flodesk.com/pages/5ffcbaa9b9d7ae50d2eb05a2

About the Author

Rachel Rawlings was born and raised in the Baltimore Metropolitan area and has always had a fascination with the strange and unusual. Although her passion for writing developed early on, it wasn't until 2009 that she published her first novel – to prove a point to her children. When she isn't writing Urban Fantasy or Paranormal Romance, Rachel can be found with her nose buried in a good book and a cup of coffee nearby. There may or may not be cookies!

Read More from Rachel Rawlings

www.rachelrawlings.com

Witch Way Home

LORI DIANNI

<u>One</u>

"You can do this, Sarah. I have faith in you, and so you must have faith in yourself. This is what you were born to do."

"You really think I can do this? Save Nicholas?"

Aggie nodded, her face solemn and practically pleading with me to understand. "You are a witch, my dear, whether you want to accept it or not." I shook my head, more confused than ever, but at the same time, I knew deep inside what she said was true. I had known from a young age that there was something different about me.

"Thankfully, in this day and age, it's accepted, but," Aggie continued, "Do not, under any circumstances, act out of the ordinary in the past. Do not even utter the word, witch." She clasped my hand. "Remember, you're going back to the Salem witch hysteria."

I nodded. If anyone in the past even suspected I had fallen from the sky, I would be most likely be accused as a witch and my fate sealed. "How did you know I was a witch?"

"Your grandmother was my best friend. We were drawn to each other like moths to a flame and as our friendship grew, our families had no choice but to tell us the truth."

"That you are descendants of actual witches?"

"Yes." She continued to watch me, her gaze lingering. "Nicholas was drawn to you as you were to him. You were fated to meet."

"I love Nicholas, Aggie. It's time he came home." As eager as I sounded, I had to admit, I was scared. "How do we return?"

Her grin split her face. She clasped my hand tight. "Thank you." It came out as a sigh. "You will read the spell and walk counterclockwise around a magic circle of stones. To return, you'll do the same, except you'll walk in a clockwise motion. It's as simple as that."

Simple. What could possibly go wrong?

Two

The following night, I was dressed in the garments Aggie had created for me in the last few weeks with the hope and intent I would accept this incredible journey to bring her nephew, and the love of my life, back home. I, on the other hand, was scared to the point of feeling sick. As we stood beneath a mammoth tree in the Salem Woods with the full moon shining down on us, I wanted to back out. But Nicholas needed me.

I had no idea how I would find Nicholas. Aggie told me to trust my inner guide. Fear clenched my stomach and I wanted to throw up. My heart slammed against my ribs, and I could feel the beginnings of an anxiety attack.

"It's time." Aggie touched my clenched hands.

I jumped at the contact and a cry spilled out. "I don't know if I can do this, Aggie. What if, what if Nicholas isn't there? Maybe he tried to come back and maybe ended up, I don't know, somewhere else? In another time period?" The thought was frightening. What if the same fate was to happen to me? I slumped to the ground. Aggie followed.

"You can do this, Sarah. I know you can." She hugged me and I sagged against her and cried. She lifted me up, still held against her. "Follow the spell. Do exactly as I instructed you. It won't fail you."

With tears in my eyes, I looked at her. "Can't you go?"

"No. Although he's my nephew he's not fated to me." She clasped her hands on either side of my face. "It was fate that brought you and Nicholas together. Fate is on your side." She kissed my cheek. "You are to be a part of my family and I couldn't have asked for a better woman than you to be at Nicholas's side." She smoothed her thumbs across my cheeks, wiping away the tears. "It's meant to be, and I know you'll come back." She smiled, nodded, and lifted my chin.

I smiled back then pulled her against me. "If anything happens and I don't return, please know how much I love you."

Aggie whispered, "I love you, too." Then with firm hands, she pushed me away from her. "It's time, Sarah. We must do this." She cleared her throat and turned away quickly. I had a feeling she had tears in her eyes and didn't want me to see how this affected her. "Now, I've drawn the symbol like this," she pointed to the ground at the base of the tree. "Try to draw the symbol ahead of time, if possible. And don't get caught."

"Right."

"I put a drawing of this in the pocket of your skirt along with the spell."

That made me feel better. I wasn't sure I could remember the symbol or even the spell if I was under any sort of duress. Then a thought occurred to me. "How will I know which tree?" I turned and lifted my hand to the massive oak before me. "I'm sure this tree wasn't this big back three hundred years ago."

Aggie pointed upward. "See that mark?" She pointed the flashlight to it, although the moon was bright.

"Yeah."

"This will be the same tree you'll pass through. As soon as you get to the other side, look at the tree. You'll see the same symbol, although the tree will be a bit smaller."

"So, this tree is the portal to the past that you mentioned last night?"

Aggie nodded. "We don't know why, but it's the only tree in these woods that we know of that holds the power to send people through time, but only with the spell and under certain conditions."

My heart skittered. "What conditions?"

"Once you pass through the portal, you cannot turn around and come back. Several hours must go by before an attempt can be made again."

"This isn't going to be easy, is it?"

Aggie shook her graying head. "Unfortunately, no. That's why you must keep your head low."

"How long do I have to find Nicholas and get him home?"

"Two days. Three days at the most."

"Two or three days?" Was I supposed to work a miracle?

"Follow your intuition, Sarah. And it will lead you home."

I nodded, inhaled and said, "Okay, let's do this." I pushed down my fear and pressed a hand to my chest. I said a quick prayer to the heavens that I could pull this off and return safely.

Aggie had me stand at the top of the small circle, facing away from the tree.

"Think of this circle as a clock. You are standing at the twelve and by moving counter clock-wise, while reciting the spell, it will open the portal. Once you see its glow, you must step through. It will only stay open for a minute or two. If you wait, you cannot return until the next full moon." Aggie continued, "I think that's why Nicholas couldn't come home, Sarah. He missed his chance. Now he has the chance again."

"I'll make sure we both make it home, Aggie."

She nodded. "Now read the spell and walk counter clock-wise."

I pulled the spell from my pocket and read the words, forcing myself to feel calm.

As I recited the spell, I sensed a change in the air. There was a buzzing like a hundred bees spinning around my head. I glanced at Aggie who seemed to blur at the edges. My mind screamed to stop, but I bit my lip and continued reciting. My head started to pound, and I winced, crying out.

"Don't stop!" I heard Aggie yell. As I walked, I noticed a glow appearing from the large trunk. It grew as I chanted the spell. By this time, I had it memorized. There was a sudden burst of light as I said the last word and there in front of me, the entire tree glowed. And, to my horror, I could see another world on the other side. Dark woods, also lit by a full moon seemed to go on forever. A deer shot through the trees.

"Go, Sarah. Now!"

I snapped my head around and saw Aggie moving her arms in a shoving motion. Anxiety flooded her face. I did the only thing I could think of. I ran.

Three

I stumbled, landing on the ground, and winced as my knees hit a protruding root. I stood and dusted off my skirt. The light had disappeared. A cacophony of crickets sounded all around me. Off in the distance, I heard the croaking of frogs. I looked up. The full moon shone down lighting up the tree. I twisted around, looking for Aggie but she wasn't there. Had I actually gone back in time? Something in the air seemed different, yet by all accounts, the woods didn't look any different. Except for the tree. Aggie had told me to look for the symbol so I would know which tree to return to with Nicholas. I glanced up and noticed the symbol carved into the tree about fifteen feet up from the base. Most people passing this tree would never notice unless they knew what they were looking for.

And then I heard a voice in the distance.

"Look for the witch!"

I couldn't get caught. I lifted my skirt high and started to run.

"There she is!"

I turned, seeing lanterns swaying in the distance and coming closer. I bit my lip, forcing myself not to scream. My breath came in spasms and my chest heaved. I darted to my right to hide in some thick bushes.

"You! Halt!"

Suddenly, someone grasped me roughly around the waist, his other hand slapping over my mouth, and hauled me up against him. I pummeled at him as he ran off the path. He pulled me down to the ground, into some thick bushes and pounced on top of me. Blackness surrounded me in a whoosh of his cloak.

I could feel his heart pounding against my breasts. His entire body pressed against me, and if it hadn't been for the threat so close to us, I would've thought it a bit too intimate. His rapid breaths were warm against my cheek. His fingers dug into my shoulders, keeping me from leaping up. For some unfathomable reason, I couldn't begin to understand, I knew I could trust this man. My intuition told me so. Isn't that what Aggie had said? To trust my intuition? Well, I'd better start now.

The horses came to a stop on the path, several yards from where we hid.

"Where is she? I saw her." The voice sounded close. Too close for comfort. I heard the snort of a horse and a whinny, followed by another. How many were looking for us?

"She's a witch. She might have made herself into a wee animal of the woods and we wouldn't know," another man said.

"All the more reason to find her and hang her!"

I almost gasped but couldn't due to the stranger's weight on top of me. He was heavy, suffocating me, and I needed air. The man breathed against my face. He smelled of woodsmoke and a hint of spice. Although the scent stirred my senses more than it should have, I still needed fresh air. I felt stifled, closed in and the first stirrings of anxiety clawed at me, wanting release. I pushed against the stranger's chest.

He pressed his hand against my mouth. "Shush!"

His words stilled my hands. His hand smoothed across my cap in long soft strokes. I calmed and forced myself to slow down my breathing.

Heavy footfalls came close. "Look closer, men. I heard something."

"Over there. A movement, I saw," another man yelled.

"Are you sure?"

"Aye, I'm sure."

"Hurry, men! Don't let her get away." Several sets of footfalls hurried away from our hiding spot.

"We'll meet back in town and think this through. We'll find the witch!"

When the horses galloped away, I sighed. The stranger eased his hold on me, his sigh a whisper across my cheek. It tingled and stirred something low in my belly. The stranger opened his cloak, and I breathed in a huge lungful of forest air. God, it felt good. He pushed his way out of the shrubbery and stood then reached out to help me.

"Are you hurt?"

When I heard his voice, I wanted to collapse in relief. "Nicholas?" I wrenched off my cap, letting my long red wavy hair spill over my shoulders.

"Sarah?"

I nodded then emptied the space between us and jumped into his open arms. I clung to him as he clutched me hard against his chest, kissing my eyes, my cheeks and then my lips. I kissed him back, plunging my fingers into his long hair. Tears flowed down my cheeks. I had found him. A moment later, Nicholas released me and set me down on the ground.

"How did you—" He shook his head. "We'll talk later. We need to leave." He grasped my hand, pulling me toward the path.

"Nicholas," I started, "Why were you here?"

"I was trying to get home, to you." He stroked my cheek and I turned into his hand. "But when I saw the lanterns, I had to hide." He brushed a hand through his hair. "I tried it a month ago. The portal will only stay open a few minutes for two days during the full moon, and once it closes—"

"You had to wait another month." I sighed. "That's why you didn't come back."

He nodded, brushing my hair back. "I tried, Sarah. Really. I missed the chance by one night."

"We have two more nights." I looked up at his handsome features and clasped his hand. "Promise me we'll try tomorrow."

He kissed the tip of my nose. "I promise."

Four

A

s the horse walked through the forest, I shivered. Nicholas wrapped his cloak around me, the lingering scent of woodsmoke wafting over me, reminding me of long-ago campfires from my youth. I started to lean forward, needing to lay my head down, so Nicholas wrapped an arm around me and nudged me against his chest.

A whisper in my ear and a stroke of hand down my face, awakened me. I startled, gasping and would've fallen off the horse, if Nicholas hadn't had his arm around me.

"We're here." He got off the horse then lifted his arms up to help me down.

When my feet hit the ground, I looked around. "Where are we?"

"At my lodgings here at the boarding house."

"Um, how am I going to get in without it looking…odd?"

He smiled. "Everyone's asleep. Besides, no one locks doors here like they do in our time."

I hoped he was right. Nicholas opened the door and ushered me through. He lit a match to a candle and holding it high, he walked to the stairs. Quietly, I walked on tiptoe through the large room and followed him up the staircase. He turned left and halted at a door. This time, he pulled out a room key, unlocked the door, and with a sigh of relief, I walked through. Nicholas followed behind me.

The room was sparse with a bed, an armoire in the corner, a table and chair by the window. It didn't look any different than any room in our time. I yawned. I was beat and it had to be near one in the morning.

"We need to talk, but I know you're tired. You can have the bed and I'll sleep on the chair."

Guilt swept through me. "No, you take the bed. I'll sleep in the chair."

"Sarah, please. Just take the bed."

"Okay." I was too tired to argue. Not having a change of clothes, I crawled into the lumpy bed, not caring if it was a bed of nails and promptly fell asleep.

A loud banging and a hand shaking me, woke me up from a dead sleep. I bolted upright, gasping. Nicholas grabbed my arm.

"Hide behind the armoire. Now!" Although he whispered close to my ear, I swore his demand could be heard throughout the room.

I scrambled out of the bed, knowing whoever was on the other side of the door couldn't be good. The look on Nicholas's face said as much. I hurried to the armoire and scrambled behind it.

"Stay there until I tell you to come out," he whispered.

I nodded, panic rising, causing my head to ache. What I wouldn't give for an Advil right now. He moved away, leaving me with a hammering heart.

Another bang on the door caused me to jump.

"By God's grace, wait one moment," Nicholas called out. I heard him open the door then immediately two sets of heavy footfalls stepped into the room.

"Good morning, sir, but we have need to speak to you this very moment."

"What is this about?" Nicholas said, acting as though he had just woken from a sound sleep. "Can a man not have a night's sleep before being woken by one of the constable's deputies?"

One man laughed low, bordering on a growl. "When the constable wishes to speak to someone, he has no need to worry if one has had enough sleep."

"Come good sir, dress yourself. You are wanted at the constable's office immediately."

Nicholas yawned. "And why would the constable have need of me?"

Footsteps came close to the armoire, and I held my breath.

"We needed your assistance last evening on a peculiar case and you were nowhere to be found."

Nicholas chuckled. "I was in Ipswich, visiting a friend."

The other man with the growling laugh, spoke. "Well then, good sir, you must've arrived home late as we called on you last evening around eleven, needing your assistance to find another witch."

"I arrived home late and went straight to bed."

"Can anyone vouch for you? Say, the owner of these lodgings or a house maid, perhaps?" One of the men chuckled obscenely.

"Unfortunately, no. They were abed when I arrived."

"So, other than your distant friend, you have no one to speak on your behalf."

"Are you accusing me of—"

"No. Nothing of the sort," the other man said. He sounded older, nothing like the growling laughter man who she believed still stood a mere few feet from her hiding spot. "But, had you been home when we first arrived, we might have been able to find this witch." He cleared his throat. "You have been known to be quite useful in tracking down witches."

I whipped a hand to my mouth to stifle a gasp. Nicholas was hunting down the accused witches?

"Come now, we can't keep the constable waiting."

There was a slap of a hand on someone's back. "Perhaps, good sir, we will find our witch this day!"

Five

I paced the floor, agonizing over what I had heard and if it were true. Was Nicholas really a witch hunter? If he was one of the several men who rounded up the accused, then I might be next. Maybe Nicholas would come back after talking to the constable and have me arrested. No! I couldn't believe Nicholas would do such horrible things. Aggie had said he wanted to go to the past to help save those who were accused. Had she been wrong? I prided myself on giving people the benefit of the doubt, so I'd do the same for Nicholas.

I stood and paced again, chewing on my thumbnail. I had to think of a way out of this. I had one day, maybe two, to bring Nicholas back to our time or I was stuck here. I pulled the paper with the spell written on it along with the slip of paper showing me how to draw the symbol for my return to the present. I wanted to set it to memory, just in case. Setting them on the table, I closed my eyes, reciting the spell.

A knock sounded and I jumped out of my skin. I almost screamed but ran to the armoire as a second knock came.

"Mister Abernathy, are you awake?" It was a woman's voice, soft, almost meek.

The door to Nicholas's room opened and a young woman, around the age of sixteen, walked in. She looked around then rushed toward the table. I peeked from behind the armoire and inhaled sharply. The girl peered down at the slips of paper. Damn! Maybe the young girl wouldn't know what it meant and would leave. She lifted the paper, appeared to be reading it, then tossed it down on the table as though it burned her skin. She hurried from the room, slamming the door behind her.

Something, my intuition if I were being honest, told me I had to leave. Now. But where would I go? I hurried to the table, grabbed the notes and stuffed them back in my pocket. A moment later, Nicholas stepped into the room. Panic gripped me. Perspiration seeped under my arms, dotted my forehead and upper lip. My stomach churned and my hands shook. Was he here to have me arrested? And what would the maid say? I was doomed. I was going to die here.

Nicholas rushed over to me, probably noticing my distress. He grasped my upper arms. "Sarah? What's wrong?"

"I...I..."

"Here, come sit." He led me to the chair, and I sat, my back straight, ready to stand and bolt from the room if I had to. He knelt in front of me and smoothed a hand over mine. "Your hands are cold and they're shaking. What happened?"

"I need to ask you something and you need to tell me the truth, no matter what."

He looked at me, his deep brown gaze holding my own as though he was trying to read into my soul. "Sarah, what is it?"

I heaved a sigh and yanked my hands out of his grasp. "Are you working with the constable to hunt down innocent people accused of witchcraft?"

Nicholas leapt up. "What?" His brows rose to his hairline and his mouth gaped open. He shook his head. "No! Why would you even think such a thing?"

"Because you seemed pretty chummy with the constable's men."

His brows crinkled and he sighed, lowering his gaze to the floor. He rubbed a hand down his handsome face. He hunkered down, his gaze pleading with mine. "I'm not hunting witches. I'm trying to save them. You have to believe me, Sarah."

I sighed in relief. "I do." I smoothed a hand down the side of his face. "But, I think we have a bigger problem."

"How so?" He stood, lifting me up with him.

My body shook in fear. "While you were gone, the maid came in. She was young, about sixteen, I think. She found my papers on the table and read them. She tossed them back on the table as if they had burned her hands, then she ran from the room."

"Damn!" He twisted around. "That young woman was not the maid. There is a maid, but she's much older, in her sixties I believe." Nicholas looked worried. His brow creased and he pinched his nose. "I think the girl who came here is one of the of girls going around accusing others of witchcraft."

"Oh God." I stood, my stomach clenching. "We have to get out of here, Nicholas. Now." I grabbed his hand and pulled him. He wouldn't budge. "Nicholas. Come on, we have to go." I was desperate to leave this room, to leave Salem and go back to our own time.

"Where are the papers now?"

"I have them," I answered, then squinted. "Why?" I pulled my hand back; afraid he had lied to me and would bring me to the constable.

"We're going back to the tree and going home." He held his hand out. "Let me have the papers."

I shook my head. There was a commotion from downstairs.

"Go to the tree. I'll stall and do the best I can to—"

I flung myself into Nicholas's arms. "Please Nicholas. Don't do this! They've come to arrest you."

Loud footfalls climbed the stairs.

His face was full of anguish. "Hide. Now." He pushed me toward the armoire. I scrambled behind it as the sound of heavy footsteps stopped outside his door. A second later, the door was wrenched open.

I peeked from behind the armoire. There were four men, and they surrounded Nicholas, while one bound his hands with rope. Nicholas squirmed, but he was no match against the four of them. I bit my lip hard until it drew blood. I wanted to scream. I wanted to run to Nicholas's aid, but what good would it do if I was also arrested?

"You are under arrest as you've been accused of witchcraft."

Nicholas fought against his bonds. "And who are my accusers? You know this is not right!"

One man, heavy set with a round pale face drew close to Nicholas. "You will meet your accuser during your trial."

My heart jolted. I knew the young woman would accuse Nicholas. Why hadn't I stopped her when I had had the chance? To my horror, they led Nicholas out of the room. He never looked back. If he had, he might have given away my hiding spot. At that moment, I knew Nicholas had told me the truth. If he was truly hunting witches, he would've given me away and saved his own life.

I had to trust he knew what he was doing. And if I couldn't save him, I had to save myself and go back to the present and tell Aggie her nephew had died as an accused warlock. I shook my head as tears streamed down my face. It was all my fault! If I hadn't come back and hadn't left the papers out in the open, this never would've happened. I had been stupid. I had cost Nicholas his life and I would never forgive myself.

<u>Six</u>

Think, Sarah! I paced. I knew nothing of the layout of the town, and I certainly couldn't go out and walk around. But I had to. I'd keep my head down and walk out of town the way we had come the night before. It couldn't be more than two miles by my guess.

I opened the door, peeked into the hallway and seeing it was clear, I made my way to the staircase. Quietly, I walked down the stairs. The house was too quiet. With a sigh of relief, I came to the front door, opened it and peered outside. I was astonished to see a crowd gathered at the far end of the road. This could be a good thing. I'd hide in plain sight. I closed the door behind me and scampered down the concrete steps to the cobbled street and walked in the direction of the crowd.

I found the crowd assembled outside of Beadle's Tavern. I had read that accused witches were tried here and kept prisoners locked in the upstairs rooms or chained to the walls in the basement if the local jail was full. My stomach clenched as I hurried past the crowd, toward the side of the building. Two men lingered by the door. They didn't pay any attention to me, thank goodness. When I heard the word, 'warlock', I scooted behind the building, where I could still hear them.

"Heard Judge Corwin is inside, listening to testimony from Goodman Abernathy's accuser."

"He'll hang you know."

Tears sprang to my eyes.

"I was told to have the wagon ready to transport the warlock." The man spit on the ground. "They'll hang him from Gallows Hill soon enough."

"You going to travel through town?"

"Will most likely go by way of the woods on the way to the jail in the village. No room here in town with all the witches they been catching."

I covered my mouth then turned away from the tavern. I couldn't help but think of Nicholas rotting away in some cell because I had left evidence on the table. And, if I wasn't careful, the same fate could happen to me. The thought caused my stomach to churn with nausea.

If I could get to the tree before the wagon, I would have a chance to save us both. The woods weren't too far away. I wasn't sure how I would save Nicholas who would have guards with him, but I had to try. I loved Nicholas and wasn't about to let him die without putting up a fight.

I walked by way of a dirt road leading out of town. I passed several colonial style homes and realized most of them would still be around in my time, only surrounded by more houses. A wagon passed me, and the driver tipped his hat. I gave a quick nod, my insides turning to jelly, wondering if I would be stopped and questioned. I jumped when a horse and its rider galloped past me, heading in the same direction. I wondered why he was in such a hurry. It didn't matter. I was the one who needed to hurry. Time was of the essence.

<u>Seven</u>

heaved a sigh of relief when I finally found the tree. I don't know how but I did. Something inside guided me when I thought I was lost. The tree was like a beacon home, and I grinned when I stood in front of it.

No time to lose, Sarah. I found a stick strong enough to allow me to draw the symbols into the ground as Aggie had shown me. I pulled the paper from my pocket and winced. This scrap of paper with unusual symbols and a spell, was the cause of Nicholas's demise and guilt swept through me. A tear splashed onto the paper, blurring one of the words of the spell, but it didn't matter. I had it memorized.

I chanted the spell and turned clockwise around the symbol. I repeated it for a second time when a shadow crawled over me.

"Gotcha now, witch!"

I screamed and twisted around, staring up at a heavily built man. My breath caught and fear caused my heart to beat so fast, I thought it'd come out of my chest.

"And what do we have here?" The burly man bent down, picking up the paper I had set on the dirt. His eyes bulged. He looked at the tree where there was a soft glowing light. "You've conjured the spirit of the devil!"

He reached for me, but I was faster and lurched out of his grasp, rolling into the shrubbery. I shivered, knowing it was too late. He grabbed my leg and yanked me toward him. The sound of horses and the squeak of wagon wheels stopped him.

"We have you now, and your devil consort. They approach now." He laughed.

The wagon creaked to a stop as my captor lifted a hand in greeting.

I sprang into action and chanted the spell a third time, moving in a clockwise direction.

"I bring you another witch!" he cried out to the guard and the driver. "See? Here is the proof. She speaks in a devil's tongue."

From the corner of my eye, I saw Nicholas standing in the back, his hands bound in front, but as my accuser approached the wagon, Nicholas lunged for the guard, head butting him in the gut causing the guard to lose his balance. The horses whinnied and shifted as the wagon tilted.

Nicholas jumped from the wagon, running toward me. A light grew in the trunk, growing bigger and brighter.

"Go through, Sarah!" Nicholas shouted.

The guard had regained his footing and ran after Nicholas as well as my accuser. I screamed, watching in horror as Nicholas tried to fight off the men. The swirling light grew brighter, engulfing the tree and I could see my future waiting for me.

Nicholas was so close. His bound hands lifted and then I was shoved into the light as a shot rang out. I screamed, tumbling into the bright light.

"Nicholas!" I reached out, but there was nothing. Only emptiness. I fell in a heap on dry ground, sobbing. Nicholas was gone. I had caused his death. As I knelt there, crying, there was a blaze of light. To my dismay, a man stumbled through. Could it be?

He tumbled to the ground, groaned and twisted around, facing up.

"Nicholas!" I cried out and swooped down on him, my dress flaring around me.

"Did we make it?" he asked. He looked dazed as I hurriedly loosened the rope.

"Yes, we're home. We made it home." Tears streamed down my face.

When his hands were free, he lifted them to my face and pulled me down on top of him. He kissed me with a hunger I felt deep inside. I tasted the salt of my tears as my lips danced with his. Nicholas was my heart and soul. Aggie had been right.

"I knew you could do it, Sarah."

I looked up to see Aggie smiling down at us. Nicholas stood, grinning at his aunt. Then he swept her in his arms and kissed her cheek. Aggie pulled me into the embrace and held both of us tight against her.

"Welcome home."

THE END

Thank you for reading my first short story! I hope you enjoyed it. I had a lot of fun writing it. I write small town contemporary romance as well as paranormal. I currently have three books published in my Misty River series, set in Maine available on Amazon. I also have two time-travel manuscripts I hope to have published in 2024. Visit me at www.loridianni.com

LAST MINUTE MATE

SEDONA ASHE

<u>One</u>

I slumped against the staircase, watching my fiancé dip and swirl my best friend around the stage. The two most important people in my life were gazing into each other's eyes, while their every move oozed red-hot chemistry.

They looked like they were in love.

"You were such a fool, Emilee," I whispered to myself.

Biting my lip, I fought to keep back a deluge of tears. Yesterday morning I'd been on top of the world, and last night it had crumbled around my feet.

I'd been invited to compete for a spot on a new dance reality TV series. The show would feature eight professional dancers and their partners as they waltzed and twirled their way through various challenges.

This type of show would no doubt involve intense drama and insanely long hours of work, but it was an opportunity I couldn't turn down. The contestants would be well paid and receive free publicity, while the winning couple would win half a million dollars. With that kind of money, I would be able to achieve my dream of opening my own dance studio.

To make things even more exciting, the producers had noticed photos of my stunning, blonde bestie dancing with me in my social media reels, and had instantly offered to cover her costs to fly to Atlanta to audition along with me.

Thanks to our moms' lifelong friendship, Salli and I had been best friends since we were in diapers. When we turned three, our moms enrolled us in the same dance school, and we'd been dancing every free moment since. We'd grown up as close as sisters, going through growth spurts, periods, first loves, and first heartbreaks together.

William and I had met at my first dance competition. He was six, and I was five… and we fell head-over-heels in love. His family had just moved to our town, and enrolled him in our studio the next week. We'd been paired as a couple and had won countless dance competitions together.

No one was surprised when we eventually became boyfriend and girlfriend. When William proposed three months ago, our friends and family had been there to celebrate our storybook romance. It had been a dream come true.

Now that dream was a nightmare.

As part of the competition, both Salli and I were to bring our own partners. Salli had brought her dance partner, Tucker, while I'd brought William. Unfortunately, while we'd been eating and exploring the city yesterday, Tucker received a call that his father had been in a car accident.

Tucker had rushed to catch the next flight back home, leaving Salli alone and partnerless for the competition. We'd spent the day trying to call in favors and find her an alternative partner, but no one was able to get into the city in time. It was devastating.

It was nearly midnight when a teary Salli headed to her hotel room across the hall to try and sleep. William was still on the phone trying to find a local male dancer of a high enough caliber to partner with Salli.

Too anxious to sleep, and needing to let it all out, I'd decided to take advantage of the hotel's gym, telling William I'd be back in an hour. Running several miles always helped to relax me, and that night was no different. My exhaustion caught up with me quickly, and after only twenty minutes on the treadmill, I was ready for a shower and bed.

I'd made my way down the hall to find Salli's hotel door hadn't latched completely. Thinking she must have not noticed it in her distress, I grabbed the handle, intending to close it for her. Then I heard her whimpers, followed by a man's low rumble. When she screamed, my heart stopped. My best friend was being attacked by a stranger.

Not stopping to think, I flew into action. I flung the door open hard enough that the handle embedded itself into the drywall. Rushing to the bed, I swung the water bottle into the back of the attacker's head...

A very familiar head.

William's golden blonde head.

"What the hec—" William roared.

Grabbing his head, he turned to face me. Even in the dim light of the room, I could see his face pale and nude form, as he jumped off the bed and held out his hands to me. "Hey. Calm down. It's not what it looks like."

I choked on a sob and staggered backward.

"Stop lying, William! Why should I be the only one who had their life destroyed on this trip?" Salli slid naked from the bed with the gracefulness of a—well, of a dancer.

Moving behind William, she circled his waist with her arms. William grabbed his shirt from the bed and held it over his junk, but Salli didn't bother to hide her nudity.

"How long?" My body had begun to tremble, and the room was spinning.

Salli grinned, and for the first time in my life, her mask was pulled away and I saw the person beneath. This wasn't my childhood best friend. This was a person who cared only for what she wanted.

"Hmmm." Salli pretended to count, ticking off one red-manicured finger after another. "I'm twenty-three now, so I've been doing the nasty with your man for about five years."

Her words hit me like a physical punch to the stomach, and I clutched at the wall to steady myself. There was one more thing I needed to know.

Turning my tear-filled eyes to William, I asked, "Why?"

"Because you're boring." Salli answered when he didn't, a malicious grin spreading across her face. "He had to stay with you because you're everyone's favorite couple. If he broke it off with you while you were an internet sensation, it would have damaged his career. What happened today changed everything, though. And tomorrow will change our lives."

"Tomorrow?" My voice cracked, and my brain was struggling to put all the pieces together.

How many times had he stopped to help Salli with something that had broken at her house? Were they having sex then, too? And what about the times he offered to help her practice her routines late into the evening when her partner had to work overtime?

I'd been a soft-hearted, idiotic fool.

William refused to meet my eyes, and made his way to the bathroom. Salli stepped forward, pushing me toward the door. As I stumbled into the hotel's hallway, she delivered the death blow to my every hope and dream.

"It seems you're without a fiancé and a dance partner. Such a shame you came all this way and won't even get to dance tomorrow." Salli made an exaggerated sad face, then giggled. "Now, I really have to go. William and I need to work on our *chemistry* for tomorrow's competition."

She'd slammed the door, leaving me frozen in the hall. I wish I could say I'd done something dramatic and mic-drop-worthy. But I hadn't.

I'd sagged to the floor and sobbed. A staff member must have gotten a complaint because he'd kindly helped me to my room. He'd figured out from my babbling what had happened, and had been kind enough to gather William's things and take them downstairs for William to claim.

Now I sat in a dark stairwell watching the two people I'd thought I knew best dance their hearts out.

"I shouldn't have come." I wiped at the wet steaks on my cheeks.

"Then why did you?" a male's voice drifted from the stairs above me.

Spinning around with my heart in my throat, I was shocked to find a man sitting behind me a few steps up. "Who— What?"

"I'm Jude. And I asked why you are here if it is causing you so much distress?" His smile was gentle.

A sob caught in my throat. "Because I hoped it had all been a nightmare, and I'd show up here to find everything was back the way it should be."

"Are you going to dance?" Jude handed me a tissue, which I greatly accepted.

"With who? The competition is for couples, and as you can see, my best friend stole mine." My eyes trailed back to the stage where they couldn't seem to keep their hands off each other, and I mumbled, "She can keep him."

"Do you want to dance?" Jude asked, his eyes glowing the eerie yellow of a wolf shifter and giving away his species.

For a moment, I forgot about his question. Paranormals were old news in today's world. They lived and worked among humans, but it was rare to meet wolf shifters, as they were elusive and tended to stick to their packs.

Not wanting to be rude by continuing to stare, I dropped my gaze to my trembling hands. "Of course I do."

It was the truth. I'd wanted to compete in this competition more than I'd wanted anything else in a long time. After the stress of the past twelve hours, I needed to dance to relieve my pent-up emotions.

"What if I dance with you?" Jude's question was soft, and I almost missed it.

My eyes shot up to meet his glowing ones. "You dance?"

Jude scratched the back of his neck, looking adorably shy. "Yes, for many years. I teach in a studio for shifter pups."

He clicked a few buttons on his phone and turned it toward me. I watched in surprise as Jude danced expertly across the screen. The wolf was good. *Really good.* Probably better than William.

Checking my watch, my heart dropped. "We'd only have two hours for you to learn a dance I'd worked on for months."

"I assure you, I am more than capable of learning your dance before they call your name," Jude rumbled. "But there is one issue."

I had so many issues I might as well have been *Vogue* magazine. Sighing, I rubbed my throbbing forehead. "Let's hear it."

"You're my mate, I can sense it." He hesitated. "And the moment I touch you, skin-to-skin, my wolf will attach to you. No matter how much I might wish to give you space, the wolf won't let me. My drive to mate you and claim you will be overwhelming."

I forgot how to breathe. This guy I just met was willing to dance with me, but in exchange, I'd be banged, bitten and bred by a wolf shifter… for the rest of my life.

The crowd erupted into wild cheers and applause, and I turned just in time to see William and Salli locked in a passionate kiss. William's hand slid to squeeze Salli's butt.

My sadness bled away, leaving nothing but burning rage.

They'd broken my heart, but I refused to let them crush my spirit. If they wanted to win the competition, they'd have to beat me.

Straightening my spine, I looked back at the wolf hiding in the shadows behind me. "Let's do this."

Two

The producers were more than willing to sign Jude up as my partner. I suspected they might be eating up the drama of mine and William's last-minute split. They eagerly assigned us to an unoccupied warm-up room. With no time to waste, we locked the door so we could rehearse without being disturbed.

"I need to make a request, but I swear I'm not trying to be creepy," Jude began.

I burst out laughing. With revenge on my mind, and music flowing through my veins, I was beginning to feel better. I was sure the memories and heartbreak would crowd back into my mind later, but right now, I was running on black coffee, adrenaline and bad decisions.

"It's probably too late for that. Besides, I'm going to be your mate. Isn't that like the werewolf version of a soulmate or bride? Just say whatever it is that you're tiptoeing around."

"Yes. My mate—my wife." Jude's face softened.

He was slightly on the muscular side for a dancer, but his shifter abilities seemed to make him paranormally light on his feet. His hair was the color of raven feathers, and his eyes hadn't stopped glowing their golden hue. Jude's face was chiseled, like a Roman statue, making him unnervingly beautiful.

My stomach twisted, and my lady parts clenched. This was ridiculous. I'd just had my heart broken. Sure, I'd agreed to hop in bed with and basically marry this guy, but that didn't mean I was supposed to be picturing him naked. It wasn't like me.

So why was it growing harder to remember what William looked like the longer I was near Jude? Was that what the paranormals called fate? Or what the humans called delusional?

Jude cleared his throat, looking uncomfortable. "I need to hold you for a few minutes. We can dance, but my wolf is going to need a chance to calm down before I will be able to focus on memorizing the dance. I know that probably sounds crazy to a human."

"It might if I hadn't spent a portion of my childhood watching paranormal reality TV shows." I smiled. Pulling my oversized hoodie off, I held out my arms. "I always found it sweet that male wolves were so obsessed with their mates."

I didn't tell him that before I started dating William, I'd daydreamed about finding out I had a long-lost werewolf mate. Forget wishing for a prince charming, I'd wanted to have a wolf claim me as his.

Jude didn't hesitate. Closing the distance between us faster than I could blink, Jude pulled me into his arms. He pressed his face into the curve of my neck, and his warm breath blew across my skin as he took in my scent. It made me glad we did this before I worked up a sweat.

On reflection, my body relaxed into his. Looping my arms around his neck, I pulled us tighter together. I was wearing nothing but my leggings and sports bra, which left a lot of exposed skin.

Jude's hands ran along my bare back, his body vibrating. "I never knew it would be so incredible to hold my mate."

I was silent, unable to speak if I wanted to. With Jude gently rocking me in his arms, I felt whole. All my stress, sadness, anxiety, and anger faded away. It was surreal, and I never wanted it to end.

Jude held me close, slow-dancing me around the room. Our bodies moving as though we'd been dancing together for our entire lives. Eventually, we flipped on the performance music and I began to guide him through the routine.

What should've taken every last second of the ninety minutes to prepare took only half that time. Neither of us wanted to stop dancing... or touching.

We had to separate for a few minutes to change for the performance, and I found myself antsy to get back to him the entire time. Humans definitely underestimated the pull of the werewolf soulmate.

When my name was called, I felt more confident in the routine than I'd felt practicing it with William the past week. I cringed to even think of his name, but it wasn't just because he was a jerk. No, after dancing with Jude, the idea that I'd ever danced with William felt wrong.

I glided across the stage, with Jude holding my hand, and a brilliant smile on my face. My eyes landed on the shocked faces of Salli and William. They clearly hadn't expected me to show up. Salli's knuckles whitened, and her jaw set.

Jude and I took our positions. The music began, and as cliché as it sounded, the world faded away. I poured everything I'd felt in the past day into the dance, and Jude matched my energy move for move. He was a dream to dance with.

When I twirled into his arms and the music faded, I met his glowing eyes. Jude had dropped his guards, allowing me to see his raw emotions. He was staring at me like I was the only thing that mattered to him in the entire world.

Riding the high of dancing my heart out, and more than a little turned on by this sexy wolf shifter, I went up on tiptoe. Leaning into his body, I slipped my arms around his neck and trailed my fingers through his shoulder-length wavy hair.

"Kiss me," I purred, my lips brushing against his.

Jude didn't need to be asked twice. He kissed me like a man starved. Tilting me back, Jude deepened the kiss, giving the crowd a movie-worthy moment. The crowd, who had been silent, lost their minds. Standing to their feet to applaud our performance, they whistled and cheered.

The announcer's smooth baritone sounded through the intercom. "And it looks like we have a crowd favorite! Thank you, Jude and Emilee!"

"You were incredible, my beautiful Emi," he growled into my ear.

That growl did insane things to my insides. Sweeping me into his arms, Jude strode from the stage.

It wasn't until much later that I realized I'd never looked back at William or Salli. I may have started the performance looking to have my revenge moment, but I ended it by losing my heart to my werewolf partner.

__Three__

Jude carried me backstage to the lockers where we had stored our things. He paused, seemingly hesitant to put me down.

With the performance over, I didn't want to be there anymore. I didn't want to have people try to talk to me. There was only one thing I wanted, and that was to be alone with Jude.

Grabbing my stuff, I hurried to slither out of the heavily beaded red mini-dress and heels. I slipped on my thong and leggings. Not bothering with a bra, I pulled the oversized hoodie on and rushed out of the changing room.

Jude caught my hand, and we ran from the theater. Laughing breathlessly, we hopped in a taxi and I gave the driver my hotel's address.

"Emi?" Jude kept his voice low, trying to keep the driver from overhearing.

"Mm-hmm?" I slid my hand into his and squeezed, enjoying the calm that washed through me every time we touched.

"I won't be able to sleep away from you. We can try to get a room with an adjoining door. Wolves usually claim their mates within minutes of meeting, and I am working hard to keep mine under control. I want to give you time to get comfortable with the idea"—Jude licked his bottom lip—"of us. But I won't be able to restrain my wolf if he feels separated from you before you are marked."

"Thank you, Jude. I don't even know where I'd be right now if not for you." Leaning my head against his shoulder, I stroked my thumb along the back of his hand.

I spent the car ride searching through my tangled emotions. Ten minutes later, the driver dropped us out in front of the hotel. Staring at its glass doors, a harsh dose of reality smacked me in the face, and I froze.

The last thing I wanted to do was to go back to the room William and I had shared. Nor did I want to walk by Salli's hotel room door and remember the things I'd seen the night before.

I'd cried myself to sleep in that room, but now that my mind was clear, I didn't want to stay in that room another minute.

"I need to get a room. Let's see if my brother has two with a connecting door." Jude weaved his fingers through mine and led me into the hotel.

I nearly died from embarrassment when the host working at the desk turned around. It was the guy from the previous night.

The one who had picked me up off the floor and helped me to my room. Ducking my head, I hoped he wouldn't recognize me.

"Ms. Emilee! You are looking radiant today."

Crap. He'd definitely recognized me.

Jude growled. "Back off, baby bro. My wolf is already on edge without you flirting with my mate."

Surprised, my eyes darted between the two men, noting the similarities in their features. "Brother?"

Jude nodded. "Lex is my brother, and he's how I found you."

My jaw hit the floor. "What? How?"

Lex answered, looking slightly guilty. "When I saw you crying in the hall on the security film, I came to help you. When I got a sniff of your scent, it triggered something in me. A protectiveness. It was odd because while I felt connected to you, I wasn't feeling the pull of a mate bond. It was all I could do not to pace outside your door all night."

Jude cut in. "Lex called me, confused about what he was experiencing. I'd heard of this happening with other siblings, so I had a pretty good idea of what was going on. He recognized you as family—as my mate. Lex just didn't realize it."

"That's how you happened to be at the theater," I whispered, the pieces falling into place.

"Yes. Lex told me what you had relayed to him through your tears, and I've never been so angry in my life. I was out of town on business, but drove all night to get here in time." Jude brushed a strand of my hair behind my ear.

My eyes burned with unshed tears. I'd been feeling so alone while sobbing my heart out in an empty bed… and all the while this stranger was pushing himself to get here for me.

"Oh, Jude!" I sobbed, throwing my arms around his neck.

He caught me against his chest, holding me tight. Once again, comfort flooded my body at his touch. At this rate, I was never going to leave his arms.

Lex cleared his throat. "Here's two keys. The rooms have a connecting door. I'll have the staff bring your things from your old room, Emilee."

He handed us the keys.

"Thank you, Lex—for everything."

Lex winked. "You're family. Just try to keep it down, okay?"

"Shut up, Lex," Jude growled, guiding me toward the elevator.

"Hey! Emilee!" Lex called.

"Yes?" I spun around on the polished floor to face him.

A mischievous smirk spread across his face. "I just wanted you to know there was an unfortunate incident with William's suitcase. Such a shame."

Laughter bubbled in my chest. Before I could respond, the elevator door opened and Jude gently pushed me inside.

Four

Walking into the room Lex had assigned to me, I collapsed on the bed. Jude had opened the door between our rooms, and I watched as he lowered himself onto his bed. We were less than fifteen feet apart, yet I missed him.

I was already longing to be in his arms again. Son of a motherless goat! This werewolf fated mate stuff was no joke.

"Jude?"

His glowing eyes bore into me, but he didn't move.

"You're too far away." I patted the bed beside me.

Jude's forehead creased. "Emi, I'm not sure that's a good idea. I'm having a hard enough time with my wolf as it is."

"What if I don't want to wait?" The words were out before I could stop them.

He sucked in a harsh breath, and his eyes flickered like actual flames were inside them. "Is this rebound sex? My wolf doesn't care, but I find I do. I loved dancing in your revenge dance, but I can't do revenge sex. Love, I need you to want me."

I rolled gracefully from the bed and padded across the carpeted floor. Channeling my inner stripper, I slipped off my leggings and hoodie as I closed the distance between us. Jude's body was tense, and my stomach quivered. What if I was making a fool of myself?

It wouldn't be the first time.

Gathering my courage, I straddled Jude's lap… wearing nothing but my favorite lime-green thong.

"Emi." His tone was pained, and his breathing was coming out in harsh pants. "If you don't want this, you need to leave now."

"My mate," I purred. Placing my palms on either side of his jaw, I pulled his head down to mine. "I want you."

That was all it took for Jude to lose control.

His mouth met mine in a kiss that had heat rushing between my legs. I gasped in surprise when Jude nipped my lip, and he used it as an opportunity to delve his tongue inside my mouth.

While he was busy tasting my mouth, his hands were exploring my body. His long fingers trailed down my back and over my hips. His touch left me feeling raw and needy. I needed more—so much more.

I quickly unbuttoned his shirt, opening it to display the lean, yet defined, muscles I'd felt while dancing in his arms. Jude shivered at the touch of my hands across his abs. Unable to help myself, I leaned in and pressed a soft kiss to his chest...

Followed by a quick lick...

And then a playful nip.

"Mate," Jude growled, his fingers digging into my thighs. "You're playing with fire."

I felt like I was already on fire, so how much worse could it get?

Trailing my hands lower, I undid his pants, sliding my hand inside. I froze. Either the guy carried around a pet python in his pants, or wolf shifters were freaking hung.

When I attempted to curl my fingers around his girth, they didn't even make it halfway around him.

Jude's hips jerked at my touch, and he thrust into my hand. "That feels... unreal."

Yeah, it did. I couldn't remember ever being that turned on.

Unable to wait any longer, Jude flipped us around. My back bounced against the bed, and I tried not to drool as Jude shimmied out of his pants. Once undressed, he crawled onto the bed and positioned himself over me.

"I want you, Emi," Jude growled.

I hooked my legs around his waist, pulling him closer. "Then stop talking and show me."

Lining himself up with my entrance, he buried himself inside me with a single hard thrust. I moaned and my eyes crossed as his thick girth stretched me.

"Mate." Jude pulled his hips back before thrusting forward again. Over and over, he thrust into my tight heat. Jude's hand slid to the small of my back, pressing me tighter against him.

My release began to build low in my stomach; the need coiling tighter. I clung to him, my breathing rough as he rocked against me, rolling his hips to rub me in all the right places.

"Jude." I moaned his name, my body rushing toward climax. "Please."

"I want to mark you, Emilee," Jude whispered against my neck.

Even though I was human, I knew what that meant. He wanted to bite me, forever claiming me as his. It was the werewolf version of a wedding ring... one you couldn't ever take off.

If I wanted to back out, I had to do it now.

I kissed his chest and tightened my legs around his tapered waist. "Mark me. Claim me as yours, Jude."

His hips thrust harder and faster, his previous gentleness turning rough. Just as my orgasm ripped through my body, Jude's long canines sank into my neck. I'd expected it to hurt, but it only added to my ecstasy, and a second orgasm rocked my entire world.

Jude's teeth disappeared from my neck, and he roared his own release as he followed me into erotic bliss.

A strange warmth rippled through me. "Jude, I feel…" I couldn't find the words to explain everything going through my mind.

"It's the mate bond, my love. It's weaving our hearts together," Jude rasped between sucking in harsh breaths.

Closing my eyes, I buried my face in the crook of his neck and savored the absolutely magical moment.

Five

We spent the next two days between the sheets. Rather than bothering to get dressed and go out for food, we simply ordered room service for all our meals.

Not wanting to risk my family calling the National Guard to start searching for me, I'd sent my parents a text. I'd kept it simple, letting them know I was safe, that William and I were no longer together, and I would explain it all when I returned home.

Rolling to my side, I threw a leg over my sexy werewolf man. "Good morning, handsome."

William turned his head, locking sleepy eyes on me. "Well, hello, little mate." His rough morning rasp had my insides quivering.

"This has been amazing. I'm already dreading turning on my cell." I cuddled into his side, breathing in his clean, woodsy scent. "It almost felt as though we were on a honeymoon."

Jude stroked a finger across my cheek. "Then let's make it a real honeymoon."

My heart skipped a beat. "I don't understand?"

"Let's get married. I claimed you, so we are already bound in the eyes of the wolves. Why not go ahead and make it official with the humans as well?"

I stared at him, waiting for a laugh or a punchline, but he was serious.

Jude's brow wrinkled. "Unless you want a big wedding? I'm fine with that too!"

I thought about it for several minutes before answering. "No, I don't want a fancy wedding. I just want to be yours, and to know you are mine."

Jude squeezed me tight. "Call your parents and see if they can make it to the city for our wedding tomorrow. My assistant will take care of their flights and arrangements."

Turning on my phone, it buzzed like crazy as text messages and missed calls blinked on the screen. There were nearly a hundred messages from William and Salli, and a dozen from my parents.

The last notification was from the producer. Clicking the voicemail message, I listened as the producer excitedly relayed that Jude and I had been selected to be on the show. She gushed on and on about the positive feedback we'd gotten.

When the voicemail message ended, I snuggled against Jude with a grin on my face. My life had been flipped on its head, but in the end, I'd gotten everything I'd hoped for... and so much more.

THE END

185

Magical Destiny

J. TRUESDELL

<u>One</u>

"Why, mother? Why must I marry him? I don't want to marry." I folded my arms over my chest as I waited for my mother's answer, although I had already known what it would be. For the sake of the coven, I needed to marry.

"Esmeralda. We have gone over this countless times before. This marriage had been arranged a long time ago, on the day you were born. It is to bring our coven and that of the Circle together. It will make us more powerful and we need that to defeat our enemies."

"But why me? Our coven is full of young women, all of who dreams of marriage. You know I have no interest in it." There was no hiding the frustration in my voice. I have pleaded with my mother frequently and each time it had fallen on deaf ears.

"You are the daughter of the high priestess. You are royalty. That is why it has to be you."

"But what of Rebecca? She is your daughter as well." I wanted to scream to the gods and goddesses at the unfairness of it all.

"Rebecca is twelve years old." My mother stated, clearly having enough of this conversation.

"But I..."

"No Esmeralda. It is done. You will marry him come the full moon." My mother said sternly, ending the conversation. She knew I would continue to argue it until I somehow managed to get out of doing something I did not want to do.

I know I sounded like a spoiled child, but think about it. Who would want to marry? I had just turned twenty. I had my whole life ahead of me and now I was being told I would be tied down with a mate. I would never be able to do the things I've wanted to do, live the life I wanted to live. Or marry someone that I actually loved. It was so unfair.

"The ceremony will take tomorrow evening as planned. During the full moon. The Circle of Equinox has already started to arrive. Now go find your sister and make sure she is not into any mischief."

With a sigh, I spun on my heels and walked from the house. I stepped out into the bright afternoon sunlight. Closing my eyes, I lifted my face to the sky, enjoying the warmth on my skin. Why did everything always have to be so complicated?

"You should try doing that when the moon is full. Like the sun, you can feel its rays, only cooler."

My eyes snapped open, and I turned my head to see a man leaning against the edge of the building. He had chestnut hair that hung in waves down to his shoulders. His jaw was covered in a tight beard, his eyes the color of the sky. He smiled at me and I felt a tingle within my belly.

"The moon?" I asked as I turned towards him.

"Oh yes. I definitely recommend it."

"I'll keep that in mind," I replied as I started down the path that led from the main house. Next thing I knew he fell into step beside me. I glanced at him, my brow raised. " Are you looking for someone?"

"Not at all." He replied, his hands clasped behind his back as he strolled beside me. "Are you?" he asked.

I paused and stared at him. "My sister." Another pause as I looked at him. "Who are you?" then the light bulb went off above my head. Figuratively. My eyes lit up. "Oh, you're from the Circle."

He grinned and wow it was a beautiful sight. "Yes, I am."

"Let me take you over to the meeting hall. I'm sure my father is there and my mother will be along soon. They can show you where you will be staying so you can get settled."

"I've already been there. I'd much rather walk with you." He smiled again and I swear my heart did a tiny flip.

"I'm Esmeralda. My friends call me Esi." I said as I started forward again.

"It's nice to meet you, Esi." He replied, keeping in step beside me. I frowned when he didn't tell me his name.

Before I commented on that, telling him it was rude not to introduce yourself when someone gives you their name, Rebecca suddenly appeared, jumping out from behind a tree and yelling Boo at the top of her lungs. Because I was so engrossed in my companion, I hadn't expected her to do that and I jumped.

Rebecca burst out into a fit of giggles. "I scared you, Esi." She said in between breaths.

I frowned and sighed. "Ha, ha. Mother wants you back at the house."

Rebecca frowned. "But I was just going to go to the lake for a swim."

"Maybe later, right now you have to get ready to greet our guests." Rebecca's eyes went from me to the man standing beside me then back. I could see the question in her eyes. "Rebecca, this is..." since I was never given his name, I couldn't introduce him to her. "I'm sorry, I never did get your name," I said, hoping he would tell me.

He smiled and held out a hand to her sister. "It's nice to meet you, Rebecca." He leaned in closer. "Great job scaring your sister." He whispered. Rebecca beamed with pride. But before I could ask him once more what his name was, I heard my mother calling for us.

"We better get back," I said, motioning to Rebecca to walk up the path back to our home.

Without another word towards the newcomer, I started forward, muttering under my breath how rude some people could be. I heard a faint chuckle behind me and glanced over my shoulder to see him following, a grin on his face. I turned forward and continued on, not wanting to speak to him. After this week, I'd never have to see this guy again.

We approached my house, my mother standing on the porch with another gentleman. She smiled when she spotted us. "Ahh there you are and I see you've met." I paused and looked up at her confused. My mother motioned to the rude man, who stopped beside me. "Esmeralda, meet Malcolm Carrington. Your mate."

Two

I sat in my chair, my arms crossed over my chest. How could the goddesses be so cruel as to not only force me to marry but to a man who was rude and obnoxious? I glanced over at said man, just as he looked in my direction with that cocky smirk I had thought was so sexy before, but annoying now. I huffed and returned my attention to my mother, who stood next to his father. Both were the leaders of our covens. They were completing the details of our upcoming mating ceremony. I huffed again, annoyed that my life was being planned out by everyone but me.

The door burst open and in walked Liam and Oliver. I straightened up in my seat and watched as they hurried over to my mother. Something must have happened, I thought. Those two always looked strong, unbendable. As if they dared anyone to bring harm to the coven. Now they looked panicked.

"What is it?" my mother asked and I could tell by the look on her face she had the same conclusion as I did.

"It's missing. The Chalice is missing."

Everyone in the room fell silent. The Chalice was an ancient and valuable goblet that had been used for centuries at every mating ceremony. It was said that the goddesses had cast a spell on it before they rose to the heavens and if the couple drank from it, it would protect their union from evil and shower upon them all the heavenly blessings.

I stood up and moved closer to my mother. What did this mean? I wondered. Who could have taken it? No one within our coven would dare do such a thing.

"Are you certain?" my mother asked. Even though I could see it in her eyes, she already knew the answer.

"We just checked ourselves. To prepare for tomorrow." Liam responded.

"It's gone," Oliver answered.

Everyone in the room fell silent. "We need to find it." My mother finally said. "We have to find it before the mating ceremony." She glanced up at me."There has not been one ceremony without it in over a thousand years." I knew I was against this whole mating thing, but at that moment, I agreed with my mother. The Chalice needed to be found if I were to be mated. I reached out and slipped my hand into hers. I had never seen my mother this off balance before. She glanced at me and gave my hand a squeeze. "Gather everyone. We will search the grounds. I want no stone unturned." She released my hand and lowered her voice. "Esi, go and search the room, look for any signs that someone had broken in." She motioned towards the door.

I didn't bother to question her. I gave a single nod of my head, then made my way to the door. Just as I was about to leave the room, Malcolm appeared by my side. "What are you doing?" I asked as I stepped out into the late afternoon sun.

"Going with you." He stated as if that was that.

"You need to stay here, or go back to your room," I said as I strode forward.

"This involves me as well, so I think I'll go." He retorted.

"Involves you?"

He moved closer to me, his eyes holding my gaze. "This is my mating as well." Then he turned from me and walked away.

I stood there for a minute in shock, then quickly rushed after him. "It's my coven," I said when I reached him.

He glanced over his shoulder at me, a cocky grin on his face. "That the best you got? " He said before turning away and chuckling. "You'll have to come up with something better than that." He continued.

I stopped walking, stunned by his words. Or maybe it was because I hadn't heard him correctly? "Wait? What?" I said as I once again rushed forward to catch up to him. "You need to go back," I said, but it was useless. He was completely ignoring me.

"Are you afraid that I'll find something that will tell us where the lost Chalice is? Did you want to be the hero and save the day?" His voice held humor when he said the words.

"What? No." This guy was infuriating. "I just don't think it's your place to go." Now he stopped, and I nearly crashed into him.

He turned to face me. "Maybe I want to make sure you will actually look for it." He said, causing my eyes to widen. "I know you want nothing to do with this mating." He turned and started forward again, once more leaving me standing there in stunned silence.

How did he know? I wondered silently. Inhaling a breath, I rushed forward to catch up to him just as he entered the building.

"How dare you." I angrily said when I caught up to him.

"How dare I what?" He asked, not bothering to look at me.

"You accused me of not wanting to find the Chalice."

"Did I?"

By the goddesses, he was infuriating. "Yes, you did." I snapped.

"Do you?" This time he stopped when we entered the room where the Chalice had been kept.

"Do I what?" I asked, not sure I was following this conversation.

"Do you want to find the Chalice or not?" he asked. This time he looked at me.

"Of course I do." I placed my hands on my hips, not bothering to hide my annoyance.

"Good, then let's find it." He smiled, then turned to the room.

191

I stared at him dumbfounded, wondering what had just happened. It wasn't until later that I began to wonder. I never told him where the Chalice was kept, so how did he know where to go?

Three

We searched the entire house and found nothing. Whoever had taken it, knew how to get past our security measures. Past our wards. Part of me wondered if it had been someone within my own coven but I quickly shook that thought away. None of them would ever do something like this. I was sure of that. The Chalice was ancient and every single member respected the ceremony.

After we searched the house where the Chalice had been kept, everyone gathered in the main meeting house. All the coven elders were present as well as my mother, the high priestess. I was there because it was my mating, which also meant that Malcolm and his family were present.

As we sat at the table, figuring out what to do next, I kept looking across at Malcolm. The questions I had about how he knew where to go kept replaying in my head repeatedly. He raised his eyes and met mine, the corner of his mouth curling up in a grin. I glanced away, my attention returning to my mother, who stood at the end of the table.

"There are no clues as to who may have taken the Chalice, but I will not rest until we have it back." My mother said with a firm voice. I knew how she was when she got like this, determined. She was an unstoppable force. Many have said that I was like her in that regard. She turned her eyes to mine. She was just about to say something when the door to the room opened and in walked Oliver. We all watched silently as he approached my mother and spoke to her softly. I wanted to lean in, to get closer so I could hear what was being said, but I remained in my seat. I glanced over at Malcolm, once again finding him watching me. He noticed I was looking and smiled. When I quickly looked away, I heard him chuckle softly.

My attention returned to my mother when Oliver turned and walked from the room. She lifted her eyes to mine, then to the others seated around the large table. "The Chalice has been taken off the property." There were murmurs from the others before my mother raised a hand, asking them to settle down. Her eyes returned to mine and suddenly I had a feeling I would not like what was next. "Esmeralda. You and Malcolm will go after whoever has taken it, and bring it home."

"Me?" I quickly sat up, wondering why my mother would send me. "Mother, there are others much more qualified to do this. What about Oliver?"

"It will be you and Malcolm. This is your mating ceremony, you will be the one to bring the Chalice home." She said the words in a stern tone, which told me there was no point in arguing. Her mind had been made up. I turned my head when I heard the sound of a chair scraping against the floor and saw Malcolm rising to his feet.

"My intended and I will find whoever was behind this and bring the Chalice home to its rightful place." He said the words so regally as if he was some high lord of something like that.

"We have people that do this and are good at it. I know nothing of how to track." I quickly tossed out there as I rose to my feet, determined to stop this craziness.

My mother looked at me, then at Malcolm, then back to me. "You will leave immediately." She stated, then turned and started for the door. I stood still and silent as I watched everyone rise to their feet and exit the room, leaving only Malcolm and me behind.

I turned to him, not bothering to hide my anger. "Why did you agree to this? If you had spoken up, she would have listened."

He gave me that cocky smirk as he turned to me. "Why are you so against this? Do you not want to find the Chalice?"

Those words only angered me more. "Of course I do. How dare you imply otherwise." I crossed my arms defiantly. "Aren't you afraid they may discover who took it?"

He grinned, then started for the door, ignoring my question. "We should get started," I grumbled underneath my breath and rushed after him.

We exited the building when he paused and turned to me. "Do you have a car?" he asked.

"A car?" His question confused me.

"Yes. A car. Transportation?" He chuckled. "How else did you think we would travel? By broomstick?"

I rolled my eyes, then started past him. "Yes, I have a car." I moved around him and headed toward my home. "I'll need to pack a few things. You should as well. We can leave in an hour. Meet me at my home." I added. I continued walking away, not bothering to wait for his response.

"Don't be late." He yelled after me, then I heard his laughter.

'Bastard." I muttered as I climbed the porch steps and enter my home.

I find my sister there waiting for me. Her eyes were wide, and she was filled with excitement. "Is it true Esi? Are you really going away to find the Chalice?" she followed me as I started up the stairs to my bedroom.

"Yes, it's true," I said as I reached into the closet to pull down a suitcase. I placed it on my bed and began to pack my things.

Rebecca jumps onto my bed and bounces. "Can I go with you?" she asked, her voice filled with excitement.

"Not this time." I finished what I was doing and closed my suitcase. I glanced up at my sister, who sat on the bed pouting. I sighed and touched her hand. "Next time. I promise." She smiled at me, then jumped off the bed as I lifted my suitcase and headed for the door.

<u>Four</u>

It had been a week since we left my home in search of the Chalice and we weren't any closer to finding it than we were the day we left. There had been no leads, no signs of it at all. It was as if the trail we had all but vanished. The only thing left was... Malcolm. I still suspected he knew more than he was letting on. It was odd how he knew things he shouldn't, yet he had no explanation for how he knew. Every time I asked, he would simply look at me with that cocky, arrogant smirk of his. I turned from the window and fought back the feeling that came over me whenever I thought of him and that smile. It made me feel things I didn't want to feel. It made my body react.

I moved to the bed and kicked off my shoes and climbed on, situating myself in the center and crossing my legs. Malcolm had gone out to get us some food, so I had a moment to myself. I decided to try something, a spell to locate the trail we had lost, or at the very least, a hint of where the Chalice may be. I squared my shoulders and inhaled a deep breath, forcing my body to relax. I rested my hands on my thighs and I pulled on the magic that was coursing through my veins. I felt it pulse, to spread out through my body. My eyes closed as I pictured the Chalice in my mind. I pushed forward, whispering the ancient words to the spell, sending the magic out in search. Slowly it widened, to expand. My skin tingled with all of its energy. I felt a shiver rush over me, but I continued with my words. It was working; it had to be working.

Suddenly I felt something I have never felt before. Magic. It was an energy unlike anything else, and I felt it mix with my own. It wove around, wrapping itself around my energy, strengthening it, making it more powerful. Soon I felt myself inside a bubble, surrounded by all of the energy. I felt fingertips brush along my arms, then a presence behind me, pressed against my body, then a deep voice whispering the words I had been speaking. A warm breath brushed along my skin, followed by the feel of warm lips tenderly peppering kisses along my neck. I felt a surge of desire rush over me, sending waves of tingling sensations throughout. I gasped and opened my eyes, breaking the connection. The magic quickly faded, and I turned my head to see Malcolm behind me, his body melded against mine, his arms around me.

I quickly scrambled away, jumping off the bed and turning to him, angry. "What the hell are you doing?"

He grinned, then stretched out on the bed, his hands rising to fold behind his head. ""Helping you."

"I don't need your help." I snapped.

"I think you do. In many ways." His voice turned silky.

"No, I don't think so." I huffed and crossed my arms over my chest, feeling exposed. I still felt his arms around me, his warm lips against my neck. The tingling sensation it caused. How it rushed over my body, settling..."You should have made your presence known." I snapped.

He chuckled. "I thought I had."

Ignoring his remarks, I turned to the table and the bag resting on top. I pulled out the items inside. Suddenly, I felt him behind me. He placed his hand on my arm and spun me around until I faced him. "You need to admit it felt good. Our magic combining. How powerful it became." He raised his hand and brushed his fingers against my cheek, causing that tingle to spread further down.

"I don't need to do anything." The words came out in a soft whisper as I tried to sound stern. I lowered my eyes, refusing to admit anything. The truth was, it had felt good. I had never felt anything as strong as when our power combined. But I was not about to tell him that.

"I think you do." He placed a finger under my chin and gently eased my head until my eyes met his. His palm cupped my cheek, his thumb brushing along my skin. It sent a tingle racing through me, settling in my nether region. I licked my lips and saw how his eyes followed the movement. I stood completely still as his head lowered, his lips pressing against mine. The kiss was soft, gentle at first, but when I didn't pull away, his arms snaked around my body, pulling me flush against his, as he deepened the kiss.

I knew I should push him away, tell him to stop, yet as he lay claim to my lips, I realized I didn't want him to stop. For the first time in my life, I was experiencing something that was mine and mine alone. All my life, it has been things my mother has wanted, things that were expected of me. This somehow felt different.

Malcolm pulled back to stare into my eyes. It was then; I felt the energy I had before, wrapping itself around us, like a warm blanket on a cool winter's day. Malcolm smiled. "You feel it, don't you?" I nodded my head yes. Every nerve ending in my body sparked and flamed with the feel of it. "It feels good, doesn't it?" Slowly, I nodded my head. His smile widened. "Once we are mated, it will grow, becoming so much more powerful." His thumb brushed along my cheek, sending delightful shivers throughout my body.

"How do you know?" I whispered.

"It is what happens when a Witch and a Warlock become one. Become one with me, Esi." He pulled me closer, his head lowering once again to lay claim to my lips.

Five

We returned home after another week of searching, only to not find anything. The Chalice was lost to us. Even with our magic combined, Malcolm and I were unable to locate the one who had taken it. So, with our heads hung low, we returned. It had been late when we arrived, so we retired for the night, knowing come morning, we would face my mother and the rest of the coven.

Even with knowing what was coming, knowing that I let my mother and my coven down by not recovering the Chalice, I could not help the smile that spread across my face. I felt at peace for the first time. Malcolm and I stood together, waiting for what we knew would come. Malcolm reached out, taking my hand in his and clasping it. He offered me a hint of a smile when I glanced at him, then together we faced the elders of the coven.

My mother rose to her feet. "Esmeralda."

I noticed my mother glance down at our joined hands. The corner of her mouth curled up in a grin. "Mother," I said, my eyes turning to the rest seated before us. "I..." My mother held up her hand, halting any further words.

"You have not found the Chalice, nor discovered who has taken it." It was said as a statement rather than a question. Was that anger I heard as well?

I sighed, feeling ashamed that I had let my mother and my coven down. "No. We have not." My voice was low, nearly a whisper.

"But you have discovered something else instead, have you not?" I raised my eyes to my mothers. She smiled and motioned with her head to my hand, held tightly in Malcolm's. I felt myself blush at her words, and I glanced away. "Fear not, Esmeralda." I turned my gaze back to hers, the question clear on my face. "The reason you did not find the Chalice is that it was never gone."

"What? I don't understand."

"This was a test, Esmeralda. One, you and Malcolm have passed with flying colors."

"A test?" Her words confused me.

My mother took a few steps closer to where I stood. "Yes." She clasped her hands in front of her as she continued. "You were against the mating, and wanted nothing to do with it. Afraid that by joining with another, your life would be over." She took another step closer, her eyes softening. "I knew you would never listen to me if I told you how wrong you were. You would have entered this mating with your heart and mind closed. I did not want that for my daughter." She reached out and took my hand in hers. " You needed to see for yourself that by joining with Malcolm, your life will be brighter, fuller, and stronger than before."

I was stunned by her words. If I was hearing this right, my mother played me. She pretended that the Chalice was stolen and sent me out on a wild goose chase all so I would spend time getting to know Malcolm?

"I can feel your anger, Esmeralda. I want you to stop for a moment and think about all you have learned while away."

"You used me," I said, pulling my hand from hers.

"No, I did not. I showed you what could be if you would just open your heart and mind. You did." She reached for my hand again. "Look at the man beside you. Think about how you felt while with him, not knowing the truth."

I glanced at Malcolm, who looked just as shocked as I felt. "You didn't know?" I asked him.

"No, I did not. I'm just as surprised as you are." I stared into his eyes for a moment, seeing the truth. I turned back to my mother.

"Malcolm had nothing to do with this." She gave my hand a squeeze. "Esmeralda. I only did this because I wanted you to be happy."

"What if your plan didn't work?"

"That was never a worry. I saw the spark between you even if you didn't."

I stepped away. Turning from my mother. She was right. I did not want a mating. I wanted to live my own life, but these past few weeks with Malcolm had shown me what I would be missing. I would still have a life, only it would be richer, fuller than anything I could have on my own. I turned to Malcolm and took a step closer to him. I reached for his hands. "I would be honored to be your mate if you'll have me."

The smile that spread across his face lit up the entire room. He tugged on my hands, pulling me closer to him. He wrapped his arms around me and placed a gentle kiss on my lips. "Was it ever a question?"

Later that evening, we stood among our covens, vowing to the gods and goddesses above our love and devotion for one another. I may not have wanted this mating, but just as my mother had hoped, during our quest, I allowed my heart to open and see what could be. To see how much stronger I would become with someone by my side. A man who loved me as I loved him. I see now and I realized why my mother did what she did. I was set on a dark path, one that would close me off from the world around me and take me to a place where darkness would reign.

I turned to my mate and smiled. I knew the life ahead would never be easy, but as long as he was by my side, we would conquer anything the world will toss at us.

About the Author

J. Truesdell lives in the wilds of upstate New York, where she professionally fights trash stealing bears in the summer and battles her way through 10ft snowdrifts in the winter. She spends most of her time taking care of her family, which consists of three cats, two dogs, one husband, two kids, and a Hellhound named Bob. Before you ask, yes, she is an animal lover, which explains her full house, but NO, she is not looking to add. The house is too crowded as it is. At least that is what she says until she stumbles across the next stray.

When she is not busy fighting the elements, hungry bears, or taking care of her family, she enjoys falling into the pages of a good book or is in front of her laptop, where she hopes to create the next greatest American novel. No, not really, usually she is just trying to write down all those crazy ideas her brain manages to come up with.

The Academy of Magical and Mythical Creatures

A.M. MAHLER

<u>One</u>

One thing I hated more than anything in the world was being thrown into a situation with hundreds of people, and I didn't know anyone.

I was on my way to my new school. A private school. An exclusive school. I didn't want to go there. I was perfectly happy with the way my education was going. I was comfortable with my teachers. I had friends and felt like I belonged.

Then all hell broke loose.

It came as no surprise to anyone when I started showing magical aptitude. My parents were witches. Their parents were witches. Everyone in my family were witches. I had grown up with magic. Everyone knew that one day I would come into my own power. It was expected.

My elementary lessons consisted of the history of magic, respecting magic, defensive spells, dark witches and how to spot them, covens and how they were governed. Everything I needed to know about the magical world.

Well, almost.

I came into my magic early for a witch. I was three years old when I first started practicing. I learned what a dog was, and I made one appear in my living room to play with. Then I did that with a cat, a bird, a rabbit. Every time I learned what a new animal was, I conjured one to play with. You can imagine how much my parents freaked out when a bear cub was in their house.

After that, I was setting things on fire. Then I was making it rain. Then I was conjuring wind when we had to go someplace that I didn't want to. Then I was levitating. Then I was traveling.

My parents could barely keep up with me. I was far more advanced than any other child my age. I had all the markers of an elemental witch—earth, wind, water, and fire. I could weave my own spells—if I even wanted to use them.

I never knew I was an anomaly. Nobody treated me differently—or so I thought.

My father was one of our coven leaders. Coven meetings rotated between the leaders' houses. I was always sent to bed early on the nights they were at my house. Usually, I'd just go to sleep. But one night, the meeting at our house was particularly heated. I couldn't remember ever hearing raised voices during a meeting before. But I did that night.

That was the first time I heard the name Azriel Serphent.

And he was not a nice witch.

What was worse than hearing about the world's most powerful dark witch, was the fact that he was after something.

Me.

Because apparently, I was the world's most powerful light witch.

That was unwelcome news for me.

Well, not at first.

At first, I was pretty full of myself. I mean, *I* was the world's most powerful light witch. That was pretty badass.

But my conceit was short-lived. Azriel Serphent wanted to drain my power. That night, I learned if my power was drained, *all* the witches would be weakened. They wouldn't be powerful enough to mount a defense or defeat against Serphent. Without the witches, the magical world wouldn't be protected from the dark witches. And if the magical world wasn't protected, the human world was pretty much toast.

All because I was born.

After much argument that spanned several coven meetings, it was decided that I would be sent away to the one place Serphent couldn't get to me.

So, here I was. On my way to the Academy of Magical and Mythical Creatures.

The Academy was a big deal. It wasn't a primary school. We're not talking about Hogwarts here. It was a college for magical and mythical creatures, just like the name said. A place to hone our craft and learn about the other creatures that inhabited the magical world. Of course, I knew of these creatures: werewolves, dragons, shifters, fae, but I'd never met any of them.

Our coven kept to themselves, and until then, I didn't know that I was the reason why. Our coven didn't want anybody to find out about me, but that was an unreasonable thought process. Especially since someone in our coven was a traitor and we didn't know who. Somebody had told Azriel Serphent all about me.

I knew magic, but I didn't know how to fight with it. Not really.

And so, I was sent to the Academy to learn.

This place was in the middle of nowhere. Literally. You couldn't stumble across it. There were powerful spells and enchantments protecting it, and it was in the middle of an ocean.

But the most powerful defense of all, were the dragons.

Dragons were the witches' guard. For as long as both have been in existence, the dragons protected and defended the witches. So naturally, the Academy was the safest place for me.

Or so I thought.

My thoughts were empty as I stood on the front steps of the school surrounded by my stuff. My parents hadn't travelled with me. They weren't able to do it. In fact, I was the only one in my coven that could travel through space—and supposedly time, but I'd never tried that, and I'd never been able to take someone with me. In theory, I should be able to take whoever and whatever I wanted with me, but I hadn't mastered that yet.

There were two large, burly, and muscular men standing on either side of a witch holding an iPad of all things. She was checking students in.

This witch was tall, red-headed, slim, and wearing a black, fitted suit. Because, of course, she was wearing black.

But she wasn't wearing a pointy hat, so there was that at least.

She looked down her nose at me. "Name?"

"Mia Duncan," I croaked. Damn, but this lady was intimidating. I very much doubted I was more powerful than she was.

Her eyebrows hiked up her forward. "Are you really? Well, things will certainly be interesting with *you* here."

I didn't know what that meant. I just continued to stare up at her wide-eyed like a doe.

"You are not to tell anyone who you are, is that understood?" She asked.

"I can't tell anyone my name?" I shook my head in confusion. What was I supposed to tell people then? Was I to make up a fake name?

"Your name, yes, but not *what* you are," she said. "No one is to know about your power. You will have an escort at all times."

That didn't sound like fun. What eighteen-year-old girl wanted a guard around?

"That won't make people curious?"

"No," she said. "It is normal for future coven leaders to have personal guards. One will be assigned to you."

"O-okay." I stammered. I actually tripped over my words. Though I wasn't my coven's future leader. At least, I had never been treated as such. "Um, who are you?"

"Professor Testa," she said simply. "Any other questions?"

"No, ma'am." I said quickly.

"Good, follow me. The guards will see your things are put in your room." She spun on her stilettos and sauntered off into the castle. I cast a glance at the behemoth guards, who did not look at me at all, before I scurried after the indominable Professor Testa.

Once I crossed through the brown, stone walls of the castle, I came to a screeching stop and stared around in awe. Inside the castle walls was a massive courtyard and grounds. It didn't look this big from the outside, but there must have been some kind of charm on the place that hid its actual size.

There were multiple buildings surrounding the main castle with covered stone walkways connecting them. The outside grounds were beautiful, with rolling green hills, and even a forest.

Students were everywhere I looked. Witches practicing magic, shapeshifters showing off the many animals they could change into, werewolves running around the grounds.

"Michael Rodigan!" Testa shrieked. I followed her line of sight to a fluffy gray wolf peeing in the grass near some bushes. Since Testa wasn't amused, I did my best to stifle my laugh. "You have been told numerous times not to urinate on the grass when you are in wolf form! There are brown spots everywhere because of you. Shift and go to the headmaster's office at once."

The wolf cocked his head to side and there was a pause before Testa spoke again. "I understand if you shift back, you'll be naked." My eyes swung in the professor's direction and back to the wolf. How did she know what the wolf might have been thinking? "You should have thought of that before you relieved yourself on the grass. Again!"

I couldn't help it. I smiled at the wolf. When he shifted back to human form, I saw a tall, muscular dark-haired boy, with dark skin and shocking green eyes. I snapped my gaze back to the professor when I saw that his full anatomy was on display for everyone to see.

That was the first time I'd seen a male naked body in person. Feeling my face heat with embarrassment, I dropped my eyes to Testa's amazing shoes.

Michael Rodigan gave me a wicked grin and said, "Hey, new girl," before he turned and streaked into the school. Laughter and squeals followed him.

Shaded black blobs began moving across the grass and cobblestones of the ground. I looked up, expecting to see airplanes, but what I saw froze my body in place. There above us, in strikingly beautiful, jeweled colors was the most amazing sight I've ever seen.

The dragons.

Two

"The school needs more dragons," Headmaster Roberts said to my father.

My father arched a brow at the headmaster. He was the only person I think the headmaster was afraid of. And as well he should be. As King of the Dragons, my father was a formidable man.

And a bit of a dick.

"I sent you twenty more just last year," my father replied. "All the dragon warriors I could spare are on protection assignments all over the world. You've already got the largest thunder next to my personal forces."

"This year is different," the headmaster said.

This was only the second time I'd met the headmaster. The first being when my father summoned him to our palace to discuss my enrollment in the school. He seemed a little young to hold the headmaster post, dark hair, graying a bit at the temples, strong facial bone structure, blue eyes. I pegged him for mid-forties.

"Why, because my son is here?" My father gestured to me, sounding bored with the conversation, and it had only just started.

"No, because of another student that is here."

Cocking my head to the side, I studied the headmaster. If the *Prince of Dragons* didn't rate more security, just who did?

"Who?"

"I can't tell you that, Your Majesty."

Whoa. This guy had a death wish. Retreating out of range of my father's flame, I stood up and began to wander the room. Dark paneling covered the walls that weren't floor to ceiling bookcases. Portraits of what I assumed were past academy headmasters were scattered about the room. The floor was a rich, emerald green—my favorite color.

To one side of the room was an oak conference table surrounded by twelve leather chairs. On the other side, was a sofa, the same color as the carpet and three, high-back chairs surrounding a glass coffee table. I was sure the chandelier was Baccarat crystal. I only knew the name of it because all the crystal in the palace was Baccarat, and I heard my mother talk about it before.

When she was alive.

A pang settled around my heart when I thought of my mother. She died when I was eleven years old. With the loss of his mate, my father grew cold and angry. I knew it was because of the loss of his one true love. That's what happened when a dragon lost its mate, but he still had his son and heir. Was there really no love left for me?

My mother's name was Sorka, and after her death, her name was never mentioned in the palace. Hearing my mother's name sent my father into a fit of rage, so the palace inhabitants never spoke of her around him.

But I was treated differently. The palace staff and warriors liked me. And Rita, our head chef, loved to tell me stories about my mother. They knew each other growing up, and she was never in short supply of tales of their exploits in their younger days.

I wished I was sitting at the kitchen table with her right now. I started taking my meals in there a few years ago. My father worked late into the night. A king's work was never done. Rather than sit at the dining room table that could seat a hundred people, in a vast hall all by myself, I started wandering down to the kitchen and eating with the staff. I was pretty sure my father didn't know.

Then again, he usually always knew what went on in his palace.

I didn't want to come to this school. I was being groomed to take over as ruler of the dragons when my father died, but I didn't see why I needed to be *here*. I had the best tutors growing up, and my magical education was complete.

Or so I thought.

Turned out, I was also supposed to learn diplomacy and have a full understanding of magical creatures. I had acceptable knowledge, but I needed to know each species as well as I knew my own.

Especially witches.

One day, I would oversee their protection. That was essential to our existence. It's what we did. It was what dragons were created for. We protected the light witches from the dark witches and threats from other species. Every species had magic. It was how we transformed after all. But witches were basically seen as gods and goddesses in the magical world. They could do a lot of shit, and if you got one under your control, you could fuck things up good.

So, we protected them, made sure they didn't go dark.

And if they did. We killed them.

That was the unpleasant part. Thankfully, I never had to kill a witch.

I walked over to a globe in earth tones and gave it a spin. It wasn't a globe of our planet. Well, it *was*, but it showed the magical territories instead of the human territories. I was pretty good with the geography of the creatures, but not proficient.

I was supposed to learn that, too.

"I'm not sure I heard you, headmaster," my father said. His tone didn't sound pleasant. "Did you just refuse to tell me who the student is that needs more protection than the prince?"

Rolling my eyes, I turned away from the conversation. I didn't need protection. I was a protector and one of our strongest warriors.

"I apologize, sire." The headmaster tripped over himself to explain. "It's a very sensitive situation. Only Professor Testa and I know of the student's real identity, and it is a matter of life and death that we keep it that way."

Well, now, this was getting interesting. I turned back to face the two men and crossed back over to the desk and chairs but didn't sit. I was concerned my father was going to vaporize this poor fool.

Also, *sire?* Headmaster Roberts wasn't a dragon. He didn't have to use that word. *Your Majesty* was more appropriate.

But honestly, I couldn't give a shit about propriety.

Another thing I was apparently here to learn.

Fuck me, but I wasn't looking forward to this.

"I need at least fifteen more of your warriors. She'll need round the clock protection."

She, was it? My curiosity was piqued. Who was this elusive princess? She had to be a princess, right? I mean, to warrant this level of protection and secrecy, she had to be extremely important.

But dragons only protected the witches and our own thunders. Witches didn't have a royal family. The werewolves did, the fae did, the shifters, well, they were a hot mess. It was like a free for all in their world. If ever a species needed order enforced, it was those guys. They either lived in harmony or were all at war with each other. There was no in between.

"You can't have them," my father decreed. The headmaster sputtered.

"What? Why?" I knew better than to question one of my father's edicts, but we could spare fifteen of our warriors and still be a heavy force. "Can't you pull them from other thunders?"

My father pinned me with a hard stare, and I knew I'd fucked up. I immediately dropped to my knee and looked at the floor. It was an apology. Though I really wasn't sorry. I just didn't want to get my ass beat or my wings clipped. That shit hurt.

"You are dismissed." My father's voice was low and even. Had we been alone, he might have backhanded me for my insubordination.

I snapped my head up and looked at my father. "Where am I to go?" We got to the castle; we came here. I didn't know my way around.

"Here." Headmaster Roberts produced a small ball of light. Nifty little trick, that. "Follow that light. It will take you to your room. Later, there will be supper in the great hall to welcome all the students back. There are no other responsibilities today."

Easy for him to say. Just because I was a student here, didn't mean that I didn't have to do guard duty. I was a dragon after all, and this place was crawling with witches.

"I think what you meant to say was, there are no other responsibilities today, *Your Highness.*" My father's tone got deadlier if that was possible.

207

"My apologies, Your Highness." The headmaster tipped his head at me. After my father left, I'd tell the headmaster royal titles weren't necessary. After all, I wasn't the man's prince, and my father wasn't his king. I was here to learn, not to be catered to.

I turned and left the room without saying goodbye to either one.

When I entered the headmaster's reception area, a dark-skinned boy with eyes the color of my scales was sitting there.

"Dude, you're Devon, right?" He said to me.

"Yes, and you are?"

He held out his hand. "Michael, your new roommate." I shook his hand and studied his face. This guy was as stoned as the castle walls.

"I look forward to getting to know you."

He chuckled. Well, at least he was going to be entertaining.

Just as I opened the door to the corridor, I heard the headmaster yell, "Good fucking lord, how many times have you been told not to piss in the grass, Rodigan?"

Chuckling, I shook my head and started following the cheery little ball of light.

I didn't make it two steps before an emotion I'd never felt before took control of my senses. The most incredible scent permeated every part of my body, seeping into my pores and very essence of life. It smelled like the air after a rainfall, a dewy and misty morning. Everything in my body suddenly settled into a feeling of complete contentment.

My dragon wanted to shift, but I couldn't do that inside the castle walls. I was gigantic in dragon form. I would destroy this entire section of the building in the process, and my happy, stoned roommate probably didn't deserve a crushing death.

My father on the other hand …

A face appeared in my vision. A girl with hair the color of chestnuts and melted chocolate eyes. She was the most beautiful creature I had ever seen. A bond was forming between us, an unbreakable tether that joined us together in a way I'd never been connected to anyone in my life before.

The little ball of light began to float down the corridor. I turned in the opposite direction. I had a new path now. One I couldn't stray from even if I tried.

And I didn't want to try.

As I began to stalk down the corridor, my dragon hissed.

Yessss …. Mate.

<u>Three</u>

Well, as rooms went, this one was pretty nice. It was bigger than mine at home, but judging by one side of the room, it looked like I had a roommate. I briefly wondered if she would be a witch or a different species. I didn't know if the school put different species in a room together.

I was surprised I even had a roommate. I assumed I would be in my own room, given my super-secret status, but I didn't mind sharing.

As long as they weren't a dark witch.

Or, you know, a jerk.

I had my own room at home. My parents' first child was a boy, so they really couldn't put us together, even though we got along very well. It was rare for my brother and I to fight. Matthew was such a gentle soul. He got along with everyone and was popular in the coven.

But *he* didn't have to come here. He was going to regular college.

Taking a deep breath, I let my annoyance go. Then I began to picture my side of the room the way I wanted it to look. Closing my eyes, I held up my hands, palms toward my side of the room. The familiar feeling of magic rippled through me, and my palms began to warm and tingle. The smell of peat rose in the room, and I knew a cloud of smoke was forming in front of me.

I sure hoped it didn't set off the fire alarm.

When I opened my eyes, my vision had come to fruition before me. The room looked exactly the way I wanted it to.

"Wow," said a female voice. Spinning around, I came face-to-face with a beautiful Japanese girl with purple hair. "I sure hope you can clean our room that easy, too."

"You're my roommate," I concluded.

She held out her hand, stepping toward me. "I'm Hana."

"Mia." I shook her hand. I hadn't encountered her kind of power before, but I was almost certain she wasn't a witch.

"That was some bomb ass magic you just did there." She walked to her bed and sat down on a purple comforter.

"Uh, thanks."

Turning, I inspected my handiwork. It looked exactly like my bedroom back home. Well, how my bedroom used to look anyway. Those walls were bare now. Fairy lights hung on the wall over my bed, with a colorful rust-colored scarf. The comforter was white, and the head of the bed was filled with fluffy pillows in a rainbow of colors.

Next to my bed stood a nightstand, where a lamp sat with my cell phone charger. Next to that was my desk. My laptop computer, textbooks, and desk supplies were all set up. At the foot of the bed was a trunk that had extra blankets and bulky sweaters and sweatshirts. The dresser stood against the opposite wall of the bed.

I turned to the various boxes and suitcases that still stacked near the door.

"Time to unpack." I grinned at Hana. Yeah, I was showing off a little bit. I was warned to be careful about showing too much of my power, but I could still have a little bit of fun.

I swirled my hand at the wrist over the pile of my remaining belongings before pointing my finger at a suitcase. It disappeared. I didn't have to check my dresser to know that the clothes packed in that suitcase were neatly piled in its drawers. I went box by box. Books appeared on a shelf over the long side of my bed. Dresses hung in the closet. Shoes slid under the bed. Hearing a clink from the bathroom, I knew my toiletries were also put away and my towels neatly folded under the sink. I even had my plush pink robe hanging on the door.

When the last box disappeared, I looked over at Hana. My final trick was a television sitting on top of my dresser.

Hana was suitably impressed.

Maybe even a little gob smacked.

Her jaw hung open, and she didn't blink.

"Yes, I'm happy to handle the cleaning," I said.

"Wicked," she said on a breath. "Sometimes, I really wish I was a witch."

"What are you?"

"Fae."

"I've never met a fae before. Are you a fairy?" I knew there were many different species of fae, not the least of which included, mermaids, banshees, brownies, elves, changlings, nymphs, and pixies. There were many more than just those classifications, and I was here to learn about them.

She nodded, "A water fairy."

"I bet you can do cool stuff, too," I said.

She shrugged. "I can't unpack in three minutes."

"Well, at the end of term, I'll pack up for you."

"You're my new best friend."

I laughed. I liked Hana. She seemed genuine.

"Which element are you?" So, she knew a little bit about witches.

210

"Um, all of them." I was hesitant to answer, but if we were going to be rooming together, she was going to see some stuff.

"No shit. Really?"

"No shit." I liked to curse sarcastically.

Before she could ask for a more in-depth demonstration, there was a pounding on our door. I instantly went on alert. Maybe it was just the guard I was supposed to have. I was escorted to my room earlier, and the guard told me not to leave my room until my escort came to pick me up for supper.

"Expecting someone?" Hana asked me.

"I don't know anyone here."

She leapt off the bed. I noticed as she crossed the room that she was very light-footed. She almost bounced with each step. So far, I was as charmed by her as she was by me. I hoped that this was a sign of good pairing. I could really use a good friend here, a confidant. I was still cautious because I wasn't sure how trustworthy fairies were. I had heard they were very secretive.

The pounding came again before she got to the door.

"Keep your pants on! We're coming!" She scolded whoever was on the other side of the door. Maybe we were late for something? I thought it was still too early for supper.

When she opened the door, she immediately took a step back. Whoever was on the other side, pushed the door open the rest of the way and stepped into the room.

And that's when I saw him for the first time.

There stood the most beautiful boy—or man really—that I had ever seen. He was tall, muscular, with chiseled muscles and a face I could stare at all day long. He was dressed in a black T-shirt and well-worn jeans. Damn, this guy could wear a pair of jeans. My heart jumped in my chest, and I was surprised by my body's reaction to him. It felt like every single nerve ending in my body stood up at attention.

I knew at that moment, that this person was going to be very important to me. I just didn't know how much.

He looked at me, and I felt a tugging in my belly, like my body wanted to go to him. I held firm. I didn't know this guy. I didn't know what he wanted. Despite what my body might want, I wasn't just going to this guy to offer myself up on a platter like some sort of witchy sacrifice.

Faint colors began to surround him as he stared at me. A green, mist-like outline appeared around his body, and what looked like a flame crown materialized softly over his head.

Who *was* this guy?

Hana looked between us before stepping in front of him and blocking his view of me. He held out his arm and gently pushed her aside.

"Look, creeper—" she started, but I jumped in and cut her off.

"Who the hell *are* you?" I demanded. If this was the way students in this school behaved, I was going to have to put wards on the door to keep them away. In fact, I was going to do that anyway. Just another added layer of protection from Azriel Serphent. I would make it so only Hana and I knew where this room was and could get in. I could even keep it hidden from the headmaster and school staff.

But not from the dragons. The dragons would be able to find me. As the witches' guard and my best defense against Serphent, I needed them to know where to find me in an emergency.

I grew irritated when he didn't answer. "Hello!" I called out. "Who. Are. You?"

He finally spoke. Words I'd never thought I'd hear slid from his perfect lips.

"I am your mate."

BLOOD MEETS BONE: Songs of Blood and Bone Short Story

ARTEMIS CROW

"Such was she

In aspect ruthless that I quaked to see,

And where she lay among her bones had brought

So many to grief before, that all my thought

Aghast turned backward to the sunless night

I left."

Dante Alighieri

Leslie Bird Nuccio

It is at the time of dawn that we must commune with the gods.

-Apollonius of Tyana

<u>One</u>

Their bones sang to her. The bass of the os, the baritone of the marrow, the tenor of the blood, meshed then pythoned through the deep thrum of the bar music, seeking her through the continuous hum of the television anchored high on the stone wall, through the tinny voices of the humans competing to be heard. The cacophony of the songs slammed into her, wrapped around her, and squeezed, choking her.

Nova white-knuckled her whisky glass, her shoulders hunched against the incessant call, the bone songs so varied she could pick a thread and walk to the person generating it. The magic of the os gave her power, gave her purpose, gave her life, but tonight she sought a sliver of solace instead of a symphony, sought a finality to the burning ache of her failure, sought oblivion in her Oban.

She sought an answer to the question: Why didn't his bones—ancient and containing the power of a god—sing for her?

Nova threw back her whisky, winced at the welcome burn, then set the empty glass on the bar. She wiped away the summer sweat beaded on her forehead that no ceiling fan could dry.

"Another?" the bartender asked, his English accented.

He popped the top off a bottle of beer and handed it to the man three stools down without breaking eye contact with her.

She patted the smooth, wooden bar twice. "Long day tomorrow. Let's settle up."

She pulled out her wallet, startling when a new bone song wove through the crowd, this one malevolent, oily, teeming with the tortured screams of a thousand damned souls.

Head down, she scanned the humans for the inhuman creature walking among them. The crowd parted as if unconsciously sensing the malignant force in their midst, revealing a man, still and searching. Tall, heavily muscled in a hulking, heavy-browed, heavy-lidded kind of way, his black aura pulled and repelled her.

Time to go.

His roving gaze brushed past her. He did a split-second double take before moving on, but she'd seen his interest. He was good at the hunt, but she was better.

Without another glance, the man walked to the bar and sat to her left, placing himself between her and the front door.

Subtle he is not.

Nova paid her tab then pulled the strap of her leather messenger bag over her head and settled it across her body. She pushed the bag to the small of her back and set a foot on the floor, ready to push off, pivot away from the man, and disappear into the crowd.

He raised a finger. "Beer."

Nova shifted her weight but before she could stand, he turned his head and nailed her with a hard, flat stare.

"Going somewhere, bone witch?" he asked, his deep voice vibrating through her.

Recognition slammed into Nova, and with it a lodestone in her gut screaming her world had changed and not for the better. Her dead-on instincts had been slow tonight, but now she understood what his corruption meant.

"What do you care, demon?" she asked, still poised to bolt.

He took a long pull of his beer, set the bottle down, and shifted his gaze to the mirrored wall behind the bar. "Stay. I have a proposal."

Nova stood. "Not interested. I work alone."

His eyes still forward, he held her stare in the mirror. "You haven't heard me out."

"Let me define 'work alone' for you. Never interested, not with a Hell spawn trying to pretty up what he is by possessing a human."

She stepped back to get clear of the stool. She needed to escape his reach, disappear into the crowd, then get beyond it and lose him in the Old Souq, but before she could put distance between her and the demon sitting inches away, four more demons stepped into view at the front door. Their solid black eyes locking on to her then rolled back to human.

It was a warning and she heeded it, freezing in place.

Her hands dropped to the outside of her leggings-covered thighs, her fingertips brushing the long, deadly weapons she'd hidden in the custom-made pockets. The femurs she'd harvested from the last angel—one of the Powers, no less—who had tried, and failed, to stop her had been sharpened into stakes and carved with magic sigils to harden the normally brittle bones.

The stakes hadn't been tested against a demon—an angel blade would have been better—but they would kill the human meatsuit the demon wore. Dropping a human in public wasn't ideal, but in this case it could prove necessary.

Nova eased away, wondering if the back door was unlocked and uncovered. "Keep your men back and I'll listen."

The demon snorted and held up a hand, stopping his men. "We want the same thing. I've been following you for months, hoping you'd find them, hoping to make a deal."

Curiosity stopped her. She sat on the edge of the stool, her back to the bar, and waited. The demon couldn't know what she'd searched for all this time. She'd never discussed it, not even with Bane, her researcher sister. In her business, the less people knew about what she sought, the better for their survival.

"What do you think I want?"

The demon took another long drink, finishing his beer. He nodded at the bartender for a second. "Treasure hunters are always so cagey. Zero trust."

The pesky zing of irritation made her twitch. "I'm not a treasure hunter; I'm an archeologist. As for trust, it must be earned, and hunting me has put you in the negative points column."

He sipped the second beer as if his thirst had been quenched with the first. "You hunt for ancient and priceless bones that you don't share with museums, that you never talk about. They're there when you come into a town; they're not there when you leave."

He set down his beer and shook his hands. "Kind of the definition of a treasure hunter. Your subterfuge makes me wonder what you do with the bones."

"Jazz hands, really?"

The demon cocked his head. "Smartass, really? When there are so many humans here, and my men are so hungry?"

For once, Nova remained silent; no good could come from pissing off a demon. *Time to stow the mouth.*

"Have your say and leave. I've had a long day."

He smirked. "Leave Byblos and don't come back."

Her heart thudded, her breath caught. There was only one reason to warn off another party. The demon knew something she didn't.

"First, that's not a proposal; that's an edict. I don't like being told what to do. Second, why?"

"You didn't let me finish."

Nova's right hand itched to draw her weapon and bury it into the demon's face, but she couldn't, not here. Instead, she rested her hand on the stake's grip in case she was forced to do something she'd regret.

Nova yawned. "So finish what you have to say. I need sleep."

"You're a mouthy thing," he said with a chuckle. "I like that, especially in a woman with fire-red hair."

"It's been said, but eww."

"Keep it up." He leaned close and looked into her eyes. "The more you sass, the more I want you."

216

He smelled male with an added tinge of sulfur. Despite her revulsion, she shivered under the weight of sexual promise. It had been too long since she'd been with a man. Her body hungered for touch and taste and satiety. Even knowing there was a demon riding the man didn't quell her body's longing; sometimes a gal needed an up-against-the-wall hard fuck to soften the rough edges.

He gave her a broad smile, smug and sure, as if aware of her train of thought, and *poof*—her lust vanished.

Nova gripped the stake tighter and pulled it out a few inches, almost clearing its spandex sheath. *I'll show you sass.*

"Well? Are you going to finish your *proposal?*"

He turned away and caught her gaze in the mirror again.

"Leave…or work with me. As an *archeologist*," he said, using air quotes, "and a bone witch, you're uniquely qualified to help."

"To what end?"

The demon shrugged. "Oh, I don't know, locating the bones of an Egyptian king, the first vampire. Osiris."

Nova pulled her stake free and stabbed the man in the thigh, pinning him to the wooden seat of his stool. The shaft of the bone flared with light; the weapon quivered in her hand. She leaned into him.

"No one touches those bones but me," she ground out.

He shuddered. "Ouuuuch."

Nova grinned, waiting for the stake to do what it did like nothing else.

He smiled, exposing all of his too-white teeth, the expression inhuman.

Her gut clenched, sweat beading on her skin. He should be screaming and writhing and getting sucked back into Hell.

The demon gripped her hand and pulled the stake free, no worse for the assault other than a bloody, gaping hole. "You thought the bone of an angel would hurt me? You'll have to do better than that." He raised his left hand and signaled. "I'm a prince, one of Lucifer's own. And I never travel alone."

Nova whirled away from the demon. She caught the bartender's eye, her eyebrows raised in question, hoping he understood.

The man jerked his head to his left.

Nova shoved through the barflies, ignoring their complaints, until she reached a hallway. Running down the short stretch ending in a small, utilitarian kitchen, she saw the open door leading to the alley. Pushing past the protesting cook, she ran outside and turned left, ignoring the wall of heat the night hadn't assuaged.

She had to get to her hotel and the safety of her protection circle.

The alley was quiet, save for a few people lingering in doorways smoking, allowing Nova to run flat out on the uneven stone. The trip from the Old Pub to Byblos Sur Mer was half a mile. Fast at a walk, even faster at a sprint.

Two shadows stepped out of a side street and blocked her path.

Nova stumbled to a stop and turned back. Two more shadows appeared.

A solid wall to her left, on her right closed doors. She reached for the closest door. Locked. The demons had trapped her.

Two

The figures advanced, closing much of the distance in seconds. They'd be on her soon.

Nova checked the only other door between them. It held fast. "Crap."

She flattened her back against the wall, pulled the second stake, and waited for the demons to get into stabbing range.

Fear and joy unfurled inside her, filling her. She'd trained in self-defense since childhood, had used her skills more than once to escape a rival with her find in hand, and more than once to save her life.

She glanced from one pair of demons to the other. In this case, she'd have to fight to save her life. Whether from death or servitude, she wasn't sure, but both were undesirable.

Nova spun the stakes in her hands and grinned—*fake it 'til you make it*—forcing her body to relax. She planted her left foot ahead of the right and bent her knees, shifting her vision from narrow focus, where she could watch her opponents' eyes telegraph their next moves, to a wide view, allowing her to see the movements of multiple fighters. Like seeing a game board at a glance and knowing your next move. Wide focus was necessary here, but riskier, especially once fatigue set in.

"You demons really don't know how to take no for an answer, even after I staked your leader," she said.

They didn't respond, not a blink or a flush of temper; hell, she would have settled for a laugh. Not good. Taunting an opponent was a great way to throw them off balance, but the Hell spawn weren't going to make it easy. It would be an all-out fight, no words, no tricks.

Okay then.

Nova's grin faded. Quiet descended.

She reached out with her magic and found the four, felt the differences in their bones, made note of the old breaks, the chips, the arthritis forming in the joints. Any weak point she found in the os could make the difference between surviving or not.

The closest man reached for her.

Nova beat his arms and head in a whirl of motion before stabbing his gut with both tips, but holding back, only pushing them in a couple inches. Not enough to kill the human, but enough to give the demon pause.

Please don't be a demon prince too.

He cursed and backed off the stakes, one arm wrapped around his waist, protecting the duel wounds.

Nova glanced at the other demons then slowly raised a stake. "Wait for it."

The other demons stopped their advance, their attention shifting to their wounded comrade.

The demon looked at his bloody belly. "What the—?"

Light burst out of the holes. He screamed and staggered back, black smoke jetting out in twin plumes, the angelic power in the femurs destroying the demon.

He fell to his knees, his scream slowing to a gurgle. The demon's amorphous form hovered just above the human who'd hosted him, as if unsure where to go, what to do.

Nova raised both stakes above her head. "Let me make that decision for you."

She stabbed the smoke, sinking the stakes into it.

The femurs glowed white hot, the power building, shaking Nova like a rag doll. She'd ended a ghost once—that had been difficult enough; this was so much harder. The stakes locked on to the demon soul, a battle for supremacy waging.

Either the demon or the angel would be destroyed. Hopefully, not taking her with them.

She held tight and rode it out. Just when she thought the demon would prevail, when her muscles had had enough, an explosion of white, black, and red lifted her up and threw her against the wall.

Nova slid to the ground, blinded, shaking from the effort and its result.

The world took its time righting itself. *Nasty side effect, that.*

When her vision cleared, she saw the remaining demons in a heap several feet away. "Get up, Nova."

She climbed to her feet, her legs wobbly, the alley spinning, her stomach threatening to heave. She took a step in the direction of her hotel but faltered to a stop.

The demon prince leaned against the stone wall, his arms crossed, his face red, his mouth open.

"Stalking isn't attractive," she called out.

They stared, locked in a battle of wills, one she couldn't afford to lose.

His gaze shifted to a point beyond her. "Swarm."

Nova whirled. The three demons had untangled themselves and stood ready to attack. Behind them, four more had arrived. Seven against one; the odds stank.

She positioned herself for the attack and spun her stakes again. If she was going down, she'd take as many as she could with her.

"Come on, if you're ready to go back to Hell."

The demon prince laughed. "Haven't you heard? There's a hellmouth now. This is Hell on Earth and we're just getting started. There are hundreds of thousands of starving demons just like the one you ended, all expendable."

The seven demons advanced.

"Not good at motivation, are you?" She jutted her chin at the seven. "Are you willing to be destroyed for him? Because these stakes aren't going to send you back to Hell so you can rise again; they're going to destroy you. That's forever in case you don't understand."

Despite her generous warning, the demons picked up speed. At this rate, they'd be on her…

The group lunged as one, their hands reaching.

Nova rolled away and ran toward the leader. If she could get past him, maybe his minions would stop.

Feral roars warned her a split second before a crushing weight slammed into her. She fell forward, pinned to the ground, the stakes still in her hands, but useless. The demon leader had been smart. Swarming her had been the right move; her need to escape had distracted her.

Stupid.

Fetid breath swamped her, the scrum of seven making it hard to breathe. She choked, the need for air blinding her to everything else. She bucked and kicked, panic driving her. Fingers clawed at her forearms, trying to steal the stakes.

One of the demons grabbed her hair and pulled her head back. Lips touched her ear, his hot, rancid breath repulsive.

"I've longed to possess a woman," he hissed.

Black smoke curled in front of Nova's face, gathering.

The sharp tang of fear filled her, the icy, razor-sharp edge slicing through her courage, a foreign sensation. Possession couldn't be allowed. A demon knowing all her secrets, her plans, having access to her bone magic would be catastrophic for her, for her people, for the future.

She turned her head and snapped her teeth at his face.

He grunted and the scrum shifted.

She jerked her arms forward and rotated her wrists until the stake points were raised. If she could kill the demon before he took her…

Hands gripped her throat and squeezed. Within seconds, the scant light in the alley dimmed, her already-oxygen-deprived body burning. The stakes clattered to the ground. Nova sagged, the fight draining out of her.

The demon prince laughed.

Mother Goddess Chaos, please help me.

A shout rang out, anger and alarm barely registering.

A rapid *pop, pop, pop* sounded around her, like popcorn in a microwave, the weight of the men

easing. The grip on her neck disappeared.

She sucked in a deep breath, hoping the weakness would pass quickly so she could fight.

More shouts, more pops. Then silence.

Nova rolled onto her back and sat up. She blinked, trying to understand what she was seeing. Seven bodies were strewn around her, their necks broken, the demons gone; they had either escaped or been destroyed.

She stood, looked for the demon leader.

He grappled with a blur, something or someone moving so fast she couldn't tell if it were man or beast. Supernatural, yes, and the demon was having trouble holding his own.

Did Chaos actually answer me?

Curiosity made her pause, but the need to survive broke through. Time to clear out before more demons arrived.

Nova staggered past the bodies, going back the way she'd come, to escape the fight.

She ran inside the first open door, hitting a wall of warm cinnamon and cloves, tangy orange and lime, the tear-inducing heat of peppers. The scents of her childhood slowed her heart, giving her time to think, as she wormed her way through the patrons.

Traversing the spice market, she raised her hands, muttered her apologies, her smile broad to appease the shouting, gesturing proprietor. She pushed her way to the front door and stepped outside, losing herself in the crowd-choked street, finally able to take a deep breath.

She turned right and ran through the Old Souq until she reached her hotel, the lobby cool, and quiet. Only then did she settle into a floor-swallowing stride, her focus on the open elevator.

She ran in and pressed the "close door" button repeatedly, staring at the hotel's front doors, expecting the demon prince to appear, until the elevator complied with a *ding*.

Nova sagged against the wall, braced to stay on her feet; if she went down now, she might not get up. She rubbed her sweaty hands on her pants then froze. Lifting her hands, she stared at them in disbelief.

"My stakes."

The weapons were priceless, irreplaceable, but she couldn't go back. She had other weapons, but the bespelled, angelic stakes were the most effective tool she had against demons. Except for demon princes, damn it.

Nova staggered to her room. A cold numbness washed through her until she couldn't feel her fingers, her feet. She fumbled with the hotel keycard—how she'd managed to keep that and the messenger bag but not the stakes was beyond her—and unlocked the door. She stepped inside the dark space, shut the door, and leaned against it. Closing her eyes, she tried to ignore the building aches overriding the numbness.

"Ahhh."

Pushing off the door, Nova pulled the strap over her head and dropped the bag, her first stop the bathroom. She flipped on the light and started a hot bath, her fingers lingering in the water until her sweaty clothes set up an itch.

She reentered the main room and unbuttoned her torn shirt, dropping it to the floor. Sitting on the bed, she pulled off her boots, taking a moment to find her calm. She leaned over and turned on the lamp.

She flung herself back, fell off the other side of the bed, and hit the wall, the surge of blood to her brain so piercing hot she thought she must be stroking out.

The balcony door was open.

A large man sat in the shadows, barely visible against the deep black of the Mediterranean behind him. The soft lights of the seaport below outlined his form, yet his face remained obscured.

Nova rose from behind the bed, and backed away from him. She sent her magic out, seeking information from his bones, needing to know if he was a demon, but her senses failed her. They registered nothing, which was impossible.

"Who the hell are you?"

Three

He crossed his legs, and her bones sang for him.

Raw power came at Nova in waves, the vibration shaking her, rocking her back until she stumbled and hit the door. In all her travels, with all the people she'd met, she'd never had a reaction reach inside her core and batter it.

For the second time tonight, her magic had failed. At least with the demon, she'd felt his malevolence, the darkness in him giving her warning until her magic had a chance to catch up.

This man? She had no clue who or what he could be.

Fear exploded inside her, feeding her rage, fueling her hate. No one had the right to possess her so fully, to make her want so deeply. It couldn't be allowed, even if it meant destroying him.

Still silent, he raised a hand.

Her magic broke through whatever had blocked her, as if with a gesture he'd given it permission to return. She choked on the audacity of the man. Her fingers curled, her nails digging into her palms. She wanted to attack, to punish him for the assault, but caution held her back. He was no ordinary opponent.

Sand and heat and spices flooded her senses. Images of a life impossibly long-lived slammed into her, sucking her down. Stones stacked on stones forming the Great Pyramids, kings and queens and priests, so many people flooded her mind, the passing of the ages flying by like a flip book.

This man was unlike anyone she'd met, his bones speaking a language she didn't understand. Panic swamped her anger and she reached for the door handle, the need to escape him driving her to run.

He rose and spread his hands wide. Step by step he entered the room, the lamplight revealing him as he advanced. Tall, at least 6'5" of stunning in a black, pinstriped, three-piece suit that hugged his broad shoulders and chest, tapered waist, and long legs. His starched, white shirt, open at the neck, exposed smooth, light brown skin she longed to trace with her fingertips.

Nova raised her gaze to his face and flinched at the superhuman beauty.

Thick, wavy, black hair skimmed over his head, ending at his shoulders. The day-old scruff accentuating a strong jaw and high cheekbones made her sigh, but his wide, amber eyes mesmerized her. They pulled her in and held her until she shook her head to break the spell he'd woven.

Her body ached for him, longed to go to him, the nearly irresistible pull making him dangerous in too many ways to count.

"I'm not here to hurt you," he said, his voice a deep croon meant to soothe.

"I don't believe you," Nova managed to squeak out—to her mortification.

Damn dry mouth.

He kept his right hand raised and reached behind his back with his left. He pulled out her stakes and showed them to her before tossing them on the bed.

"I wanted to return your weapons, and talk."

"That was you? In the alley?" Nova asked, gauging the distance between her and the stakes and him.

Needing the power the stakes would give her overruled her fear, her caution. She lunged for them, scooping them up with one hand. She backed away, the stakes pointed at him, her roiling gut settling somewhat.

She could have defended herself with her bare hands, at least for a little while, but that would have required touching him. The battle raging inside her bounced between that being a very bad idea to being a very good idea. So. Distance.

He pointed to the chair across from the bed. "May I?"

Nova kept her stakes pointed at him and nodded once, waiting to see what he would do.

He sat, crossed his legs, and folded his hands into his lap. "Yes, that was me."

"How did you move so fast? I've never seen anything like it."

He tilted his head to one side. "How did you come across angel femurs? That's not a standard weapon." His gaze dropped to her chest. "Nor are you a standard archeologist."

Heat welled inside her then barreled straight to her breasts. She could have sworn they grew a cup size under his sure-as-a-touch stare. She glanced down and cringed at the sheer tank top basically baring her all.

She forced her head up. Nothing to do but brazen it out until she could get him out of her room.

His gaze flickered to the bathroom door. "Your bath."

A puff of air blew over her face and flipped the ends of her long hair.

He shifted in the chair as if he were merely restless, and not some cousin of the Flash who'd blurred again.

Her bath was no longer running. *Holy Goddess. What is happening?*

"Don't do that," she said, pointing her stakes at him, the tips shaking.

He shrugged, his legs crossed as if he hadn't done the impossible. "It's in my nature to fix things. Let's cut to the chase instead of wasting time with small talk that addresses nothing important."

He rose, walked to the nightstand, and picked up the television remote.

"Why didn't you blur?" Nova asked, her back against the door again.

This had been the weirdest night, maybe of her life.

"Blur is a good word for it. I do prefer blurring to going at this snail's pace but moving that fast takes a toll. I haven't had time to recharge."

He turned on the television and flipped through the channels until he reached the news.

Sitting on the bed, he turned his focus back on her. "Name is Calder. I'm an archeologist, too, of a sort." He pointed to her stakes. "You can put those down. I'm not here to hurt you."

Nova sheathed one, but kept one pointed at him. No one gave her orders, and she wouldn't start with him. "What does 'of a sort' mean?"

"I have a short list of very specific antiquities that I seek. You are Nova Os, bone witch and renowned archeologist of paranormal artifacts. I need your help."

Nova crossed her arms. "You're the second man asking for my help tonight."

Calder's lips twitched. "I don't think the demon was asking."

She tipped her head and sat on the opposite corner of the bed. "I'll give you that."

Not that any distance could save her from a man who could move so fast he was essentially invisible. Nor make him less stunning to look at. Goddess almighty, the man was even more beautiful up close.

A tingle started in the small of her back and it wasn't from his looks. *Well, it is partially. Who am I kidding?*

This man and the demons were after what she had sought and failed to find. She wanted him to offer her that information, as well as the rest of his short list, but his silence made it clear he wasn't going to explain further until he showed her something.

"What do you want me to see?" she asked, dragging her gaze back to the news.

A breaking news banner scrolled across the screen, a reporter coming into view outside of Mabaj Grotto, a tourist attraction an hour from Byblos. Multiple ambulances and police cars had parked yards from the entrance, the area cordoned off. A pair of paramedics passed the camera, the body carried between them covered with a blood-stained white sheet.

"Spell it out for me," Nova said, turning to Calder, her focus on his only flaw, a slightly crooked nose.

"Access to that grotto has been closed to tourists for months. *Those* tourists were outside the entrance." He pointed to the television. "They were slaughtered."

She watched the rest of the report, her heart sinking. "The demons?"

He scowled. "A lot of them. More than the eight who attacked you."

Nova's free hand clenched the bed coverlet, bunching it. "Tell me why you're here."

"I think you know."

"Say it anyway," she snapped.

"Osiris's bones. That's why you're here, why the demons would slaughter innocents to keep them away from the grotto. I propose we work together to find the bones before the demons do."

"And the rest of your list?"

He shook his head. "Not until we get the king's bones."

She stared at him, willing him to cave, but he returned her gaze with a flat expression. He would wait an eternity without giving her a thing. *Damn him.*

A scream sounded down the hall.

Nova jumped up. "What the hell?"

Doors slammed, cries and whimpers echoed outside her door as people ran by.

Calder cleared his throat. "That would be the demons."

Nova whirled and pointed the stake at him. "What did you do?"

He rose and walked forward until the tip of her stake pressed against his chest, right over his heart. "I told the demon leader where you were staying."

"You son of a bitch."

She reared back to plunge the stake into him.

He grabbed the shaft and forced her arm up, his strength unnatural. He pushed into her, pressing her body back until she hit the wall. Heat and the scent of male filled her, warming her, enticing her to acquiesce to any demand he might make.

"Agree to work with me, Nova. Only then will I get you out of here."

"Tell me why. Otherwise I'll take my chances."

Calder bent down and pressed his mouth to her ear. "Because Osiris needs me, and I must answer his call."

More screams, much closer this time.

She could jump off the balcony, but she was on the top floor. That would be suicide, or broken bones leading to her capture. Again, suicide.

Calder and the demons were pushing hard for her help, so they must believe Osiris's bones were here. She couldn't leave now, and if she had to choose between an unknown like Calder and the demons who'd attacked her, she would choose Calder.

Nova shoved him back and held out her hand. "We find the bones, together."

He took her hand in his.

Shockwaves rocked her back. She would have fallen again if he hadn't had a firm grip.

227

Double damn him.

His amber eyes dilated until they were nearly black. Seeing him affected steadied her.

He pumped her hand once. "Deal."

Someone pounded on the suite across from hers. Calder released her hand, and they broke apart.

"We have seconds," he whispered. "Grab only what you need."

Clothes she could replace. She ran to her messenger bag and draped the strap across her chest.

Calder pointed to the stake still in her hand. "Put that away. I don't want you accidentally stabbing me."

She slid the stake into the leggings sheath and slipped into her light jacket. "How do we get out of here?"

Before she could blink, she found herself cradled in Calder's arms, the man balancing on the balcony rail overlooking the port.

"Have you lost your mind?"

He didn't speak, just stepped off the rail and let gravity pull them down.

Nova gritted her teeth and hoped she landed on top of him so his broken body would shield her from the same fate, but he floated down like he was wearing a parachute.

They landed and Calder set her on her feet. Shadows converged on them and swarmed.

She clung to Calder's side. "Demons?"

Calder chuckled, the rumble vibrating through her. *Triple damn him.*

He snapped his fingers and the shadows shimmered. Seven solid-black dogs appeared, pacing around them in a tight circle, their gazes pointed outward.

Lean like a Doberman with erect, pointed ears, they stood taller than any dog she'd ever seen. As much as she loved dogs, these she would have crossed the street to avoid. She raised her gaze to Calder.

"They're Anubis dogs. They're my charges, but they've assumed the role of protector." He inclined his head. "When the Egyptian deities fell to Hades and were trapped, I assumed responsibility for the animals they revered. Anubis dogs, Bast cats, and so on." He grimaced. "It's a zoo, but the dogs have proven useful. The scarab beetles, however." He shuddered.

"W-what the h-hell are you?" she stammered.

The port lights defined the angles of his face. His frown shifted to a lazy smile.

Seriously, somebody help me.

"I'm an Osiris vampire, the first of my kind, and the last, I'm afraid, unless we can find Osiris's bones and help him rise."

The End

Look for the Songs of Blood and Bone series in 2024!

Witch's Dance

CREA REITAN

<u>One</u>

I stand outside the Salem Witch Museum and stare at the people walking in and out. About every third person is magical, belonging to my world and not that of the mundane. I can see the little shimmer when someone enters the school and not the museum that is our façade. It's late in the day, which is the only reason there are more non-magical people than there are students.

Sacred Tongue Academy looms overhead and I'm silently correcting my thoughts to 'Satan's Touch.' While witches are rarely one of the species that have been going missing within these walls, every day that goes by is another breath of relief that it wasn't me or anyone I know. But then, there's always tomorrow.

Inhaling deeply, I walk back into the school. My magic lets me walk through the veil into the college instead of the witch museum. While there are dozens of species within these walls that attend classes, and the student body is all pretty inclusive, sometimes a particular species likes to gather as a means of bonding with their community. I'm pretty sure that's how the recent disappearance of a demon was noticed. The demon community realized that one of theirs was missing.

Tonight, I'm heading into the courtyard within the center of the school to mingle with anyone who holds magic in their veins, regardless of what level that is. Witch, warlock, sorcerer, etc. I'm a witch and it's always good to connect with other witches. You know, networking and shit.

Internally rolling my eyes at the thought of mingling, I step outside and am immediately hit with all the magic at work. The space is already large, but the center where the fountain usually is has been replaced by a bonfire that soars to the height of the roof. Every now and then, the flames flash different colors.

Around the fire are dancers. Mostly dancing to their own beat regardless of what the music is playing. They dance for themselves and sometimes in couples, throuples, or small groups. Sensually. Erotically.

As I'm watching, the beat changes and the dancers shift naturally into a more choreographed dance. Moving with the words and worshiping the fire, the spirits, the source of magic. Paying their dues, their respect, and asking for something in return.

I blink, and the moment has passed. The sweaty bodies are back to dancing how they wish. A shiver races down my spine as I smile. Beautiful. I fucking love being a witch.

To the right is a long table with three large cauldrons. Witch's brew. I know it for what it is. Primarily water. You put some in your chalice and add the extracts that you choose. There are vials and bottles lining the table as a bar might display bottles of alcohol.

Most of these additions are alcohol, yes, but also flavors and the fun elixirs that witches are known for. They offer different kinds of buzzes. Exotic flavors. Temporary but heady effects. Heightened pleasure.

There are high-top tables all around and witches mingling. The many feminine and masculine voices drift towards me, and I can't help the feeling that it's all just *right*. Like when you're walking around the city and something inside you is so settled that you can't help knowing that you're right where you should be.

Silly for this moment, maybe. Because really, I'm a junior at a fucked-up school, single, and with average grades. I have nothing to write home about. Yet, it feels as if the stars are aligning tonight. There's nowhere else I should be but right here.

I step further in and catch sight of the group of girls with the magic sex toy shop, A Lick of Magic. They're dressed as they usually are, all sexy and filled with smiles. Their rainbow array of hair and pretty flesh glowing in the firelight. Of course, there's also the shape of a dick across their chests as they advertise their company. Confident in their product and enthusiastic about advertising it.

There's a small crowd around them as they speak and while it's primarily the five of them, there's a few guys there as well. I don't recognize them but they're all graduate students whereas I'm an undergrad. We don't exactly run in the same circles.

However, I wasn't immune to their shop. Did I buy a couple magic dildos and dick sleeves? Hell yes. And are they worth the money? Let's just say that my orgasms have totally improved from the time when it was just my hand and me. I think I might like another body to share an orgasm with once in a while, but I am definitely enjoying my silicone dicks and fleshlights.

Shifting my gaze away, I move to the beverage table and fill a chalice with a ladleful of the base brew. Then I meander through the additions and drip a few into my cup. Though these cups are meant to go in the fire when we're done with them—magic recycling—they feel solid, like real metal.

With drink in hand, I head for the fire and watch the bodies move. I'm not in the ring of dancers as I sip my drink and admire the bodies before me, but close enough to feel their erotic energy as they wind, bend, and sway with whatever tunes they hear. Enough time must have passed that once again, they shift into the choreographed set. I watch, entranced, as the man in front of me pays his respect to whatever it is he practices in particular.

It's sexy, and his eyes meet mine as he turns. A smile flicks across his lips before the dance makes him pivot away. There's a woman in front of me now and her glassy eyes say she's had a couple drinks, but also that she's completely lost in this moment.

The dedication lasts maybe three minutes and then breaks; the dancers moving back to their own steps without missing a beat. Taking another sip of my drink, I step into the ring and feel the music sing to my blood more than hear it in my ears.

Magic is potent.

Dancing has never been my thing, but I let my body go as I move to the rhythm, absently wondering if everyone hears the same tune. Taking another sip of my brew, I'm not sure I care. It's freeing. Yes, others can see me, but I have to think that I look as carefree and sexy as everyone else does out here. Maybe that's the point of the magic in the music. To remove your inhibitions and let yourself relax.

Which is probably why the witch gathering was organized. Introduce yourself to your peers and be yourself completely. Swallowing the last of my drink, I toss the cup into the fire. The flames streak to the sky in a bright pink and I grin before I close my eyes and move to the music that I'm fairly certain only I can hear.

I'm so lost in myself, in the dance, that I barely register when a body presses against my chest. When I realize, my breath catches but my eyes don't open. Instead, I rest my hands on their hips before sliding one around to their hard, flat stomach.

The moan is low and masculine, making me grin in appreciation. His arm reaches back, cupping the back of my head as he presses his ass into my hips, getting my blood flowing south. I drop my mouth to his neck and let the music move us together.

But I hear the moment the music shifts and we're pulled apart. Not forcefully. It actually feels natural, like we'd intended it the whole time. The melody is almost hypnotic as I feel the pulse of magic reach up and tug on the source inside me.

Licking my lips, I send up a prayer to the place where all magic resides, giving appreciation. Offering my thanks. My breath of promise to use magic wisely and not always selfishly. I don't ask for anything in return this time. I'm not in need. Except maybe for continued good health. But that is kind of a blanket request I lay for everyone.

The music releases me and I find the body pressed to mine again. Hot. Breathing heavy. I grunt as I turn him around and pull him close. Opening my eyes, I meet deep blue ones. Dark orbs that remind me of the velvety night sky. He's a strong sorcerer.

A gorgeous sorcerer. Olive skin and curling brown hair. The corner of his lips quirk up as he stares at me. The flush on his cheeks does not go unnoticed. Neither does the ever growing bulge pressed against my thigh.

"Hi," I murmur.

The music pumps in my blood but I'm certain that I spoke loud enough to be heard. As if it were only the two of us.

His voice is deep, sexy. "Hi," he returns, his smile quirking bigger. He licks his lips, and my eyes drop to trace the movement. It's only then that I realize he's a bit shorter than me. Three or four inches. Enough that he fits perfectly in my arms. Perfectly against my body.

His lips part. I think he's about to say something when his eyes flicker over my shoulder. The flirty smile drops, and he stiffens in my hold. Before I can ask what's wrong, I feel his presence and scowl as big hands drop on my hips. Possessive. Threatening. Biting in and threatening to leave bruises.

"I-I'm sorry—" the man in front of me starts, trying to back away, but I hold him close.

"Don't be," I say, and push him forward so I can move out of Maddox's hold. But his grip doesn't slacken or loosen as he follows. Frustrated, I wrap an arm tightly around the man in front of me and turn us so Maddox doesn't have a choice but to drop his hands.

He's a big man. Like a goddamn bear. The look on his face, all obsessive and possessive, used to make me feel wanted. Warm and giddy and all sorts of mushy shit. But I've come to realize that I don't like Maddox or the games he plays.

Oh, I'm all about big guys and being manhandled. I like when someone feels possessive of me. I like that they can get jealous as long as it's not in a toxic way because I like knowing that their desire for me is real.

What I don't like is being hidden. Being a tool to make someone else jealous. I don't enjoy being a third or fourth priority, only important enough when all other plans have fallen through.

Casual is fine, but messing with someone and leading them on is not.

And that's what Maddox does. So he's a dick. And not the kind I like, even if he's got a rather impressive cock. I hate everything else about him.

"Go away," I tell him.

"No," he says, voice deep. Sounding like a fucking animal. His gaze drifts to the man I'm holding against me, and I feel him flinch. I don't blame him. Looking at the monster that is Maddox would have made me flinch once upon a time. He's just that big and intimidating. He reaches for me again and I back away. "Come on, baby. Don't make me chase you."

"I'm not," I say. "And don't call me that. I'm not your baby or any other cutesy name. I've told you a dozen times to go away and leave me alone. Now is no different."

That last part was for… damn, I need to ask this guy his name. But it was for his benefit.

Maddox frowns, then brings his hand up, and out of the evening air, he conjures a rose that glows. It crackles and burns with energy, filling the surrounding air with a heady pleasant scent. Offering it to me, his dark eyes intense on mine. "Stop this," he says quietly, taking a step closer. "You misunderstood."

Rolling my eyes, I pull this guy in my arms further down the fire, but not willing to turn my back on Maddox. He moves quickly for such a massive man. Can't let him out of my sight because I know he hasn't given up yet.

"I really don't want to be caught in the middle of ex drama," the guy says quietly.

I shake my head. "What's your name? I can't keep mentally referring to you as 'this guy.'"

He laughs, and the sound makes me look at him, pulling a smile to my lips. I study his face—so damn beautiful. "Caro," he says. "Yours?"

"Rue. And for the record, he's not an ex. He was an... occasional, casual fuck who turned out to be crazy."

Caro looks warily over his shoulder. I don't blame him. Maddox is already approaching again since we've stood still. We aren't really dancing right now. Only gently swaying to the music that had faded because we weren't paying it attention.

"I don't want to play games tonight," Maddox says, reaching for me. I shift away and he releases an irritated growl. Fucking animal. "I'll be good to you. I've apologized. Let me—"

"You need to learn to take no for an answer," I snap.

Maddox's eyes flash dangerously. The flower in his hands decays, turning black and then to ash, which catches on a breeze that I don't feel and drifts away. "Rue," he warns, his voice low and dark.

No longer comfortable putting Caro between us, I shift, so he's now behind me. Magic crackles at my fingertips, my heart racing in fearful anticipation. I'm a decent witch. But I'm not as powerful as Maddox.

Before anything else can transpire between us, the music pulls us into the sacred dance. I catch Caro's eyes and he flashes me a nervous smile as our bodies move identically. On my other side, I hear Maddox growl.

Though I'm stupidly distracted, I throw myself into the ritual, send up my thanks and vow of servitude. This time, I ask for something in return. Not to harm anyone, of course. You don't wish for ill lest it be turned around on you. No. I ask for strength and speed.

When it stops, I barely slip free of Maddox's sudden lunge for me. He stumbles, looking up at me with predatory intent.

Fucking crazy man, I think as I grab Caro's hand and pull him away from the bonfire.

"You sure he's not an ex?" Caro asks once we're away from the fire and music, our voices only contending with the quiet murmur of chatter surrounding us. I lead us to the brew and pause.

"He's not," I tell him, looking into his deep, dark eyes. The wariness that had been there at Maddox's appearance and the exchange is gone. And once again, his lips quirk up. "He's a mistake and a lapse of self-confidence," I admit.

Caro licks his lips, and my eyes track the tip of his tongue. "Want to get out of here?" he asks.

I look around, knowing that Maddox is in the crowd somewhere. He's a fucking possessive asshole. When I told him I didn't want to be his plaything anymore, that if he wanted to keep climbing in my bed, then I needed to be it for him, he chuckled, brow raised, and flatly told me no.

Maddox hadn't been expecting me to grow a backbone. He had every bit of evidence to say this wouldn't end differently than every other time I'd told him I've had enough. The words 'I'm worth more than a pity fuck' rang loud in my head, even though I couldn't bring those words to my mouth. Because the way he looked at me said I wasn't.

And I believed him.

It's not that my confidence has improved from then until now. There's still a voice whispering in the back of my head that he's as good as I'm going to get. If I want to be wanted, being a fuckboy backup is all I'm good for.

But Caro looks up at me, asking me to go. Though I just met this man and I'm weak enough to let him use me, I nod. Everything in my fragile heart hopes he'll be different from every other fucking person I've met since I was a teenager.

"Yeah," I say.

He takes my hand and pulls me to the door, but we come up short as I run into him. Maddox zeroes in on us and now he stands in our path looking like a stone wall. Arms crossed. I can almost *see* the smoke coming off him with how angry he is.

Caro stares at him, frowning. I sigh, squeezing his hand tightly before letting it go. "I'll give you my number," I tell him. "If you want to call me later, you can. But he's just going to keep following us because he's a psycho."

I know that he can hear the self-deprecation in my voice, though nothing I said was about me.

His fist clenches before he grabs my hand again and yanks me to his side. Maddox growls like a pissed off mama bear, taking a menacing step toward us.

"No," Caro says. His fingers push between mine and my heart gives a hopeful jump. It's only at this moment that I realize how much I've been faking confidence since I walked in here tonight. But then I'm distracted by the thrum of magic pulsing off Caro. "He wants to measure cocks. I can assure him that mine is bigger."

Maddox snorts, making it obvious that he's looking at Caro from head to toe. Sizing him up. Dismissing him as a threat.

"Do you want to leave with me, Rue?" Caro asks, not taking his eyes off Maddox. I bite my lip, his magic brushing over my skin like a caress.

"Yeah," I repeat. "But I don't want—"

My words cut off as the bonfire flares brightly. The courtyard fills with surprised screams. Even Maddox's head snaps in that direction. Which is a mistake.

The magic wafting from Caro shifts until it circles him like a cyclone. I can almost see it, little glimpses of bright spots that glitter in the dim courtyard. When Maddox turns back to us, Caro lifts his arm, swirling his finger in the air and then points at Maddox.

His eyes go wide as the magic surges forward, sending Maddox shooting through the air and slamming him into the wall. He slumps, falling into a heap. I'm still frozen in shock. We're being watched now as Caro lowers his hand and sniffs.

Maddox lifts his head, his eyes glaring irately at Caro. Hot bursts of magic are shooting over him like fireworks.

"Looks can be deceiving," Caro says and somehow, I know his voice reached Maddox as if he were standing two feet away.

Caro turns, looking at me. "Rue? Ready?"

I'm still staring wide-eyed, my gaze flickering between them as I try to process what I just saw. What just happened.

"Yes," I tell him, voice quiet.

His smile is small when he gently pulls me toward the door. We walk in silence for a bit, through the building and then out onto the quiet streets of Salem. There are people milling about, breaths wafting in clouds of steam in the chilly December air. A shiver races down my spine as Caro leads me down the road.

Hawthorne Boulevard is lit by street lights made to look old and give a soft glow. I glance into Salem Common as we pass. There are shadows moving, as if ghosts of generations gone linger and haunt the green. I think it's more likely they're just students or residents, maybe even some tourists, moving about the cool, quiet winter night.

We cross the street to Hawthorne Hotel, a façade for the five story dorm building that belongs to Satan's Touch. When we step inside, we pause. My skin prickles as the cold from the outside is penetrated by the warmth of the lobby.

Caro watches me as he rubs his hands together. I don't meet his eyes at first as I observe people milling about and moving from one place to another. Leaving the dorms or returning. When I finally look at him, he gives me a tentative smile.

"No pressure, Rue," he says quietly.

"I *knew* you were a powerful sorcerer," I say, instead of anything that has to do with following him here. I mean,my dorm is on the second floor, but still.

Caro smirks. "I have old blood," he says, shrugging. "Long line of magic in my family and way back when, there was some interbreeding to keep the line strong and pure." He makes a face but shrugs again.

By interbreeding, he means conception between close relations. You know. Think the old dynasty Egyptian pharaohs. Or European royal bloodlines. Not something commonly practiced today, but things that happened once upon a time. Magicals are no different except that when a magical species interbreeds, it fortifies the magic, power, or strength of that particular family. It's not just a sense of royal blood. It's compounding magic.

I glance behind me towards the door. "Let's go upstairs. He lives here, too."

Caro nods and I follow him to the stairs. "My room or yours?"

"I'm on the second floor," I say instead of answering directly.

He gestures for me to lead the way, so I do. Conscious of the fact that I'm once more leading someone to my room that I don't know, I'm internally begging that this won't turn into another Maddox situation.

I'm still chewing on my lip as I lead Caro to my door. My hand is surprisingly steady as I insert the key and open it, revealing a room like all the others.

My bed is on stilts, with storage underneath. It's pressed against the far wall, under the window, so I can look out at the stars on a clear night. I have a desk, bookshelf, and a chair that I like to curl up in.

Moving aside, I let Caro come in and shut the door behind me. As soon as it's closed, there's pounding on the door. It is so loud, I jump away from it but lunge forward to flick the lock as Maddox's voice fills the room.

"Rue!"

Scowling, I turn my back on the door, hoping that it stands up to his fists. I can feel his magic thrumming over my walls, trying to work its way inside. Fucking psycho stalker.

"He's rather insistent," Caro states.

Sighing, I nod and try to block out Maddox's yells. Maybe I can call campus security on him. Maybe I should. Would that make him understand that I'm serious? He's probably simply not used to being told no. He always gets what he wants.

When I turn, Caro is looking at my bookshelf. It's not until I look beyond him that I realize my mistake. It's been a while since I had anyone in my room, and after Maddox, I had no intention of bringing someone here for a while.

My face heats as Caro studies my collection of A Lick of Magic sex toys. Not just heats. Burns the fuck up.

"Uh," I say. There's no coming back from this now. Should I tell him that I am in a dry spell? That after the madness that's banging on my door, I swore off all intelligent people. But I sure as fuck wasn't going to go without orgasms.

Caro looks at me with a smirk and my face heats further, but as he licks his bottom lip, my cock twitches in my pants.

A flurry of angry magic shudders through the room, pulling me out of falling into a heated place. Maddox's slamming on the door echoes louder, his voice like needles against my bones. A scowl replaces the heat on my face.

"Would you like me to get rid of him?" Caro asks.

I look at him. He isn't tiny, but he's smaller than average. Something I actually really love since he seemed to fit against me so well while we were dancing. And I *know,* not just because he explained his bloodline, that he is a powerful sorcerer. I can feel his magic, even when it's just simmering under the surface.

But that familiar sense of not being good enough sits heavy on my shoulders. If he takes care of my problem, he'll see just how pathetic I am. He may have come home with me, but that doesn't mean he isn't just here for a lay like Maddox.

And yet, I invited him inside anyway.

His fingers brush against my cheek, pulling me from my thoughts as another raging wave of magic flutters through my room. I'm staring down into night velvet eyes as he smiles softly up at me. "Whatever you're thinking, it's not true."

"What makes you think that makes sense with what I'm thinking?" I ask.

His smile is soft and sweet. "Because I can see it written all over your face." Before I can ask what he sees, he says, "Self-deprecation." I flinch and turn away.

Caro turns my face back, his fingers grasping my chin and guiding my attention to his. "Let me get rid of him. And then we'll hang out, okay?"

I nod because I'm not sure what else to do. I can't make Maddox go away. Ignoring him doesn't seem to be working tonight. Before too long, he's going to break down my door.

Flashing me a cheeky smile, Caro saunters to the door and flings it open. I shift just in time to see his magic explode out of him, covering him in a monstrous shape full of claws and spines and fire. Within the magic storm is Caro, standing still. I can barely make out his bemused face.

There's a brief moment of struggle from Maddox before he basically shrivels and then drifts off into the air as his body unravels into a curling line of smoke. I'm wide-eyed when Caro shuts the door and turns back to me, his magic having sunk back into himself though his dark eyes are still glowing with little white starry specks.

"That'll take care of him for a few days," he says, moving back into the room.

I'm pretty sure I'm looking at him in awe. How did he just do that? What kinds of secrets do the old families have?

"Want to watch a movie?" Caro asks when I just blink at him with my jaw hanging against my chest.

"Uh." I look around the room as if I'll see something monumental. Something out of place. A change in time. I see none of that. "Sure?"

When it leaves my mouth as a question, Caro chuckles and moves toward me. He stops in front of me and smiles up. "Or we can dance some more?"

"I—" I have no idea what to say. So I just look at him, dumbfounded but impressed. So damn impressed. And now wondering why he's here with me. Why waste his time on a nobody?

Seeing that I can't answer him, Caro moves into my space and presses against me as we had been around the fire. He links his arms around my neck, body flush to mine, and waits for my broken brain to catch up.

My hands move to his waist all on their own. I wrap around him, hugging him close and bringing my forehead to his. Is he real? I didn't just make him up?

The absence of Maddox slamming into my door leaves a serene silence wrapping around us. It's so peaceful, so welcome, that I sigh and close my eyes. "Thank you," I whisper.

"You're welcome," he answers. "I'm glad I finally ran into you."

At first I don't answer. Then his words register and I open my eyes to look at him. "What do you mean?"

There's a faint blush on his cheeks. I'm mesmerized when he bites his bottom lip. "I've had a crush on you since we shared a class together last year. When I saw you dancing alone, I thought I'd finally grow some balls to approach you."

Again, I find myself staring at him. I want to ask why. Why would he have a crush on *me*? But the words don't leave my mouth. Instead, I feel as if I can't catch my breath. All tingly and lightheaded.

He has a crush on *me!*

My arms tighten around him as I close my eyes to breathe him in. I can feel him. Smell him. See him. Hear his words and his breathing. He's real. All my senses tell me he's real.

"I know," he says, pulling away from me slowly. He kicks off his shoes and motions for me to do the same. I do, but pause as I watch him crawl on my bed. He lays sideways, facing the window. "Come up, Rue."

My heart is racing as I move next to him. When I'm settled by his side, Caro taps the glass of the window with his socked toe. In the span of a blink, the entire wall and ceiling disappear and we're laying on my bed under the stars.

I crane my neck to look around, amazed at what I see. At the endless sky and infinite stars twinkling overhead. "Wow," I whisper.

Caro smiles at me, shifting closer.

I'm not a very confident person but I move in, pulling him against me. We wrap around each other, so we're all tangled limbs, and stare into the clear night sky.

We don't talk much but in this moment, I think that maybe my life won't continue to be a series of unfortunate circumstances. Maybe I've finally met the single person in this life that will like me as I am. That I'll be enough for someone.

"Yes," he murmurs. I shift my eyes from the sky to look at him. Softly, Caro brushes his lips to mine. "You're more than enough."

"Did I say that out loud?" I asked, cheeks heating.

Caro grins. "Maybe."

I close my eyes in embarrassment. But he shifts so his face is aligned with mine. His lips a breath from mine. "You're enough, Rue. You're perfect. And I'll spend every day showing you that for as long as you'll have me."

My heart shatters, each tiny piece stuttering in my chest in a witch's dance.

I'm enough.

Binding Incantations

BRANDY SLAVEN

Myra LuRox has always had a way with her witch magic. A disastrous, back-firing way that is. Her move to Vixen Falls is her one last attempt at some semblance of control over it. The only thing she didn't account for is Zane, a warlock with his own magic who has been sent to keep an eye on her. Will the power of both his and the falls be enough to save Myra from herself, or will her past finally catch up with her?

One

MYRA

They say in Vixen Falls you can be anyone you want to be. I've come to learn this as truth. That may have something to do with the fact that I keep my distance from everyone. People speak to me in passing, but I never go out of my way to make friends with any of them. The only place being friends with me will lead you is to the hospital or straight into the ground.

With that cheery thought, I stalk down the stairs of my apartment building. Casting a glance over my shoulder, I take a second to be thankful that this place was open at the time I came rolling into town on one of those big grey buses. Things are like that here, though. Small miracles when you need them the most. As long as I keep a tight leash on my magic, they stay miracles and don't turn into monster disasters. Trust me when I say that I've had enough of those to haunt me for a lifetime.

I turn and head down the narrow alleyway that leads toward the main street running through town. Vixen Falls isn't very large, so you don't have to go very far to get where you want to go. Even the falls themselves are just a quick hike outside of town. Turning left, I pass several of the main touristy shops before coming to the door of Caroline's Candle Cove. Her main windows display the normal candle scents of the seasons and souvenir knickknacks you can find in almost every store in town. It's what she keeps in the back is the real Caroline's. She keeps anything and everything anyone could ever need for a spell back there. My first instinct was to stay as far away as I could until I could get my magic under control, but as they say, 'a girl's gotta eat'. As per my luck, Caroline was the only one hiring and I couldn't afford to turn her down.

I get so wrapped up in my head that I completely miss the box sitting right outside of the door. The toe of my thigh-high boots catches on the side, and I go stumbling forward. My face looks to smash right into the glass portion of the door right before it opens. Instead, I find my face buried into plaid and a very hard chest. I still don't have my footing underneath me, and it causes us both to go tumbling to the ground in a messy heap of tangled bodies.

Bracing my palms against the floor, I push myself up and brush my dark blue hair out of my eyes. It's then that I get a good look at my rescuer and tragic victim. Zane. Of course. If there was ever a time for me to be clumsy, which is all of the time, it would be in front of him.

I try to untangle us as I stand, "I'm so sorry."

A deep chuckle starts in his chest, "Myra, I thought we had this discussion last time we ended up like this on the floor."

There's a couple that has been standing a ways away from us that must have been distracted away from their browsing to see what the fuss was. At Zane's words, the woman purses her lips and pulls the man away from us. It takes me a minute to catch on and then my face goes as bright red as the plaid on his shirt.

I finish pulling myself away from him as I stand and offer him a hand up. There's a zap of energy that flows from his palm into mine. The first time that it happened, I almost knocked over an entire candle display holding hundreds of tiny glass candles. This time I am expecting it and choose to act like it's not there, even as he takes his time letting go.

"Well, it's been a pleasure as always," he says dusting pretend dirt off his pants.

I pick up the bag that he was carrying and hand it to him as I mumble, "Sorry."

He laughs and takes the bag from me. His voice goes down even further into a deep offering, "I'd gladly be underneath you anytime."

At this, he leaves me standing in the doorway to Caroline's with my jaw unhinged on the floor.

"You're catching flies, honey," Caroline calls out as she swishes by with a smile. I try to distract myself watching her. She can't be but about thirty, which puts her eight years my elder. The way that she carries herself, though, makes her seem so much older. One of the best things that I love about her is she always looks like she just stepped out of a plus size Romani magazine. Today's choice of dress is an emerald thing that flows down her body and accentuates it in all the right places. Paired with a gold bangled belt and a scarf in her hair, she looks every bit the gypsy she claims herself to be today.

The staring couple side-step me to get out the door and I realize that I must look like a fool just standing here. I quickly close the door behind them and catch the eyes of Zane across the street. He sees me staring and smirks as he waves. I throw a disbelieving look in his direction and turn on my heel. I'm going to need a whole lot of caffeine and mindless work to get me through the day because his words are playing on repeat in my head.

Two

ZANE

A few months ago, when I was first assigned to Ms. Myra LuRox and this town, I just knew that my life would be changing. I never would have seen it happening like this, though.

I had everything back at my coven. A good job, respect, and most of all, a beautiful woman to warm my bed every night. One slip up and I'm the pariah of town, only worse. I was given this assignment to keep an eye on Myra, but it was closer to banishment than anything else. There really isn't anyone to blame but myself really. Or, if we wanted to get technical, the blame torch could always be passed to my ex and the warlock I found her sleeping with. It was for no other reason than pure rage over seeing them together that I beat him senseless.

Karma always comes back in spades, so I can only hope that they are getting theirs. As I watch Myra through the window of the candle shop, her mouth sings an unheard song, and she dances to the beat as she sweeps the floor. I can't help the idiotic smile that crosses my face. Ever since I laid eyes on this sexy creature in front of me, I haven't had one moment thought of going back to my coven. I know she feels the sparks when our magic touches. She may not know what it is yet, but she will soon.

I try not to act like a creeper staring at her through the window, but I get busted anyways.

"You ever going to ask her out, son?" Caroline's voice says from the door.

I look to her then back inside only to see that Myra has disappeared somewhere in the back. Answering Caroline I say, "I'm working up to it, sweet Caroline." I don't comment on her son remark. Not many people know Caroline's true form, or that she's much older than she looks. If there's one person in town you don't mess with it's her, and probably the dragon shifter, but he's more bark than bite.

She nods to me as if she can read my mind, "I wouldn't wait too long if I were you. I've got a feeling this one is going to need all the help she can get soon. You feel her power now, yes?" I nod and she returns it and continues, "As it should be. It is done."

Her words have finality to them that have my brows pulling down in worry. Before I can say anything, she is gone, and Myra comes skipping out of the shop. Probably not the best idea for someone as clumsy as she is, but I wouldn't have her change it for the world. I love the smile that lights her face as she takes a deep breath of air. Just not so much when it falls into a frown as she sees me standing there.

Without giving her a chance to say anything, I hold up the paper sacks that I'm carrying. I send a small push of wind her way and get the satisfaction of watching hunger glaze over her eyes.

Freeing the smile I've been fighting I ask, "Dinner?"

__Three__

MYRA

I

'm not so sure that I fully trust Zane, but I forgot to bring lunch with me today and I'm starving. As if my belly hears my thoughts, it lets out a loud growl at the smell coming from those bags. He would have to be deaf not to hear it. It's confirmed as his smile gets even wider.

"Come on," he says turning on his heel. Looking back over his shoulder he teases, "I won't bite." I smile at his back and fall in behind him.

The view from the back is just as good as from the front and it kickstarts my heart into overdrive. I forget for one second that I am a witch blessed with an uncanny knack for mishap and misfortune. As that thought crosses through my head, I come to my senses. Zane starts across the street towards a small park where I know that there are small picnic tables. I take small steps backwards in hopes that he won't hear me until it's too late. As I come even with the alley leading towards my apartment, I shove my head down and take off at a dead sprint. My name is called out, but I ignore it and keep running. It isn't until I'm securely behind the locked door of my apartment that I wonder what a fool I've made of myself. I stare at the door as if the inanimate object is the true reason for my guilt. Of course, at that moment a loud knock rings out from the other side and I squeak as I jump back in alarm. I barely manage to keep on my feet as I trip back against the table behind the small couch. The cheap wooden furniture isn't so lucky. It tips over and spills a few books and candles across the floor. Watching one of the candles roll all the way into the kitchen, I pray to all that is holy that Zane will just leave.

I'm not sure how long I stand there, but when I don't hear any noise coming from the other side, I decide to make a risky move. There's no peephole in my door. I should probably try to convince the landlord that I need one, but I'd rather just pay my rent and keep off the radar.

With the chain still connected, I make a small crack in the door. There's no sign of Zane, but the smell from the food still lingers in the air making my stomach growl again. Looking down, I see the reason why. He left one of the bags on the stoop.

I close the door and with a deep breath I release the chain. When I poke my head out, I look left and right to make sure that this isn't a trick. The coast is clear, so I yank the bag inside and slide the lock back in place after the door is closed.

I wish I could say that I was so ashamed of my behavior that I didn't eat what was in the bag, but I can't. Barely making it to the table, I devour the contents and nearly lick the aluminum foil that the delicious meatball sandwich was wrapped in. If that wasn't enough there's also a huge slice of baked cheesecake and I eat it without a fork like a barbarian.

It's then that the guilt hits. This didn't come from the diner. Zane made this himself to bring to me. "Shit," I say to the empty room.

I throw my trash in the small pail under the sink. Grabbing my keys, I head back out into the night.

Aware of my surroundings, I make my way over to the grocer. The one or two patrons that I run into either nod or voice a hello to me as I make my way back towards the wine section in the corner. Anyone watching probably thinks I'm crazy, because I stand there for a good twenty minutes or so not able to make up my mind.

I can't really afford the good stuff, but I owe Zane for his kindness and for how I acted. My face turns bright red and he's not even here for me to relive it. Screw it. I pick up the more expensive black colored bottle of dessert wine and take it to the counter.

Shockingly, I make it out of the store with no slip ups or hassle. Lyle behind the register had just given me a knowing smile as I paid and said to have a good night. I simply passed him a tight-lipped smile.

Back out into the night air, I breathe the clean scent into my lungs. There's nothing like being outside here. I don't like being trapped inside. The scent of emotions that roll off people have a tendency to float around long after they've gone. Then they find me and cling on like a second skin.

The magic that trickles down the mountainside at the falls whispers to sister magic in the air, so every breath I take washes away that negative energy residue.

Starting down the sidewalk, I set a fast pace knowing I've got at least a mile walk ahead of me. Would have been smart to change out of my long boots and throw on a light jacket, but I was in too much of a hurry. Then again, there's also the question of how I know where Zane lives. I've never been to his house before and I don't even know his address. The best way I can explain it is the residual energy thing. Plus, it helps that my magic recognizes him on some basic level. Makes tracking him so much easier.

I'm so lost in thought that I don't realize the faint trail has led me to a quaint two-story log cabin right outside of town until I'm standing right in front of it. The falls aren't too far from here and I can feel their magic call to me as it caresses my skin.

I shut myself off from the feeling and immediately regret it. The amazing dinner is in danger of making an appearance as my stomach rolls. Looking up at the dark windows of the cabin, I decide just to do this quickly and run, tail tucked back to my safety nest.

Taking the steps two at a time, I then set the bottle of wine on the welcome mat. As I contemplate ringing the doorbell, a dark voice from the shadows of the porch makes me jump out of my skin, "That would taste so much better if I weren't drinking it alone."

My hand jumps to my heart as I watch Zane unfurl himself from a porch swing. He marks his place in his book without dog-earing the pages. That's good because I don't know if I'd be able to be with someone who defiled books that way. *Wait a minute...be with someone? What am I thinking?*

I try to cover up the inappropriate thoughts running through my head with the first thing I can think of, "Can you even read that? It's pitch black out."

He chuckles, "I have my ways. I'd be glad to discuss them with you if you'd stay for a glass of wine with me." He scoops the bottle off the porch and holds it out as if he's the one that has something to apologize for.

Going against all of my better judgment, I nod to him, and a huge smile lights his face, visible even in the dark. Doing one of the most reckless things I can think of, I follow him into his house.

Four

ZANE

Leading Myra into my now home, I can't help but to steal some glances over my shoulder at her. The night vision spell I cast a short while ago will last throughout the night, as it does every night. Myra is a stunning beauty even in the dark. All dark blue hair flowing in waves down her back and ice blue eyes that suck you in the moment you catch them. She's got a tiny pixie-like face that most wouldn't think attractive. As for me, I find it more than appealing.

There's a small sound from behind me and a short curse. I turn around and try my best to hold in my laugh. She would find the only catch on the entry rug. Even with the lights on, it would be inevitable.

I decide to put her out of her misery, "Freeze."

Her eyes go wide at the authoritative tone in my voice. I'd be lying if I said that wasn't the biggest turn on of the night to watch her comply without question. Trying to dislodge those thoughts, I snap my fingers and several candles around the room light. Myra gasps and I smile. With another snap the fireplace blazes to life. I see the envious daggers she shoots at the fire.

I step into her space, "I could teach you to do that you know."

Those ice blue eyes turn up to me and I see longing in them before it's quickly shut down with fear. We have plenty of time, so I take a step back before I have her running scared again.

I walk backwards toward the kitchen, "I'm going to put this in the fridge so it can get cold. I may have some extra cheesecake leftover if you'd like some more."

Indecision is clearly written across her face, so I smile. "Come on, I can't eat all of it by myself."

I sigh inwardly in relief as she starts walking again. After depositing the wine, I take two plates out of the cabinet and scoop us both a good slice. Setting it down in front of the barstool across from me, I remain standing. Myra sits and pierces my heart with a stare before starting in on her plate.

Her soft voice brings me out of my head, "Why are you being so nice to me?"

"Hmm," I say with confusion, "Should I have a reason to be neighborly?"

She shrugs, "If this was a white picket fence kind of place I'd say no, but nothing here is quite normal, is it? There's a reason for everything and to be honest I'm not the kind of person who you should make friends with."

I'm interested in being more than friends with Myra LuRox, but she doesn't need to know that just yet.

249

Before I can reply she says, "Honesty is our best option and I'm going to lay it on the table for you. I'm now one hundred percent sure that we know what the other is, but I'm not like you. Everything my magic touches turns to ash and some quite literally. So, I'm not sure what your end game is here but it will only end in agony. I promise you that."

Hmm, some things are starting to make sense now. I've been all but chasing her for months, doing everything I can to squeeze any attention from her and she avoids me like the plague. I want to ask her if that's the reason she runs from me, but instead I feel my eyebrow lift in response to her declaration. Getting the feeling like she's getting ready to take flight again, I change the subject as I nod my head towards her empty plate, "Cheesecake was good?"

Her head tilts to the side like she's trying to understand me, and it's so damn adorable. When I don't say anything, she realizes that I was actually expecting an answer.

"I'm still here, aren't I?" she asks.

I laugh as I grab the plates and put them in the sink, "Yes. Yes, you are. You have to tell me something though, because the curiosity is killing me." Her body stiffens and she glances at the door. I move quickly around the counter to sit on the stool between them. Locking eyes with her, I reach my hand out to her hair. My fingers run straight through the strands as I ask, "I'm curious as to if you've had this color from birth."

She lets out a physical sigh of relief and says, "No. I wasn't born with it. It was a rebound spell. When I was younger, there was this girl in school who bullied everyone."

I rest my hand on her shoulder with my fingers still in her hair as her eyes never leave mine and she explains, "I could do a little magic by then, so I thought that I could teach her a lesson."

"Did your parents never teach you about the three fold law?" I ask interrupting her story.

She smiles sadly at me, "They never had the chance. My parents were killed when I was two."

I don't recall hearing that before I was sent here, but I was so pissed about leaving my coven that it's possible I simply missed it.

She continues and I pull out of my head to give her my undivided attention, "I lived with my aunt for a while, and she taught me everything that I know. This was my first big spell, and it was the only one that I had ever done towards someone. It wasn't meant to hurt her or anything, just turn her hair blue. So, the night that I cast the spell everything went as planned, then the next morning I woke up with this." She grabs the blue strands from my fingers and holds them up for example.

"Ever since then, any time I cast a spell, even small things, something always goes wrong with it. After the one time I lost my eyebrows and sliced my finger almost clean off, I stopped using my magic. All except the last time."

"What happened the last time?" I ask quietly, not wanting her to feel pressured into talking.

She shakes her head and stares at a non-existent spot on my counter. Then surprising me even further she admits, "I didn't mean for it to happen. My aunt went crazy there at the end. Everyone said she was dabbling in dark magic, but I lived with her. I think I would know better than anyone if she was. Our minds are such fragile things. Most of them said I was crazy for telling them that someone had taken over her body. She tried to kill me that night." Stopping there she looks back up at me, "I never meant to kill her. I knew that something wasn't right, but she had me against the floor with a knife to my throat. My magic reached out automatically. It was only supposed to be a little wind to push her off me. Well, it did that and much more. She busted through the window of my room and fell three stories to the ground. You know, that's not even the crazy part. I was only a few inches from falling out myself when I went to try to help her and maybe I'm nuts, but I could have sworn that she whispered thank you as she fell through the air."

I'm not sure which shocks me more, Myra's story or the fact that she shared it so willingly with me. There's more here, I'm certain of it. It's going to take some digging to find out, but I make a promise to myself right in this moment that I am going to find out for her.

My hand moves from her shoulder to her chin, and I pull her to face me, "It's not yours or your magic's fault. Just from what you're telling me right now, I can honestly say that it sounds like something dark was at work here."

A tear slips down her cheek and that is my complete undoing. I wasn't going to rush her into anything with me, but I can't sit here and watch as big tears roll down her beautiful face. Swiping them away with my thumbs, I lean down and press my lips against hers

<u>Five</u>

MYRA

My neck aches from the odd angle in which I've slept all night. Lifting it to work out the kink, my face rubs against something soft. The masculine smell that hits my nose has me wanting to burrow into it further. I catch myself just before I do, and my eyes fly open. At first, I don't understand where I am and start to panic. Then last night comes back into focus. Anxiety strikes through my chest as memories flash through my clouded early morning logged brain. I cannot believe that I spent the entire night on Zane's couch. We sat up for hours way into the night just talking about anything and everything. I also cannot believe that I told him about Aunt Summer. The blame should be placed entirely on the cheesecake. If I didn't know any better, I'd say that he spelled it. Sitting down at his kitchen bar I spilled the beans of who I am and what I'm running from without hesitation. Not only had Zane not even flinched, but when my chest felt like it was going to explode with anxiety and sadness, he had cleared my tears away and kissed me.

That thought has me bringing my fingers to my lips. I still feel him pressed against me. As if he knows my inner thoughts a voice deep with sleep says, "I let the fire go out a few hours ago. If you're cold, you can come over here with me."

For the first time since waking up, I take a look around to see that I've been sleeping sideways on the couch, and he's laid back in an oversized chair that faces the door. His kiss last night wiped the bad thoughts clear in my head, but I never would have initiated. If I do as he says and go to him, it will be of my own free will and all of the bad things that happen to him in turn will be my fault. My stomach churns at the thought, so I am going to do what I do best. Get the hell out of Dodge.

Standing is pure torture. Throbbing, my neck cries in protest as I try to stretch. Add that to the cold of the house and I want nothing more than to cross the distance and crawl inside the blanket beside Zane. Again, I feel as if he's in my head. He lifts the blanket away from his side beckoning me over.

"How do you do that? You're not reading my mind, right?" That sounds silly, even to my own ears.

He chuckles, "No, little bird. Sad to admit that isn't one of my abilities. I've just lived in this house long enough to know what standing there without the fire feels like."

It can't be but like in the upper fifties outside, but cold air feels like it seeps up through the floorboards just enough to make it chilly inside. A quick glance at the clock tells me that it's still a few hours before I normally wake up and still a few more yet before I have to head into work. My brain says run like a madwoman while you can, but there's something niggling inside my chest that keeps me rooted into place. Before I know what is happening, I find myself standing next to the chair.

He cracks an eye and grins at me. It's so comical that I find myself laughing and crawling into his side for warmth. My feet feel like popsicles, and I try not to laugh as I press them against his warm legs.

"Ahhh, damn it woman! You're so cold!" he cries out. Giggles promptly burst from my lips uncontrollably. I can't even stop laughing long enough to catch my breath. It isn't until a different kind of tears than last night roll down my face and I start to warm up a bit that I notice that Zane is fully awake watching me.

It makes me self-conscious, "What?"

"Nothing," he replies a little more gruff than usual. "I've just never seen you laugh like that."

My smile stays in place with strain, "Not much to laugh for anymore."

The gruffness is still in his voice, "Well maybe we can change that."

I can't help the way my gaze drops to his lips. Anyone could see that Zane is a handsome man. His dark brown hair is cut close on the sides with more on top that tends to lie to one side of the other. His honey-colored eyes don't need any light to accent them. They do enough of that all on their own. I can't figure out which one mesmerizes me more, hip lips or his eyes. Letting my own wander down his face, I take in the sharpness of his jawline that leads down into a cleft chin.

With no thought behind it, my fingers find that small groove, "I've never realized you had this." To my defense, it is one of the smallest that I've seen.

He lets out a low hum in the back of his throat that makes my heart skip a beat. The side of his mouth twitches almost as if I'm tickling him. I go to pull my hand away, "Sorry."

His hand strikes out to capture mine. Rubbing my palm across his cheek, he says, "I love the feel of your hands on me."

He's got a five o'clock shadow that does funny things to my stomach as the tiny hairs tickle my palm. Of course, my dirty mind takes me somewhere I'm not sure that I'm ready to be yet. Instead, I settle for pressing my hands against either side of his face. When our lips touch this time, it is all my doing.

You know, I've always wondered why it was a thing to close your eyes while kissing someone. Do you not want to look them in the eye? I never understood until now. Even with all of the other guys that I've kissed, I've never felt these feelings coursing through my body. With my eyes closed, my other senses kick into overdrive. The sound of his breath hits my ears as the speed of it picks up. That masculine scent from the blanket is so strong here that it wraps me up in a cocoon. I must say, however, his taste is my favorite. His tongue begs for access and I don't deny him. This time kissing Zane, I am the one in control. He lets me set the pace, and I take my time exploring. Only once we're both breathless do I pull away. I open my eyes to find him staring at me with wild eyes and a smile on his face. The scrutiny makes me a little uncomfortable, so I lay my head down on his chest and his hands find my hair. I fall back asleep at the feel of his fingers running through it while his warmth surrounds me.

<u>Six</u>

ZANE

The very last thing that I want to do is wake this sweet little witch curled almost on top of me. I spent an hour after she fell asleep thinking about all the things that she had revealed to me last night, before dozing off again. Something doesn't sound quite right about her story. I'm not sure why, but I'm getting a really weird vibe from it. At least I know how to pass my time today while Myra is working. I'm going to make a few phone calls to see what I can find out.

As much as I really don't want to, a glance at the clock says Myra will be late if I don't get her up and moving.

"Myra," I say softly as I run my fingers through that blue hair that I love so much. She snuggles further into me, burying her face into my shirt. Dear gods, she wouldn't make this any harder on a man, would she? I try to angle my lower body away from her. I'd hate to send her running scared again. Even though, her kisses in the hushed hours of this morning say that may very well be the last thing on her mind.

I run my hand up her back in another attempt to rouse her, "Myra. Sweetheart. It's after seven. You'll be late to Caroline's if you don't wake up." Caroline's name does the trick.

She stretches like a cat against me, and I am grateful that I made the decision to angle away from her. When her eyes open, they don't show the confusion they did earlier. She's well aware of where she is. Trying my best to refrain from making the first move with her again, only sets me up for failure. As those ice blue eyes look to me with dreams still in them, I can't help but to lean down and press my lips against hers.

It's short and sweet, but nonetheless satisfying, "Good morning, sweetheart."

She smiles shyly up at me, but doesn't comment on the pet name, "Good morning. Thank you for keeping me warm."

Her eyes spark with mischief and I can't help the laugh that slips from my lips, "Sweetheart, you are more than welcome to crawl under my covers anytime." I'm rewarded with her laugh as she throws the cover back. Counting backwards from three in my head, I wait until she puts her feet on the floor.

"Holy Jack fucking Frost!" she yells, falling back into my lap. My deep laughter earns a scowl from her. "It's hardly funny," she growls at me. "Is it always this cold in your house?"

My laugh dies down and I grin at her, "Most of the time. It's poorly insulated underneath, among other things, so unless I keep the fire blazing, the floorboards feel like the arctic."

She nods in understanding, "What's the other things?"

With her focused on my face, I give her somewhat the truth, "Ghosts." I don't know why I say it. Maybe to gage her reaction and to see if she'll just laugh it off.

Eyebrows sinking as low as her frown, she looks anything but amused or scared even. "Why do you have spirits here?" she asks quietly.

If there is ever going to be anything between us, honesty will have to be first priority, so I admit, "You're not the only one running from something."

At this, her expression turns wary, and then it hits me how bad that sounded. "I haven't killed anyone or anything. I've just pissed off the wrong people in the past." When that doesn't change her frown, I say, "Look, I'll tell you all about it tonight if you'll have dinner with me here."

I expect more hesitation from her, so it shocks me when she outright agrees.

"But only one condition," she says fighting a smile.

"Anything," I tell her seriously.

The smile breaks loose on her face, "You have to get up and get my boots."

I tilt my head back and laugh, "Done." Moving the blanket reveals thick socks covering my feet.

Holding in another chuckle at her mouth hanging open, I hear her mumble something to herself as I grab her shoes and bring them back to her.

"You know what's weird?" she asks as I hand them to her. She doesn't wait for my reply. "I don't even remember taking them off."

I smile down at her, "That's because you didn't. I did."

Her face turns pink, "Well, thank you for that. And everything else really. I've been alone for a while now and I'd almost forgotten what human interaction felt like."

Waiting until she laces up the boots, I pull her to her feet, "No need to thank me, sweetheart. I'm just glad you came to find me." It's my turn to be surprised when she stands on her toes reaching her face up towards mine. Even with the added height of her shoes. I have to lean down to her, and I fucking love it. There's nothing wrong with taller women, but I've never had one push my buttons. Especially not as much as this little firecracker in front of me.

"I have to go," she whispers against my lips.

Nodding, I release her and watch as she makes her way to the door. Just as it creaks on purposely unoiled hinges, I stop her, "Myra." She turns to me.

"What changed your mind about me?" I ask.

The smile she sends me makes me want to pull her back to our little blanket party on the chair and keep her there for the rest of the day. But, it's her words that leave me in an amused speechless state of mind, "It was the cheesecake."

Seven

MYRA

I crash into a wall carrying a basket full of potpourri packs, which end up heaped on the floor. Unfortunately, this isn't the first time that it has happened today. The other times I was lucky enough not to be carrying anything. Rubbing an already forming bruise on the top of my arm, I sigh.

"You okay today?" Caroline asks as she walks by with a grin on her face.

I shrug, "I guess so. Why do you ask?"

"Honey, you're clumsy, but never have I ever worried more about the safety of my store before. That poor wall will never be the same again. Neither will poor Zane," she cackles and walks away leaving me standing gawking at her retreating form.

Should have known that I couldn't squeeze by on that one. Caroline knows everything. Zane. I blame Zane. It's all his fault that I can't seem to not be distracted today. That and his lips. I was shocked beyond all that I've ever known when he kissed me last night. I could seriously spend days wrapped in his arms.

Picking up all of the little baggies and putting them back into the basket, I stand up and run into what feels like another wall. Only, I know that it isn't because I physically feel my magic flinch away as soon as I make contact. I save the basket in the nick of time before it tips over and spills again.

"Oh, excuse me, ma'am," a gravelly voice says. He reaches out to steady me and I flinch back at the same time I look up to find his face. It takes a minute because he's so tall, at least seven foot and wide to boot. His dark hair is laid back on his olive skin and almost black eyes stare back at me. The face gives the impression of a happy man in a moment of contrite embarrassment. Something is way off, though. There's a monster underneath there and it scares the shit out of me. Normal circumstances, I'd run but this is anything but normal. He's not human and I know better than to show a wild animal my back.

I slowly retreat towards the counter where Caroline is checking out a customer. Never taking my eyes from the beast in front of me, I hear the front door chime as the customer leaves.

"Myra? What are you…" she starts then cuts off mid-sentence.

Her voice goes deeper than I've ever heard before, "You are not welcome here." Even if it wasn't the words, I'd know by the tone that she isn't talking to me. I refuse to take my eyes off the stranger. As he takes a step towards us, I back around the corner to stand at Caroline's side.

The smile drops from his face and his true form moves underneath the surface of his skin. I've never been one to be scared of the dark or anything in it, but this stranger is truly terrifying.

I wish he would just leave or that Zane was here. Wait, what? Since when have I ever relied on someone else for my protection?

My inner thoughts are interrupted by a deep raspy sound. It takes a minute before I realize that it is the monster speaking. What shocks me more than anything is Caroline's own voice taking on those same qualities. Holy creepville. This is still the same Caroline. I know she won't hurt me, so I keep my body from flinching away like it so badly wants to do.

Their tones become angry and his face flashes from that of the human to something else again. Just as quickly, his back straightens, a smirk crosses his lips, and he is out the door without another word.

Caroline moves faster than I've ever seen as she zips around the counter to the door. She flips the open sign to closed and engages the locks. Taking an extra second to look outside, she turns back around to face me. I'm sure I've still got the shock written all over my face.

"Come dear. I'm sure you have tons of questions and deserve an explanation," she says walking towards the back of the store. Sitting the basket still clinched in my fingers up on the counter, I follow behind her through the curtain covered in tiny silver stars.

Caroline points to a chair at the round table, "Sit."

In all the times I've been back here, I've avoided this table. There are weird inscriptions all the way around it and through the center. Even standing from a distance, I can feel the magic pouring out at me. I ignore the push I feel against my magic and sit where Caroline pointed. She mumbles to herself as she hurries around the room pulling out glass jars. Once she is satisfied with what's in her hands, she seats herself across from me.

Her hands fly over all the things as she grinds some ingredients and binds the others, "Ask me your questions."

There are two front and foremost in my mind, but I know that when she answers one, it will answer the other, "What was that?"

She places her palms down on the table as she gives me her undivided attention, "That, child, was a demon." Even though I'm expecting it, the answer still leaves me more than a little shell shocked. Before I can say anything, she says, "He wasn't supposed to be here. There are many protections and wards on the shop. I'm not sure how he was able to get in without my noticing him."

I find my voice, "Do you know him?"

At this, she sits back in her chair and stares at me. She looks as though she's debating on how to answer, "I'm not going to lie to you, Myra. Yes, I knew him once. I will not use his name, but on this plane, he goes by Amir."

That name triggers something in my memory, but as quick as it's there, it's gone again. "Wait," I tell her, "Doesn't that mean prince?"

A dark look passes over her face, "That it does. It also means that there can be no lax in these wards."

__Eight__

ZANE

It took me most of the morning and a few favor call ins, but I finally tracked down Myra and her family. All the way to Southern Mississippi. Which is odd because Myra doesn't have any kind of accent at all. Her aunt didn't live too far from her parents either. It's quite apparent, just from the few people that I spoke with, that her upbringing, by far, left something to be desired.

The parents were complete lunatics who had themselves sunk lower than the Titanic in dark magic, which may explain a few things regarding her own magic.

Sitting on the porch waiting for her to come home to me…damn I love the way that sounds. I glance at my watch. She should have been here an hour ago. Just as I get up to head over to Caroline's, my lovely witchy wonder comes into view. A stupid-happy smile crosses my face as I watch her, but it slowly melts away as I notice that she keeps looking over her shoulder. I want to go caveman and beat someone's head into the ground as she makes it to me and I see the fear in her eyes.

I meet her at the bottom of the steps, "Are you okay?"

There's a moment of hesitation before she visibly shakes herself and she smiles up at me, "Yeah. It's good I think." She looks to the light fading in the sky and there's a flash of that same fear, "Can we go inside?"

"Sure. Come on," I tell her wondering what has her spooked so bad.

I lead her into the kitchen where dinner sits already cooked, "Are you hungry?" I ask her.

She nods in reply, and I set about making our plates. I don't fill the air with idle chit chat in hopes of her telling me what happened.

Coming around the island, she takes a big jump up to the counter on my left. She looks so hot sitting there swinging her cute little legs, wrapped in those sexy ass boots. What's a guy to do? I stop with dinner to go stand between her knees. She parts her legs for me, so I am able to go face to face with her. Her arms go around my neck and my hands find the outside of her thighs. I'm fighting the urge to lay her back on this counter and feast on her instead of dinner. Our lips touch and her magic sends a spark through me. It feels like dragging my sock feet over the carpet then touching a metal surface, only through my entire body. I'm sure it's meant as a warning, but my magic ignites in response. Literally. Every candle wick around us blaze to life.

She pulls away and wonder fills her eyes as she looks around, "Why did you do that?"

I grin at her, "Didn't happen on purpose. I think it might have been a ricochet of your magic."

A worried look crosses her face as she chews her bottom lip. Grabbing her chin, I force her to look at me, "It's nothing you did, sweetheart. Simply natural magic, only yours has a default setting of self-destruct."

"I tried to warn you," she whispers closing her eyes.

"Look at me," I tell her. She shakes her head, so I let my voice slip into the authoritative one that I normally save for the bedroom, "Open your eyes, Myra." I try to hide the thrill that her obedience sends directly under the belt, "I made some calls today and what I found out, leads me to a possible theory." I kiss her again before I slip away and go back to the task of dinner.

Sighing loudly, she asks, "Well?"

"Dinner first," I answer.

I hold in my smile at her impatience as she sighs again, "Okay, fine."

Nine

"Is there a reason you're dragging this out as long as possible?" I ask Zane after he's cleaned up after dinner and done everything else but answer my question.

He cuts his eyes to me over his shoulder, "Maybe I just like having you beg."

I feel my face flame first at his words and then the wink that follows. My heart feels like it's going to pump right out of my chest and there's a weird fluttering sensation in my stomach. No one has ever come close to making me feel the way that Zane does, and he's got just the right amount of arrogance to know it too.

As he grabs a dishwasher thingy from under the cabinet, I get a full-on view of his backside. Yeah, there's those flutters again. His body fills those jeans out just right, from his waist and bum, all the way down his legs. He ditched the flannel tonight for a soft grey shirt and I'm having a tough time deciding which I like on him more. The flannel makes him look like a rugged sexy mountain man, whereas the soft tee leaves nothing to the imagination. It hugs tight to a chest and arms that's definitely seen their day in the gym.

Then I realize why I'm able to see his chest so well. He stands propped back against the sink in front of me. I should feel embarrassed to be caught ogling but I'm not. His fingers beat a rhythm against the side of the counter, bringing my attention to the muscles working in his forearms. When I manage to lift my gaze to his, he's grinning down at me.

"Are you ready?" he asks, still smirking.

"Sorry," I say not really sure why I'm apologizing.

He tilts his head back and laughs before he moves to stand in front of me. Twisting my body to face him, I look up to a serious expression. His hands caress the sides of my neck as he steps into my space, "Nothing to be sorry for, sweetheart. I like you checking me out. Does my body meet your approval?"

I smile mischievously, "Meh, it's okay."

"Is that so?" he challenges.

My skin feels like it's on fire as his eyes slowly track down my body.

When his eyes finally make it back to mine, I feel like the wicks from the candles from earlier. Like he's set me on fire.

"Maybe all you need is a little more persuasion," he says slamming his lips down on mine. Forget being on fire, this wild dominant side of Zane has turned me to straight ash. I groan into his mouth as I come to the conclusion that he has pulled a full-blown distraction. The worst part is I don't care, because I don't want him to stop kissing me.

It's a few minutes before he pulls away with a shuddering breath, "Do you want to know what I found out today? Because, if not, I'm okay with moving this to a more comfortable spot in the house."

My brain is on Zane overload. All I want is to take him up on his second offer, but I need to know that information. Especially after what happened today. I shoot him an apologetic smile.

His lust filled expression slowly falls away as he takes my hand, "Let's move to the living room."

Making quick work of it, he soon has us set up on the floor in front of the fireplace. It's fairly warm since the fire has been burning for so long.

Zane's butt has no sooner hit the small pillow and I'm already asking, "How bad is it?"

His eyebrow lifts in question, "Why do you assume that it's something bad?"

"Well, let's see," I say with snark, "You've kept your lips sealed shut all night, so obviously it's not good."

He watches me for a second, "How much do you know about your parents?"

"Umm," I reply, "Not much really. My aunt would never speak of them. There have always been rumors, though."

"What kinds of rumors?" he asks softly.

I close my eyes not wanting to see the condemnation on his face, "That they were doing stuff that is forbidden."

Zane's fingers brush against my jawline and when he doesn't say anything, I open my eyes to find his intense stare.

"Whatever they did, sweetheart, has nothing to do with you. There's a theory with your magic, but that doesn't make you responsible for their bad decisions. Do you understand?"

A pressure falls off of my chest as I realize that he's not going to judge me. I nod to him.

"Good," he says, "I hate to be the one to tell you, but since it's relevant to our current situation I have no choice. Those rumors were true, sweetheart. They were involved in the worst kind of magic. From my sources today, it sounded like the forbidden magics were just the start of it. Do you know how your parents died?"

This one I do know, so I nod again, "It was a house fire."

He returns my nod, "That it was, but what was covered up was the fact that it wasn't a normal house fire. They summoned a demon that night and reneged on a deal."

263

After what happened in Caroline's shop today, his words make my skin crawl. "What happened to it?" I whisper, feeling if I asked any louder it would materialize right in front of us.

At this, he shrugs, "I'm not sure. That would take us digging a little deeper and possibly contacting the other side. I'd rather not go that route. Here's where we come to my theory. I do believe that whatever incantation they used was in some way meant for them to gain your powers, only it bound them instead. That's why all of your spells have gone horribly wrong."

His theory makes sense, but there's just one problem, "Do you know any binding incantations? Or, unbinding I should say."

He nods, "I do, but we'd have to wait until the next full moon, and I would need a lock of their hair.

My hope deflates faster than a balloon in cold air, "But they burnt in the fire." Clearly stating the obvious.

"Very true," he says calmly as if he didn't just offer my magic on a silver platter and rip it away again.

He grabs my hand and kisses the back of it, "Luckily, my theory isn't finished. I think there's a way to get your powers back, but you have to trust me."

Do I trust him? We've been awkward friends for months, but that doesn't mean that I truly know anything about him. I eye him warily, "What were you talking about when I was getting ready to leave this morning?"

Looking to the fire he says, "Almost a year ago, I found my fiancé in bed with a warlock from our coven. The guy started mumbling under his breath like he was going to try some magic on me, and I shut that shit down. Between him sleeping with my fiancé and whatever he was trying to do, I saw red." Zane's face turns regretful, "I beat him up pretty bad. I've spent the last year watching over my shoulder, because you don't piss off the wrong people and just walk away from it. There was a lot of the coven that wanted me stripped of my powers."

I didn't mean for the conversation to turn as dark as it has so I try to change it, "What do you do for a living anyways? I see you around town all hours of the day and you never seem to be working."

He grins like a maniac, "Keeping tabs on me, sweetheart?"

My face goes pink, and I start to defend myself, but he interrupts running a hand through my hair, "I was just kidding. I helped design a software program and an app spawn from that, so most of my work is via the internet and phone."

"Makes sense then," I say closing my eyes at the feel of his hand touching the bare skin between my neck and shoulder. Oh, I see myself getting into so much trouble with this man.

Ten

ZANE

"Oh, there's no way in hell, sir," Myra says rooted in place beside me.

I smile, "I told you that'd you'd have to trust me."

"But this?" she asks incredulously. "I don't see how submerging my body in freezing water, that is probably harboring no telling how many wicked critters. Did you know that I can see the future? That's right. All I see is hypothermia and a snake bite coming from this."

My laugh echoes around the little clearing that we are standing in, "Sweetheart, trust. I just happen to know that these falls harbor more than just hypothermic spring water and snakes. It is one of the last places of pure magic. Can't you feel it calling to you?"

She shrugs and I watch as her doubt turns to misery and starts pulling off the top layer of her clothes, "I swear. If I die, I'm coming back to haunt you."

"I'll take my chances," I smile.

"You could at least come in with me, you know," she says laying the guilt on extra thick.

"What? In there?" I ask, matching her tone from before.

She looks ready to slap me and I find myself more turned on than I've ever been in my life. A super sexy, not to mention exasperated and half clothed, little witch in front of me. Yeah, I'm screwed.

I watch her walk to the edge of the water and I can't help but think of waking up with her in my arms earlier. There couldn't possibly be anything better than that. She's so perfect in every way. Tone in all the right places while soft in others.

"You know, it's probably best to rip it off like a band aid and just jump in," I tease as she toes the water. She throws a look over her shoulder that puts wicked thoughts back into my head. Then she surprises the hell out of me by walking up an outcropping of small rocks before launching herself cannonball style into the water. I chuckle to myself. Honestly wasn't expecting that.

After a few seconds, I start counting. I make it to thirty before I begin to worry.

"Myra? Myra?!" yelling I take off at a dead sprint. What if I was wrong and her magic tried to drown her instead. Nothing matters except getting her out. Baywatch diving into the water, I curse myself for being so stupid. Please be alive. The murky water makes it hard as fuck to see through, so I have no choice but to surface and get my bearings.

"Looking for me?" an amused feminine voice asks from the small rocks. My mouth opens with a pop. She duped me, and I fell for it.

"I'll give you a twenty second head start," I warn.

The words haven't even left my mouth before she's grabbing her clothes and dead sprinting on the short trail that leads back to my cabin.

"One, two, three…"

Eleven

MYRA

Oh shit. I've really done it now. Maybe pushing Zane that far wasn't such a good idea. Even still, I can't help the thrill of excitement that shoots through me at the cat and mouse game that we are now playing. All I know is when he gave me a head start, I took it. Clouds roll in thick in the sky as I streak through the woods in my bra and panties. I'm only halfway to Zane's cabin when the bottom falls out of the sky. The cold rain seeps down to my bones and the wind that has picked up out of nowhere threatens to knock me over at the same time chills rack my body.

I throw myself at the back door of the cabin. Thankfully, Zane left it unlocked. Rushing in, I don't bother to close the door. Zane should be right behind me. My hands shake as pressure builds in my chest. This started out as a fun little game, but something is happening inside of me. *I'm so cold.* The thought barely crosses my mind before the fireplace roars to life. My mouth falls open in shock. A few seconds later a low rumble starts underneath my feet. An earthquake?

The blood rushing through my veins is letting out a low hum and I fear that I'm going to be sick all over Zane's rug. I have to contain my scream as the backdoor slams against the wall. Zane, drenched both from the falls and the rain, marches through.

Holding my palms out beside me, I feel tears streaking down my cheeks, "Zane? What's happening to me?"

His determined steps never falter as he makes his way to me. Without saying a word, he grabs my face and pulls me to him. Our mouths crash together as a bright light fills the room and a clap of thunder rattles the windowpanes. Everything goes silent as his tongue explores my mouth. The only sound I can still hear is the rain beating against the side of the house. My magic reaches out to Zane, and I feel his push back fully dominating mine. Letting go of the last of my reserves, I allow both Zane and his magic to take control.

He must feel the shift, because he growls into my mouth. I gasp as his hands lift me against him so that I'm left with no choice but to wrap my legs around him.

We are moving, but I couldn't honestly care any less as to where we end up. All I know is I can feel him and not just physically, but also on the inside. Only, there's a thin line stopping him from completely consuming me.

My back hits a soft mattress and Zane's scent wafts up from the blanket. I love the way that his body presses down onto me. His mouth moves from mine to a spot underneath my ear that causes another moan to escape me. Grabbing double fist-full of his hair, I hold on for dear life as he makes his way further down.

He moves to my breasts, and I can feel my hardened nipples scratch against the lace of my bra as if begging for special attention. When his mouth closes over the left one, my back arches off the bed and his name comes out as a whisper. This elicits another growl, and he doesn't even bother to unclip my bra. He jerks it over my head like a shirt. My panties follow suit landing somewhere behind him. Lying naked in front of him, I should feel self-conscious of all of my flaws, but it's the exact opposite. The look on his face as he scours my body with his eyes is empowering.

Taking my foot into his palm, he begins a very slow torturous crawl back up my body as he kisses every inch of available skin. When his lips find that sweet center spot of my body, my toes curl as a strangled cry leaves my lips. I grab fistfuls of his hair again, only this time I'm trying to pull him back up to me.

"Zane, please," I whisper, begging.

He makes this 'mmm' sound and it vibrates through me louder than my magic earlier. I don't think anything has ever felt this good, until he slowly works his fingers inside of me. Seeing nothing but stars behind my eyelids, he pushes me to the brink and I almost cry in frustration as he pulls away.

I open my eyes to see his gloriously naked form perched between my legs. My center clenches as he raises his fingers to his lips and sucks them into his mouth.

His eyes never leave mine, "Mmm. You taste just as I thought you would, sweetheart."

All I can manage is another whisper, "Zane."

It must be the final straw for him trying to take it slow. His eyes turn dark, and that wicked fucking growl comes from his mouth. Then one second he is above me and the next his body is pressing me down into the mattress. He enters me in one swift stroke. His movement is so quick, that the tiny barrier inside of me stands no chance against the assault. I cry out again, only this time it's the pain mixed with the pleasure.

"Fuck," Zane says, lying as still as he can on top of me. "Why didn't you tell me, sweetheart?"

The feel of him stretching me so fully like I've never been before leaves me breathless. Somehow, I manage a few words, "Please, don't stop."

Zane's right-hand worries down my side, "I don't want to hurt you, baby."

Something takes ahold of me, and I feel my magic begin to fight back for dominance. This time it's my growl that fills the quiet of the room. I push against his chest and in his shock, I'm actually able to move him. In one swift move, we've traded places with him under me instead. I rock my hips and groan as it fires up those nerve endings again. Zane's warm hands close around my breasts before he rolls my nipples through his fingers and gives them a slight pinch. My back arches pushing further into his hands and my hips rock a few more times in response.

My control begins to slip, and Zane's magic doesn't miss a beat. It folds around me like a blanket. Flipping me over to my stomach, he enters me from behind. Oh. My. God. His alpha attitude and the pace that he sets quickly pushes me right to the edge. I fall right over as I feel his teeth sink into my shoulder. Then he is falling right over after me.

A bright light inside of me flashes quicker than the lightning outside and something snaps like a rubber band. There's a scream, but I can't be sure that it isn't me. For the first time in my life, I feel free. Almost like a weight has been lifted from my chest. The only thing I feel now is my magic that has settled thanks to the blanket Zane's is providing.

When we collapse, it's to my back against his chest. His arm goes around my stomach, and he tucks me closer to his body. I'm vaguely aware of the storm having died down outside. It raged with us all the way through the end. It's now nothing more than a trickle against the window pane. Between that sound and Zane's warmth, I feel his lips against my back and I fall into a deep sleep.

Twelve

ZANE

Rain pounding against the window wakes me. Myra's head is propped against my chest and her arm is thrown across my waist. I would die a happy man if I could wake up every morning just like this, and last night…I knew she would be amazing in bed. I just didn't realize what a little firecracker I actually had on my hands. Add that to the fact that I am her first, and last, if I have anything to say about it, I am certainly the luckiest bastard in the world.

I feel pretty horrible about passing out last night and not cleaning her up. It was impossible to stay awake after the beating my magic took from Myra's. On the one hand, my theory worked. Her magic is now unbound from the forces that were holding it. On the other hand, from being caged for so long it was all over the place, causing all of the crazy weather and even an earthquake. The other downside is that I felt someone else with us last night. I heard it scream as their tether broke to Myra. I just hope that whoever or whatever it was is long gone now. She may not like it, but whatever curse she was under may never go away. She got her magic back, but I'd bet fifty bucks that the binding spell left her connected to one of her parents. Either way, whoever it was is not happy right now and in turn she is now bound to me. I'm more than happy with this development. I just don't want her to feel like I handed her freedom and snatched it away again. We're going to have to talk about it as soon as possible.

Her breathing changes and I watch as she stretches sleepily before looking up to me, "Good morning."

I brush my thumb across her cheekbone, "Good morning, sweetheart. Are you feeling okay?"

She hesitates for a few seconds as if she's taking stock of everything then smiles up to me, "Better than okay. Thank you for last night."

It may have started as an innocent thanks, but she blushes at the end letting me know that she means everything.

Tilting her chin up, I place a lingering kiss on her lips, "You're most welcome and thank you. Ready to start the day?" She nods and I pull us both up to our feet, "Bath or shower?"

Her face turns pink, "If I say shower, will you join me?"

I grin, "You read my mind, sweetheart."

A little while later, after a scalding hot shower and a round of smoking hot sex against the wall, I flip bacon over in the frying pan in front of me.

Arms snake around my middle, "A girl could really get used to being spoiled like this, you know?"

I grin like a fool, "That's what I'm aiming for."

She laughs and swats my ass before making her way over to the coffee pot. I left her favorite creamer out on the counter beside her cup and it doesn't go unnoticed.

"Thank you," she says walking to me for a quick kiss. I love the smell of coffee on her breath. Between that and the scent of my soap covering her, makes me want to say, 'Fuck breakfast' and take her on the counter instead. A drop of grease pops me in the arm. Shit. I rub the spot and flip the switch to turn it off. Moving the bacon over to the other plates in front of Myra, I take a seat across from her. There are several things that we need to talk about this morning, but I'm going to let her get some food in her belly first.

Leaning back in her seat, she looks at me over her cup of coffee, "Thank you for breakfast."

I nod to her as I sip at my own cup, wondering which of the subjects is safer to start with, "What would you say if I asked you to move in with me?" She goes to open her mouth, but I hold up my palm, "Just wait. I still want you to keep your job at Caroline's and everything. It just doesn't sit right with me to have you over at your apartment where I can't protect you."

"But we still don't know about my magic, and I need to tell you about something that happened yesterday," she admits sheepishly. I nod at her to continue. "A demon came into the shop yesterday."

I want to shake her and Caroline both for not telling me sooner, but instead I say, "What happened?"

She shrugs, "Nothing big. He was just there. He and Caroline had a conversation in a weird language, and he left. She did some cleansing rituals on the store that she said would strengthen the wards."

"That's really good," I say trying to contain my rage at the fact a fucking demon was so close to her and I had no idea, "Please tell me sooner next time if something like this happens. From now on I'll walk you to and from work. And I'm really hoping you will make things easier for me and just say yes to my other question."

I see a wicked gleam in her eyes, and I know she's making me wait on purpose. After a minute or so she says, "Okay."

She's lucky that there are other subjects on the table, otherwise I'd have her over my knee for that.

"There's something else, sweetheart," I start. Her slim eyebrow pulls up in question, so I spit it out, "Okay, so I know you've felt that crazy influx from your powers. Hopefully, it will settle down in a couple of days. They were bound to something, but it's gone now."

She nods, "I felt it last night, heard it scream actually."

"Me too," I admit. "You're no longer bound to it. I wish I could say that you are completely free, but your powers have been bound for so long that they were out of control last night. The only way to help you was to bind them to mine so I could help you control them."

She looks at me with a serious expressions that I'm sure is for my own safety than anything, "So I'm bound to you now?"

"Yes and no," I say. "It's not like before. Your magic is yours. The curse has been lifted so all spells shouldn't backfire. But your magic is leaning on mine for a crutch right now. Does that make sense?"

She nods and I say, "When or if you're ready, we can always try to remove it."

Spinning her coffee cup in front of her she says, "That's good, honestly. I couldn't do anything against them last night. I've never felt so out of control. I'm just really freaking out over this demon."

I open my mouth to respond and a loud thump echoes through the house. She just about jumps out of her skin, and I have to fight my smile. "It's just the paper, sweetheart."

Her face turns red, "Sorry, I'm just a little jumpy. I'll get it."

I watch as she carries her mug through the doorway, shaking her head and mumbling to herself about being a scaredy cat. The front door opens and the next thing I hear is her mug shattering against the floor. Thinking the worst, I come so quick around the counter that I bang my hip on the corner.

She is standing there looking down at the mat. I limp over to her and when I touch her lower back, she jumps back and screams.

I pull her into my arms, "You're okay, sweetheart. What is it?"

Her hand shakes as she points to the paper lying on the doorstep, "That's him. That's the guy that was in the shop."

I let her go long enough to pick up the paper. Front line reads 'Man Claims Blackout of Memory for Slain Family'. This isn't good. Reading the rest of the article, all signs point to him being possessed. The only problem now is, if it's not with him anymore, where the hell is it?

<u>Thirteen</u>

MYRA

For the next week, I spend my time either at the shop or with Zane. I must admit, the latter is more fun, even if I did have my reservations with him at first. There's just something about the way that he is with me. He doesn't treat me like I'm as fragile as an egg or like a spoiled one that's just a ticking time bomb waiting to happen. I don't think that I'm even close to saying the 'L' word, but I know that I could see myself getting there with him.

Between the magic practice, late nights in the sheets and the constantly looking over my shoulder, I am exhausted. Which of course means that I am extra clumsy and why Caroline sends me home telling me to get some rest.

It's only lunch time and Zane isn't due to be here until I get off tonight. Surely, I'll be okay enough to run down to the store real quick and grab some groceries for dinner. It would be nice to cook him dinner for a change. Even if he'll probably end up taking over anyways, because he's more dominant in the kitchen than in the bedroom. That thought has me putting a little more pep in my step to hurry.

I walk through the tiny little market and stuff my basket full of things that I'll need to make chicken alfredo. It's one of the few dishes that I know I'm damn good at. As I make it to the meat section in the back of the store, a tingle goes up my spine and not the good kind either. Freezing my movements, I try to be nonchalant about scanning the mirrors in the corners of the store. From what I can see, there's only me and one other person in here. He isn't doing anything threatening, but his build and biker gear do enough on their own.

Grabbing a pack of chicken, I make my way up towards the register where the only other person in the store is supposed to be. I get about halfway down the aisle and a little old lady pushing a shopping cart comes around the corner of the next one over. Weird. I didn't even notice that she was in here.

She looks at me with a sweet smile and I return it. As she passes, I want to warn her about the biker guy, but what do I say. I'd look like an idiot accusing someone for doing nothing, so I don't say anything. At the last second, she reaches out and grabs ahold of my arm causing me to drop the basket in my hands.

I reach out for her thinking that she slipped and needed me to catch her fall. When I look at her face, I know otherwise. Those eyes have haunted my dreams for the past week. Just as I suck in a breath to speak or scream, my brain hasn't decided which, a thick muscled arm reaches out and smacks the old lady's arm away from me.

It's the biker. He mumbles a few words under his breath that sound like a lot of hissing noises and she collapses and falls right into his arms. Turning to me, with a voice deeper than a grave, he says, "You need to run along now little witch. I don't know what you've done to piss that demon off, but he'll be back and he won't be happy. Make you some talismans or if you can't, go see Caroline a couple of blocks over. She'll be able to help you."

He lays the woman on the ground and checks for a pulse. I want to ask him more about the demon, but I don't want to press my luck. Picking up my basket, I make my way to the register.

Once I make it to Zane's house and explain what happened, to say that he's pissed would be an understatement.

"You can't be running off without me right now, sweetheart," he chastises. "I couldn't find out anything more on the demon or why he's taken an interest in you, so I need you to stick close right now. Even if that means not going to work until we figure this out."

He drops the subject quickly when I say, "I'm not leaving Caroline stranded with no one to help her. I'll go back and stay at my place before that happens."

We spend hours into the late night going through old books that Zane has stashed on a bookshelf in his closet. When I ask him why he would keep books in the closet like a dirty little secret, he tells me that these books are a secret, and I can see why. The very first book I pick up talks about reanimating a corpse, or necromancy as it's called in our world. It's one of those taboo no-no's that everyone is scared to even talk about. The book gives me chills just flipping through the pages. I tuck it underneath several others spread out on the floor, so I don't have to look at it anymore.

"I need a break," I tell Zane standing up to stretch. He nods and makes a mmhmm sound, but he's hunched over and completely submerged in a book that looks to be a hundred years old.

The wine that we had with dinner added to the warmth of reading by the fire with Zane makes me feel drowsy. It's only around eight, so I go to the kitchen to make a pot of coffee in hopes that it'll keep me awake.

Zane's voice startles me so bad that I almost drop the box of k-cup coffees, "I think I found him."

He sets the book down on the counter beside me, "There's only mention of him right here on this page, but it's enough and it's not good."

His phone vibrates on the counter, and he leans over to look at the screen. The number says Alexandria, Kentucky.

"Who is it?" I ask.

He shrugs and answers, "Hello?"

There's a woman's voice on the other end of the line and whatever she says has him motioning for me to wait a second. I try not to listen, but the mention of vampires peaks my interest. I've known they existed, but I've never met one. By the way Zane is talking, he knows one personally. A local club owner, Kyran or something. I wonder if I could get him to introduce us one day, or that might be awkward, 'Hi, I wanted to meet you because you suck people's blood.'

"Hello?" Zane says snapping his fingers in front of my face, "Earth to Myra."

I shake my head, "Sorry. I'm back."

He smiles down at me, but it's quickly lost with his next words, "Okay, so back to the demon. I'm glad Caroline told you part of his name. One of my ancestors apparently had a run in with him." He points to the page where a crude drawing of a half-man, half-bull is drawn. I look away and pretend to be focusing on starting the coffee so that I don't have to look at the page.

"My great great great Uncle John was a bad warlock, known for his dealings in dark magics. Everyone turned a blind eye to him, until one day when his niece came up missing. When they finally found her, it was too late. Uncle John summoned this very demon and used her to do it. He requires a blood sacrifice, only it's the soul he's after not the blood," he tells me.

"So does that mean that he's after you, because he already has dealings with your family?" I ask.

I can tell by the look on his face that his answer won't be good, "Not exactly, sweetheart. I'm pretty sure that he was summoned the night that your parent's died. If I had to guess, I'd say that he's the reason they did. Only, instead of going back to hell where he belongs, he attached himself to you somehow. I believe that he was the binding on your powers. He fed off of them for years and now that he's free, he has all of that to keep him fueled. At least for a little while anyways."

My heart races a million miles a minute, "Does it say in there how to stop him?"

He shakes his head and I try my best to not feel defeated, "Myra, look at me."

When I do as he says, he lifts my chin and gives me a kiss on the lips, "You're not alone anymore, sweetheart. I'll do everything within my power to make sure that we send it back to hell where it belongs."

The only thing I fear is it dragging one of us back with it this time.

Fourteen

ZANE

I'd like to say that life is damn near perfect. I get to go to sleep holding Myra every night and wake up next to her beautiful face every morning. The only thing hanging over our heads is this demon thing. I didn't want to tell her last night, but she's been kept in the dark for more than enough of her life and I'm not keeping it from her.

Between the demon and that phone call that I got last night, I'd say that things are going to start going to hell in a fucking hand basket fast around here. No one just randomly calls and asks for a vampire prince for no reason. I'd normally tell them to stick it where the sun doesn't shine, especially considering he's not one of the bad ones, but I had to share it or go against witch code. Being this close to the falls on a ley line, has it's perks for trying to get Myra's magic up to par, but it also brings in the crazy shit. I wonder if I can convince her to move away from here. I'm not one for being a coward and running, but it's not about just me anymore. I'll do anything it takes to keep her safe.

When I walk her to work this morning, I pull Caroline aside and tell her my assumptions for the demon's attention and about the prince of darkness. She isn't happy about either but promises to keep Myra safe. It lifts some weight off my shoulders. The devil himself would be insane for messing with the likes of Caroline's kind.

With all of my work being internet bound, I have the time to run errands all day. I find myself not wanting to stray too far from the shop just in case. Eventually, I finish everything I need to do and still have a few hours to kill. Deciding to set up in a coffee shop and knock out some stuff I've been procrastinating, I head home to pick up my laptop.

It takes me about a second too late to realize that something is wrong inside the cabin. A warm hand closes around my neck and I'm shoved to the floor. I try to flip back over to see who it is, even though I've got a pretty good idea, but my attacker is sitting on top of me with a knee in my back.

His breath fans out over my face and smells like rotten eggs as he says, "You should have just stayed away."

"I won't let you have her," I say with what little breath I have in my lungs.

The sulfur smell washes over me again as he laughs, "I can smell your fear warlock. Your wards here in the house weren't strong enough to stop me and neither are you."

Something crashes into the back of my head and I can do nothing. My last thought is of Myra as darkness consumes me.

<u>Fifteen</u>

Distractions are against me today as I knock over yet another display in the shop. At least this one is only potholders and hand towels. I broke a few glass figurines on the one earlier.

"Girl, if I didn't know any better, I'd say that you were doing this on purpose, so I'd send you home," Caroline says with a smile.

I wince and apologize for at least the tenth time today, "I'm really sorry. I swear I'm not doing this on purpose. I just don't feel too good Caroline."

"Well, you're not pregnant, so talk to me and tell me what you're feeling," she says.

My mouth makes a popping noise as her words take me by surprise, "You can tell that?"

She shrugs, "One of my many abilities. Now, back to you not feeling well…"

"I don't know," I say wringing my hands. "There's a pressure kind of sitting on my chest and it feels like it's trying to suffocate me."

Her face turns to worry, "I need you to do me a favor and close your eyes."

Without any questions, I do as she says. Something fans against my face and I smell the scent of one of her incense sticks that she uses in the back part of the shop. I haven't even taken a full deep breath of it, before I feel it. Panic and it's not mine. Zane.

Caroline's hand closes around my upper arm to keep me still long enough for her to ask, "What is it?"

I only say one word. It's all that's needed to set us both in motion, "Zane."

Taking off at a dead sprint out of the shop, I couldn't possibly care any less if I trip and fall on my face. All I can think about is something is wrong and what if I don't get there in time.

When I finally make it over to the cabin, I see smoke pillowing out from the windows and it sends me into even more panic. Zane is in there and I know it. Not bothering to wait for any emergency crews or even for Caroline to catch up, I rush up the stairs and in through the front door.

The air is already so smoky that it makes it hard to see and I have to pull up the top of my shirt hem to cover my mouth as I call out, "Zane?"

A weird shuffling noise comes from his room, and I make my way in there carefully. The nob burns my hand when I turn it, but I'll be damned if I don't try to get him out.

I kick the door right underneath the handle and flinch away just in case. More black smoke billows out. Once it clears enough to see, the sight laid out before me makes me want to throw up.

Zane is face down on the floor with his hands and feet tied behind him while the room is on fire like the inside of a furnace. Standing over him is the demon in what must be his true form. I'd love to say that I'm not scared, but I am. More so than that, though, I'm pissed. Zane is an innocent bystander in this whole mess and his death will be on my hands if I can't think of some way out of this.

He stirs on the floor, and I see a puddle of blood underneath his head. His eyes find mine and he starts moving around trying to stand up. The demon reaches down and grabs him by the back of the neck and pulls him to his knees. When he speaks, it's English, but hard to understand, "We can do this the easy way or we can do it the hard way. You willingly hand yourself and your powers back over to me and I'll set him free. Don't and I'll bleed him slowly while you watch."

There's no way in hell that he's letting Zane walk out of here no matter what I do or don't do. I feel my magic shift under my skin and the demon must feel it too, "Don't try anything witch. I'll slit his throat and take you willing or not."

Zane tries to mumble something around the gag that's in his mouth and the demon materializes a dagger in his hand. I scream as he runs Zane through with it. There's a spot of red on his shirt that gets bigger by the second. I look to the demon, but all I see is the red. My powers ripple out away from my body trying in vain to search for our saving grace. It latches on to a pipe running underneath the house. I pull with all that's in me and feel it burst as it rushes up through the floor boards. The fire hisses as the water begins to put it out. The demon growls right before I feel another presence behind me.

I'm not sure how I know it's Caroline, but I step out of the way to make room for her. She says something under her breath and a bright light fills the room. I let my magic keep the water flowing to finish with the fire, even if I can't see anything. The only thing I can make out is a ball of light hovering directly over Zane's body. After a few seconds, it moves over to the demon who's frozen in place somehow. The next thing I know, I hear the demon scream as it did before when he was ripped from me. A blast throws me back against the wall and breaks my connection with the magic. At least the fire is out for now.

I look around to see no sign of Caroline or the demon. Zane stirs on the floor, and I crawl over on my hands and knees. The bindings are gone from around his wrists and legs, but more than anything, the blood is missing from the front of his shirt. There's no way I imagined that dagger. I lift up the bottom hem and inspect his shoulder just to confirm for myself.

Zane's chest rumbles underneath me, "After everything, the first thing you want to do is strip my clothes off?"

A relieved half laugh, half cry falls from my lips and I throw my arms around his neck. I press my lips against his as I feel warm tears trekking down my cheeks.

"What happened?" he asks sitting up.

I wipe away the tears on my face and shrug, "I have no idea. Caroline and the demon were here one second and the next there was this bright white light, and they were both gone. Oh, and it healed you where he stabbed you."

"Yeah, I remember that part," he says rubbing the spot on his shoulder. "I just can't recall what happened after. You said Caroline was here?"

When I nod he says, "Okay, that makes sense then."

"What does?" I ask.

He shakes his head without answering my question, "I think it's time that we talked to the Arbiter."

That gives me pause, "Who?"

About the Author

Brandy Slaven lives in Tennessee with her husband and two wild children. If you can't find her creating worlds with her words, you will find her with her nose in a book at the beach or hiking at a state park.

Also By Brandy Slaven

Other Books By This Author

Omegaverse

Building My Pack

White Trash Trilogy

Reviving Kendall

Refusing Kendall

Reclaiming Kendall

VanPelts: A White Trash Trilogy Prequel

Logan: A White Trash Trilogy Novella

Lady of Darkness Series

Of Death And Darkness

In Dreams Of Despair

Divinely Damned Series

The Arbiter

AntiLove Bookclub Series

Love Bitters

Love Starves

New Year Surprises: An ALBS Novella

Saga of Evanescent Realms

Sunken Empire

Standalones

Identity: A Villainously Romantic Retelling

Sidra

Zombie Queen

Burying Blayke: An Underground Omega Syndicate Novel

Bewitched

(Prologue)

Fated Book One (excerpt)

Kelly Moran

This excerpt is a work of fiction. Names, characters, places, and incidents either are the product of the author's imagination or are used fictitiously, and any resemblance to actual persons living or dead, business establishments, events, or locales, is entirely coincidental.

Content Warning: Not intended for persons under the age of 18.

1718: Puritan Island, Royal Province of Massachusetts Bay

"The villagers are coming. We must hurry, dear sister."

Celeste Galloway, with a heavy heart, tore her gaze away from her one-day-old babe nursing at her breast to peer into the hearth's flames. Using strength from within, she pulled magick from her core and channeled the elements. Heat wrapped around her, teased the hair off her nape. Her sluggish, foggy mind parted and the vision became clear.

The villagers were, indeed, afoot. However, they weren't yet at the forest edge or near her little stone cottage in the clearing. She had time to prepare, but not much.

Gently, she swaddled the baby she'd named Hope, and rose to set her on the straw pallet by the fire. Her body ached from rigorous birthing, but she relished the pain. From agony came love, even though it had been love's betrayal that had set them on this course.

With a kiss to her daughter's sleepy brow, Celeste chanted a protection spell and faced her sister, Mara. Blessedly, they looked similar in coloring and stature. Characteristics and the enchantment would keep both her daughter and sister protected.

Mara twisted her fingers. "We have to prepare for the journey."

"No." Celeste took her sister's shoulders, remembering the long travel aboard the ship from Ireland, all the illness, the death. Their own Ma and Da hadn't survived. But, Mara would thrive and so would the baby. Celeste would see to that. "You are to stay with Hope."

Mara's blue eyes, the same shade as Celeste's, widened in fear. "They'll kill us both. And what of you?"

"They're coming for me, not you. And I will let them."

Tears dampened Mara's pale lashes as she trembled. "No, you mustn't."

"Aye. It is what the Fates deem." Celeste had seen the future, all the outcomes, and had meditated long nights. This was the only way. "From this day forth, you will mature until your sixtieth year, then you will age no more until the cycle has come to pass. You will watch over our heirs, their heirs, and protect them. Promise me this. Vow to me."

"I...don't understand."

Time was short, but Celeste drew upon patience. "I put a potion in your tea, love." Much magick had been conjured to create it and had left her weak for two fortnights while she'd still been with child. "You, Mara, will forever be the Galloway protector. And when the curse is broken, we will be reunited in the afterlife."

Mara fretted. "What curse? You do not make sense."

Straightening, Celeste glanced at Hope. "The curse I'm to cast this eve. The Meath Clan has turned the settlers against us, have instilled fear in their hearts. They know I'm a witch, but they do not know you practice. Keep secret, and all will be well."

Blessed be, Hope didn't resemble her father. She'd come out of Celeste's womb looking just like her ma. That would protect her from the Meath Clan, as well. They wouldn't suspect she was one of them, conceived from a forbidden passion. A love that was doomed to end the moment criers had outed Celeste and Finn to his father. The puritan minister was intolerable to change of any kind and had been on a witch hunt since his rise to power. Fear and hysteria held the villagers ears and, hence, Celeste's time on this plane was dwindling.

"Come, gather the boxes we fashioned."

At the table, Celeste took a quill and dipped it in the inkwell. Quickly, she scrawled the spell she'd perfected in her mind while Mara gathered the three small pine boxes no larger than her hand and set them beside her. Spell completed, Celeste ripped the parchment into three sections and laid them each in their respective boxes. Removing three of her rings, she placed one in each, as well—a sapphire, an emerald, and a ruby, all having the pentacle of their craft etched in the band underneath the gem so it was visible through the stone. The heirlooms had come from their homeland and had been passed down for three generations.

Securing the lids, Celeste closed her eyes. White heat and light poured from her hands as she called upon her magick. Hands hovering over the first box, she whispered the incantation, then moved on to the other two. When finished, she waited, and moments passed. Then, a trinity knot emerged onto each of the lids, searing into the wood and creating a yellow glow before dimming.

"It is done." Celeste nodded, her heart pounding. She set each of the boxes on the floor in front of the hearth in a neat row and used an incantation to hide them from this plane until they were needed some distant day. "Fetch the grimoire, love."

Confusion marring her brow, Mara scurried to the sleeping pallet and lifted the corner. Prying the floorboard loose, she pushed it aside and removed their family's leather-bound book brought over from Ireland. It had been blank on the journey, but was now partially full with spells and potions Celeste had achieved with success.

Mara placed the heavy volume on the table. "Tell me your plans. I'm frightened."

Remorse clutched Celeste's chest. She hadn't expected this all to be happening tonight. She'd known the end was nearing, but not that it was here.

Cupping Mara's pale cheeks, Celeste looked at her flame red hair so like her own and gazed into her younger sister's wide eyes. "I know you're scared. Let me finish my tasks, as this is of great importance. I promise you, all will be well."

Turning to the table, she drew breath and closed her eyes once more. Hands outstretched over the grimoire, she channeled magick, having to pull more from her fading reserve. Weak from all the spells and childbirth, she fought dizziness and focused.

Light and heat radiated down her arms to her fingertips. Whispering the incantation for protection, she added a spell for longevity, too. When her eyes opened, a trinity knot was seared into the leather cover just below the pentagram.

Wiping her damp brow with her forearm, Celeste slumped into a chair. "Put the grimoire away, love, would you? I'm spent."

Mara, always dutiful, did as she was told and then knelt by Celeste's feet. "I beg you. Tell me of your plans. They are coming for you as we speak."

"I know." Celeste ran her fingertips through her sister's soft, wild hair. They'd buried Mara's husband of only a year just a week ago. Poor, dear Mara would be tasked with such a great burden.

"You will raise Hope as your own. No," she said as Mara tried to object. "You must, to keep her safe. A recent widow, they will not suspect you as her ma." Their cottage was isolated from the village and most left them to be. It had been easy to hide Celeste's condition. "For me, do this."

Tearfully, Mara nodded and tightly clasped Celeste's hands. "Where will you go?"

"Nowhere, love. I will let them come."

"No! Please, do not—"

"Aye. It's in the Fates." Celeste brushed Mara's tears. "Raise my daughter as your own and teach her our craft. Every generation must learn from you, the truth and our ways. Never let them forget where they come from, their history." She pressed her lips together, fighting the pressure behind her breasts. "When the time comes, the curse I am to cast will be lifted, the boxes revealed. The path is set, forged in love."

"I can't bear this burden without you." Mara's chest hitched with a sob. "Don't leave me."

Tears burning Celeste's eyes, she gazed at her sister, wishing hate and love weren't such a fine thread of difference. "I must, but you are strong. I have faith in you."

Sniffing, she closed her eyes for a moment to gather herself. "Hide the grimoire, keep it protected always. Have my child, her children and thus forth, build upon what I started. After they've taken me and I'm gone, write my last words in the book. Don't let them forget what was done to me."

Gathering Mara to her, Celeste held her sister one last time and soothed her as she wept. When she'd calmed, Celeste drew away and rose. Warning knells shot up her spine, wove around her heart.

The villagers were nearly here.

Swiftly, she moved to Hope and knelt by her precious little one. Taking her tiny hand in hers, Celeste grazed her fingertip over Hope's inner wrist and chanted. The babe fussed a bit as the trinity knot she'd conjured branded her skin, but Celeste cooed and sent her pain away with a flick of her hand.

284

"I love you, my daughter, my life." She kissed her brow, leaving wet tracks upon her baby's cheeks. "Blessed be."

Shouts rose from outside, and Mara shot to her feet. Panicked, she glanced wide-eyed at the door and then Celeste.

"Let them come. Remember my instructions and let them come."

The door burst inward and wood splintered. Minister Gregory Meath stood outside the threshold in his black robes, a crucifix in his outstretched hand. Behind him were villagers, a hundred of them, at least, their faces angry and frightened. Torches illuminated the cool darkness.

Her baby cried, and Mara rushed to pick her up, holding Hope against her bosom.

Slowly, Celeste rose to her feet and stepped forward. Nerves wrought, she waited.

"You have been charged with witchcraft, Miss Galloway. What say you?" Shaking with fury, Minister Meath glared at her through green eyes the same shade as her dear Finn's, his black hair just as thick and beautiful. But there was no adoration or acceptance in the minister's eyes like she'd gazed upon so many times with his son. "Speak, witch."

She drew a breath for courage. "I do not refute your claim. I, and I alone, have practiced the art of magick."

"Celeste, no." Finn shoved past his father and gripped her arms. Such a handsome boyish face of twenty, but he'd grow even more into a man soon. "Deny their accusations. Let them try you."

Her life, her one true mate, stared pleadingly into her eyes. But their love wasn't meant to last. Their destiny was to come together to bear a child and lay the path. They'd accomplished that. Nothing else could be done now. If the villagers put her on trial, they'd only find her guilty. It would make his agony worse. Draw it out.

Forcing her anger at their unforgiving circumstances aside, she removed his hands from her shoulders and kissed them. "Do not let them taint what we had, my love."

"Step away from her, lest she cast another spell on you, boy." Minister Meath grabbed Finn by his arm and dragged him outside. Finn fought and wailed, but villagers held him. "Celeste Galloway, you are sentenced to death." He turned to his son when Finn screamed. "When she is dead, you will be free from her devil's hold and you shall understand. This is through no fault of your own, boy. She is evil in the flesh."

Heart breaking, Celeste stepped forward.

Minister Meath seized her elbow and led her. The new moon made sight difficult, but torches chased the shadows. Villagers bound her wrists and ankles with rope, the coarse threads abrading her skin. Rocks scraped the soles of her bare feet. Cold from the damp spring earth sent a shudder through her bones.

Mara called her name. From the doorway, she wept, pressing a hand to her quivering lips and holding a crying Hope with the other.

"Is the child yours, witch?" Minister Meath glared from Celeste to the baby.

Panic gripped her. "No. Her name is Hope and she is Mara's. My sister was with child after she wed her husband."

Minister Meath eyed Mara. "Does she speak the truth?"

Whimpering, Mara nodded. "Yes. The baby is mine."

"Very well."

Celeste looked at her sister one last time. "Don't let them forget. Blessed be."

They dragged her across the clearing and to the cliffs, where a post waited around a pyre of branches. Fear stole her breath and froze her limbs. They wouldn't be hanging her this night. They'd *burn* her.

Frantic, she closed her eyes, shaking against a gale as it whipped her gown and hair. As they bound her to the post with iron shackles, she recalled every sweet kiss and embrace with Finn, the feel of Hope's soft skin against her cheek. To keep herself calm, she breathed in the salt-scented air from the unforgiving ocean and pine from the nearby forest. Roar of the tide crashed against rocks and wind whistled.

"Have you any last words, witch?"

Celeste opened her eyes and met Minister Meath's scornful, righteous glare. She had to complete her mission or all her preparations would be for naught. Somehow, she must find the courage.

"Yes." Tilting her face toward the inky sky, she channeled the spell she'd written and pushed into Mara's mind so her sister could document her words.

"In this the darkest night, I bring about a curse to life. Love has been stolen because of hate, and in this act, they have sealed their fate. Until three-by-three shall walk this earth, these two families will forever search. No love will last or ever be found. In this I seal, in this they're bound. Upon when three sets of eyes of green are born alongside blue of the brightest morn, only then will the Fated see the secrets I have hidden from thee. Three tasks await to set the cursed free." She brought her gaze to the minister, whose face had gone ashen. "As I will, so mote it be."

Gasps were muttered and bellows howled, but Celeste held onto her power and cast it out. Light poured from her into the night, rippling over the bluffs, the forest, the village, and straight through to the other side of the island. She struggled to hold onto the magick long enough to saturate the ground and souls on it, then she slumped against the pole. Drained, she heaved air.

"Torch the pyre." Minister Meath clasped Finn by the back of his neck and forced him to face Celeste. Eyes red, tears streaming from his eyes, Finn's tormented gaze met hers. "Watch your witch burn. Let this be a lesson to all. Evil has no place here. We will smite darkness in the name of Him Almighty."

She held Finn's gaze a moment more, mouthed *I love you*, then pinched her lids closed as the kindling caught fire.

Read the rest of the epic book, *Bewitched* by Kelly Moran, today!

ABOUT THE AUTHOR:

Kelly Moran is an international bestselling author of enchanting ever-afters. She gets her ideas from everyone and everything around her and there's always a book playing out in her head. No one who knows her bats an eyelash when she talks to herself. She is a RITA® Finalist, RONE Award-Winner, Catherine Award-Winner, Reader's Choice Finalist, Holt Medallion Finalist, Book Excellence Award Finalist, and landed on the "Must Read" & "10 Best Reads" lists at USA TODAY's Lifestyle blog. She is a former Romance Writers of America® member, where she was an Award of Excellence Finalist. Her books have foreign translation rights in Germany (where she is a Spiegel Bestseller), the Czech Republic, Romania, and the Netherlands. Her interests include: scary movies, all kinds of art, driving others insane, and sleeping when she can. She is a closet coffee junkie and chocoholic. Tell no one. She's originally from Wisconsin, but she resides in South Carolina with her significant other, her three sons, their wily dog, and their sassy cats. She also writes haunting page-turners as Kelly Covic. She loves hearing from her readers. FOLLOW HER HERE.

She is His

Marcie Shumway

Chapter 1 ~ Planning

"Remind me again why I continue to do this every year," I huffed to my best friend as I checked another item off the list on the tablet in my hand.

She laughed.

"Because it reminds you of how you met your husband," she pointed out with a gleeful smile.

My best friend, Gabby Adams, wasn't wrong. It was a homage of sorts to how we'd "accidently" come together and eventually admitted how we felt. A shiver ran up my spine at the thought of the events of that night.

Another laugh from beside me.

I rolled my eyes at her, and she shook her head sending her long deep brown waves dancing. She was as tall and thin as I was short and curvy. My blonde locks complimented her brown ones, and my green eyes twinkled along with her blue ones. Our personalities also couldn't be more different, mine quiet and reserved to her outgoing and bubbly one. We were Thelma and Louise.

"What's next?" she questioned, taking a sip from the coffee cup in her hand and letting out a low moan of pleasure from the taste.

"We got the catering squared away, linens, tables and chairs, DJ, and decorations," I rattled off going down my checklist. "All that is left are costumes."

"Yes!!!! My favorite part!" she exclaimed.

This time it was my turn to laugh. Her excitement was contagious and honestly, it was my favorite part too. I tucked my tablet into my purse, grabbed my coffee, and the two of us got out of my Jeep. The cold Maine October air sliced through my jacket, and I picked up my pace to the front of the store.

The jingle from above the door when it was opened and the warmth inside made me smile. This was one of my favorite shops and one of the state's unknown secrets. Gabby and I's kindergarten teacher had decided that she wanted to open a clothing boutique when she retired, and her husband had obliged her. It was a sweet shop with a little bit of everything. One of the best parts about it, in my opinion, was that her lingerie section would change depending on the season and holiday.

"Hello girls!" Mrs. Palmer sang out as she came from the back of the store, her skirts swishing.

As long as I'd known her, she'd worn long skirts. They ranged from bright happy colors to dark brooding ones. It was almost like they depicted her mood. Today, they were a deep purple with white polka dots and a tight white blouse. Purple circles hung from her ears and a white one from her neck. Her smile was big.

"Hi!" Gabby and I greeted her.

"It must be costume time."

"That it is," I told her.

She grabbed my free hand and led us both to the back of the shop. The lingerie section was littered with black and deep purples and reds. I smiled. Halloween colors. We passed the lace and moved to a small portion of the back that was filled with costumes. She gestured for Gabby to look around but continued to lead me. I shrugged at my friend and followed Mrs. Palmer to the dressing rooms.

Once there, she pointed a finger at the first one. I followed her gaze and it landed on something hung against the wall. All I could make out was a black corset top with deep red accents and black lace. Knee high boots leaned up against the bench below. I turned and raised an eyebrow at her, my lips tipping at the corners.

"It was meant for you," she whispered, squeezing my hand briefly.

She released me and whipped away to go back to the front to help Gabby. I stepped into the dressing room and closed the door behind me. Putting my purse and coffee down on the bench, I admired the outfit. It was sexy with a witchy tone to it, just what I was looking for. There was a mask dangling from the hanger as well. Perfect.

I stripped and with my back to the mirror, I slipped into the fabric. Its soft touch against my skin made me feel empowered and sexy. The corset top in place, I looked down, there were slits for each leg to peek through in the lace dress. I grinned wickedly. My husband would love this. I sat down, still not looking in the mirror, and put on the boots. The leather squeaked as I zipped it. This was why I kept planning the party.

Standing, I looked up. My eyes widened. It was just what I'd been thinking of in my head. I tied on the mask and an evil smile parted my lips. Letting out a little squeal of happiness, I let myself out of the dressing room and made my way to the front.

Gabby was chatting away to Mrs. Palmer as she pawed through the costumes. My former teacher's eyes caught sight of me first and a knowing look covered her face. My friend noticed her gaze and followed it over to me. Her eyes got big, and her mouth dropped open.

"So?" I asked, posing for her, one leg slightly forward to show the slit.

"Woman." She whistled. "Turn."

I did as instructed, rolling my hips a little for her benefit. She cat-called and I grinned wickedly when I faced her again. Gabby's eyes sparkled.

"It's perfect."

Chapter 2 ~ Teasing

I turned in front of the mirror, my freshly curled waves bouncing and the lace around my legs floating. The costume fit better than I remembered it fitting in the store. My make-up was done, my mask was in place, and my boots were zipped. It was almost time to go downstairs.

Base from the music could be felt upstairs and the aroma of food wafted up as well. I was ready to mingle, but the game Cain and I played required me to wait until most of the guests had arrived. It was all a take back to the night oh so many years ago when we got together for the first time. Nerves flitted through me at what I knew was coming.

"Almost ready?" Gabby asked, coming into the guest room behind me.

I looked at her in the mirror to admire her costume. She was dressed as Cleopatra, gold and sparkles covering her lean body. Her long legs were accented by her gold shoes that had criss cross laces climbing them. I whistled at her, and she laughed.

"Think Elliot will approve?" she questioned.

Gabby was married to Elliot Smith, Cain's cousin.

"He hasn't seen it yet?"

She shook her head.

"We decided to pull a little Cain and Allie tonight."

This time I laughed.

"Have fun," I told her with a knowing smile.

We chatted a little longer, mostly just her filling me on those people that had already shown up. Together we made our way to the window and looked out over the driveway, it was packed. Time to head down.

"Let's go lady."

We looped our arms together and headed out of the room to the hallway. The sound of the guests got louder as the stairs came into view and my excitement amped up. Despite the stress of planning the party each year, I loved when it all came together. I was a social butterfly and enjoyed being surrounded by friends and family.

"There you are!" a voice gushed as soon as my foot hit the floor at the bottom of the stairs.

I didn't make it far before I was aware I was being watched. I soaked it up, putting an extra sway into my hips as I greeted friends and socialized. There was a mixture of old and new money in this room, yet on a night like this, that didn't matter. People were laughing and having a wonderful time, which was the other reason we did this. So many of those around me worked 60-70 hours a week on top of juggling a family and businesses. Tonight, they got to let loose a bit.

For the first hour of the party my husband and I never came in contact. We teased each other from afar, circling on opposite sides and sending glances across the room. My skin felt hot just from the looks alone. He was dressed as Dracula and the dress pants and top fit him like a glove. While I knew exactly what was underneath them, they still teased and taunted. Cain had rolled up his sleeves and his forearm muscles danced in the light. I glared at him for that move, he knew his arms were my favorite.

Shifting to distract myself, I let myself get caught up in a conversation with Elliot and two other gentlemen that worked with my husband. Cain wasn't a jealous man by any means, he knew I was his. However, the dance we'd been doing had him keyed up. Putting my hand on one of the man's arms, I leaned in and put in my two cents. I continued this the whole conversation. Elliot was laughing and his eyes sparkled at me, knowing exactly what I was doing.

I'd barely stepped back from the group when I felt heat at my back. His scent filled my nostrils and heat pooled between my legs. A strong male hand gently squeezed my hip.

"You're playing with fire," he growled in my ear.

A shiver ran through me before I could stop it.

"Oh?" I asked innocently.

Since part of the buildup was very little touching, I pulled away and strode toward the bar to grab another drink. How I did it without showing the weakness in my knees was beyond me. Some years I could be the strong one and give it right back to him, tonight I was a hormonal mess. Need coursed through me. We'd upped the ante this year. We were a very sexually active couple; the physical part of our relationship came so easily. However, leading up to this, we hadn't touched in two weeks beyond a quick hug or kiss. I'd ached for him before we'd started the party.

"Shot, please."

The bartender didn't ask what I wanted, just filled a shot glass with an amber liquid. I downed it and closed my eyes at the burn, feeling it all the way to my toes. When I opened them, I found Cain watching me as he now talked to the men I'd just been with. I smirked, licked my lips, and winked at him. His jaw clenched. I had his attention, and he was hard already based on the subtle shift he took to adjust himself. I turned back to the man serving, making sure to put one hand down to hold the slit in my skirt open and letting it ride up my leg.

"Hard cider," I requested.

Seconds later he handed me a glass with the lighter liquid. I took it gratefully and sipped a little. The sweetness danced across my tongue, and I took another deep breath before moving to a group just off the bar. I felt my husband's eyes following me and my lips curled.

I left the leg in his view bent slightly, baring it with lace on each side. I watched out of the corner of my eye as he shifted again. Gabby was part of the group of women I was with, and I heard her giggle slightly beside me. I took another sip from my glass and ran a finger down my thigh slightly to the top of my boot. Another shift in my peripheral vision. It was almost time.

"You're killing the man," my best friend whispered in awe.

"That's the point." I laughed.

"Elliot and I have nothing compared to you two." she sighed.

"Girl, we've been doing this for years," I reminded her softly. "It takes practice as well as a good knowledge of what turns your man on."

That was one thing Cain and I took pride in, knowing what the other one enjoyed in the bedroom. Though, sometimes it took just the right look, and I was putty in his hands. I joined in with the conversation for a bit as the ladies discussed a girl's night soon and which movie we would watch. It wasn't long before Gabby nudged me, and I knew I needed to head to my post.

Slowly, I disengaged the women and started a slow stroll toward the door at the side of the large living room. My husband leaned against the wall near the hallway watching me like a hawk while he talked with Elliot. I put my glass down on a table for empties near the closed door and made a production of looking around to make sure no one was watching me; I saw his lips quirk up. Turning the knob, I slipped inside and closed it behind me. It wouldn't be long now.

Chapter 3 ~ Capturing

Leaving the lights off, I made my way carefully down the stairs. I could walk this path with my eyes closed. I'd done it so many times. I put one hand out to make sure I didn't run into the corner I knew was coming up and followed the wall down the short hallway. Counting my steps, I turned into the makeshift bar room, a soft glow came from the back, and I smiled. He'd turned on the battery powered lamps we had in the corners.

Shadows danced on the walls. The bar stood to my right with mirrors behind it, stools lined the wall on the left. In front of me was the pool table and behind that a leather couch. My senses tingled when I heard the rustle of fabric and soft footsteps. I closed my eyes and took a deep breath.

I felt him directly behind me, his chest to my back, barely touching. Taking in the sensations he evoked in me; I left my eyes closed. His scent surrounded me, calming and exciting me all at the same time. Versace filled my nostrils as one arm wrapped around my waist to pull me closer. His free hand snuck down to toy with the lace and pulled it over so that the slit exposed my thigh. Fingertips traced the rose tattoo that lined the outside of the muscle.

"You've upped your teasing game this year, baby," he growled, low and breathy.

I felt his erection between my butt cheeks and let out a sigh.

"I've learned from the best," I purred.

Reaching a hand back between us, I stroked a finger up his length. The arm that had been at my waist slid up and he cupped a breast. I arched back into him and brought my hand back to halt his on my leg.

"What's the matter, Lee?" My husband questioned, turning us slightly so that I was facing the bar.

His hands came out to grab mine and put them on out to grip the pad that wrapped the wood. Only he could use that nickname and not make me mad. He used it most in the bedroom or when we were intimate, and it never failed to send a shiver through me.

"I want you," I admitted on a breath.

"Open your eyes all the way."

My eyes were open, but the heat he was sending through me had them in slits. I widened them as I heard the zipper on his pants. Mine met his in the mirror and I saw the slow smile that took over his lips. Cain's brown eyes were dark with lust and his jaw was ticking. His control was barely in check.

I turned and looked at him. He didn't instruct me to turn back around, instead, he moved back to me and lifted me. Wrapping my legs around him, I locked my mouth to his. Our tongues went stroke for stroke in a frenzy, while my hands tangled in his hair. Cain moved us, putting me down on the pool table. His mouth pulled from mine long enough to assess what I was wearing so he knew what he could access.

While he took me in, I leaned up to loosen the top enough for my breasts to spill out. A sucked in breath from my husband egged me on. I shifted the lace on my legs and pulled my panties aside with one finger to expose myself to him. This time he hissed, and I smiled. He pulled his cock from his unzipped pants, and I licked my lips as he stroked. He was throbbing and ready for me. Precum sparkled at the tip.

"I need you, Cain," I whispered.

He leaned in to pull me to him and while his mouth came back down on mine, he slid home. Sighing, everything slowed. His hands gripped my ass and moved me ever so slightly. My legs locked at his lower back and my pelvis shifted slowly all on its own.

Releasing his mouth, I brought my hands from his shoulders to my chest and massaged my breasts. His groan had my inner muscles tightening around his dick. His mouth curved into a naughty grin before he lowered it to the spot just between my boobs and kissed. I bucked and begged for more. He obliged, nibbling his way across one to the nipple. Watching me from under hooded lids, he took it into his mouth and suckled.

Still holding that one breast up for him, I took the other hand down to grab his hips. The pace started to pick up. Grunts and groans became louder, and I finally had to give up both hands to hold him from pulling out too much on his thrusts. The tingles were coming, and I could feel him pulsing inside me as he got closer as well. One little change would set us both over the edge. Releasing my hands, I pulled away from him to lean back and arch.

"Fuck, Allie," he panted.

He flicked my clit with his skilled fingers, and I clamped around him like a vice. That was enough for him, and his seed started to spill. My legs shook from the effort of holding him in place, but I did so until he stopped thrusting. We both remained still for a moment catching our breath.

"How does that continue to get better every year?" He asked, pulling me back up to hold me and put his forehead to mine.

"Damned if I know." I giggled, cupping his face and running my thumbs back and forth on his beard.

"Did you know El and Gabby were trying to do the same thing?" he asked with a chuckle, his hands running up and down my sides.

"I did," I nodded. "They got nothing on us."

"Hell no, they don't," he agreed with a wide smile.

Finally, he pulled from my body and scooted behind the bar to return with two cloths, one wet and one dry. Cain cleaned me up and kissed my forehead. As I gained my legs back, he went back behind the bar and did the same to himself.

"Okay my hot little witch," my husband taunted coming back over to me. "Time to return to the party."

We'd created the rule from the start that we'd sneak back in individually. Melding back in without a fuss and hoping no one noticed. The only ones that ever seemed to were the ones that knew our little secret game. I always went first.

Giving him a hard kiss that sent him reaching for me before he could stop himself, I pulled away and sashayed toward the door. I heard him curse under his breath and I smiled. Five years together and I still had it.

Chapter 4 ~ Aftermath

"So, how did the little teasing session end up?" Gabby asked a couple hours later.

We'd changed into comfortable clothes and were helping the vendors clean up. The bartender, the caterer, the servers, and DJ were forever grateful. It had been a busy night for all of them and as hostess I never felt like it should be all up to them. Pulling a cloth off a table I folded it and turned back to her with my eyes sparkling.

"Pretty damn good," I told her. "Yours?"

"Sex with us is always good, but it wasn't what I expected," she laughed. "I think we need coaching."

I laughed too, looking over at Cain and Elliot who were folding tables and putting them on a rolling cart. My husband must have sensed me watching him and he looked over his shoulder, throwing me a wink when his eyes found mine. I blew him a kiss in return.

"You two are ridiculous," my friend muttered under her breath good naturedly.

We continued on with our cleaning. It took a couple hours, which probably would have gone quicker had the four of us not been acting like teenagers and throwing stuff at each other, but the rooms were finally put back into place. Taking the living room in, I felt the exhaustion of the past few weeks kick in. I plopped down on the couch with Gabby and leaned my head back.

"Another successful Halloween party."

"Yep," I nodded, fighting to keep my eyes open.

"Come on, lady," I heard Elliot's voice ring out from the doorway. "Let's leave the love bugs alone."

She rolled her eyes at him.

"You've got a year to teach me how to torment him sexually," she whispered.

I laughed.

"Talk to you tomorrow," she said as she got to her feet and headed toward him.

I waved half-heartedly at her and let my eyes close. It felt like seconds later, I was being lifted into strong familiar arms. I snuggled into his chest and wrapped my arms around his neck. He chuckled.

"How are you doing, baby?"

"I'm tired." I yawned.

"I know, but otherwise, you good?"

"I am," I told him. "It seemed like everyone had a good time and you know that is all I ever want."

"They did," he agreed. "You always do an amazing job."

He put me down on the bed and I opened my eyes. Cain had his back to me and was pulling off the sneakers I'd replaced my heels with. I rubbed a hand down his t-shirt, feeling the muscles bunching beneath. Once my shoes and socks were off, he took a minute to rub each foot, knowing I wasn't used to wearing anything other than flats and that my feet were probably tender.

I wasn't sure how I'd gotten so lucky to meet him in that bar room all those years ago when I'd been invited to his Halloween party, but I was grateful for it every day. My wedding ring glinted in the light off the bedside lamp as I continued to rub his back and I smiled. He continued to massage, and I sighed.

"Same place and time next year Mr. Smith?"

"You'd better believe it Mrs. Smith."

I already couldn't wait, and my body heated at the thought. One year to plan another perfect costume and ways to torment him. Maybe I wasn't so tired after all.

A Familiar Conundrum

Martina Marie

For many generations, families living in the small town of Nokturne Cove have all possessed a unique quality. Ever since the founder of the town, Ender Moone, built a cottage between the never-ending mountains and the endless sea, the families that reside there have all been moonkissed. They're all specially chosen by the moonlight and granted an animal familiar and magical powers. Some of these special powers include strength, healing, control of the elements, transformations, and many others, each power celestially selected for the family to best help maintain the town. For if the town should fall, humanity would fall with it.

Tap. Tap. Tap.

The mid-April thunderstorm rains down onto the metal porch roof like a midnight lullaby. Raising my fist to my mouth, I try to cover another yawn. I love these nights with my grandma, the both of us sitting in the rocking chairs on the porch with a fuzzy blanket and a big, warm cup of tea listening to the thunderstorm, her pet ferret, Max, laying at her feet. We both sit there in silence, listening to the rain fall to the roof and then through the gutters. Grandma sat in her chair with her salt and pepper curly hair in a loose bun, her cat eye glasses halfway on her nose. I like how big her glasses are because they show her blue eyes more. She fixes the tie on her fluffy pink bathrobe, before crossing her feet in her matching slippers.

Grandma picks her mug up off of the wrought iron table my grandfather had made for her almost ten years ago now. She takes a sip of her special homemade nighttime tea blend, and then sets the mug back down gently.

"Danny, hunny, I think it's about time I'm more honest with you."

I sit up a bit straighter, turning to look at her better. My brown curls bounce as I turn my head, one of them falling in front of my brown eyes. Mom always said it seemed like my hair and my eyes were competing at who could catch someone's attention first. I was a bit cold, when we first came out, in my blue and green camo pajama pants and dark blue night shirt, but now a nervous feeling set in, making my whole body feel warm. "What do you mean? You've always been honest with me, haven't you?"

"You're twelve years old now. Things are about to get a bit … confusing. But I will try to help you out as much as I can." She rubs her hand across her forehead, and for once she actually looks a bit nervous.

"Ugh. Ew. I had health class in school last year, Gammy, you don't need to have *that* talk with me. I know what's going to happen." The warm feeling quickly goes away, but the nervous feeling remains. I look down into my own mug, watching the little bits of fruit swirling around, hoping that she won't want to keep that conversation going.

She brings her hand up to her mouth, laughing to herself. "No, no. Nothing like that. You've probably learned more from the other kids here in town than I could talk to you about. No. I have to be honest with you about your family's history in this town. I'm not sure what the other kids may or may not have let slip, but it's time you are told the truth."

Scrunching my eyebrows together, I can't hide my confusion. *What could the other kids know that I don't? What has she been hiding from me?*

"That is the same face your mother used to give me when she was a little girl and I asked her to help name the herbs in my store. She couldn't wait for the day when she could give you this talk. She always wondered what your abilities may be." She takes her handkerchief from her pocket and wipes at her nose.

"Abilities? Like talent? Like art or music? I have been practicing my trombone more." I pick up my mug, cupping the lower half of it to warm my hands.

She places her handkerchief on her knee, laughing as she whispers something to Max. "Not exactly, but you are very talented in those aspects. I know it's been hard since we lost your mother and grandad four years ago, but you have me, your friends at school, and the rest of the town to help support you."

"Gammy, you're making me more confused. What's going on?" Setting my mug back down on the table, I look from her to Max and then back to her.

After spinning around in a few circles, Max gives up trying to lay down and climbs up onto Grandma's lap.

She pets Max from his head to his tail before turning toward me and leans in closer. "What I am about to tell you needs to stay here at the house. Most children do not know, and tourists to our town *will never* know. The history of our town that you have learned in school is a watered-down version our ancestors compiled for us to teach without causing new fear or panic. Have you ever wondered why we don't have much crime? Or why the town seems to work together really well? Our whole town is … based on … magic."

Whatever was going through my head when she paused through that sentence, I never would have guessed that she'd try to say the town was magical. *Should I be worried about her? She is getting older. I see her talking to Max more than most people talk to their pets. My friends think she's a bit weird, but how bad is it if she's saying the town has magic?*

"Okay, Gammy. That may be enough tea for tonight. Why don't we head in and go to bed, and you can talk to me more about this tomorrow?"

She reaches over and places her hand on top of mine. "Danny, this is serious. I didn't say that to try to be funny."

I pull my hand away, and for a minute, I thought it looked like Max was shaking his head at me. "I didn't think you were joking, Gammy, but it definitely sounds a bit … crazy. How could our town be magical?"

Max leans into Grandma and nudges her arm with his nose.

"Yes, yes, Max. I'll make sure to tell him." She pats his head as he lets out a little squeak. "This story was told to me by my grandmother, and her grandmother told her, and her grandmother told her, through the generations. Back when the town was first founded—"

"By Ender Moone," I interrupt her, causing her to let out a sigh.

"Yes, by Ender Moone. He built a cottage, where the museum now sits, and did what he could to protect the land from others who wanted to harm it. Nearby villages heard about his troubles, and wanted to come help him. They soon built a small village around him and helped him protect the beach and forest. One night, an invader came into the new village and tried to burn down Ender Moone's cottage. Something woke up the villagers and they gathered water to help extinguish the fire. That night was a full moon, and they say the glowing rays were so bright that the villagers were moonkissed, their bodies encased with glimmering, silver auras. Soon afterwards, the villagers touched by the moonlight were showing signs of extraordinary abilities. One could quickly grow crops to make sure they had enough food for the winter. One had the ability to heal the sick and injured. Others started coming forward with talents that helped not only their families, but also everyone else in the village. As new generations became of age, they were also granted magical talents that further helped the success of the village. The village grew and grew until it became the town we know today."

She pauses to take a sip of her tea. Max's little nose nudges her again. "Yes, yes. I'm getting to that part."

I stand up and rearrange my blanket before sitting back down. The lullaby of the rain has stopped, and the silence is almost deafening. Bringing my hands up to my head, I try to understand this new truth. *Ender Moone's protectors were ... moonkissed? People got powers to help protect the village? New generations got powers when they became old enough? Well, that explains why some of the kids in school got weird and kind of distant. If she's telling me about this, then she has powers, my parents must have had powers, and I will soon get a power, too! Whoa, this is crazy. It ... it can't be true.*

I stir my tea with my finger and take a sip, hoping to get rid of the dry feeling in my throat. I'm not paying attention when I put the mug back down, and it almost falls off the edge of the table. "Wh-What? That can't be. That means everything they teach us in school about the town is a ... a ... lie?"

"Oh, hunny." She grabs my hand with hers, placing her other hand on top. "Not a lie, exactly. More like a half-truth. I know this can be a lot to take in. There is one more thing though."

I look at her with wide eyes, pulling my hand away and placing it in my lap. "There's more?"

"Each person that possesses a magical ability is granted an animal familiar. A friend to help them learn their new abilities and to help protect them. Like Max, here, he is my familiar. We can talk to each other quietly with our minds, or he can talk to me as you and I are talking now. If someone else is around when he talks to me, they will only hear his squeaks and normal ferret noises. Once a familiar is bonded to you, they are your companion for life. They will live as long as you do, and they will feel when there is something wrong. Our tomorrows aren't promised, so make sure you protect each other. And remember, over everything, do not talk to anyone about this. Each family has their own way of telling the next generation. As far as other kids are concerned, there is nothing special about us or this town."

I take a couple deep breaths, still trying to process this madness. *Magic is real?* "So, wait ... everyone in our family has had magical powers? What is yours? What was Mom's?"

"Yes, they have. I have the ability to heal people. As you know, I own the apothecary in the town square, and I help heal people with herbs and tonics. The hospital was built for long-term care or if I need to see more than a few people at a time, but people mainly come to me when something is wrong with them. Your mother was very smart and had knowledge that most of us will never understand. She was a teacher, trying to help pass the knowledge she had to you youngins, or really anyone wanting to learn something new."

"She was amazing. I miss her. Does that mean our cat, Solara, was her familiar? I thought she ran away. I hated that we lost her the same night we lost Mom." A tear falls down my cheek, and I use the edge of my blanket to wipe my nose.

"I miss her, too. Max and I found Solara laying on the driveway and knew instantly your mother had passed. I couldn't handle the thought of you waking up that next morning and seeing Solara like that, so I buried her underneath the willow tree out back."

Unable to hold back the tears anymore, I sob into my blanket. Max squeaks at Grandma before jumping off her lap and running back into the house.

"You have a lot to process. I just gave you a ton of new info. Why don't we call it a night and go to bed? We can talk more in the morning."

I sniffle and sadly nod my head up and down. She grabs my tea mug with hers and helps me up, following behind me into the house.

I drag my blanket up the stairs, stopping on the middle step. "I love you, Gammy."

"I love you, too, bug. Get some sleep."

Reaching my bedroom, I push the door open with my foot. I then crash onto my bed on my stomach and fall fast asleep.

A couple of days go by, which then turn into weeks. Grandma and I haven't talked about magic much, but lately I've been feeling weird. Not like I'm getting sick or something, just like there's a low-lying hum of electric waves flowing through my skin. It started about a week ago. At first, it was weird, kind of like the feeling that happens after your foot falls asleep and the feeling comes back, but not as strong. Now it is becoming more of an annoyance, and I have to tell Grandma about it. I find her sitting on the couch, crocheting another sweater for Max. Standing in the doorway of the sunroom, I wonder how I am going to bring this up.

"Is that you, Danny? I heard that left floorboard squeak."

"Oh. Uh … yeah, it's me. Are you expecting someone else today?" I rub my hand up and down against my shorts.

"Not 'til later, dear. Is something the matter?" She puts her project down and turns her swivel chair toward me.

"I … uh … need to talk to you. But I'm not sure how."

"Speak from your gut, hun. Just be true and the words will find their way."

"How did you know you got your powers? Was there a sign or a … uh, feeling? Just wondering." I lower my head and tap my toes on the floor.

She laughs to herself. "That was a good long while ago. Oh, geez. I think I remember a weird feeling. Yes, like a buzz. Almost as if a bee was flying around me, but every time I looked for it, I couldn't find it."

I gasp, raising my head to look at her. "I've kind of been feeling a little like that this past week. Like my skin is full of electricity, as if I just rubbed my feet on the carpet and I'm about to shock you, only it doesn't go away."

"This is it! Have you felt like you're being pulled toward a certain trait more than another? Strength? Smarts? Healer? Maybe?" Her smile is huge and contagious. She gets up from the chair and walks over to me, scooping me up into a big bear hug.

Smiling back at her, I squeeze her tighter. All of the anxious, nervous feelings I had before are instantly gone and replaced by a happy, calm feeling. "I don't know, Gammy. That electric feeling hasn't gone away, but I don't feel nervous anymore. I feel happy, almost excited."

She lets me go but keeps her hands on my shoulders. "That's how I feel right now, bug. Let me know how you feel over the next couple of days. It sounds like you may be an empath. Makes sense, actually, with how easy it was to calm you down when you were little. Or how you somehow always knew when someone was upset. I don't know why I didn't guess that one would be your talent sooner. Have you met your familiar yet? Have any animals started talking to you?"

"No, not yet. At least, I don't think so. I haven't seen any today other than Max."

Stepping back, she takes a deep breath. "Oh! Good idea." She looks over her shoulder at Max's bed on the floor beside her chair. "Max. Wake up, sleepyhead."

He stretches in the sunlight before jumping up and running over to Grandma.

"Want to help us out? Can you do me a big favor?"

He nods his head up and down.

"Can you talk to your friends, or do a little run through the woods, to see if Danny's familiar may be nearby? I have a feeling they'll find each other soon, but maybe we can give them a little help." She smiles and winks at him.

After squeaking at her again, he runs through the backdoor, goes past the barn, and then into the woods.

Lowering my head, I'm overcome by a sudden sadness. "Is he upset with me?"

"No, hunny. Not with you. He's upset his nap got cut short. Now," she pulls me in for a quick hug, and then grabs her purse from the nearby table, "I need to run out and make sure I have his favorite treat ready for him when he gets back. Why don't you take a walk through the woods, too? You might even find your familiar while you're out there. If you see anyone while I'm gone, don't tell them about our magic. I love you." She smiles at me and heads for the front door.

"I love you, too," I call out toward her.

I walk through the sunroom to the screen door in the back. The trees aren't directly behind the house. I have to walk through the small field with the old, reddish-orange barn. We tried to raise goats once, but they kept escaping through the fence somehow, so we mainly use the barn to store things like the lawn mower lately. Just past the field, diagonal to the house, is the tree line to the biggest forest in Nokturne Cove. It's home to all sorts of animals.

Maybe my familiar is living in the woods? I hope it's a raven ... or a bunny, maybe even a deer. I wouldn't mind it sleeping in my room with me. Anything big like a bear or a mountain lion will scare the crap out of me. I spend a couple hours walking around the woods, but don't find much. There's some birds singing here and there, and a frog or two, but not much wildlife out today.

The rest of the week I try to do what I can to find my familiar without causing the townspeople to be concerned. I check out the animal shelter and pet stores in town, but I haven't come across a talking animal yet.

"*Trust your familiar, Danny. They will find you when the time is right.*" Grandma's words echo through my mind.

How am I supposed to trust an animal I've never met? Why haven't I felt the connection with them? My determination to find my familiar grows, and I resolve to check out the woods again. Waking up early the next morning, I decide this time when I go out, I will be better prepared.

I pack a small backpack with some granola, a bottle of water, and one of Max's toys with a bell that jingles. *Today will be the day!* I set out for the woods, nervous but excited that I may be coming home with a new friend. The woods are so beautiful today. It isn't too hot or too cold; there is just enough of a breeze flowing through to keep you comfortable. I see a couple squirrels running through the trees, but they don't want to come anywhere near me. The trickling sound of water calls me deeper into the woods. The creek is always one of my favorite spots to relax. I'd go down there, take my shoes off, and walk through the water looking for rocks and to chase the fish.

Suddenly, I'm pulled into a memory of me and Mom trying to find the shiniest rock. I found one that outshone all of the others I had previously found, but when I reached down to try and grab it, I slipped and fell forward. I was soaked. Mom told me to get out and shake like a dog to dry off. I tried it, but it didn't work.

A hissing sound brings me out of my head and back into the woods. I wasn't paying attention to the trail and almost stepped on a snake.

I jump back, letting out a quiet, breathy scream. *Please don't be my familiar. Please don't be my familiar.*

It hisses at me again before slithering off of the trail into an old, hollow log.

Thank goodness! I reach the edge of the creek and look at the sun glistening on the water. I could spend hours ... no, days out here listening to the songs of nature. I thought Grandma was a bit crazy talking about magic, but after gaining my ability I've been seeing more and more of the everyday magic all around us.

A croak beside me reminds me why I'm really out here.

"How about you, Mr. Toad? Could you possibly be my familiar?" I pick him up to see if he'll talk back to me, especially since he doesn't make any motion to jump away.

"Were you about to kiss that toad?" a voice asks from behind me, breaking through the silence, causing me to jump and drop the brown-colored toad I had just picked up.

"What? No. Me? Kiss a toad? Blech!" Making a disgusted sound, I turn around and wipe my hands on the front of my pants. *Of course, it's Lucy, my next-door neighbor. What is she doing out here?*

"Having a little trouble?"

"With what?"

"You know …" She twirls a piece of blonde hair around her finger, her blue gaze bouncing around the forest.

I look around nervously. *Grandma said to keep our magic a secret. Lucy can't possibly know I'm trying to find my familiar … can she?*

She walks over to a tree beside us, places her hand on the trunk, and closes her eyes. "She's not here, by the way."

I scrunch my face at her in confusion. "What? Wh-Who's not here? I'm not looking for anyone." *Is she talking about Grandma, maybe? Can she hear what I'm thinking? Get. Out. Of. My. Head!*

"Yeah, you are. How else do you expect to find her if you don't get out there and look?"

"If you're talking about my grandmother, she's at home. I'm just exploring the woods in my backyard." I open my arms out beside me and lift my head to soak in a bit of sunshine coming in through the canopy of the trees.

She snorts, shaking her head, her ponytail swinging behind her. "And I'm just out here hunting for dinner. Your grandmother asked me to come out here and find you. She said you may need some help, but I didn't think you'd need this much help."

I can't hold in my frustration any longer. "I don't need any help. You can go do something else, somewhere else. I was about to go back home anyways."

"Oh, come on. Don't be such a crybaby. How long have you been out here? How hard have you actually looked? Or are you just out here playing around?"

"Why does it matter to you? Only a couple of hours … maybe. I'm just out here enjoying the forest, like I said. I'm not looking for *anything*." I drop my head and kick a rock next to my foot. It bounces off of a nearby tree, making a loud *thump* that echoes through the oddly quiet forest. A breeze rolls through the leaves as if the forest just sighed at my attempt to act normal. No one in this town is anywhere close to 'normal'.

Shaking her head, she inhales deeply. "I know why you're really out here. Why your family didn't tell you about everything sooner is on them, but I was asked to try to help you. Do you want my help or not?"

Panic sets in, in the pit of my stomach, and I hate the thought of losing Grandmother's trust because I told someone about our magic. I continue to play dumb. "I'm fine. Thanks." I bend down to pick up another rock to skip across the creek. "Ew, why is this one hairy?" I look it over in my hand before gently pulling it apart. "There are small bones in here. I think I found an owl pellet. Don't they try to hide these things?"

"She's close. You're at least on the right track this time."

"This time? What do you mean this time?"

"I … uh, may have seen you at the pet store one time talking to the cats."

Has she been following me? I thought I heard someone last time I was out here, but I thought it was just an animal. Could it have been her?

I drop the pellet and rub my hands on my pants. The sun is starting to go down and I don't want to be out here in the dark. "It's getting dark, I'm going home."

She glances around, watching the last of the orange sunbeams breaking through the canopy. "Yeah, okay. I have a feeling, though, that you'll find her soon. Follow the clues."

"Clues? What clues?" I turn around to ask her more, but she's already running back through the forest toward our houses. I've only been looking for my familiar for a week. Grandma said that some people are connected to their familiar right away, whereas others don't connect until their familiar feels that they are ready to. Lost in thought, I almost trip over a root hidden in the fallen leaves at the tree line.

"Danny!"

I step through the tree line just in time to hear Grandma calling for me. Running past the barn to reach the back of the house, a random shiver flows through my body. "What was that?" I whisper to myself. I shake my head at whatever that feeling was and run to the porch to meet Grandma.

"Here. I'm right here, Gammy." I bend over and put my hands on my knees, trying to catch my breath.

"Any luck in the woods?"

Max runs up and rubs against Grandma's leg, squeaking fast about something.

"That's my boy." She bends down and rubs his head before pulling a treat from her apron pocket. She looks back up at me and pats her jean-clad legs like she's looking for something. "I thought I had it on me, but I can't seem to find it."

"What's the matter? What are you looking for, Gammy?" A new burst of energy flows through me and I feel excited; it must be Grandma that feels that way.

"I thought I had your grandfather's pocket watch on me, but it's not in my pockets. I was going to clean it up and give it to you. I must have placed it in one of the boxes with some of his other things in the barn the other day. Be a dearie and try to find it for me please." She brings her hands together and positions them in front of her mouth to hide her smile.

I hope there's a way to learn how to turn down people's emotions, because I'd still like to feel mine from time to time. "Yes, ma'am. I'll go look for it, but I won't be happy about walking all the way back over there, even though I'm feeling a burst of energy and excitement ... for some odd reason," I add that last bit a little too sarcastically before running off back toward the barn.

The barn is a decent size—not quite big enough for horses, but not small like a shed either. After the goat fiasco, Grandpa would bring old tractors or cars in here to work on. I loved sitting in the hayloft above him, listening to him work while I made birdhouses for Mom.

The sun has just started to set, casting brilliant hues of red and orange across the clouds. The barn never really scared me before, but this time I'm hesitant to slide open the door. As I push the door to my right and step inside, a flash of white flies in front of me from one side of the barn to the other. "Aaaaaahhhhhhhhh! A-A-A ghost!"

The sound of flapping wings and a breathy sigh fill the barn. "I'm not a ghost! And you just scared away my dinner." She turns around and quickly flies toward me. Bringing her wings together in front of her, she pushes a big gust of wind into my face, before landing on top of a box.

"You're a ... a barn owl. You're beautiful." *I didn't really know what my familiar would be, but I never thought of them being an owl. This is exciting.* "I'm ... I'm Danny." I'm so nervous, I put my hand out for a handshake.

She laughs to herself, making a sound like a purr. She extends her wing to my hand, and we awkwardly shake them up and down. "Nice to meet you, Danny. My name is Stella."

Please keep an eye out for the full version of this story in the future. There are many more adventures for Danny and Stella to get into.

Daddy's Girl

By K.O. Newman

Lesleigh

The moment she walked through the door, she struck me dumb. Leather jacket, emerald green highlites in her hair, and a fucking attitude that hung around her like smoke. It was almost as sexy as the scent of her. The second her musk hit my nose, I knew it was all over.

"Looking for something, darling?" I asked, putting my pencil down and sitting up straighter.

"Told to come look for someone named Vick." She popped her gum, her little pink tongue slipping from between her lips to lick the bubble off her lips, before blowing a bubble, and repeating the process. I'd never been so fucking hard in my life. "Have an appointment."

I nodded and pulled the ledger over to where I had been sketching. "Vick had to leave early," I said, just loud enough that the grizzly in the back of the shop heard me. Ain't no one tatting up this piece but me. "What were you thinking of getting?"

She pulled a folded piece of paper from out of her pocket. Dropping the drawing on the counter, she gave me a raised brow, clearly not buying what I was selling. "Called twenty minutes ago. Vick run out that fast?" She leaned over the counter, getting right in my face and giving me a straight look through the collar of her shirt, all the way down to the little piercing in her belly button. Fuck me. "You think I can't smell the bear in the back?" she whispered. "That I can't smell you?"

"Then you know." I picked up the paper and took it to the scanner, making a copy. "Vick won't be touching that porcelain skin, baby girl." I pulled the new page off the printer and slapped it on the light board I had been working on, taping it down with a blank sheet on top. "You're fucking mine."

"Don't do that macho bullshit, sweetheart." She snatched up the paper from my board and stuffed it in her pocket along with her drawing. "I made an appointment with Vick."

"And you are my mate, gorgeous." I stood, using my height to look down at her. "You want that little cherry tat, you're getting it from me or no one."

With a shrug, she turned on her heels and went to head out the door. "There are other shops in the area."

"Ain't one who will give any cherry tats today." I rounded the counter, grabbing her hand and pulling her back. "If you don't go for fate, what do you go for?"

"You prove yourself to me, prove to me you'll make me a good partner, then I'll think about mating." She slipped her hand out of mine and crossed her arms over her chest. "Fine. You do the cherries. But if you fuck this tat up, I will remind you about it for the rest of your fucking life, got me?"

"Names Les." I winked and took the paper she offered again, going back to make another clean copy, free of all the fucking wrinkles she had put in the other page. "And I don't fuck up tats. Especially not on my mate's skin."

"Sophia." She dropped her ID on the counter for me to scan and swiped a clipboard, dropping down on the old leather couch that took up most of the front of the shop. "And no mate crap until I'm ready."

"Got it, Cherry."

I could feel her roll her eyes at me, even though I couldn't see them. But the scent that bloomed in the room told me she liked it.

*****

Sophia

The buzz of the machine set my adrenaline running the second it started. Les gave me a heated look as he dipped the end of the machine in his cap of ink. The scent of the ink mixed with the hormones he was giving off were heady. My mind swam as the needle hit my skin, the first line of my new tattoo vibrating its way in, the sharp bite of the needles only heightened the entire experience.

"You good?" he asked, whipping down the ink and blood that dripped from my skin.

"Fucking fantastic." My head rolled back on the chair, and I let the mix of hormones and chemicals racing through my body take me away. The truth was, any time Les had his needle in my skin I was fantastic. Anytime Les was touching me, I was fucking high as a kite, my body humming under his attentions.

"Good girl," my man purred, and my skin broke out in goose flesh. "You gonna be daddy's princess tonight?" Les pulled the needle from my skin and went back to his cap of ink. "Or you gonna be a brat like you were last night?"

"I'll be good," I sighed.

"Promises, promises," he chuckled. "When you gonna let me mark you, babe?" His voice went serious, and I opened my eyes to look at him. "It's been months." The growl of his bear rolled up his throat, making shivers run up my spine. "Your panda has to be losing her mind, too."

"Wanna make sure it's right," I shrugged, looking down at the design he was inking into my skin. I was more comfortable letting him put his name on me, than I was letting him bite me. Bites were far more permanent. "You know why."

"I ain't your Pa." Les set down his machine, the buzzing stopping abruptly. "I am not your father, Cherry." He leaned in and tipped my chin up. He pressed a quick kiss to my lips before leaning back. "True mates don't cheat. We don't walk away."

"I know." Pulling myself out of his grip, I curled into the chair, pulling my legs up to my chest. My wrist stung as I moved it around, leaving blood and ink on my shirt. "But I'm not ready, okay?"

"Yeah, baby." Slowly he inched his hand down my arm, fingers still covered in the black latex gloves. "We'll wait." He threaded out hands together, and just held on for a moment. "Let's get you marked, then baby. Like my name on you."

"Only fair." I leaned up and pushed his shirt down over his heart. My name was curly and bright red right over his heart. The little cherry blossoms incongruous with the hard as nails tats that covered the rest of his skin. "I'm on your skin."

"Wanna fuck you so bad, Cher." He growled, leaning over and changing me to the chair. "You better fucking sit still until I'm done, cause you're going to be bent over this chair the second the last line is laid.

"Yes, daddy." I purred, already feeling myself heat up for him. Les was the only man who could ever give me what I really needed, and he fucking gave it to me in spades. I could still feel the red of his hand on my ass as I sat there, and couldn't wait for him to make the otherside match.

*****

Lesleigh

The sun set slowly in the summer. The last red rays colored the lake bloody. And with my mate under my arm, there wasn't a more beautiful sight. "You sure about coming to the party tonight?" I tipped up her chin, pressing a kiss to her brow. So far we had kept our dating life out of club life. Cherry had grown up in a club, but not like ours.

LOKI was born out of the fires of shifter experimentation in the sixties and seventies. Monserious things that had been done to the grizzlies in the care of Ironwood Heights Psychiatric Facility. And our bears were a different breed for it. My grandparents had been the few who pulled themselves out of the rubble and started our clan. Granddad was a founding member of Lords of Khaos after the Korean War. I was a legacy.

"Nothing I haven't seen before." Cherry snuggled down into me, tucking herself under my leather cut, getting her musk all over it. Just the way I liked. "Anyway, I know Kai and the twins." She shrugged. "And skank ass ain't gonna bother me none. Long as my man keeps his mitts on me."

"All of me is yours, Cher." I pressed my nose into her hair, breathing her in. She was starting to smell like me. Not enough, but a little. Once she let me lay my teeth on her, we would smell like the mates we were. "I told you, grizzlies mate once. Can't even get it up for anyone else."

"Still think that's an old wives tale." She sat up and rolled to her feet. "Better take me home if you want me to wear something other than this shit." She dusted off her ass, wincing a little.

"Still sore from last night?" I growled and turned her around so I could admire my handywork. "Fuck, Cher you are so sexy."

"I like feeling you." My mate leaned into me with a shrug. "Reminds me who I belong to all day long."

"We belong to each other, princess." I stepped into her space, backing her up until her ass hit the trunk of a tree. "I can't wait to feel you under me again. You pretty ass painted red from my hands."

"Yes, daddy," she simpered, her hands reaching for my belt.

"No." I stepped away and huffed out a laugh. "Maybe we not show the entire park my cock. Wait til we're home, baby."

"No," Cherry whined, reaching for me. "I'll be real quick, daddy. I promise."

"It's the unfinished bond that's messing with your head, Cherry. You cannot stick your hand in my pants in public." I pinched my nose. "Let's get you home. Wear a skirt tonight." Fuck. Titan was under my skin going insane. The scent of my mate's arousal would haunt me for fucking weeks. The bond wanted to be complete, no matter what we wanted. It was pulling at me to sink my teeth in deep, even if she protested. But I wasn't that fucking kind of animal. "If you hurry we can be quick and dirty at your place." I held my breath and counted to ten. "Take the edge off of this, mate."

"I'm sorry." And she really sounded like she was. "I just want to touch you. I need your scent in my nose. On my skin."

"OH, Cherry, I fucking want that too." I threaded my fingers through hers, trying to ignore the fact that my cock was hard as fucking steel in my jeans. "I love you, you know that, right? Don't make me something I'm not, but fuck do I want to bite you."

"If I ask for it?"

My world stopped. Right there in the middle of Battery Park, my brain froze. Slowly I turned to look at her, catching her eyes to see the sincerity behind them. The raw need that coursed through me every second of the day.

"Do you really mean it?" I whispered, knowing we were getting looks from other park goers. "You ready to have my mark? Just like that? You want this to be forever?"

"Don't you want it?" Cherry asked in the smallest voice possible. I could almost hear the fluttering of her heart as we stood there, her scent filing the air, making Titan roll around under my skin, trying to catch it on his fur. "It's time isn't it?"

I closed my eyes, feeling the adrenaline rush through me, my bear roaring in triumph as our mate finally chose us. Finally she wanted that one thing we had been waiting for. "Let's get to the party. We can even leave early if you want to. Make our own party up in my room."

"I love you, too, you know?"

"I know, Cher." I kissed the tips of her fingers and grabbed her helmet from the handlebars of my bike. The rush of potential bubbled under my skin, Titan was high on the hormones that flooded our system and my cock was throbbing with the beat of my heart, desperate to be inside my mate. To feel that final piece of the puzzle lock into place "You gonna be a good girl, and do as I say?"

"Yes, daddy." She took the helmet from my hands and put it on. The cheeky grin on her face didn't go unnoticed. My girl might follow my rules in the bedroom, but all bets were off until the moment that door closed. It would definitely be a party to remember.

Fuck.

Sophia

The music was thudding along under the din of voices. The bar at the Ironwood clubhouse was packed tight with brother, clan and hangarounds. Sweetbutts with varying arrays of clothing rubbed up against any and all members they could get their hands on, slinging drinks that were barely mixed. There was a woman in the kitchen who's aura spelled trouble for every girl who left her kitchen with food, only to get distracted by club dick.

Our table wasn't much better. Kai was completely engrossed in a pair of blondes who didn't look like they had a brain cell between them. Just thinking that made me feel bad. I wasn't that kind of girl, but the way they giggled and fucking everything he said, and bobbed their heads back and forth, it felt like the personification of bimbodom. The twins were entertaining their own pair of girls, one of which kept kicking our chair as she curled up under the table, with Finn's cock so far down her throat you would think he was checking her oil.

"You done?" a chick in black mesh and very little else asked, rolling her eyes at me, as I sat in my mate's lap, very much not putting on a show, despite the fact that he had his hand up my skirt. Not doing anything interesting, just touching my skin, tracing patterns on my thigh. He was rock hard under my ass, but he had been a warm comfortable presence since we walked through the door to see a guy he called Exorcist choking out some girl in the hall, slamming his cock into her so hard, she was going to have bruises on her ass. "You know, the guys like it when you wiggle around a bit," she whispered helpfully as she took my glass and placed it on her tray. "You want a chance to go up to one of their rooms, you should at least give him a hand first." She shrugged as she walked away.

"Really?" I laughed behind my hand and Les's arms came around me, hugging me to his front. "Is that what the guys like?" I looked over my shoulder at him, to see his amused grin. "Should I wiggle around a bit, get you interested?"

"Baby, I'm far past interested," he growled in my ear, shivers going down my spine. His fingers worked their way up my thigh under the table, tweaking the elastic of my panties. "I'm just enjoying a beer with my friends before the real fun begins." He said the last part loud enough that Kai tore himself away from the girls he was playing with to give Les a glare.

"To friends," Finn shouted, lifting his beer, while he grunted and twitched under the ministrations of sweetbutt number three, who was still working hard, kicking the chair again. "What say you, brother?"

"Fuck off," Fitz grumbled, picking up the chick he had been playing with and tossing her over his shoulder. The fact that she had no panties was very much evident to the entire room. Her skirt flipped up over her ass, Fitz's fingers deep inside her. "I have plans." He stalked away, straight up the steps. The girl didn't even protest the treatment.

"You know, they're more fun when there isn't a party," I stage whispered to Les. "Maybe we go to the house tonight?"

"Doesn't got electricity," my mate said. "But it will be quieter."

"And more of our toys are there," I reminded him. "The whole trunk is just waiting for us."

With that, I was also up over Les's shoulder. "Don't do anything I wouldn't do," he said, slapping Finn on the shoulder. "And maybe take this upstairs. Mamma keeps looking out the kitchen door, and she doesn't seem to be pleased."

"Fuck." Finn shoved back from the table, shoving his wet cock back in his pants. "Cock blocker."

"Pretty sure it's only cock blocking if you don't actually get your cock wet." I laughed from over Les's shoulder, which earned me a light tap on the ass, that just made me more determined to leave. "Take me home, mate."

"My pleasure, princess." Les gave one last wave to his friends, and strode out the backdoor of the clubhouse with me bouncing on his shoulder. "I assume you have plans?" He asked as we walked down the dark road.

Every single street light was out. None of them worked, and hadn't since the club took over the property, in a bid to keep them from going public with the supernatural, after the uprising at Ironwood Heights Psychiatric. It served the grizzlies who were trying to find their feet not to dive directly back into the human world and all its evils. It was easier to stay hidden, to live in the shadows and not be bothered.

"Of course I do." My hand ran down the washboard perfection of my mate's chest, and flicked the button of his pants open, before slitting it inside. "Fuck, Les." He was hot and heavy in my hand, his cock pulsing in time with his steps, bringing us closer to the house, and the trunk filled with goodies that we had set at the foot of the bed.

Les and Kai had been working to restore the house that Les had inherited from his father. Most of the houses dotted along the streets of Ironwood Heights lay empty. Husks left over from when the staff lived on site. The only reason Les was determined to fix his up was me. He didn't want us both living in the rooms above the clubhouse.

"You planning on sharing, baby?" He hand came back up and tapped me on the ass again, this time a little harder. My pussy clenched, wanting that hand back, the feeling of him touching my skin, making it warm and pink. "You want a spanking, or we gonna go right into the mating, cause I'll be honest, I want you on my cock like yesterday."

"I was on your cock yesterday, daddy," I teased, tightening my grip around the base of his shaft, tugging him inside his pants. Les's steps faltered, and he had to stop for a moment.

"Cheeky," he growled, leaning over to catch the skin of my shoulder between his teeth, giving me a playful nip. Nothing that would break skin or solidify our bond, just enough to sting a little. He had been nipping more often. Testing his boundaries, and making me scream as he fucked me. The pain making it all the better, deeper. "Maybe we do need to have a little time over daddy's knees."

"The silk rope came in yesterday," I breathed, drowning in the heady rush of lust that rolled through the air. "Tie me up? Make me scream before you mark me, please?"

"Please what, baby girl?" Les asked, his boots making hollow thumps on the old wooden stairs that lead up to the front door. "Please what, Cherry?" he growled when I didn't answer right away.

"Please daddy?" I breathed, my sex weeping for him, needing to be filled. "Please daddy, I want you so much."

"Good girl."

There were no lights, so once we were inside, Les set me carefully on my feet and found the old camp torch that we left by the front door. The weather was mild enough that not having any heat wasn't a problem, the breeze flowed through the open windows, bringing in the scent of leaves and growing things.

Once the hallway was illuminated by a fleet of lamps and my mate had our lantern in his hands, we went up the old staircase. Every other stair creaked and moaned under our weight, but we had been assured that the structure itself was completely sound. Just old.

Each step forward, my heart rate kicked up higher. The anticipation swirled in my gut with the realization that we were basically headed for our marriage bed. Once his mark was on my skin, I was his. Forever.

Les waited at the double doors to our room, the shadows from the lantern playing across his face, giving him a hauntingly sinister look. My man was all marshmallow on the inside, but the longer he grew his beard, the more he worked with Kai at his father's construction business, the harder he got.

"Cherry." He tipped my chin up until I was looking into his shadowy face. "You sure about this?" His voice was soft, warming me from the inside. "We can just…"

"I'm sure, Les." Pushing up on my tiptoes, I captured his lip between mine. "I want your mark. It's time."

"Then get undressed and lay on the bed." He put the lantern on the bedside table, turning on its twin on the dresser, so that the mirror reflected the light all over the room. "Now, mate," he said after a moment, when I stood frozen in the doorway.

Les watched as I crossed the room, pulling my dress over my head, then dropping it on the floor, followed by my panties and bra. The wind whistled through the open windows, making me shiver. "How do you want me?" I asked as I crawled up onto the big four poster. The bed had been hand made by Les and Kai. It was very specifically made for our proclivities, and the iron rings were hidden not only on the head and foot boards, but also at the top of each newel post.

"Lay back, mate." He crouched down at the end of the bed, unlocking our trunk with a distinct snick of the lock, and creak of the old hinges. "Arms over your head." I did as he asked, feeling my belly turn to liquid fire as he pulled out a long length of silk rope. "Safe word?"

318

"Pineapple," I said automatically.

"And if you can't say it?" Expertly he wrapped the cord around my wrists, securing it to the ring in the center of the headboard. Tight enough that my hands wouldn't slip through, but loose enough that I could move them around a bit. I had watched my mate study for hours, pouring over different knots, tying and re-tying them when I asked to be restrained.

"I knock on the wood." I demonstrated rapping my knuckles against the headboard. The sound rang through the room, satisfying him.

"Good girl." He tucked the extra rope down behind the mattress where it hung behind me. Out of the night stand he pulled a wicked pair of fabric shears, just in case. "I'm going to keep you restrained for the entire time. If you feel uncomfortable or your hands start to go numb, you tell me. If you need to stop for any reason, you tell me. I'm going to start with some light spanking. Then I want to feed you my cock."

"Yes, daddy," I breathed when he stopped expectantly. "But you'll mark me?"

"Patience, little one." He helped me turn over so I was up on all fours, the ropes moving easily with me. Once youve got me nice and hard, I'm going to fuck you. Hard."

"Please." My hips moved back of their own accord, searching for contact. It earned me a mild smack on my upturned ass.

*****

Lesleigh

Even in the dim light of the lanterns, the flush on my mate's skin was clear. She was ready. The scent of her filled the room, and I almost wanted to forgo any foreplay, and just cut to the chase. The way her sex glistened in the light, there wasn't much if any foreplay she needed. But she loved the weight of my hands on her, the thick slide of my cock down her throat, almost as much as the main attraction. The only thing better was having her sitting on my face. The musk of her desire imbedded in my nose, covering my beard. It was the reason I was growing it longer. I wanted to smell her for hours.

With a careful hand I positioned her on her knees in front of me, checking one last time that her hands looked good, that the knots I had tied were secure. And then my hand came down on the rounded part of her ass, making the flesh jiggle. My cock was rock hard, but her cry made my desire spiral up higher.

My hand rained down on her, warming her flesh and making her drip for me. Her pussy shone in the lantern light, as if calling me. It was calling me.

With a reluctant sigh, I pressed kisses to her flesh, the heat of her skin warming my hands and face, as I took a small taste. Cherry jerked when I pressed my face between her spread legs and licked her from clit to asshole. Humming at the flavor of her on my tongue.

"You taste like honey, baby girl,"I purred as I pulled away. Rubbing her ass once more, before I helped her turn on to her back. "You ready for my cock, baby?"

319

Cherry bit her lip, looking me up and down with fire in her eyes. Those pretty orbs landed on my weeping dick, and she nodded.

"Words, mate," I growled, tipping her chin up as I straddled her chest. Her full breasts pressing against my ass, arms up over her head, pushing the generous mounds together. The little metal rings were cool on my skin, but that would soon change. "What do you say? Are you ready for my cock?"

"Please, daddy," she moaned, wiggling on the bed beneath me. "I want your cock please. I want it in my mouth, I want to choke on it, please."

"Anything for you, baby." Folding nearly double, I pressed my lips to hers, letting her taste her own arousal on my tongue. "Anything for my mate." I nipped at her mouth before pulling away, and pressing my cock to her lips. "Open up." Painting her face with my dripping precum, I waited until she opened to me, silver tongue ring winking at me, before she wrapped her lips around the head of my dick, sliping up the arousal that waited for her. "Ain't gonna last long here, Cher." I grunted as she took me deeper, her tongue working me over until I touched the back of her throat. "Shit." She swallowed, squeezing my cock until I nearly saw stars.

I pushed myself up onto my knees, leaning over her, gripping the headboard as she sucked my cock with a satisfied hum. My girl was perfect. Every inch of her was built for me. From the way she sassed me back at every turn, to the way she bowed to me in the bedroom. Spectacular.

"Baby, stop," I growled, starting to pull away. Her knees came up behind me, holding me in place. "Cherry," I warned, the pressure of my orgasm coming too hard. "I said stop."

With a pop she let go of my cock, letting it bob between us. "But you taste so good, daddy." Her voice was all sugar, but the look in her eyes was anything but. "I can get you ready again, why not come in my mouth?"

"Cherry," I warned again, lifting myself off of her and going to help her turn over. "You want a spanking instead of a dicking, mate?"

"No, daddy," she whined, letting me move her once again. Once she was up on her knees, I pet down the marks I had left, already starting to fade. "I want your cock, please. I want your teeth. Please, Les." Her hips moved of their own accord, but this time I let them, slicking my cock through her arousal until I was coated, and she was squirming with need.

"Fuck, Cher," I sighed as I pressed the head of my cock into her warmth, letting the game go. I slammed myself as deep as I could go, having to bite my tongue to keep from cumming right then. My own blood filled my mouth as I fucked her. My fingers sneaking between us, to play with her clit. "I love you, baby."

"Love you too, Les." Her hips started to stutter against mine, losing the rhythm I had set. "Harder, please!" She screamed. "Fuck daddy."

With one last thrust, we tipped over the edge and I struck. My teeth sank deep into her skin, the copper of our blood mixed in my mouth as her body convulsed around me again in a harder, sharper orgasm.

"You're all mine now, mate," I whispered against her throat, bathing the bite with my tongue.

"You're mine too."

I reached up and loosened the knot around her wrists, undoing it so we could lay in our bed together. The rope fell behind the bed as I rolled us onto our sides, my body spooning hers. "I wouldn't have it any other way."

With a kiss over her shoulder, her eyes drooped heavily. She always needed a nap after a scene, and this time was no different. I would take watch over us while she rested, our bodies still connected, just as the threads of our soul joined in an unbreakable knot.

"I love you, Sophia. More than you could ever know." I placed a kiss on the top of her head, and held her close. "Nothing will ever change that."

"Welcome Home Scones"

Victoria Perkins

The thin man with wire-rimmed glasses followed his badger down the familiar path, his thoughts far away from his present state of being. This was not an unusual occurrence for Co-headmaster Corakin Gibberish, neither the absent-minded walk, nor the animal with him. In fact, most of the students at Audeamus had come across both man and beast on one of their nightly promenades, especially over the last few years. Tonight, however, the pair were alone.

Or so it seemed.

Then, suddenly, a sound came from the bushes lining the path, and the badger was off at a brisk trot, disappearing into the foliage before Corakin had even registered the noise. When he finally did, he sighed, withdrew his wand from his sleeve, and ventured into the darkness after his badger, casting his illumination spell after only a few steps.

He thought about calling for Ziege, but the badger never came when called if it knew it was in trouble. If he walked around shouting for it, all he would do was disturb his students. So he watched and listened, following the broken branches and the sounds of a bulky creature crashing through the underbrush.

When he finally caught up to the animal, however, it was something else that caught his attention.

A dark-clothed figure was climbing up one of the hayslip trees. One that had a branch very close to a fourth-floor balcony. Students had curfews, but that didn't mean they always abided by them, and this wasn't the first time Corakin had caught someone trying to bypass the magical measures used to keep track of anyone out later than they were supposed to be.

He pointed his wand at the figure and muttered the words that would freeze the figure in place, and then bring them back down to the ground to face the consequences for breaking the rules. This was the part of being in charge that he liked the least. Not because he didn't appreciate the importance of enforcing the rules, but because he didn't think he was any good at it. Yes, the students received the same punishment as they would have if someone else had caught them, but he'd always felt that he lacked the gravitas of his co-headmaster, Professor Durand.

"You should have taken the consequences for breaking curfew," Corakin said, his voice kind but firm. "The penalties for sneaking in are a bit more severe."

Just as he was about to suggest that they go to his office for a conversation, the figure turned toward him.

"Oh," Corakin said, surprised. "I don't know you."

Short copper-colored curls and a heart-shaped face, she looked about the age of his younger students, but he knew she wasn't one of them. He might've been absent-minded in a lot of areas, but when it came to the young people under his charge, he knew the names and faces of each and every one.

"Ten points to you," the girl said. Her blue-green eyes glittered as she folded her arms. "And since I'm not a student, I can't have missed curfew."

"And yet you were attempting to get into my school." Corakin kept his voice mild and his eyes sharp. He knew some people thought he was a pushover, someone easy to deceive and manipulate, but he wasn't a *goblok*. Something was wrong here, and if it put his school in danger, he would do whatever was necessary to protect it.

"I was climbing a tree." Her face took on a mutinous expression. "You can't prove I was trying to do anything illegal."

Ziege chose that moment to butt his head against the girl's leg and she let out a little yelp, jumping backwards.

"Ziege, bad badger," Corakin scolded. "No treats for you tonight."

When he looked up again, the girl was gone. He sighed but didn't go rushing after her. He didn't need to. It was common practice to cast a silent tracking spell whenever someone was caught breaking the rules. Tomorrow, he would find her and find out why she'd tried to break into the school. If she meant harm, he'd deal with it, but intuition told him that it was more likely that she was the one in trouble. If that was true and she needed help, he'd find a way.

Too many times in his life he'd been useless when people around him put themselves in danger. This girl, however…maybe he could do something for her.

****

Ade Thayer breathed a sigh of relief as she emerged from the woods and heard no one following her. The stranger hadn't really seemed like the sort to conduct a full-on pursuit for a breaking and entering that hadn't actually happened, but then again, most normal people didn't have badgers as pets either. For all she knew, he liked using the creature to scare people or something. She'd run into enough crazy and cruel people to know that anything was possible.

In the shadows of the city, Ade made her way through the streets and alleys, most of which were empty, but even the few people out and about didn't look her way. Used to people simply not seeing her, she hadn't bothered casting a cloaking or invisibility spell, something she now realized had been a mistake. She'd gotten complacent, and it'd almost cost her.

When she reached the run-down hotel at the edge of the city, she stopped and muttered the spell necessary to muffle her steps. A quick look around confirmed she was alone, but she took the extra time to make sure that was the case. After what had happened outside the school, she wasn't taking any chances. She had too much to lose.

The room at the very back had been empty for weeks before the Thayers had arrived and in the last month, the spells they'd cast had kept the miniscule staff from realizing that the room they used for storing extra supplies was occupied. Anytime someone ventured that way to get something, they'd remember a better place to find what they needed. Ade didn't know how much longer they could continue the deception, but she didn't want to move the family again unless absolutely necessary. She'd learned the hard way that more moves meant more risk.

It'd taken her nearly six months to get all of her siblings back after they'd been caught that time. Shashi still had nightmares about it.

At the door, Ade used her wand to trace a pattern and then tapped the center of it. The lock clicked and she opened the door.

"Ade!" A four-year-old bundle of dark copper curls and freckles launched herself off the closest bed.

"Narisa." Ade caught her youngest sister. "What are you doing still awake?"

"She refused to lay down until you got back."

Twelve-year-old Mladen looked exhausted, and Ade felt a pang of guilt. She knew she didn't really have another choice but to leave the twins in charge – not that Ezer shared the responsibility equally with his twin – but that didn't mean she liked it.

"Narisa." Ade gave her sister a stern look. "You have to sleep."

"You was in trouble." Narisa's bottom lip jutted out.

Ade felt a familiar chill go down her spine. This wasn't the first time Narisa had said something like that, but it never failed to shock Ade.

"Well, I'm here and safe, so it's time to go to sleep," she said.

"What 'bout Rajya?"

Ade froze mid-step. "What?"

"You go get Rajya first," Narisa said matter-of-factly.

"Mladen?" Ade looked over to see wide blue-green eyes in a stricken face.

The lights came on and Ade cast a quick spell, but her gut was already telling her that her ten-year-old sister was gone.

****

This had been a very bad idea, Rajya told herself for the hundredth time. All she'd wanted to do was be with her sister and then she'd gotten distracted by the *garflag* and when she'd finally remembered that she was following Ade, she'd looked, and Ade was gone.

Rajya had frozen then, locked in that place where she didn't know what to do and had too many options but there was obviously a right one and she didn't know what it was.

That had been a long time ago. She didn't know how long but it was dark and cold and she wanted to go home. Well, not home to a place because the Thayer kids hadn't had one of those since Rajya was six-and-a-half-years-old and her mother died.

She didn't like to think about that and usually she could distract herself by talking to one of her siblings but they weren't here. She was all alone. And being alone made her think about her mom again and that made her sad.

"One, two, three…" she whispered the numbers all the way to hundred. Then she started again, this time in Spanish. "Uno, dos, tres…"

She'd gone through French, Welsh, and Japanese when she heard the first new sound. A snuffling and rustling. An animal, she realized.

Before she could decide if she wanted to scream or run, a little brown face popped out from the bushes and gave her such a look of curious surprise that she found herself doing the strangest thing.

She laughed.

The laughter broke her paralysis, and she reached out to what she now realized was a badger. It sniffed her fingers, then butted its head against her hand. She scratched its head and then watched as it backed away. It kept watching her though and she decided that it wanted her to follow it.

So she did.

****

Ade tried not to curse or panic when her second attempt at using her tracking spell failed. She'd cast them on each of her siblings, but they didn't last forever, and she'd forgotten to renew them recently. All she could get now was a very faint indication of which way to go. Fortunately, that was enough to make her suspect that Rajya had followed her from the hotel.

She retraced her steps at a faster pace than before, trying not to let panic set in the longer she went without seeing any trace of her sister. All of the kids knew how cover their tracks, even Nasira to an extent, but Ade hadn't ever thought what that would mean if she was the one trying to find them.

So focused on where she was going, Ade failed to notice the slender figure in dark clothes until a hand wrapped around her wrist. She jerked back, reaching for her wand as she debated the wisdom of shouting for help.

"*Dawel.*" The man's voice was familiar. "I'm not going to hurt you."

"Wait." Ade frowned. "You're the guy from earlier. The one with the badger."

"Corakin Gibberish," he said. "And my badger is missing."

"Well," she countered, "my little sister is missing, so I think I win."

326

Corakin's eyebrows went up and Ade was surprised to see something that looked like approval in his eyes. Most adults didn't have that reaction to her smart mouth.

"I believe we're likely to be headed in the same direction," Corakin said. "My badger has a sense for when children are distressed. If your sister was upset, I am sure that Ziege went to comfort her and then led her somewhere safe."

"It's a badger." Ade gave Corakin a disbelieving look.

"They're very loyal and intelligent creatures," Corakin assured her. "Shall we follow your tracking spell or mine?"

Ade appreciated the fact that he didn't just make the assumption that he was in charge or that his magic was better than hers. Unfortunately, because her spell to track Rajya was shaky, she had to concede to him.

"Yours," she said shortly. "That way I can focus on using my eyes."

They'd gone only a short way into the woods when Corakin asked how many siblings she had. "I know it's not really any of my business," he added. "You just seem to have a lot on your shoulders for someone so young."

"What do you know about it?" Ade snapped.

Grief crossed his face. "I've known a few people your age who carried far more weight than they should have been expected to."

Something about his words made Ade believe that his concern was genuine, and she was surprised by her instinct to trust him. She hadn't felt like that toward any adult since her parents had died.

"Five," she said. "I have five siblings."

"I'm not going to ask about your parents," Corakin said. "But once we find Ziege and your sister, I'm going to ask you if you need any help, and I would like you to think very hard before you tell me no."

Ade shot him a look, but he still seemed focused on his tracking spell. As they came out of the woods, he turned toward a warehouse. Before Ade could tell him that Rajya would never go in a place like that, they heard a shout. The voice was too deep to be Rajya, but Corakin and Ade both started running in that direction.

****

Following the badger had been a good idea. Deciding to go into the warehouse as soon as she heard unfamiliar footsteps had not been. Rajya had thought there would be somewhere to hide until the strangers passed, but instead, the place had been completely empty. She'd still been trying to figure out what to do when the door burst open and three men came in like they owned the place but she didn't think they did.

"Told ya she came in here." The man speaking had a funny accent and a big mole on his cheek.

"All right, little girl, here's what's going to happen." Another man had his wand out and pointed it at Rajya which she knew wasn't a nice thing to do. "You're gonna come with us and do everything we say, and we won't hurt you."

Rajya knew she wasn't always great at reading people but even she knew he was lying. They were going to hurt her no matter what she did and that scared her because she didn't like being hurt. Her hand shook as she reached for her wand. It was a little one, a kid's wand, barely powerful enough to help her direct her magic, but it was all she had.

Then something bumped into her leg and growled, reminding her that she wasn't alone. She had a badger and that made her straighten and square her shoulders.

"What is *that*?" The third man took a step back.

"It's dead is what it is." The man with the wand glanced at his partners. "Get ready in case I miss."

Rajya wanted to tell them that they shouldn't hurt the badger, that she'd stop them, but her voice didn't want to work. In fact, nothing wanted to work. She was frozen again and it was so much worse than before because now she was in trouble and so was the nice badger who helped her not be scared.

Suddenly the man with the wand moved toward her and the badger jumped. The man let out a shout as the animal's teeth buried in his leg which had to hurt but Rajya didn't feel bad because he was a mean man.

"Get it off!" He started to shake his leg, trying to knock the badger loose.

His friends had their wands out but didn't seem to be able to figure out where to direct their spell. Rajya knew she should use their distraction to run but her knees were locked and her legs refused to obey her and she wanted to make sure the badger was okay as much as she wanted to leave.

The man managed to shake the badger free and gave it a kick, making Rajya angry and that feeling was enough to help her voice push through the ice keeping it inside.

"Don't do that!" The words exploded out of her, shocking her with their boldness.

All three men turned toward her, but before any of them could do anything to her, someone else's voice rang out.

"Get away from my sister!"

Rajya felt relief rushing through her as Ade came running in. She didn't know who the man was with Ade but Rajya was glad to see him too. Even her strong, wonderful sister was no match for three adult men and Rajya didn't know what she'd do if Ade got hurt because Ade was the one who took care of them now and kept them together. If something happened to Ade, Rajya and her siblings might be split up again and Rajya didn't want that to happen.

She prayed in her head that everything would be okay.

328

****

Ade's blood turned to ice when she saw the three men stalking toward her sister. She'd never seen them before, but she knew what they were anyway. They were predators and people like her siblings were their prey. They'd either use them or sell them...or both.

She was barely aware of Corakin beside her, rushing forward with his wand out. She'd always been good enough with magic to take care of her family, but now she realized that the years of schooling she'd missed might be the difference between life and death. And not just for her.

She dove out of the way as her spell rebounded back on her, wincing as she slammed into the ground. When she looked up, a man with a mole loomed over her, a chilling leer on his face.

"Looks like this is my lucky night," he said. "You stay right there like a good girl and maybe we won't hurt you too bad."

"You're not going to hurt her at all."

Ade blinked as the owner of the voice stepped between her and the man. She had to be dreaming. Angels weren't real, but here was someone who had to be an angel. He had wings, after all. Massive blue-black wings, streaked with slate gray.

Except, weren't angel wings supposed to be white?

"What are you?" the man with the mole asked.

She could almost hear the smile in the angel's voice when he said, "Justice."

And then he pulled out a sword.

Ade stared as the angel of justice went on the attack. Not with a wand, but with an actual *sword*. A sword that sliced through the man's wrist and sent both hand and wand dropping to the floor.

She should've been sickened by the gush of blood and the man's pained scream, but all she could think was what he would've done to her and Rajya.

Rajya.

Thoughts of her sister got Ade moving again and she scrambled over to the girl's side. Ade could hear the angel behind her and moved so that Rajya couldn't see what was happening. She had no doubt it was violent and bloody.

Only a minute later, everything was silent. Bracing herself for what she might see, she turned around, being sure to keep herself in front of Rajya. Just in case anyone got any bad ideas.

"Bram, thank you." Corakin greeted the angel. "How did you know I was in trouble?"

"I didn't." The angel named Bram shrugged and his wings suddenly disappeared. "I've been tracking these guys for days. They had a warrant out on them for trafficking, *darnau ffiaidd o fudr*." He spat on the ground at the end of what was clearly an insult of some kind.

"Still, thank you." Corakin turned toward the girls. "Are you all right?"

Ade nodded, her gaze darting back to Bram who didn't seem at all concerned that he was covered in blood.

"Don't worry about him," Corakin said. "That's Bram Grimm. He works security at my school."

That didn't explain the wings, but Ade was more concerned with getting her sister home safely and avoiding all questions that could lead to her and her siblings being split up again.

"Badger!" Rajya exclaimed.

Ade turned to see Rajya hurrying over to where the badger was limping toward them.

"Ziege!" Corakin immediately went to his pet.

"Good badger." Rajya threw her arms around the animal and then looked at Ade with an unmistakable question on her face.

Ade's heart sank. She hated that she was going to have to tell Rajya that they couldn't keep the badger, but at least they were both safe. That was going to have to do for now.

"You know," Corakin spoke before Ade could. "Ziege gets lonely sometimes, when I'm working." He glanced at Ade. "He might like having some kids around."

"We can't take in an animal," Ade said, deliberately misunderstanding.

From the look on Corakin's face, he knew what she was doing, but he didn't call her on it. "Well, you'd all be welcome to come stay with Ziege instead."

"Ade, please?" Rajya gave her older sister a pleading look.

"Rajya, I don't know…"

Corakin put a hand on Ade's shoulder and gave her a soft smile. "You're far too young for this responsibility. You should be allowed to be a sister, rather than mother and father both."

Ade swallowed hard and tried to push down how much she wanted what he was offering. She couldn't trust it.

Could she?

"You would all be automatically accepted into Audeamus, of course," he continued. "Further education for you and your siblings as soon as they reach the proper age. Until they, they'd have a place at the closest primary school."

"They really do need to be in school," Ade agreed, her resolve wavering. She'd been doing this for so long and she was so tired.

A still, small voice whispered in her head that she could trust this man. She'd heard that voice a time or two before and it had never steered her wrong.

"And you'd have a home," Corakin promised. "Whatever that may look like, it'd be a home for all of you. And I won't ever let anyone separate you from each other."

That was it. The last reassurance that she needed. She supposed she'd eventually need more at one point or another, but for right now, it was enough.

"All right." She nodded as she stood and reached for Rajya. "Let's go get the rest of our family."

"Wonderful!" Corakin beamed. "And then I'll make welcome home scones!"

Ade had no idea what those might be, but since they had the word 'home' in them, she figured she'd like them just fine. After all, it was a word she hadn't thought she'd ever hear again. She had a funny feeling, though, that it wouldn't be the last time.

Home.

It sounded wonderful.

Wolf at the Door

Scarlett Kol

The whinny of horses rang through the treetops. Distant. North, maybe. But still far too close. I stilled, resting against the rough bark of a birch tree, then listened to the noises swirling on the breeze. Above my head, autumn leaves rustled in a slow percussion, but soon drown out to the far away stomp of hooves and broken branches. I closed my eyes and placed my hand over my pounding heart.

Oh Goddess, bless me with the good fortune to find the beast before they do.

I whispered the prayer thrice, then clutched my satchel strap tighter across my chest. Most of the coven laughed at my plan, but if I failed, it would only be my life on the line. One more casualty when we'd already had so many.

No one in my circle cared about the wolf attacks. The number of times those same villagers condemned and threatened my sisters for our beliefs, didn't warrant sympathy when a stray animal began peeling off their numbers. We simply strengthened our protection spells and let nature take her course.

Except I couldn't let it go. Each report of an attack on an innocent ached within my bones. They reeked of disproportion. Of wrong. Not the balance I'd devoted my life to. The balance I drew my strength and magic from. I needed to make things right, even if I might regret it. I'd brewed the poison myself. Hemlock as a base with a pinch of wolfsbane and half a dozen other herbs to ensure that it would take down a wolf, but with enough rejuvenation power to save the tortured soul inside. After all, the villagers claimed a wolf took their loved ones, but the witches knew better.

Then my race began. Another young man ripped from his home yesterday sent the villagers into a flight of panic. A hunting party. Men with muskets rushing into the mysterious forest to kill themselves a prize. Heroes of honor—and completely in my way. I'd prepared for weeks. I'd waited. The poison needed the peak of the full moon, and now I had unwelcome competition. If only they could've waited until tomorrow.

I trudged forward on my mission, scanning every dark shadow or broken tree limb for any sign of the wolf. Warm rays of sunshine beat down on my chestnut locks and soothed the pressure of stress in my skull as fall leaves whisked around the bottom of my skirt, then fluttered away on the breeze. Lofty treetops whispered. Beckoned. Invited me in with a cheery tone and mocked my baleful intentions. The idyllic landscape sang of sweet, seasonal celebration, not the harbingering of death. But I marched determined into the woods looking for just that. Hopefully, it would also bring rebirth and hope once lost to a dangerous beast.

The battle cry of hunters drifted behind me as I ventured onward. If they found the wolf first heading their direction, I'd be no match for their skills, but if they chose wrong, picked a different path, then I might be headed the exact right way.

Ahead of me, the trees thinned and streams of daylight grew brighter, nearly blinding outside the canopy. As I continued on, the soft lapping of the running water called out ahead.

Bursting out of the woods, the creek lay out for miles in either direction. Crystal blue waves glittered in the sunshine and my muscles relaxed as the awe of the beautiful day worked its spell upon me. If only I had time to linger here for a few hours.

But the allure of serenity wasn't the only voice drawing me closer, instead, I moved on calculated strategy. Animals needed to drink and stalking easy prey near a watering hole seemed like a reasonable place to continue my search. Except no animals lined the banks as expected. Instead, one stray human splashed around in the water, likely scaring any timid creature away.

I glanced back into the thicker trees then inched closer, watching him from afar. Wavy, flaxen hair atop his head shone like a crown in the light as he frolicked in the water, his pant legs rolled up to his knees. His thin white shirt flapped tight against his chest, like the sail on a ship I'd once seen in the harbor. A grand thing of beauty the ship had been, and my pulse quickened thinking the same about the rogue in the creek. I peered around, but saw no one lounging near the creek bed. Just him. Splashing about with little care for anyone else.

Straightening my cloak over my shoulders, I gripped my satchel tighter and marched toward the edge of the water.

"Excuse me, sir," I said.

He didn't respond, only continued batting his hand against the surface of the water, making circular ripples that spanned out around him.

I assumed a louder, more stern voice. "I said, excuse me, sir."

The creek guardian halted and his head jerked side to side as if he'd imagined hearing me. He gazed back over his shoulder and his icy blue eyes popped open wide. His body twisted as his feet faltered.

"Whoa," he shouted as his balance slipped.

I rushed forward and extended my arm. He grabbed hold, his strong fingers digging into my flesh, as he steadied himself on his feet. A delighted smile curled across his deep red lips as he released his grip and placed his hands on his hips.

"Hello there. I didn't realize I had an audience," he said, giving a majestic bow.

The gesture teased a grin from my mouth, but I quickly pushed it back down. "My apologies, I didn't mean to intrude, but I wondered if you could be of help."

He splashed his way out of the water and dripped a puddle on the rocky shore. "Of course, what might I be of service for?"

Leaning in closer, I lowered my voice. "Have you, by chance, seen a wolf?"

"A wolf?" His nose scrunched up to match his narrowed stare. "Why would a lady like yourself be searching for a wolf?"

Good question. My rational brain knew asking was a huge mistake, but that never seemed to stop my mouth. Heat built up in my cheeks and I turned away. "Never mind."

The stranger placed his hand on my shoulder and I looked back, staring at his thick fingers on my cloak. He quickly whisked them away. "Not so fast, you can't ask a question like that then ignore it. I have heard little about wolves in this part of the woods, so I hadn't expected a slight thing like you to come searching for one."

Pushing my spine straighter, I stood tall, my nose in the air to add extra height. "It's just that... Wait, are you bleeding?" I pointed at the stranger's leg, as red drops poured down his calf and stained the ground.

"Oh, that. It's nothing." He swiped his hand dismissively through the air and slid his injured leg behind the other. "I just fell off my horse, is all. Ungrateful animal is probably halfway back to his stable by now."

I shuddered and slowly stepped away.

"So, that means... Forget I asked. I should be going."

He didn't look familiar, as I would've remembered that face about town. But clearly, the search for the big, bad wolf extended past the borders of our tiny village. And when I thought I'd been one step ahead; it turns out I was even further behind. Turning on my heel, I started for the safety and anonymity of the trees.

"Has my confession about being a lousy rider offended you, miss?"

I stopped but didn't turn around. "No. I just didn't realize you were a hunter. I'll leave you to your business." And as far out of mine as I could get.

"What makes you say I'm a hunter? And why does that worry you so much?"

I waved my hand over my head. "It doesn't. Carry on."

"But I'm not. I only went for a leisurely trail ride and my stubborn horse Dominic spooks easily. A jackrabbit crossed our path, and he tossed me to the ground. Is my shame really such a bother that you'd run without at least finishing the conversation you started?"

His voice swirled around me, and I cringed at my mistake.

"Of course not." I hesitated, but eventually turned around to face him. "But do something about that leg before it gets worse."

He crooked his eyebrow and donned a satisfied smirk. "That's what I was doing before someone interrupted me, trying to clean my wounds."

Another layer of guilt draped over me as I clenched and unclenched my fists. I sighed. "Maybe I can help."

I marched back and sat down on the rocky edge, pulling my satchel into my lap. "Sit down. It won't be perfect, but it should slow the bleeding."

He smiled, a broad, charming smile that I couldn't look at directly. Like staring into the sun. Then he sat down, his legs spread out in front of me.

I leaned forward and peeked at the injured leg. Red streaked across his skin, accented by matted leg hair. Much more extensive than I expected. "Do you have anything to cover the cuts?"

He reached back and tugged at a green coat lying beside a nearby bush. He whisked a blue scarf out of the sleeve and handed it to me. "Will this do?"

I nodded and searched through my satchel for a few herbs that might help. After crushing them in my hand, I scooped a bit of creek water and added it to the mixture, creating an earthy-smelling paste. I spread some on the deepest part of his gash, and his leg twitched beneath my fingertips.

"This looks much worse than a fall. Are you sure that's all it was?"

"I might have fallen into a particularly thorny patch of brush. I'm a bit accident-prone." He dropped his head to his chest as the tops of his cheeks tinged pink.

"Looks like it." I spread the salve thicker, concentrating on the string of puncture wounds closer to his ankle. Must've been quite the thorn bush.

The stranger's leg twitched again, and he bent forward to examine my work. "What is that concoction, anyway?"

"Sage and blackwort. They won't do a lot, but it should keep the cut from infection until you can get it bandaged up properly."

He rested back on his elbows and watched me fuss over his leg. His stare punctured holes in my concentration and I had to avoid looking at him.

"And why do you know how to do these things?" he asked. "Are you a witch, by chance?"

I froze, my hands hovering over his injury. "Of course not. I happen to be a nurse."

"Really? A nurse who wanders the forest looking for wild animals and keeps a strange supply of herbs in her bag. That sounds right."

Taking a deep breath, I continued on the wound. Running would make me look guilty. I'd played this game many times before. Denial was my most prized weapon. "Witches go against the entire moral fibre of humanity. I can't believe you'd accuse me of that."

"Even if I really don't care? Moral fibre only matters to those who never really uphold it anyway, don't you think?"

I laughed. "Clearly, you've met some of the people in my village."

The stranger sat up and edged toward me. The unexpected closeness made my mind hazy. "I'm the last person to be prejudiced against others. Especially magical ones. Your secret is safe with me, little witch."

"But I never said—"

He tilted his head and stared through me. My lies wouldn't work. He'd already devised the truth, and I'd given myself away.

"Where are my manners?" He pushed his hand near my face. "I'm Tristan Du Chambray."

"Pleased to meet you." I raised my sticky hands and shrugged, happy to have avoided a full out admittance of witchcraft. "Daniela."

"Just Daniela? No titles or airs to declare? Even witches must have their aristocracies."

Very true. The high priestess wasn't just a role model, she ruled the coven like a queen. Society didn't differ much, regardless of the altar you worshipped at.

"Good point. But, no. Just Daniela is fine."

He leaned back and tucked his hands beneath his head, staring at the sky while I finished rubbing the herbs along his leg. "All right, Daniela, why are you looking for a wolf?"

"Because a wolf has been terrorizing our village. It's already taken four of our citizens and it needs to be taken care of."

"But why you? Leave it to the men to fight the beast while you—"

"Cook and tend to children?" I glared at him, pushing rougher into his cuts.

He flinched and sat upright again. "No. While you concentrate on things like healing the sick and creating magic."

"Magic is exactly why I need to find the wolf first. But it's ridiculous, I doubt you'd understand."

"Try me. I've heard a lot of things in my short life."

I grabbed the scarf and wrapped it tight around his leg with a tight knot holding it in place.

"Have you ever heard a werewolf?"

"Only in fairy stories, but yes, once or twice."

I leaned closer as though anyone would hear me. As if the birds would take my confession and spread it among the village. "I believe it is a werewolf taking the villagers, and if they kill the wolf, it will also kill the person the wolf has claimed."

Tristan shook his head. "You're right, that sounds ridiculous."

"Maybe. But you wanted to know, and that's the answer. I'm here to find the wolf and deliver a poison that will separate the wolf from the man. It needs to be activated by the light of the full moon, so I only get once chance to do this right. Once ingested it will destroy the unnatural part of the beast and release the human. I can't just let the hunters kill an innocent life. Anyone cursed by the werewolf's bite shouldn't suffer for their misfortune."

"And what if you're wrong? What if it's just a wolf?"

I rolled his pant leg down over the scarf and rinsed my hands in the creek, drying them on my skirt. "Then the poison will kill the wolf and everyone is happy. That should take care of your leg. Make sure to get it properly bandaged when you get home."

I replaced the herbs in my satchel and stood on shaky legs. "Good day, Tristan."

"Where are you going?" He rushed to his feet and shrugged on his jacket, following me away from the creek.

"I'm off to find the wolf, remember? Or did you hit your head when you fell from your horse?"

He laughed, the joke twinkling in his eyes. He stumbled forward, too close for decorum. "I'm pretty sure my head is fine, although I feel a bit dizzy since you arrived, little witch."

A sudden lightness clouded my own mind, but I denied it. I patted him on the shoulder. "Nothing a good night's sleep won't cure."

"But you can't just leave. Have you ever seen a werewolf before? What are you going to do if you even find him? He may rip you limb from limb."

"No, I've never seen one before, but inexperience doesn't make me helpless." I pulled my knife from the sheath at my waist and slid it quickly back into its place.

"You are definitely a surprise, Daniela. But I won't let you walk away. Let me come with you."

I took a strained breath and walked on deeper into the forest. He followed close behind, matching every step. "Thank you, but I'll be fine. Besides, shouldn't you be getting off that leg, anyway?"

"It's feeling better already." He stomped his foot on the ground and fought the wince trying to crack across his face. "And what kind of man would I be to let you face this danger alone?"

I stopped short, and he kept walking, then spun around, realizing he'd gone too far.

"I don't need a man to help me."

"Fine. I understand." He nodded and crossed his hands politely behind his back. "But maybe you might want one? Besides, I do have some hunting experience, so I could probably be of help."

"Only if you promise not to get in my way."

He made the sign of the cross over his heart, then froze as he seemed to remember his pagan company. "I promise."

We walked in silence, each moving in tandem over the uneven ground. Some of the tension in my shoulders released having Tristan by my side. At least there would be someone to tell the coven if things went awry.

"All right, fearless hunter. Which way should we go?" I crossed my arms and scanned the paths ahead of us. One led into a darker part of the woods, another through a bright meadow, and the last wasn't a path at all, just inky darkness marked by a pair of dead trees that had fallen into a perfect "x".

Tristan placed his hand on his chin and surveyed each option.

"Why don't we try this way?" He pointed toward the meadow. "Wolves love rabbits and I'm sure there are several in there."

I stepped back and allowed him to move ahead. "Then, please sir, take the lead."

* * *

The sun dropped low in the western sky, and I shielded my eyes with my hand to avoid staring straight into its rays. The golden shimmer on the russet and pumpkin-colored leaves dipped into more ominous tones as the day waned, inching closer into the night.

I dragged my leaden feet forward, concentrating on each step and attempting to forget the past several hours of nothing. No wolves. No clues. Not even people, save Tristan and me. Just miles of forest canopy closing in over our heads.

"Are we ever going to find anything?" I said, as I rested on a large fallen log, my tired legs tingling beneath my skirt.

"Hunting requires patience." Tristan sighed and leaned back against a nearby larch tree, his exasperated tone draining the sentiment from his words.

My shoulders fell forward as I tried to keep my head up. "Except I'm quickly running out of it."

"You knew you'd embarked on a difficult task. Things like this don't come easy."

And they hadn't. Tristan did as he promised, leading me down pathway after pathway. Except even he had started to give up hope. The poison needed the light of the full moon, but what good was an active poison with no target? Perhaps the hunters had better luck and were hoisting the limp body of the wolf above their heads at the local tavern to the cheers of the entire town. But that would mean another unfortunate soul would be taken too soon. Cursed to die along with a killer beast. Magic taking another victim. Magic. Was it even worth the trouble it caused?

"Maybe I need to think about all this differently. I shouldn't be running around chasing shadows when I could be using my strength." I slipped off my satchel and placed it on the ground, then cleared the fallen leaves around me. "Tristan, can you find me a stick?"

He looked at me curiously, but pushed himself off the tree and obeyed my command.

"Here." He passed me a willow rod. "What are you doing?"

"Tracking spell." I traced the stick through the dirt, drawing a wide circle, then added a pentacle in the center.

"Wait a second. You could track the wolf this entire time. Why didn't you mention this before?"

I tossed the stick to the side and examined my drawing. Perfectly symmetrical. "Because I didn't know if it would work. It still might not. You typically need to have something of the person or thing being tracked, but maybe if I have something charged with enough intention it might be enough."

"I have no idea what that means, but—" he leaned closer, his warm breath fluttering across my skin and warming my blood. "What if someone were to see you? Witches are about as popular as man-eating wolves, these days."

I grabbed hold of his upper arms, locking his eyes with mine. "That is why you need to be a superior lookout. Stand here, and if you hear anyone then rush toward them and stall. That should give me enough time to get rid of any evidence."

Pushing him back a few steps, I positioned him at the top of the circle, then looped around and sat down on the forest floor. I pulled the blue vial from my satchel and gazed at the dangerous elixir inside.

"Is that the wolf-killing poison?" Tristan asked, not daring to step away from his station, his stare glued to the small bottle.

"It is. But it's really just a separation spell. Breaking the natural from the unnatural. More science than you would think." Placing the vial in the center of the pentacle, I closed my eyes and inhaled the crisp autumn air. When my breathing slowed to the rhythm of the breeze, I looked out again over my makeshift altar. I unsheathed my knife and sliced the soft part of my hand near my thumb, then squeezed, letting the blood trickle out over the vial.

Tristan flinched then stared off into the distance, either taking his lookout task seriously or potentially not having a strong stomach for blood.

"Is it working? I don't think it's working?" Tristan said, finally daring to look back.

"Give it a second. Magic takes patience too."

The vial slowly started to roll. Left, then right. Left, then right.

His eyes lit bright as stars. "It's actually happening."

"Have you ever seen magic before?" I asked, my stare still glued to the bottle.

"Once or twice, but it always fascinates me."

I glanced up with a warm smile at Tristan's excited expression. The late afternoon light shimmered in his hair bringing out the golden strands and a warm glow surrounded his face. "I've been brought up with this my entire life and it still fascinates me too."

Then the vial stopped.

I frowned.

Squeezing my fist again, the last bit of blood dripped slowly off my palm onto the blue glass. It rocked slowly to one side, then stopped again. Still frozen between Tristan and me.

"What's wrong?" Tristan said. "What did it say?"

I dropped my head into my hands. "Nothing. The vial is supposed to spin like a compass then rest in the direction of the wolf, but it didn't even move. It just sat here between us and rocked."

Tristan shrugged. "What do you think happened?"

"I don't know." I slapped my hand through the pile of leaves beside me and watched them scatter across the dirt, then place the vial back into my satchel. "Maybe I really do need something of the wolf's, or maybe it's because the poison isn't active yet. The light of the full moon is still missing from the recipe."

"Then I guess we'll just have to keep looking." He stepped around the pentacle and extended his hand with a grin. I accepted, and he whipped me to my feet, much stronger than I'd expected from his stature.

I stumbled as my feet hit solid ground and landed my head into his chest.

"Easy now." He let me linger there for a moment, then helped ease me back up straight. His eyes flicked back and forth, reading all the features of my face as his breath hitched.

"I'm so sorry." I splayed my hand across his chest and pushed myself back but he wrapped his warm fingers around mine holding it into place. The cool breeze nipped at my burning cheeks and I cast my stare away.

"It's almost nightfall, maybe we should—"

Tristan's words disappeared into silence as I caught sight of the trees in the distance. Two dead fallen trees crossed into a perfect 'x'.

I ripped my hand away and stormed toward them. The same ones I'd seen earlier that day. I closed my eyes and heard the babble of the creek just beyond the bend, and my stomach sank.

"We haven't even left the creek," I yelled over my shoulder. "Did you trick me?"

Tristan rushed up beside me. "What are you talking about?"

"You know exactly what I mean." I pointed at the trees and scowled with every bit of my being. "This is exactly where we started. Have you been leading me in circles all day?"

"No, how could I?"

"I don't know. You've been leading the way for hours. I let you pick the route over and over again because you insisted that you knew about hunting. Did you do this on purpose or are you truly that lost with directions?"

Fire burned deep in my gut. I'd wasted my whole day in probably three miles worth of landscape. How could I be so foolish? I knew I should have gone alone.

"Is it true? Did you deceive me, Tristan?"

His head dropped to his chest, the words for his betrayal choosing to remain unsaid.

"That's why we haven't seen anyone or anything, isn't it? You've been leading me astray, so I wouldn't find the wolf."

"I can explain." He stepped forward, his arms wide open, but I didn't care.

I whirled around and ran in the direction of the dead trees, not stopping once to look back.

"Daniela, come back here. Daniela, wait."

Tristan's voice faded behind me as I burst deeper into the dark wood.

No, I will not come back.

Not for him, anyway.

Branches picked at my cloak as I ran. Twigs snapped beneath my heavy footsteps, echoing in rhythm with my puffing gasps. The crimson sliver of the sun peeked through the canopy. So little time left.

How many of my hours had he wasted? And for what? I didn't even care to know the reason, I already hated it. Just another man thinking he knew better. Trying to stifle my voice, and I'd let him. Even the most devious lips could create a charming smile. Yet, I'd let him lie and dissuade me from my true goal all day.

Heavy footfalls sounded behind me and I buckled down, forcing every ounce of energy I had into my feet. Except running blindly through the forest wasn't exactly a plan. Not only did I need to find the wolf, and fast, I needed to lose the dog behind me.

The light ahead dimmed. The last light of day bleeding across the sky. My foot slammed into an exposed root, and I tripped along, fortunate to avoid a full-blown fall. Bubbles of weightlessness floated into my throat and stole my breath. My pace slowed, even against the insistent urging for my brain. The trees thinned and I stumbled forward into a small dimly lit clearing nestled lower on the forest floor.

I halted. Alabaster bones created a crooked path toward a shallow cave carved out of the hillside. Streaks of red throbbed across my vision in time with my accelerated pulse. Black flies swarmed near the entrance, devouring a ball of matted fur and blood. The dead eyes of a hare stared up from the decomposing leaves, pleading for help that would never come.

Slapping my hand over my mouth, I choked down a scream and staggered back a step.

"Congratulations, you found the wolf's den. And all on your own."

I whirled around, still holding my face, as Tristan broke into the clearing. He sauntered slowly, choosing to circle away from me instead of risking a direct confrontation. Smart move.

"Yes, and with no thanks to you." I dropped my hands to my hips and straightened my spine, the quiver in my knees hidden beneath my skirt.

"Of course, I had no intention of showing you the way here. Not until I was ready."

The cool calmness of his demeanor rattled my anger.

"Ready? For what? So I could watch you slaughter the wolf yourself? You're no better than any of the men from the village. You have no mercy, no capacity of thought that there may be an innocent life to save and not just a trophy for your den."

Tristan tilted his head to the side as if analyzing my stance, then tossed his head back and laughed. The menacing sound resonated off the treetops and crows launched into the twilight sky. "A wolf's head is no trophy to me."

He stepped closer, and I retreated in tandem. My hand shot to my waist and pulled my knife, brandishing it in front of me. "Stay back, I will succeed in my task and you will see that I was right."

He stopped his advance and raised his palms in surrender. "We'll see."

Faster than a hummingbird's wing he went for his own knife, waving it high in retaliation. Double the length of mine with a jagged, serrated edge. A tiger-sized knife compared to my own.

"Except, you don't have your story straight. I did intentionally lead you away from here, but not so I could kill the wolf." He licked his thumb and slid it across the sharp edge of his weapon, a strange joy building in his eyes. "I always planned on killing you first."

The world rippled. A tear in the landscape hazing reality and descending us into nightmares. My throat dried as the last drop of daylight glinted off Tristan's knife tip.

He lunged.

I ran.

"Where are you going, little witch?" Tristan's voice dropped to a low growl as his menacing breath followed close behind.

Scanning the treeline, I weighed my few options. All of which required running faster than the knife-wielding madman at my back. I shouldn't have told him what I was. But I trusted him. He made me trust him. I huffed and puffed as my feet glided over the forest floor, and I tried to recite every protection charm I knew. But the adrenaline jumbled all the words in my brain.

A haggard scream rose in my throat and reverberated through the woods.

"Help!"

Tristan laughed, his heady breaths falling on my neck as he stomped on the hem of my skirt. My feet fell out from under me as a sharp pain thrust through my abdomen, dragging me to the ground.

"Help," I screamed again, as I clawed forward across the dried sticks and dead leaves. Dirt caked in my fingernails, but I kept moving.

"They'll never hear you. All the hunters went home hours ago." Tristan smashed his knee into my calf. Searing pain surged through my limbs as he pressed his body over my back. "So, scream all you want."

"Let me go." I clawed my hand behind my head, but failed to make contact.

"Give up fighting, it will only make it harder on yourself."

A piece of my soul broke at his threat and for a split second my body fell limp. He took advantage of my weakness, pinning me harder to the ground.

"I'll bet you wish you hadn't stopped to help. It's always the kind hearts that summon the most darkness."

Except the young man by the creek couldn't possibly be the monster on my back. However, kind never did mean weak. I strained my neck to glimpse his position, then bit down on my lower lip and swung my heel into his injured leg.

"Ow!" he yelled and slackened his grip.

I slithered forward on my elbows, pulling my body free. The edge of the clearing grew closer. Attainable. Pulling my leg forward, I pushed to stand. A blunt smack landed between my shoulder blades. Pain splintered through my spine as Tristan forced me down onto my back.

"You are a feisty one. I'll give you that."

Hot tears seared down my face as he pushed down on my chest. Breathing ached. The air thinning to near nothingness.

"Who sent you after me? I may be a witch, but I am no threat. Let me leave and you will never see me in these woods again. I'll leave this to the hunters. Just please, let me go."

"It's not personal, just the wrong place at the wrong time." He leaned closer, covering his face barely an inch from mine. The silver moon glinted in his ice-cold eyes. "Remember when I asked if you'd ever seen a werewolf? You didn't realize you were staring right at one." He reared his head back and licked his lips. "But wasn't that exactly what you're looking for?"

My stomach hollowed. I was right. There was a werewolf, but I'd been foolish assuming he'd be in wolf form. *Stupid, Daniela.* Taking on too many causes and forgetting to take care of myself. The tears burned hotter and poured faster.

"And my tracking spell, it did work, it—"

"Was tracking me. Indeed. A nice bit of spellwork, by the way. But I won't be letting you get into any more magic, I'm afraid." He rolled off me and tucked his arm beneath my shoulder. "Now, let's get on with this." He jabbed the tip of the knife near my face, close enough that my breath fogged the metal. "And I don't suggest any more attempts at escape. You're outmatched."

He struggled to his feet, then whipped me through the air to mine.

The sun had finally set and taken the harsh lines of red, replacing them with the cool blue tones of the rising moon. It bathed the clearing in glassy light, as if acknowledging my new clarity, yet hiding my shame in its shadows. Pain seared in my muscles as Tristan's fingers dug deeper into my bicep, dragging me toward the cave. He tossed me in before him, the sharp blade resting against the back of my neck urging me forward into the darkness.

Oh Goddess, grant me the strength to face this challenge and wisdom to find escape.

A putrid warm scent surrounded my head as I tripped forward into the cave. A rotting stench. Bile rose in my throat and I gagged, choking it back down. The knife at my neck bit into my flesh and I continued forward.

"Enough." Tristan's voice bellowed as he grabbed my wrists and cuffed them in his large, firm hands. Rough ropes followed, tied tight with thick knots, each one ripping at my skin as it locked into place.

"Can't let you run away again." He tugged the last knot, then pushed me against the cave wall. My head smashed against the rock and a thick fog clouded over my mind.

The rope binding my hands raised until my arms pulled high over my head.

Tristan chuckled. A snap. A hit of sulphur. Then the warm light of a match lit a hurricane lamp in the middle of the room. The yellow glow cast over Tristan's face. The wide-eyed, carefree lightness that illuminated his features beside the creek bed had disappeared and twisted into something sinister and dark.

Beyond the lamp, few things were strewn around the room. Half-eaten bread, a flannel blanket, and a lump of clothing in the corner. I narrowed my stare. Blood stained the ground and the outline of limbs and human features came into focus. Black flies buzzed around the decomposing corpse as another waft of decay assaulted my nostrils. I struggled against the ropes, aching to cover my mouth as my stomach retched and emptied in front of me. The vile stench of stomach acid mixed with the decay, singeing the inside of my nostrils as I heaved again and again.

"You should get used to death, my little witch. As you will soon be joining the rest of them. You should understand that concept better than anyone. Nature has a balance—life and death—and soon I will take your life so you can meet death first hand." He watched my body convulse against the ropes and laughed, the evil sound echoing off the stone walls.

"So, it's true. The wolf killed the villagers."

"In a way." He stood and placed his hands behind his back, then paced. Each step, calculated and solemn. Back and forth. Back and forth. "I was there for every single one of them. I heard their screams as I ripped out their throats. I felt their hearts beat for the last time as they lay in my hands."

He placed his open palms in front of him and stared. The flicker of the lamplight roared in his eyes. "These hands have killed so many people already."

He swiped the knife from its sheath and admired the blade.

My legs shook as the ache in my arms overtook my body. The blood from my fingers had rushed away and my hands numbed. I never thought about how I might die, but this wasn't in any of my plans. Except maybe it wasn't too late.

I fought against the paralysis in my throat. "Fight the wolf, Tristan. You don't have to do this. You don't have to be a killer."

He lowered the blade as his questioning eyes scanned over my bound body. A beaming smile burst across his lips.

"You still don't get it, do you? I met the wolf last winter. That cold, lonely winter, where I ached for the rush of fresh blood to warm my hands."

He closed his eyes as his mouth dropped off, then raked an open palm over his face, his fingernails making tracks in his own flesh. I gasped. The monster flickered in his expression, reveling in the joy of his pain. A blood lust so strong and thick, it oozed sickening across my skin. I pulled harder against the ropes and slid backward, ramming my hip into the rough rock wall.

"A young man wandered into the woods. Lost in a sudden snowstorm. Delicately handsome, and oh so trusting."

Tristan stalked closer. The lamplight glowed over his repulsive smile, twisting shadows in his burning eyes. He raised the knife, and I struggled again. His hand smacked on my chin, holding my head steady. Tears soaked my face as I managed a whimpering cry. The hot sting of the blade tip traced down my cheek as I quivered in his grip.

"To his surprise, I gut him stomach to sternum while he thanked me for my help. Then that mangy wolf attacked. Bit my leg while my kill lay blubbering his last breaths and bleeding out on the clean, unspoiled snow. And since then, I have been fighting the wolf. Fighting against the furry cage it's locked me in, content to chase rabbits and foxes instead of enjoying the divine pleasure of human suffering. I killed those people. Me. But that beast inside fought me every step. It forces me to turn and rips open my wounded leg. It tries to keep my urges down. But that ends now."

I swallowed against the blade as he held it at my neck.

"You came along just in time. Your energy. Your goodness. Your abundance of life thrilled me. Each step we walked fueled by the thought of how delicious it would be to feel it all sputter out and die in my hands. Except for one small thing."

His hand flexed. I screamed, my voice ripping up my throat. The knife dropped to my chest and sliced through the strap of my satchel. He fell to the ground and scattered the contents of the bag in the dirt.

"Ah-ha. Here it is." He snatched the blue glass vial from the mess and held it above his head. "I need to get rid of this unnatural part of me. First, I kill the wolf that tears me down, and then I celebrate by making you my first kill in freedom."

He pulled up from his knees and strolled toward the entrance of the cave. The silvery moonlight glinted off the fragile glass of the bottle and the poison inside shimmered. Finally complete. A weapon lethal enough to kill a werewolf, but now even deadlier to set a more dangerous beast free.

"I almost killed you right away, you know. Drowned you in the creek and watched you struggle. But instead, you gave me the answer to my salvation, so I let you live a while. You brought me the hope I'd been looking for."

He uncorked the lid and swallowed the contents of the bottle in one gulp. I scanned the cave, looking for anything I could find to remove my restraints. Anything that might give me a head start for when the wolf died and set Tristan free. But nothing. Just the corpses and the lamp.

"I can feel it coursing through my veins," he said as he held his arms out in front of him. A blue glow started at the tips of his fingers and spread up his limbs, enveloping his entire body. I cowered near the wall, watching my own magic become my undoing.

Tristan raised his head toward the sky bathed in starlight and magic. He cackled, loud and long, each note piercing my heart and letting more dread seep in.

"The power. I can actually feel myself getting stronger. It's amaz—" Tristan's lips dropped to a frown as he bent over and grabbed his thighs. His arms shook, his entire body vibrating in front of me. White foam erupted from his lips, as his eyes rolled back toward his brain.

"Tristan," I yelled.

He didn't respond, save the high-pitched whining sound coming from his trembling body. He fell to his knees, still shaking until he folded into a ball on the ground.

"What have you done?" he mumbled, as he shook harder, kicking up a cloud of dirt around him.

Then he stopped.

"Tristan."

No response.

I fell against the rock wall and let my breathing slow. Relief washed through my limbs, cleansing out some of the fear. I must've measured things incorrectly. Made a mistake.

Good.

Thank you, Goddess, for unanswered prayers and failed spells.

The air stilled and the ominous mystery of the night seeped into my bones. My pulse quickened again, pounding hard in my temples. What if the poison didn't take, how long did I really have until Tristan came for me again? And even if the hemlock killed him, how would I explain his death to anyone who might find me? If a wild animal didn't find me first.

Questions kept coming, rolling around in my head and making the world hazy. I grabbed ahold of the ropes and pulled with all my strength, but they didn't budge. Still tied tight through the rock caverns above my head. I raised my feet from the ground, hoping sheer weight would pull them down, but again they gave no slack. How many others had he tied here, then killed, or just left to die?

I swung the ropes, jumping and twisting the restraints until my muscles screamed for me to stop. Panting, I collapsed against the rock wall as tears flooded my eyes. Would I die here anyway? At least by murder's hand, it would have been quick, but would I starve to death before nature reclaimed me in her own way?

Each teardrop tracked down my cheeks and splashed on my dress. A glowing haze covered over the cave as my head drifted, exhausted and hopeless, toward my chest. The lamp likely wouldn't even last till morning. Then I would truly be alone. Unless…

With renewed strength, I walked toward the lamp, stretching my arms as far as they would go. I reached my foot toward the lamp, trying to entangle the handle on my foot. Ropes may not break, but they would burn.

My toe grazed the outside of the glass, nearly knocking the lamp over and smashing it on the ground. A loud groan echoed through the cave. Tristan's body shuddered before me. I reached further with my foot, the joints of my shoulders nearly dislocating. But the pain would be worth the escape.

The groan grew louder. Deeper. Visceral. I stole my eyes away from the lamp and looked toward the entrance of the cave.

Tristan's shoulders arched and peaked as a gray sheen stretched out across his skin. His fingers popped and split until claws appeared in their place. His face popped and stretched into a snout until he let out a guttural howl. I eased back against the wall and stood perfectly still as the yellow eyes of the wolf stared back at me.

My lungs burned for oxygen, but I couldn't breathe. The wolf continued to glare and strut up to me. It snarled, revealing lines of pointed teeth perfect for ripping me apart.

The wolf sat back on its hind legs and snapped its jaw, then pounced right at me.

I screamed, tearing off the last shred of my voice. But its teeth never touched my skin. My hands dropped from above my head as the ropes fell from the ceiling, still clasped in the jaws of the wolf. It spat them to the ground and the lack of tension gave enough room for my hands to wriggle free.

Braids of dark red burns tattooed my skin where the rope bit into my flesh.

"You saved me," I said, as I rubbed my wrists and the blood flowed back into my fingers.

The wolf strode back to the entrance and grasped Tristan's knife within its teeth. He returned and dropped it at my feet.

"Is he ... gone?"

The wolf dropped his head, then lowered to the ground on his front paws.

"And that means you're free."

The wolf raised back on all four paws, then nuzzled his nose against my leg. I froze. His teeth snagged on my skirt, but he didn't bite. Instead, he turned and walked to the entrance of the cave. He glanced back at me and jerked his head toward the forest.

"You need to go," I said. "The hunters will be back tomorrow to kill you."

The wolf nodded and disappeared into the moonlight.

I raced out of the cave, each step taking me out of this nightmare and closer to home. Home. I doubt I'd be leaving it for a while after this. I clutched my cloak tighter to my chest and headed into the dark woods. A mournful howl hung in the night sky. My breath hitched for a moment, but I carried on.

We'd both better run.

The Haunted Tournament

By Alicia Rades

Chapter 1: Nadine

This short story takes place during The Reaper's Shadow, book two in the College of Witchcraft series by Alicia Rades.

Alchemy 101 was going to be the death of me. I was sure of it. Never mind that just a few weeks ago a reaper tried to take my soul to hell and hadn't managed it. This college Alchemy class was worse, and I was certain it would do me in.

On my first day, I exploded a cauldron. I needed today to go better if anyone was going to believe I was a real Alchemist. I wasn't, but no one except my friends knew that.

The coven was divided into five Casts, based on the type of magic a witch or warlock obtained during their Evoking Ceremony on their nineteenth birthday. Mentalists could control the mind or perform telekinesis, and Seers could get visions or talk to ghosts. Mortana were known as the Death Cast, and Alchemists could brew potions.

Then there was me. My magic had awoken a few weeks ago, and I became the only Curse Breaker in the coven— a Cast that had died out decades ago.

I had to hide it, though. If the coven found out what I was, the priestesses would demand my power, which could be catastrophic for my health. My lupus symptoms only got worse the more magic I used, and my doctors said it could take over a year for my body to get used to my new power. Luckily, I could use my power to fake my Cast using crystals infused with alchemy magic. This kind of magic was easy on me, and my power could go unnoticed by the coven.

I attended Miriam College, where witches and warlocks learned to control their magic. Everyone thought I was an Alchemist, so I'd been placed in Alchemy 101 this semester.

Isa rubbed against my leg and purred, offering comfort. I stared down at my cat for a few seconds, then I pushed my fear aside to focus on the task at hand. We were brewing a simple remedy for respiratory infections. With the alchemy crystal in my pocket and the fake cauldron mark on my arm, I could fool anyone into believing I was an Alchemist— if only I managed to brew a real potion.

"Steady," my lab partner Onyx warned as I lifted the bottle of peppermint oil above our cauldron.

My hands shook badly, but I took a deep breath and counted the drops according to the spell book. Professor Richards had described this as a simple but volatile potion. One wrong measurement, and the potion would fail.

"I'm good," I told Onyx as I counted the drops under my breath. "Four… Five… Ah!"

Gwen swept past our table, knocking into my elbow on her way back to her station from the supply closet. My hand jerked, and several extra drops fell into the potion. The mixture began hissing, and a white cloud rose from the cauldron. The strong scent of peppermint assaulted my nose, so potent that I began coughing uncontrollably.

At the front of the room, Professor Richards's face fell. "Everyone out!" he called. Students started screaming and scrambled to evacuate the room.

"Whoops," Gwen said innocently. Isa hissed at her, and I knew the bitch had done it on purpose.

"You…" I tried to catch my breath, but the smoke continued to spread across the room. I couldn't seem to get enough air.

Onyx grabbed my arm and started dragging me across the room. She coughed violently, and I wheezed as we stumbled into the hallway. Clean air filled my lungs, and I sagged to the ground.

"Nadine!" Onyx knelt beside me. "Are you all right?"

I kept my eyes on Gwen, who was whispering to Stacey. The girls shot glances our way, and Stacey snickered. Isa growled.

"Is everyone all right?" Professor Richards demanded. "Onyx? Nadine?"

"Fine," I rasped as I caught my breath.

"It's a common mistake," Professor Richards assured me kindly. "Give me a few moments to clear the room."

He went back inside the alchemy lab, and whispers spread throughout the hallway.

Gwen approached me, staring down her nose at me. "You should be more careful. You don't want to get sick before the Haunted Tournament. It'd be a shame if you couldn't compete."

She walked away laughing. It was no secret why she hated me. She was friends with *Chloe*, whose family had been in a feud with mine for generations.

I tried to shake it off, but taking a dig at my health was a low blow. After class, I sulked through the halls of Miriam Mansion, until I reached the cafeteria and slumped into a chair beside my friends.

My boyfriend, Lucas, noticed my sour mood right away, and he squeezed my hand under the table. The muscles in his arms flexed, and I found my eyes roaming over him, up his toned arms, across his cupid's bow lips, and into his mesmerizing green eyes. He gazed at me with desire in his eyes that made my heart do flips.

"Is everything okay?" he asked.

"Gwen sabotaged my potion in class," I grumbled.

Across the table, Grant cracked his knuckles. "I'm an Alchemist. I'll give her a taste of her own medicine."

Talia frowned. "What did she do?"

I quickly told my friends about what happened. When I finished, I asked, "What's the Haunted Tournament? Gwen mentioned some competition, like she didn't want me participating."

"It's a sporting event hosted every spring semester," Lucas explained. "The professors plan a different competition each year. It's like a game using magic. We never know what's going to happen, and that's part of the fun. Teams of four sign up, and whoever gets past the haunting first wins a prize."

"Let's do it," I decided immediately. "We can all sign up."

Talia looked uncertain. "The prize usually goes to seniors, because it's designed to show off their magic. It can get dangerous. I don't even have my magic yet, and your symptoms flare when you use too much magic."

I shrugged. "I'll be careful, and we'll back you up. Gwen and those bitches need to know they can't scare me."

"I guess it could be fun," Talia agreed.

"I'm in," Grant added.

"Looks like you've got yourself a team," Lucas said.

We left the cafeteria after we finished eating, and we found a group of people gathered around a sign-up sheet in the Main Foyer. We moved forward in the line. A group of girls finished signing their names, then one of them whirled around and nearly rammed into me. It was Chloe, along with her band of back-up bitches. Gwen and Stacey saw me and snickered under their breath. Camille crossed her arms and tapped her foot impatiently.

"Don't tell me *you're* entering the Haunted Tournament," Chloe sneered.

"That's really none of your business," I replied coldly.

"I deserve to know who I'm competing against," Chloe said, eyeing me up and down. "Though, I don't suppose I have anything to worry about. I heard you exploded another potion. You won't make it past the obstacles with your magic."

"At least I have magic," I stated.

Witches and warlocks didn't get their magic until they were nineteen. Chloe's birthday wasn't until the end of the semester. Her powers wouldn't awaken until then, and that's when one of us had to leave town— or suffer the fate of the curse over our families.

"I don't need magic to win," Chloe insisted. I had a feeling she was talking about more than just the Haunted Tournament.

Chloe pushed past me, slamming her shoulder into mine. The three girls beside her followed.

Lucas turned to me after they left. "Are you sure you want to do this?"

I nodded. "Chloe needs to learn that I belong here. I'm not going anywhere."

Lucas smirked. "Then let's give them hell."

***

I woke to the sound of screams the following morning. Isa jerked awake from where she slept at my feet, and Talia startled from across our dorm room. I could see the morning light coming in through the curtains, but it was shadowed by an overcast sky.

"What's going on?" Talia asked, still only half awake.

"I don't know," I said. "But it can't be good."

Another scream sounded, and I realized it was coming from outside. Talia kicked her covers off and leapt to the end of her bed to look out the window. Her face paled. "You're going to want to see this."

I groaned as I sat upright. My body ached as I made my way over to the window, and my stomach sank when I saw it. At first, I thought it was a group of witches descending upon the school. There had to be dozens of them. But then I noticed how they moved— twitchy and inhuman. It hit me. Those weren't witches. Not anymore.

They were *corpses*.

Several students raced into the school, screaming as the corpses approached. A few corpses had approached a vehicle in the parking lot and began pounding on the windows. I saw a shadow move, and I realized someone had locked themselves inside to hide. The car alarm went off, but the corpses kept pounding, trying to break through the glass.

Talia smirked. "It looks like The Haunted Tournament has begun."

My heart leapt in excitement. I didn't know what I expected when we signed up, but I certainly hadn't pictured us fighting zombies. It sounded fun!

I went to my dresser and tossed on a pair of jeans and a sweatshirt, then slapped my hair into a ponytail. Talia did the same, then we rushed out of the room, leaving our cats behind. We hurried down to the Main Foyer, where a huge group had already gathered.

Grant and Lucas were there, and we rushed over to them. They were watching the zombies through the window, awaiting instructions.

The double doors were open, and the group of corpses had nearly made it across the lawn. I could see them better now, and they looked frightening. Some still had pale skin stretching across their sunken faces, and others had rotted nearly to the bone. Old clothing hung off their bony figures, and dirt caked their hands.

A voice came over the school's intercom system. It sounded like Professor Warren, one of our necromancer professors. "Your task is to defeat the zombies. The first team to eliminate them wins. Let the Haunted Tournament begin!"

Teams began flooding out of the school, and magic whizzed across the lawn as students attempted to neutralize the corpses.

My friends and I ran outside and planted ourselves at the bottom of the stairs. A zombie reached for me, and my heart leapt. Magic sizzled in my palm, then shot toward the zombie's chest. The zombie didn't react when it slammed into him, but a sense of pride washed through me. My powers were so new that I hadn't cast a spell like that yet.

A battle orb flew past me, and the neck of the nearest corpse snapped. The skull rolled across the ground, landing at my feet. I shot a glance behind myself to see Lucas smiling proudly, another battle orb sizzling in his hand. Battle magic shot from his palms, and the corpses began falling over like bowling pins. I thought for sure we'd end them in no time… but the bodies began to rise again. Headless corpses and twisted skeletons stood, their bodies twitching as they approached.

A student flew over us on a broom, but a zombie reached up to grab his ankle, yanking the guy to the ground. His broom fell at Talia's feet.

The zombies descended upon us. Lucas threw up a shield, but it was too late. A rotting corpse in a tattered suit reached Talia and grabbed her by the front of the shirt. He yanked her to the ground.

"Get off of me, dirt breath!" Talia yelled as he nabbed her again. She kicked him in the face, then grabbed the broom and swung it at him. His jaw made a crunching sound and hung off the side of his face.

"Leave her alone!" Grant lunged for the corpse, while the rest of us tried holding off the others. He yanked the man's arm behind his back, but it snapped and tore clean off. Grant's features paled as he looked down at the dismembered arm in his hands. The corpse tilted its head, giving Grant a strange look. Then the hand grabbed his neck and squeezed.

It was more like a sparring session than anything that would hurt us, but it got our adrenaline pumping for sure. The tournament was a test to see how we'd do in a real fight.

I caught sight of Chloe's team nearby. Gwen and Stacey blasted off a few spells, and Chloe fought with her fists. A corpse reached Camille and clawed at her face. Chloe punched a zombie in the jaw, but it barely slowed down. I was impressed. Chloe looked like she knew what she was doing, even without magic.

Talia got to her feet again, but the zombie near her grabbed her hand and bit it. I lunged forward and sank my fingers into the zombie's eye sockets to pull him off of her.

"Lucas, can you stop them?" I cried.

"I'm a reaper, not a necromancer!" he replied. Reapers and necromancers were both part of the Mortana Cast, but their powers were vastly different. Necromancers could reanimate the dead, while reapers were responsible for leading souls to the other side— if the dead chose to go with them.

Corpses pushed past one another, all trying to get into the school. A few teams had retreated inside, but Lucas created a shield in front of us. The zombies hammered their fists against the shield, but they couldn't get through. We were safe— for a few moments, anyway.

"How do we stop them?" Talia asked breathlessly.

"I don't know if we *can* stop them," Lucas said thoughtfully.

I looked around. Teams were using battle magic and other spells to try to slow the zombies down, but nothing seemed to work. A few necromancers had gained control of some of the corpses, and a senior Mentalist with telekinetic powers flicked her wrists, tossing the corpses off their feet. The second they landed, they were already approaching again. The girl aimed her magic at a group of them again, and they clawed outward as their feet dragged against the ground. The tearing of flesh met our ears as her teammate used his telekinesis to rip them apart. Limbs went flying, but moments later, the bodies were piecing themselves back together again. I'd never seen anything like it.

Necromancers and Mentalists seemed to have the upper hand, but nothing could *defeat* the zombies— only slow them down.

"Lucas is right," I agreed. "Our battle magic is useless against them."

Nearby, Chloe yelled to her teammates. "How the fuck are they this strong?"

"Dark necromancy or something," Gwen panicked.

The Mentalist girl tore another corpse into pieces with her mind. Arms went flying in opposite directions from legs, but the corpse found pieces of another body to attach to.

Great, we were fighting Frankenstein's monster now. We could only hold them off so long.

"There's got to be more to it," I said. "We're supposed to be going through obstacles, right? So there's got to be some other way to stop them."

I turned to Lucas. "How would a necromancer cast a spell like this?"

"They could enchant the corpses," he said quickly. "But piecing the bodies back together... that requires skill. They've got to be watching the fight— controlling it."

"Then we have to find the necromancers responsible." I gazed out toward the trees, but I saw no movement. Whoever was doing this had to have a good view of the scene.

"They need a vantage point," I realized, looking upward. "They must be on the roof!"

My friends and I whirled around, and we raced into the school together. I turned down the hall— and came face-to-face with a dozen haunted spirits.

Chapter 2: Lucas

Ghostly moans filled the hallway as ethereal spirits swirled in front of us, blocking our path to the stairwell that led to the roof.

"This must be one of the obstacles," Nadine said. "One of our Seer professors must've summoned them."

Talia eyed the spirits skeptically. "I don't get it. They're just ghosts. We should be able to pass right through them. What's the catch?"

Grant stepped forward, but a ghost swooped down and touched him. He yelped and jumped back. "They're ice cold!"

Curiously, I reached my hand out, and one of the spirits swept through it. It was like plunging my hand into an ice-cold lake, and I understood why he'd jumped back. I wasn't risking one of my teammates getting hypothermia just for sport. There had to be another way through.

"I know how to get rid of them," I said as I conjured a bundle of clearing herbs. I lit the bundle with a lighter, and smoke billowed upward. I waved the smoke at the nearest ghosts, but they just moaned and flew away a few feet.

"Goddess, you people are scared of a few ghosts?" a voice came from behind us. I turned to see that Chloe had followed us inside. I didn't see her teammates anywhere, which meant she must've abandoned them. She tossed her black hair over her shoulder and swept past me. "Surely this obstacle was designed for the *bravest* witches."

Nadine's hands curled into fists. "Get lost, Chloe."

Chloe scoffed. "Or what?"

She walked straight into the sea of ghosts. They let out haunting cries as they swirled around her. Chloe let out a cry of pain, and I witnessed her skin turn blue with the cold. I rushed forward and waved my herb bundle at the ghosts. They backed off enough that I could grab Chloe and yank her away from them. Chloe wrapped her arms around herself and shivered.

"You're not going to win this thing alone," I told her firmly, before turning to Talia. "You come from a family of Seers. What's the best way to get past these ghosts?"

Talia pressed her lips together, looking thoughtful. "Well, the herbs were a good idea, but cleansing herbs only work alongside intention. I think we all need to set an intention together. Intention works even without magic, so I can still help."

I nodded. "All right. We can create our own spell to focus our intention."

I thought about it for a moment. "How about... *Through cedar smoke, we right what's wrong, send these ghosts back where they belong?*"

"That should work," Nadine said. "Let's give it a shot."

The four of us began to recite the spell I'd come up with while I waved the herb bundle at the ghosts. They backed off a little, but not enough to lead us to the stairwell. Chloe stood off to the side, observing.

I realized why the spell wasn't working. Chloe may not have her powers yet, but she could still set an intention, and that itself was powerful.

"If we all want to get through, we have to work together," I told her.

"Chloe's not on our team," Nadine protested.

"Well, I'm not going anywhere," Chloe sneered.

I figured as much, which meant we were stuck with her. "Doesn't matter. The ghosts respond to us all. Are you going to help us?"

Chloe sighed. "You're not getting through without me."

She began reciting the intention with us. Slowly, the ghosts began to disperse, floating through the walls and disappearing. Their moans quieted.

We hurried toward the stairwell that led to the roof. I thought it'd be a straight shot to the top, until I came to a landing with an alchemy table set up on it. A big cauldron sat over a burner, with all kinds of vials set around it. A black cat with a tuft of white fur on his tail sat on the lowest step, eyeing us curiously.

"Strange…" Grant remarked. "This must be another obstacle, some sort of potion we have to brew— though I don't know what."

"Please," Chloe scoffed. "This cat looks harmless. What kind of potion could you possibly need?"

Chloe started for the steps, but before she could reach them, four other cats appeared out of nowhere. They were all black, with that same tuft of white fur. It was as if the cat had *multiplied*.

Chloe shoved one of the cats aside with her foot, but it jumped onto her leg, while the others crowded around her feet. Four more cats appeared, then eight, multiplying over and over again until there were dozens of cats swarming around Chloe. She tried to back away, but she tripped over one of the cats and landed on her back.

"I think I know what potion we need to brew," Grant said, hurrying over to the alchemy table. A spell book lay open, and he quickly looked it over. "As I suspected. The cat's been dosed with a potion that allows it to multiply. We have to create an antidote."

The cats prowled toward us. Chloe tried shoving them off of her, but she didn't get to her feet before she tripped again.

I reached down to pick one of the cats up. It purred in my arms and licked my face. I laughed. "They're sweet."

"Um… they may be sweet, but there are too many of them!" Talia cried. She was standing upright, but so many cats had gathered around her that all I could see was her head poking out from the sea of them.

More and more cats appeared, until we couldn't see the floor anymore. Cats crawled atop one another, trying to climb up my jeans.

Vials clinked together as Grant scrambled for the right ingredients. "Nadine, I need your help."

Nadine pulled a cat off her shoulder, which had been licking her face. She smiled as she scratched his head and set him down. She carefully navigated the swarm and went over to the table to help Grant.

Chloe laughed out loud. "If Nadine manages to brew a real potion, I'll be impressed."

"Shut up, Chloe," Nadine snapped. "If you don't want to help us, you can leave. I don't see your teammates anywhere around to help."

Nadine lit the burner beneath the cauldron. Grant began measuring out ingredients while Nadine stirred the potion.

Meanwhile, more cats climbed up my jeans, meowing and purring as they tried to cuddle me. I felt their weight pressing in at all angles, until they became so heavy that I fell over. Cats swarmed on top of me, their tongues rubbing against my face as they licked me. Several cats sat on my chest, and I coughed as I tried to inhale. A cat shoved its butt into my face, tickling my nose with its tail— then promptly sat right on my face. I couldn't breathe. This cute, adorable obstacle had quickly turned into a nightmare.

I shook my head to toss the cat off of me, as my arms were held down by the others. "Hurry up!" I cried. "These cats are suffocating us."

"Almost done…" Grant replied. "There! Now we just have to find the right cat."

"You mean we can't give the potion to just any of them?" Talia demanded, her voice muffled behind layers of fur.

"We have to find the original one," Grant said.

"How are we going to do that—?" I started, but I cut off when a cat walked over my groin, smashing my balls. *Fucking hell!* I didn't want to use battle magic on these poor creatures.

"We're looking for something different," Grant said. "The duplicates aren't perfect. The original cat will have some sort of unique marking or something to set it apart."

"There!" Nadine cried. "That one has green eyes, and all the others are yellow."

I couldn't see anything, because I was encased by black fur from all sides. I projected a shield outward, pushing the cats away, and finally gasped a greedy breath. I caught a glimpse through the fur just briefly to see Nadine holding one of the cats. Grant shoved the end of the vial into the cat's mouth, and the potion slid down its throat.

A moment later, the cats disappeared; only the cat in Nadine's arms remained. The cat relaxed, and she set him on the ground. He bowed his head to us, then stepped aside, allowing us through.

"Thank the Goddess." I scrambled to my feet, alongside Chloe and Talia.

We climbed the stairs and reached the door to the roof. I opened it... but what I found wasn't the roof at all. It was a cemetery. Grass and gravestones stretched as far as the eye could see. It was like we were on ground level, not several flights up at the top of the school. It was nighttime, too, and the full moon shone down on us.

I glanced around curiously. "Another obstacle?"

Chloe pushed past me and stepped into the cemetery. "It's obvious, isn't it? It's some sort of Mentalist spell, messing with our heads."

Chloe's whole family were Mentalists, so she knew a thing or two about their powers.

"It's an illusion?" Nadine asked.

"Not an *illusion*," Chloe sneered. "Illusions project outward. This is all inside our heads, like a hallucination."

Nadine narrowed her eyes at Chloe. "So how do we get past it?"

"It's like a dream," Chloe said. "You need to get your mind to overpower the magic. We need to look for what doesn't belong, in order to *convince* our subconscious that what we're seeing isn't real."

We started walking around the cemetery, though I didn't know exactly what we were looking for. The ground felt solid beneath my feet, and the wind brushed against my skin. I'd have believed I was really here if I hadn't just walked up several flights of stairs.

Nadine stayed close to me as we navigated around the tombstones. She held my hand and leaned into me to whisper, "If we're looking for something outside the ordinary, Chloe fits the bill."

I chuckled under my breath. "She'd take that as a compliment, I'm sure."

Nadine stopped in her tracks. "Does this count as something out of the ordinary?"

She pointed to the gravestone in front of us, and I noticed the dates couldn't be right. The death date was eighty years into the future. Even if the dates were correct, it'd make the person over two-hundred years old at the time of death. I glanced around at the other tombstones and noticed the same thing.

"The death dates are all wrong," Chloe stated from several tombstones away. She'd figured it out the same time we had.

"According to this tombstone, this guy over here died before he was even born," Grant announced.

"And this lady died before her child beside her was born," Talia added.

A loud *crack* sounded throughout the graveyard, and the tombstones crumbled all at once. The hallucination faltered, and the sky brightened to reveal an overcast morning. The cemetery had vanished, and we stood on the roof of Miriam Mansion.

A man in a cloak stood in front of us, his figure appearing ominous. "You have done well, students. It's not often we see underclassmen make it past our obstacles first."

I relaxed. It was only Professor Warren, my advisor.

"So, did we win?" Chloe asked; a bit rudely, if I might add.

"You have yet to defeat the zombies," he said, gesturing to the scene below us. I glanced over the railing that lined the rooftop, and I saw that the corpses were still attacking. Students shot spells at them and slowed them down, but the zombies were still trying to get into the school.

"Warren's a necromancer. He's controlling them," I told my teammates. "The only way to stop the zombies is to stop him."

"Then you must duel me," Professor Warren said.

I'd sparred against my professors before in class, so I knew which spells to use. I planted myself in front of Nadine and tossed a stunning spell at Professor Warren. He lifted a wand, and a shield bloomed out in front of him. The spell bounced off the shield, and the five of us ducked as it whizzed back in our direction.

Grant cracked his knuckles. "All right, Professor. You asked for it."

Grant shot off a few spells, and Professor Warren deflected each one. I quickly joined in.

Professor Warren smirked under the hood of his cloak. "You'll have to push yourselves harder than that, boys."

We were going easy on him because we didn't want to hurt him, but it seemed Professor Warren wanted us to give it our all.

"Go low!" I told Grant.

Grant shot a high-powered stunning spell at Professor Warren's feet, and he was blasted backward. The moment we caught him off guard, I launched a spell at his hand. His wand went flying, and he landed hard several yards away from us.

I rushed over to him. "Professor, are you all right?"

Warren coughed and sat upright. His hood fell back, and he glanced over to where his wand had fallen. A smile spread across his face as he got to his feet. "I'm very well, actually. You've defeated me— and the zombies. Excellent job."

I looked down from the roof again and saw that the zombies had all collapsed. A few students cheered, like they thought *they* were the ones who'd immobilized them. They hadn't noticed what we'd done up on the roof.

Professor Warren reached into his cloak and pulled out an envelope. "Congratulations to your team. You're the winners of this year's Haunted Tournament."

Chloe rushed up behind me when I took the envelope. "What's the prize!?"

I ripped open the envelope to find a gift certificate to a cafe downtown. "Looks like we're going out for pizza."

"Ooh, I vote for pineapple on mine," Nadine said.

"Pepperoni and sausage for me," Talia added.

"That's it?" Chloe balked. "We went through all that for a *free pizza*? I could've done literally anything else with my day!"

"A free pizza *and* the glory of winning," Grant pointed out.

Chloe eyed him up and down. "Like I want to be associated with *your* team."

"You *did* help us get through the obstacles," Nadine pointed out. "We wouldn't have known what to look for in that last one without your help."

"The obstacles were designed for witches with different powers to work together," Professor Warren stated. "Even though some of your teammates don't have their powers yet, it appears you five work well together."

I didn't know what he saw in us, because we did *not* work well with Chloe. Not by a long shot. Though, I supposed we all played a part.

"We *did* get past the obstacles together," I said. "Nadine figured out we had to get to the roof, and Talia knew how to get past the ghosts. Nadine and Grant made the potion together, Chloe knew what to look for in the cemetery, and Grant and I disarmed Professor Warren."

Nadine smirked. "I guess I'm a better Alchemist than I thought."

She was taunting Chloe, because all those mean girls had made her feel bad about alchemy. Chloe didn't know the true nature of Nadine's powers, but it was only Nadine's first week with them. I was sure that with time, she could use her alchemy crystals to brew all kinds of potions, and Chloe would regret tormenting her.

"I guess it worked," Chloe admitted. "But it's just some dumb sporting event. This changes *nothing* about our family curse, Nadine. Enjoy your free pizza. I'm out of here."

Chloe turned on her heel and left the rooftop. It sure didn't sound like she wanted us to *enjoy* anything.

"Don't let her get to you," I told Nadine.

Nadine scoffed. "Like she could! If she doesn't want to claim her winnings, then that means more pizza for us. Who's hungry?"

"Famished," Grant said.

Talia's stomach rumbled, and she laughed. "I didn't fight those cats for nothing."

I draped an arm around Nadine's shoulder. "Let's go claim our prize."

THE END

Read more from Nadine and Lucas in the College of Witchcraft series. This series is part of the Hidden Legends Universe, which features college-aged protagonists attending magical academies, dual points-of-view, disabled and diverse main characters, and steamy, empowering romances. To learn more and get free books, visit hiddenlegendsbooks.com.

THE ONCE-DREAM

By Megan Linski

A University of Sorcery Short Story

CHAPTER ONE

The winter felt cold and harsh around me. Brisk, cutting like a knife, piercing me from the inside out, even through the hard stone walls of Arcanea University.

I was Prince Ethan Nowak, a monarch of the fae, heir to Malovia, wolf shifter by claim, and yet I'd never felt more alone than this night. School was temporarily paused due to winter break, and wouldn't resume until January. Normally, I'd be back at the palace preparing for holiday celebrations, but certain current events had left me bitter, not wishing to return to the palace and be anywhere near the pomp and circumstance. My mother, the queen, wasn't happy about my absence, but I couldn't be convinced to face her. So here I was, solitary in my dorm room, wishing that it was a new semester in my Junior year so I could focus on my classes in fae magic, rather than on the chilling feeling that engulfed me now.

The reason I felt alone was because my mate was, currently, not here. Emma was with her mother on vacation in Poland, and wouldn't be back for several weeks. I could easily reach out with a phone call, but things were tense between us lately, so I thought it best to give her space. I didn't believe Emma wished to speak with me after the events of the King's Contest, and so, I turned my mind to other matters, difficult as it may be.

I hovered over my desk, scowling at my current project. I'd hoped to get a head start on it, before classes began, but I was thoroughly puzzled. One of my classes next semester required us to write original poetry, to use in our spells. Fae magic was our intention, and through it, our words, so it was important to get this right so I could cast better spells. I'd never been very talented at poetry, so I decided to try my hand at it before I embarrassed myself in front of the class, but I found myself absolutely stuck.

There was a knock on the door. My best friend, Stefan, entered the room. The dragon shifter barely squeezed through the door frame as he asked, "You coming? Figure we could go with the guys down for a pint at *The Drunken Dragon*."

"You go without me," I grumbled. "I'm stuck doing… this."

Stefan ambled over, then stared down at my pitiful attempt at poetry. He began laughing. "You moping around in here writing sonnets instead of getting tipsy with us? Surely a waste of your free time."

"It's not a waste. I must become a more proficient sorcerer. This will help… I think."

I picked the poem up, and began to recite it.

"I am the line

I have a duty

To protect this nation…"

I sighed. "That's as far as I got. I don't know what comes next."

"Hm…" Stefan's mouth twisted, then his eyes immediately brightened as he got an idea. He snatched the paper from me, bent down and scrawled a line. "There. That should work."

I read the poem again, and immediately scowled when I got to the last stanza. "*I am the line. I have a duty. To protect this nation…* and spank the booty."

"Fits perfectly!" Stefan crowed, appearing *very* proud of himself.

I biffed him on the back of the head, and he cackled. "What? It rhymes!"

"Silly things like this aren't going to help me perform powerful magic."

"You're so moody. Lighten up!" Stefan said. "Just put some shit down on paper, and go out with us."

"I am not in the right frame of mind for partying," I growled.

He gave a dramatic sigh. "Suit yourself. But if you get tired of playing Shakespeare, I'll be down at the pub, getting sauced off my ass. Now *that's* a poetic sight to see. Bards should write about it for ages."

I shook my head as he slipped out the door. His attempts to cheer me up were appreciated, but not helpful.

I struggled with the poem for a while longer, before it became very late and it was far past time for bed. I flopped onto my mattress without bothering to change, and stared up at the ceiling. The minute my mind was off of the poetry, it immediately reverted to Emma. The thought of my red-haired, green-eyed sorceress made my stomach twist and my heart ache. I was her wolf shifter, and she was my everything, the woman I was bonded to through a powerful magical connection, the fae girl I was sworn to protect. I wasn't sure she wanted anything to do with me, because for a week now, we'd had no contact.

My eyes closed as I imagined myself with Emma, somewhere we could be together where none of the problems of this world mattered. My mind went into a stupor as I pretended that I was caressing her fiery locks, bending down to touch upon her a gentle kiss…

* * *

Awareness came upon me slowly as I stood to take in my surroundings. I found myself on my paws, my white wolf pelt standing out vibrantly amongst a grouping of green trees, which pressed in all around. I was in some kind of forest, in my wolf form. The emerald leaves of the trees around me glistened slightly in the dark, and above me, the moon shone beautifully across the plant life that blossomed here. There were tiny droplets of moisture on the branches and leaves, indicating that a rain had just come through.

I was slightly aware that this was a dream, although the dream felt realer than reality itself. For no reason at all, I began to run. My paws pounded against the forest floor, skimming the grass as I stampeded toward my destination, whatever it was. My ears pricked forward, and I smelled something lovely… something incredible. A mixture of oakmoss and amber perfume that I recognized.

I broke through the trees, and came to a clearing. Standing in a circle of moonlight, illuminated by the night's glow, was my mate... Emma.

And it appeared she was waiting for me.

CHAPTER TWO

Poland was wonderful, especially at Christmastime. Krakow was decorated with lights and glimmering garlands from the smallest city street to the tallest tower. Outdoor markets selling mulled wine under the falling snow wafted scents of gingerbread over me as I tottered through the cobblestone streets. My mother and I had spent the entire week taking in all the different festivities, and I'd hardly had a moment to pause between the pure wonder of it all.

Secretly, though, I wished I was here with my mate, Ethan, enjoying the sights. It wasn't that I didn't like spending time with my mother. But I missed my love… even if we weren't really speaking at the moment.

Krakow was a human city, so we couldn't perform magic here. I found myself disappointed that I wasn't able to practice all the spells I'd learned during my first semester at Arcanea University, due to laws on supernatural secrecy.

Even so… a few peculiar looks from humans as we walked by indicated to me that not all was what it appeared. Sometimes, I wondered if a chosen few knew what we were, and the kind of power we held as fae. Fairy tales, myths and legends held a bit of truth to them. Humankind just didn't know how much.

By the time we got back to our hotel later that evening, I was absolutely wiped out. My mother wanted to go out and do more things, but I was too tired to move; we'd been walking all day, and we'd get an early start tomorrow to go on a tour of the local sights, so all I wanted to do was rest.

Mom headed out on her own as I changed into a satin nightgown. I worried about her a little, walking around a foreign city by herself. But then I reminded myself she was a fae, and had magic. If she got into trouble, she could use it to fight back, and I didn't think there was a stupid enough idiot on Earth who'd mess with Evonna Sosna when she got in a mood.

I laid back on the bed and let my red hair cover the satin pillows. This hotel was completely grand, and I felt like true royalty as I sank into the downy mattress, pulling the silk comforter over my form.

As I felt myself drifting off, I caught myself thinking about my mate. What was Ethan doing now, and did he miss me like I missed him?

I took a final breath, and felt myself slipping into a world of dreams just as I imagined Ethan delivering a soft kiss to my lips…

* * *

Music came to me first. The soft sound of chimes, comforting notes of classical music ringing gently throughout the area.

I opened my eyes, and sat up slowly. I found myself sitting in a comforting green armchair, surrounded by books. I was in some kind of magical bookshop. There was a roaring fire in the hearth beside the armchair, making the whole room warm, and books flew around like birds, using their pages as wings as they floated around the area. There were gold sparkles hovering in the air, and a crystal ball sat on a nearby table, along with dimly burning candles. There were paintings on the walls of medieval scenes, knights riding horses and delivering flowers to ladies-in-waiting.

It didn't appear the shop was run by anyone. The counter was empty. I rose to my feet, eyes skimming over the apothecary jars of potion ingredients beside the bookshelves. I ran my fingers over the spines of books, observing the titles and knowing that if I wished, I could stay here in this vision and thumb through parchment pages forever. Every book I desired to read was here, and in this perfect room, I could become immersed in each word.

As I passed a mirror, I gazed at my reflection. I was wearing a dress, chiffon layers of light blue, pink, and white. The dress had a short handkerchief skirt that ended at my knees, and I donned no shoes. White flowers wound throughout my red hair. I definitely looked like a fae of the woodland, a mischievous sprite set to cause mayhem in the lives of those who crossed into her forest refuge.

This certainly had to be a dream, but it was a nice one, so I longed to stay in it. I found a hot cup of tea sitting out for me on the table beside the armchair, and sipped it, finding that the tea was delicious and comforting.

I wished to stay and remain cozy here in this quaint little shop, but something else called me onward. I left the bookshop, and continued my journey. All around me was a green forest, glowing under the cover of the moon. I came to the center of a clearing and stood in the middle of a circle of moonlight, basking in the calmness of the eerie evening.

There was noise in the brush behind me. I turned. Emotions flooded my veins and overpowered all senses as I watched a white wolf come near. Ethan approached me, wagging his tail slightly as his mighty paws padded across the moss and to me.

"Emma, love." His telepathic voice that he used in his wolf form echoed through the clearing, and I strode forward to take his massive head in my arms. I stroked his ears, kissing the top of his head as I held him tightly. This was all I wanted in the world, and now, he was here.

"I am glad to be with you," he stated, and he licked my cheek softly. "It already feels like it's been too long."

"You're here now. Let's enjoy this wonderful forest." He didn't bring up that we were upset with each other, and I didn't, either. After all, this was my dream, and I could create anything I wanted in it. Right now, I wanted Ethan and I to be happy, so we were. It didn't matter that he wasn't really here, and this wasn't truly him, at least, not in this moment. All I wanted was to have him near me, and that he was a fantasy my mind had conjured made no difference.

I climbed onto Ethan's back, and held on tightly to his fur. "Let's explore this forest, and see what we can find."

Ethan gave a happy rumble, and started forward. His long strides thudded through the trees as we wandered the woods, from this way to that.

As we searched the forests for whatever was hiding there, faekin began coming out of the brush. Small sprites danced in the air ahead, and nymphs melded out of the bark of trees to wave as we passed. An alicorn with a rainbow mane nickered to us and tossed his horned head as we ran by, while little trolls grumbled beside butterflies, whose wings glowed and changed color. We were far from the only magical creatures in this forest, and here, it felt like we were at home.

Eventually, the trees ended, and we found ourselves in a wide open area. A silver surface caught my eye, and I focused my attention on what was there. It was an ice pond in the middle of a springtime forest. It didn't make sense, and yet, nothing made sense with the fae, and this was a dream, so I was willing to accept it. I got off of Ethan's back, and approached the ice pond. As I did, Ethan shifted back into a man, and came near the ice pond beside me. He was wearing a loose, white cotton shirt and simple breeches, making him appear, like me, that he was living in a time long before the modern age.

I loved ice skating, and Ethan loved hockey. Without any explanation, skates appeared on our feet, and Ethan stepped onto the ice pond. He reached out a hand, to help me onto the ice.

I took it, and we began gliding together. I did a turn as Ethan spun me around, and he took me into his arms so we could skate side-by-side.

As we skated around the pond, the edges our blades made in the ice shimmered a dramatic blue, the markings rising up into the air around us. The edges glittered and vanished as the butterflies came out of the trees, fluttering over the pond. The faekin came out of the woods, cheering and applauding as they observed Ethan and I perform our dance on ice. I did a spin, then a small jump, coming to a pirouette stop in the middle of the pond. I glanced over my shoulder, and saw that Ethan had a huge smile on his face.

"You are truly an ice princess." He reached out to kiss my hand. I felt heat travel up my arm and settle over my breasts as we stepped off the pond, and our skates vanished. We sat in a bed of clover as the faekin dispersed, some heading back into the forest, others clambering onto the ice pond, to try and imitate the dance we'd performed. They fell on their faces and laughed at each other as they attempted to recreate the dance, the butterflies still flying overhead.

Ethan lounged back on the clover, and I laid beside him. We faced each other as fireflies hovered overhead, and he said, "It seems perfect, to enjoy this small world with you here."

"It is perfect." I sighed. "I wish we could stay like this forever. The real world is… scary."

"I'm not afraid of it. So long as you are there."

I felt the same way. I reached over, to stroke his muscular arms. Ethan sighed and said, "I only wish I was able to put what I feel into words. It's difficult, conveying my thoughts through mediums like fiction, or poetry. I feel wholly inadequate to do so."

I enjoyed poetry. It was a hobby I dabbled in from time to time. And I understood exactly what this dream was trying to tell me... that Ethan loved me, but he didn't know how to say it. I wanted to tell him it was okay to be vulnerable, because I felt just as exposed with him as he did with me. We had a mating bond, and he was my soulmate. I wanted to encourage my wolf to not run from his feelings, but embrace them. Because I embraced my love for him like I embraced life each morning. Why run from something that felt this good?

"You can't judge yourself for what you want to express. Say what you feel freely, and allow the words to come across the page without holding yourself back," I suggested. "If you're having trouble writing, it's because you're judging yourself. And that judgment will be restrictive to your creativity, spells, poetry or otherwise. Just let yourself be free."

"Wise words. Perhaps I will write my feelings about you," he confessed, a bit of a blush crossing his cheeks. "I could never compose enough poems to describe it."

He leaned forward to kiss me. My worries melted away as he pressed his lips to mine, and slipped his tongue delicately inside my mouth. I kissed him back with a fever, threading my hands over his chest, slipping them through the slit in his cotton shirt. He deepened the kiss, hovering over me to press his weight into my form, and I thanked the gods that he was here with me, in this perfect dream. I felt Ethan slipping the shoulders of my dress off, and I gave a soft moan as his hands wandered downward.

"Emma," Ethan whispered, and that's when I felt the dream begin to break. I attempted to hold on, but the feel of Ethan's kiss and the luxury of his hands upon me dissipated as I returned to an entirely different world, one where we were kept apart.

* * *

My eyes opened to the darkness of my hotel suite. I scowled, feeling completely cheated.

Dammit. I'd woken up right when things were starting to get good. I sat up, running a hand through my hair to sweep the locks away from my eyes. It was just a dream. Or was it?

Though we were hundreds of miles apart, there was a faint resemblance through our mating bond that told me Ethan might've experienced the dream, too.

My fingers itched to pick up the phone and call him, though I hesitated to do so. It was late, and I didn't want to wake him if what I'd experienced really was just a dream, and not something magical between us. I'd heard mates could go into each other's dreams, but I wasn't sure if that was an ability Ethan and I shared. Was it possible he'd experienced the dream, too?

I wrapped my arms around my form and held tightly. That world had been a perfect existence. A once-dream that, perhaps, could become reality someday.

I glanced out the window, and onto Krakow's streets. It was still nightfall, but a different kind of night that I'd experienced in the blessed woodland. I wondered aimlessly if Ethan was thinking of me.

And prayed that he was. Because no matter what was between us, I couldn't wait to be in his arms again.

You can read the first book in the University of Sorcery series for free, and begin Emma's adventure in The Wolven Mark: University of Sorcery, Book One.

Made in the USA
Middletown, DE
25 August 2023

37088162R00209